DANNY DRAGONE

THE
SUN
FOLLOWER

DRAGONE'S WORLD INC.
© 2024

To my wife, Jackie, for always believing in me.

I

PART ONE

CHAPTER 1

A thunderstorm glided over Long Island City, every raindrop clanking on the windowsill like the scattered array of firecrackers. James Grady stood close to it, the sound reminding him of the war that had ended years earlier. *I guess it's better than hearing all those bullets and missiles*, he thought, awaiting his orchestra of teenagers to file into the music room of the Brighter Minds Charter School. With time to spare, the students either tuned their instruments in unison or had obnoxiously loud conversations with one another. "*Congratulations Seniors, Class of 2042,*" read the digital banner above the door. James, attempting to maintain his patience, gazed out through the wet glass. He could see no farther than his own reflection. His dirty blonde beard had grown thick, its grayish-white hairs sneaking in. Without it an eighteen-stitch scar on his chin would be the topic of conversation. The lids below his steel blue eyes were sagging and sad like his father's – another sore subject he preferred never to talk about. After all, it had been ten years to the day since that coward abandoned his family.

"*The future is calling you ... Make sure to take care of your mother.*"

That was the message his father had sent him on that gloomy May afternoon a decade ago, eerily similar to the present one. Those words still lingered in his mind like a dark cloud. They were the last ones he would ever hear from Pops. That was the nickname he and his sisters had given their father back before the family fell apart. Since then, James had wasted many years searching for that man. A past he had buried away. Or at least that's what he had told everyone.

Across a foggy East River, the Manhattan skyline appeared to be the same as the one James had seen on his first visit there. The city as a whole, though, had changed drastically since then. He had lived there off and on through most of the Great Upgrade – a series of ambitious construction projects in which blacktop roads had been replaced with solar-powered panels. Vacant skyscrapers had been transformed into farms and green walls. A massive overhaul of infrastructure to combat the increasingly volatile climate effects. The controversial project, still far from being completed, was the last straw for some deniers. It had ignited what was now referred to as the Last War. An even sorer subject that nobody wanted to talk about anymore. Also one that no one who survived would ever forget.

Through the rain, one of the many holographic billboards caught James's attention.

"*LUCIDITY.*"

It flashed to the words:

"*A World As Real As It Gets.*"

Lucidity's state-of-the-art tech was supposedly beyond any previous VR, beyond any metaverse they'd ever created. It'd been hailed as the "next big thing," but James couldn't care less at the moment. He had the impossible endeavor of motivating a group of restless teenagers to focus on one task.

When a soft bell tone resonated in the music hall, his students put away their UniTabs – a stretchable and nearly transparent smart device usually worn on people's wrists. To set an example for his students, James never took his Uni out in class. Teenagers, and adults alike, were obsessed with the device. They now used holograms instead of music sheets. Metronomes clicked in their unseen earbuds. All of which made his job as a conductor seem less vital.

"All right, people, let's take our places," James said. "Today's the first day of the rest of your lives, which means our nine days of hell will start now. The National Competition is next Wednesday, and I think we have a pretty good shot if we focus."

It wasn't quite the New York Philharmonic, but the school was designed for the future of education and James wanted to be part of that in one way or another. Although far from his aspirations after graduating, it was a blessing compared to the mess he'd been in right as the war ended.

He continued, "We're going to start with 'Train Wreck' because we seem to be having the most problems with that one."

"That's because it's weird as fuck," one of the kids mumbled under their breath.

"Does someone have a problem?" Nothing but a giggle came from half of the class. "Something funny?"

"No, sir," said the entire class in unison.

"All right, 'Train Wreck,' from the top."

The first of their two pieces for the competition was difficult and eclectic, with overriding scales and parts that seemed to fall off in dissonance. Maybe his students were right. The experimental piece inspired by his worst relapse may have been a bit too avant-garde for their young minds. As they played it, he noticed his lead violinist improvising, adding notes all over the place.

"Stop!" James turned to the front row. "What are you doing, Calvin?"

Calvin Johnson – his finest protege. A seventeen-year-old junior who weighed no more than a buck-thirty. He was shy but always wore a huge smile during class. One of the few who traveled from another district, he was only able to afford the school because of academic scholarships. Lately, however, he seemed tired and distracted. That afternoon he wasn't smiling. Before he had a chance to defend himself, one of the other kids butted in.

"Yeah, what the hell happened, Johnson?"

That was Kyle Gibbs, a popular junior with a God's-gift complex, had been moved back to second violin earlier in the school year. Neither he nor his well-off parents were too happy to see their son play second fiddle, so to speak, to a kid from Tarrytown. The bias against Calvin had nothing to do with his skill or skin color, though. Kyle and Calvin were both Black, but Kyle and the rest of his classmates lived within the areas that had already been modernized – the "Interior." Those who didn't were condescendingly referred to as *outsiders.*

"He's been messing up so much lately." Kyle's invisible braces filled with saliva. "Just because he has a special pass to be here shouldn't mean that he gets away with his little improvisations."

James shrugged. "I'll decide who goes where in this orchestra."

"Then you must be half-assing it through the class just like Calvin."

James slammed his fist down. "Talk to me again like that and I'll have you thrown out of this orchestra. And this time I don't care how many times your mommy calls the principal." The class snickered at Kyle. "Calvin, do you have anything to say for yourself?"

"I'm sorry ... I was just playing around." His head was down. "Let's do it again."

Their second attempt wasn't any better.

Kyle blurted out, "God dammit, Johnson! I can play this in my sleep."

"I'm glad you got to sleep last night."

"Maybe you should go to a school in your own neighborhood – where you belong."

The two young men were in a heated stare-down. James rushed over to break up the fight, standing between them with palms on both chests, struggling to hold them apart.

Kyle cried out, "You can't touch me, Mr. Grady,"

James let him go. "That's it – we're done for today. We'll be doing an extra hour tomorrow to make up for this." There was a collective sigh from the class, hard to decipher if it was joy or disappointment. "Enjoy the rest of your afternoon."

Kyle stormed out of the classroom. "Fucking outsiders," he mumbled under his breath.

Calvin threw his violin bow on the floor.

James picked it up. "Can you stay behind for a bit, Calvin?"

The student nodded and sat down in his chair as the rest of the class filed out of the room.

James took a seat next to him. "Everything okay, bud?"

Through tears, Calvin answered, "What do you think?"

"Is something going on at home?"

"It's Teddy again."

James knew of his stepfather. PTSD could get the best of any soldier after the Last War. "What happened this time?"

"Well, Teddy came into my room at midnight and turned off the power to the system." Calvin shook his head. "You can't do that! It's frightening and can cause brain damage if it's not powered off properly."

"Wait, what system?"

"Lucidity," Calvin said. "Anyways, Teddy pulls me out of the DreamCatcher while I'm in the system. He tells me that I need to clean the apartment before my mother gets home. I was still trying to distinguish where I was, but it's mad jarring when you get pulled out like that. It can be like getting woken up while sleepwalking." He shook his head. "You know what I mean?"

"Lucidity?" James pointed to the billboards outside of the window. "That ridiculously expensive VR gaming system?"

"It's not a game, and it's not virtual reality. Its OS triggers sensory nerves in your brain so that you can live within the world they created and utilize its innovative technology. You can feel and smell and taste." Calvin finally took a breath. "Well, the tasting part still needs some work."

"So, what did Teddy say to you?"

"That drunken mother*fuh*—" Calvin stopped mid-sentence. "That jerk tells me to start cleaning up even though he hasn't lifted a finger all day. Then he calls me a loser because I play the violin and spend all my spare time working in Lucidity."

"Slow down, Calvin ... I thought you worked at the bodega in your neighborhood."

"Not anymore!" Calvin proudly grinned. "I'm employed by Lucidity now. They pay way more than the bodega and give me free access to the system. I mean, the DreamCatcher alone costs a hundred G in addition to the thousands for the monthly subscription. It's mad expensive." He looked up at James. "And you don't know anything about this, do you?"

"Apparently not. What exactly do you do for Lucidity?"

"From ten until three AM every night, I'm a guide in the Welcome Facility."

"That's why you're so tired every day." James crossed his arms, his shoulders tensing. "Maybe you need to get a more reasonable job."

"I can't, Mr. G, Lucidity is all that I have right now. Well, that and this orchestra. I have friends there that understand me." His face lit up. "There's a potential future for me there."

James remembered the excitement of new technology. At least for those years when he was that age. "My father was obsessed with Alter-World."

Calvin snickered. "It's kinda like AW – minus the lame graphics, horrible interplay, and well ... really everything. Look I know, you're, like, forty, so you don't get it."

"You know I'm barely in my thirties, Calvin."

His student laughed. "I know, Mr. G. I'm kidding. But as the billboard says, this BCI is as real as it gets."

"BCI?"

"Brain-Computer Interface."

James sighed. "Look, I can't stop what you do in your personal life, but I also can't keep taking your side if you're causing this sleeplessness. This game—"

"It's not a game," Calvin interrupted. "It's an extremely sophisticated system."

Frustrated, James reminded him, "This job in Lucidity – or whatever you call it – is hindering your performance in my orchestra. I don't want to give Kyle back first-violin because you can't keep up the pace. There will always be people threatened by others who have to work twice as hard." He checked to see if anybody else was around and whispered, "Don't let that asshole get in your head."

Calvin nodded. "I swear it won't affect my performance anymore. It's just that when I get time off on the weekend, I get to go to a world where people understand me." He sighed. "You get that, right?"

As if it were his high school days, the ones where he'd isolated himself from the world to master music theory, James understood. "You have the whole summer to play – I mean, *use* – Lucidity. Can you just give me a hundred and ten percent this week?"

"You have my word." Calvin fist-bumped him. "You know what, Mr. G? Maybe you should join."

"No thank you."

Calvin snickered, his hands holding the strap of his backpack. "Okay ... *We'll see.*"

The teenager picked up his stuff and scurried out of the class.

James wished all his students treated him with that much respect. Hell, he wished he treated himself that kindly. He stared back out the window, the rain turning to a drizzle now. The billboard that had caught his attention was clearer than before, its simplistic graphic enhanced by the same company's latest holographic technology. James, being the curious soul that he was, wondered if this Lucidity could live up to its "*a world as real as it gets"* promise. But even that depended on who ran this particular world.

Either way, he couldn't help but be intrigued.

CHAPTER 2

Before James left school that afternoon he rummaged through his bag, searching for his UniTab. Around that time every day, even a minor discrepancy would raise his blood pressure, so the heated scuffle with Kyle still had him reeling. Sweaty and shaking and unable to find the device, he slammed the bag down. And with that, the UniTab appeared on the floor. With his afternoon ending prematurely and idle time on his hands, James desperately needed to get to one of his meetings.

PS 39 was one of the last public schools of its kind in the city – now solely used for NA meetings. While his attendance wasn't mandatory, it helped him through the more difficult days. The hallways were the opposite of his hybrid charter. The handmade posters reminded him of simpler times. A musty stench filled the gymnasium where the meeting took place. He took a seat in an uncomfortable chair as the others arrived.

Some of them came to New York to get away from the insanity of the Outside, which was a haven for heavy drug use in certain areas. Heroin had regained its popularity at the height of the war and the epidemic had only grown during the Second Pandemic. The desolation people felt as those disasters had collided was devastating, and compared to other people, James had gotten off easy.

Kalen Green, the short and spunky Irish woman who ran the meetings, entered with a giant closed-mouth smile and her fiery red hair in a messy bun, never caring much for her appearance. For the most part, Kalen was kind and warm, but from time to time she'd bring out that patented Irish tough love.

"*Ay*, ya look like *gobshite*," she said, with an accent as pleasant as a parent's scolding. She glanced at James before taking her seat. "Now that we're all here, who would like to speak first tonight?"

When no one appeared interested in sharing their feelings, he prayed – if only for a brief moment of zen – that Kalen wouldn't call on him that day.

"James ... we haven't heard from you in a while." With a glower, she asked, "How's everything going with ya?"

Everyone stared at him. "I can't complain."

Kalen chuckled. "Don't be shy ... Give it a lash, ey."

"Well, I'm having a baby as you all know ... A boy."

The others memebers of the group softly clapped.

"Does that make you excited?" Kalen paused. "Or scared?"

"Sandy and I are ecstatic. Now we're trying to come up with names and such. It's a little stressful, but we're looking forward to his arrival."

Kalen was quiet for a moment, her chin resting on her fist. "Does it bring up any repressed feelings about your father and him leaving your family?" She addressed the rest of the group. "For some of you newbies, James started doing drugs after his father left his family, spending years of his life on a reckless search, only to find himself in a worse place than he started. Like many of you, he had lost his *feckin'* mind." She paused and gave James a wink. "But as you can see, he has moved on since then. A teacher, a husband, and a soon-to-be-father."

Again, everyone clapped for James as he was unwillingly tossed onto a bright stage. A naked soul for them all to see. Kalen was the one who'd persuaded him to join the program, but she didn't need to remind him of that every session.

"I hadn't thought about it until you brought it up." He purposely made the comment passive-aggressive. "I figured I'm having a baby and that's a good step in the right direction. I've put all that other stuff in the past."

"Well, that's great, James." She casually moved on after opening a scab that had only begun to heal.

As the meeting dragged on, James turned to his badgering thoughts. *Am I going to be like my father? Would I abandon my children and wife the way he did?* In hindsight, his father was a saint until he wasn't anymore, but James was never even close to being perfect. The session hadn't been productive at all. Afterward, as James poured a bitter decaf coffee into a paper cup for the road, someone tapped him on his shoulder.

"*Hoyay*, hermano ..."

It was Tomás, his sponsor for the last two years. The six-foot-tall Latin man was lean, with a hulking rib cage and a mischievous gap-toothed grin. He was ten years older than James, and the two of them had become friends at Kalen's meetings. After serving his time in the Last War, he'd come back with PTSD and an addiction to painkillers. He'd been through his ups and downs, but that day he seemed to be flying high on life.

"Well, you look like *gobshite*," said Tomás, impersonating their counselor. He let out a high-pitched cackle at his joke. "Did you let Kalen get to you today?"

"She doesn't know what she's talking about."

Tomás leaned back, scanning him like a drone. "You do look like you've seen a ghost. It's close to the tenth anniversary of the day your father left, right?"

"Something like that." Trying to avoid the subject, James looked up at the huge grin on his friend's face. "And what's up with you? Why are you in such a good mood?"

Tomás, acting strange, led him to the bleachers, away from the rest of the group. He was acting strange. "The Light Keepers." Even his lowest voice carrried across the echoey gym. "I went and saw them."

Shocked, James didn't know what to say to his friend. The Light Keepers were a cyber cult that'd been putting out anonymous videos to lure recruits. They had been using Lucidity's tech for harmful experiments. Some thought it might be remnants of the Free Folk, but most presumed it was one woman using a filter to hide her entity. In the videos she put out, she recited cryptic messages as a mesmerizing alien-like avatar. Recently, after several deaths linked to the Keepers, their status rose from cult to cyber-terrorist organization. It was now considered a felony to associate with them. Not only was Tomás his sponsor, but he was his closest friends besides his wife.

James whispered, "You need to quit with that shit, Tee." Kalen glanced at the two, who were obviously up to no good in their corner of the gym. "What good is a sponsor or a best friend if he's dead or in prison?"

"I'll be fine."

"Every dead man's famous last words."

"You should come with me one day."

James laughed. "Or maybe I should just stick a needle back in my arm."

"I'm serious, Grady. They'll help you forget about the past."

"I got a baby on the way." James made sure no one else was paying attention to them. "Are you sure you've been taking your meds?"

"I don't need the pills anymore."

"Oh, Jesus!" James scratched his beard. "It's worse than I thought."

"Trust me."

"I don't think Kalen would approve of you running off and joining a cult."

By the crooked grin on Tomás's lips, he wasn't going to budge. "I only have to go back a couple more times. I promise you I won't get caught."

"How did you find the Light Keepers anyway? The Feds haven't even had any luck."

"I can't tell you that," Tomás insisted. "All I know is that I'm finally finding myself."

"It sounds to me like you're drinking the Kool-Aid ... *brother*."

Despite how ridiculous and illegal it sounded, James was curious. The real world didn't seem to make sense to anyone, including himself. Whether it was a new virtual escape or a cyber cult, he was missing out on some secret everyone else seemed to have already figured out.

Tomás put his arm around him, pulling him into a headlock. "I was starting to lose my mind, hermano, but now I feel freer than ever." He took the last bite of his donut, and before leaving, he said, "The door's open whenever you're ready."

CHAPTER 3

As soon as the front door slid open, James staggered in and threw his handbag down onto the oak floor of the sleek and sterile living room. He partly wished their tenth-floor, three-bedroom condo in Long Island City was more cluttered. Every wall and appliance had a screen implanted in it – undetectable unless in use. Compared to the house he'd grown up in, it seemed like a futuristic palace in the sky, completed by a terrace with a panoramic view of Manhattan. If it weren't for Sandy's job, then he would probably have lived on the outside.

It had been four days since he had seen Sandy — his wife who was away at the annual Psychology and Neuroscience Conference in Atlanta. Many of her patients were terminally ill, and luckily for them, she was an empathetic angel anyone would want at their deathbed.

James happened to have been on his own the first night they'd met.

Sandy didn't usually travel for her job, and on this Thursday evening, a mere seventy-two hours since she'd left, he was already starting to get antsy without her.

"Welcome home, James." The voice of the peppy synth named Ginger made James flinch. Through the built-in audio system, it asked, "What can I help you with? ... How was your day?"

"Power off."

He didn't need another long conversation with the synth, literally programmed to talk for days. Ginger seemed bored – if that was even possible with AI. The authenticity of the tech had gotten eerie since the days of Siri and Alexa. Luckily, the EFI put in place more safeguarding regulations after the Free Folk had manipulated a highly sentient AI drone to go on a killing spree at an outdoor rock concert.

James then remembered having a reason to utilize her services.

"Ginger ... Messages, please."

The screen over the fireplace came on. A video message from Sandy. Before cueing it, James gushed at the user profile image she had set as her default. He'd taken the photo of her when they were on their honeymoon – a sunset sky in the background and the perfect glow on her face. She had a Chinese mother, and her father was a European mutt, but most people mistook her for Polynesian or Hawaiian. She was born with olive-brown skin and a full head of golden locks, hence her name.

On-screen, Sandy stood in a fancy hotel room in the background. "Hey, hun, I guess you turned off your Uni again. It's been a long day and I just wanted to say I love you and that I miss you before I go to yet another lecture." Her hair was tied up in a messy bun, but she seemed relaxed. The tone of her voice always sounded calm but that was a skill set of her trade. The conference seemed like a much-needed break from the norm of dealing with hospice patients. Her job took a huge toll on her, whether she liked to admit it or not. "I'll be back tomorrow afternoon." She blew a kiss. "And don't forget we're going to your mother's this weekend."

With the competition on his mind, James had forgotten about the trip. His mother, Mary, had recently found out she was to become a grandma. She and Sandy had gone behind his back to organize the weekend. James and his mother had hardly spoken much since her agoraphobia diagnosis, which he dismissed as psychosomatic nonsense, had caused her to skip his wedding four years ago.

SYNCDN – a holographic AR system pronounced as "synced in" – was his go-to for a couple of hours of spacing out every night. The tech only required a light pair of blue-tinted lenses. It functioned as a hub for entertainment and education. As soon as he put on the visors, a vast array of options appeared in the room. Books and magazines, ones that he could pick up and read, rested on a table. A virtual Steinway Grand sat in front of an actual piano stool, which seemed out of place when the network wasn't activated. He hid all those items, choosing the theater setting instead. He shrank the cinema-sized hologram with a simple finger motion.

Ginger was programmed to put it on the news, which was more informative than glum after the war's end – or any time since James had been alive. When he was a child everyone pretended that the country and the world as a whole would get past the growing divide. It only got worse. James, a pacifist, didn't much agree with war or any violent conflict. Eventually, however, it was the only way to defeat the extremist movement taking control everywhere. On the other end of the table, the progressive Earth First Initiative, and their Great Upgrade, appeared to be simultaneously lowering global temperatures, protecting the most vulnerable countries, and with some help from a private militia, keeping their promise to bring about peace. It was no utopia or anything but it was better. At least until a new threat began to surface.

On-screen, an anchorwoman spoke. "Despite its safety guarantee, Lucidity reported a second death today. Sasha Anderson, a bank manager residing in London, was found dead in a DreamCatcher this morning. LucidiTech's CEO, Prishna Gupta, immediately condemned the cult hackers known as the Light Keepers."

The news showed a clip of Ms. Gupta speaking at a press conference. "This anonymous threat is a danger to the system and those who access it." She was middle-aged, petite yet statuesque, her accent Hinglish. "Here at LucidiTech, a subsidiary of my father's Gupta Energy Corp, and within the world of Lucidity, we pride ourselves on safety and transparency. These terrorists only mean to harm us. They'd rather create the anarchy we once lived in before." She closed her eyes as if saying a mental prayer and then continued. "Law enforcement agencies all over the world are asking anyone with information to contact us with any possible information on the whereabouts of this clandestine enemy."

"Power off," he said, shutting down the SYNCDN.

Without drugs or alcohol, James's anxious tendencies reared their heads. All he could think about was Tomás going to jail and Calvin dying in whatever these Dream Catchers were. Since Thursdays were usually movie night in the Grady home, he put on *The Wizard of Oz* – a film that had regained popularity after its centennial anniversary. The choice would've never been allowed if Sandy were home. It was his father's favorite. She always reminded him that one memory could lead to the next, and before long, he'd be searching for his old man again. "There's no place like home," Dorothy said at the end of the film. Pops had quoted it every time he'd come back from his missions. He had never meant it. *Damn it,* James thought. *Sandy's right.* Only, James didn't want to find him anymore; now he just wanted to vent to the bastard.

For years he'd been sending messages to his father's outdated Connector account, an app so old it only ran on his office computer, but also the last place he'd heard from him. Figuring it would go unread like the others, James furiously typed out a message. Before pressing the send key, he read it over.

"Pops, this is the last time you'll ever hear from me. It's been ten years now and I'm not sure who was hurt the most. Mom's condition was getting better before you left. Since then, she's never learned to feel safe again. After Heather died, you needed to be there for us ... for her. My sister was gone — your daughter. And what did you do? You ran. The Army claimed you 'drifted' but Mom thinks you're dead. Who knows, maybe you are.

Patricia's big heart has led her to a selfless, unfulfilled life. As you requested, she took care of our mother – your wife. She spends most of her days trying to get the stubborn woman out of bed. She's never gotten to experience life.

As for me ... I'm doing fine without you. Most therapists, including my wife, believe you were the cause of my erratic behavior after college. The only thing I regret is searching for you. In that little amount of time you were around, you hammered in the fact that I needed to practice more. I needed to get into a good college. I needed to graduate. I fucking did all that for you, and you weren't even there to see me succeed. But I guess if you had actually been reading these messages, then you would know all this by now.

Here's something new, though — I have a child on the way and luckily I learned the most important lesson from you: how not to be a father. You had some good moments, but at the end of the day, you walked out on your family without an explanation. That's a pretty shitty thing to do. So fuck you and goodbye forever."

For a good ten minutes, James read what he had written to his father, over and over, questioning whether he had taken it too far. He hadn't been that angry in his messages since he began sending them ten years ago. *Pops will never see this anyway*, he thought, as he sent his words out to a man who didn't exist anymore. Right as he was about to go to bed, a *ping* came from his computer. James rushed back in and turned the screen on.

It said: *"The future is calling you, son."*

The same message he received ten years ago.

There was a *swoosh* followed by a bubbling sound, an animated ellipsis on the bottom left of the screen. According to the outdated app, his father – or someone who had access to his account, was about to send another message. James's heart pounded. He'd waited a decade for anything. The ellipsis went away, and so did the first message he received.

James sent another: *"Where are you, Pops?"*

No *swoosh*. No bubbling sound. No proof that James wasn't simply going mad with too much idle time. He stared at the screen, waiting for another response. Was it a glitch? Or was his father trying to send him a coded message? The Army's excuse had always seemed hasty, a formality during a tumultuous period. His mother's theory was only meant to help her sleep at night. But James, despite all his ill feelings, had no doubt Pops was still out there. The only issue: he'd promised Sandy, in sacred wedding vows no less, that the search for his father had to be over. It was the only ultimatum she ever gave him. The one commitment that was never to be broken.

PART TWO

CHAPTER 4

The traffic on 95 flowed with precision as Sandy Grady headed to her husband's home in Pennsylvania, taking care of a few work tasks in the AV Traveler she chose for the trip. At one point she remembered voting against the Automateds, the self-driving vehicles they used in the Interior, but now that she was pregnant, the thought of trains and taxis – or even worse, driving – was a hassle she wanted no part of. Far from a dystopia that many had predicted, the AI-run vehicles hadn't suffered a fit of road rage ... yet. Sandy set up an office in the spacious front cabin while her husband, James, napped in the rear, a glass divider between them to block any sound. Fortunately, she had a video session with one of her patients to keep her from overanalyzing her first trip to James's hometown.

Sandy fixed her hair on a screen that acted as a mirror, getting ready for her call with Monica Klein, a sixty-five-year-old patient of hers, who up until a few weeks ago had been terminally ill. Most of her patients were. Alone for weeks in the ICU with no visitors, Monica found comfort in Sandy's visits. Then one night her family had snuck her out of the hospital and when she came back a week later, the untreatable tumor in her brain had disappeared. No one bought that story, though.

"Hello, Dr. Grady," Monica shouted through the screen, her gray hair now coming through on her formerly bare skull. She sat out with a flute of champagne. It wasn't even noon yet. "Where *ya* headed to?"

Clearing her throat, Sandy replied, "We don't have much time, so I'd prefer if we continue our discussion on what treatment you received in Arizona." She jotted down details with a stylus on a stretched-out version of her UniTab. "The hospital has procedures and protocols you failed to adhere to, and they'd like the name and credentials of this magical doctor you went to."

"I already told you everything, Dr. Grady," Monica insisted, "and now that I'm not dying, maybe we can be friends."

Grinning, Sandy said, "Until the oncologists get the results back from your more advanced MRI, I'm to keep an eye on you. Which means you're still one of my patients for the time being." She finally answered the woman's first question. "I'm going to meet my mother-in-law for the first time if you must know."

"Oh, that's exciting!" As if they were gossiping brunch buddies, Monica swirled her champagne in the glass and took a sip. "How'd you meet James anyway?"

Sandy had mentioned her marriage on occasion, but had never told Monica about the fairy tale version of that cold December night four and half years ago, when she'd found her future husband bleeding out on the concrete, unconscious without a pulse. The ER doctors didn't have much better luck. James was dead for three minutes before they revived him from an overdose. The last time she'd told that story was after their wedding, and she hadn't spoken to her parents since.

"I met him at one of his concerts," she told Monica. It was partially true. Earlier on the same December night, she was mesmerized by his passionate performance on stage, and when she locked eyes with him they had a moment. "He used to play in a band."

"Oh how romantic," Monica swooned. "It would take a serenade to woo a pretty young thing like you."

"Actually, I'm three years older than him."

"Oooh ... a cradle robber."

Sandy blushed, then realized how unprofessional the conversation had become. "Now that I answered your question, why don't you tell me where your family took you so we can't get this over with? We only want to know so we can help others get the same treatment you did."

All of a sudden, Monica pretended to be called from inside her house. "What's that?" She avoided eye contact with Sandy, playing up her part. "I'm sorry, Dr. Grady, my grandson just woke up and I have to go change him." Now off camera, she said, "I'll make an appointment later this week."

The screen went black and her patient had once again avoided the questions.

Sandy didn't have much time anyway. They pulled into a checkpoint, which scanned the vehicle as they passed into Delaware County. It was easy for them to get into the Outside, but another couple going in the opposite direction was interrogated like criminals. The system needed major tweaking, she thought as the steering wheel retracted from its spot in AV mode. For the final five miles, she'd have to drive.

As soon as Sandy pulled up to the house her husband had grown up in, it dawned on her what a different childhood they'd had. While her parents owned several properties in different parts of the world, the Gradys had just a few feet between them and their neighbors. Of course, she hadn't spoken with her own parents. At the wedding, they had found out James was a former addict and made a horrendous seen. A sore subject she preferred not to talk about. James had been nothing but a good husband to her. For some reason, though, she still felt nervous, hoping her child would have at least one grandparent in his life.

"Wake up, babe," she said to James.

Groggy, he muttered, "Yay."

"It won't be that bad."

James kissed her. "Whatever you say."

Waiting at the door, Mary Grady had a huge grin on her face and was in good shape for a woman who never left home besides her walks to church, located conveniently at the end of the block. Her thin gray hair was styled and much longer than the conservative bob she'd had when they spoke a couple of weeks ago. She wore a dash of makeup and a fashionable Interior-like outfit, sprinting to meet them in the driveway.

"Welcome home you two, or should I say, you three." Mary pulled back to take a good look at him. "Jesus, you sure could use some sun, James Michael Grady."

"We're working on it," Sandy said. "I keep trying to get him to take me on a vacation."

James asked, "So what's the plan?"

There weren't many options with Mary's self-diagnosed agoraphobia – a special kind where she could only leave the house for worship at the end of the block.

"We can start by getting your bags in the house." Mary held the screen door to let them in. "Then I'd love to get to know this lovely wife of yours, who's even prettier in person. I made some of James's favorite oatmeal cookies if you guys want a snack."

Sandy asked, "And do I smell coffee?"

"Why yes you do." Mary giggled and turned to her son. "Do you mind if I steal her from you?"

"Be my guest." He hugged her. "It's good to see you, Ma."

The kitchen-slash-dining room reminded Sandy of a café she used to visit near Brown's campus in Rhode Island, which was meant to feel vintage. In the Grady home, though, it was most likely how it had always looked, quaint as the late 1900s. She was nervous, and not sure if coffee would help, but let Mary pour her a big cup anyway. James had told Sandy of his mother's quirks, so Sandy was prepared, making sure not to bring up Mary's condition, knowing most phobias fascinated her.

Mary signaled for them to sit. "So how many weeks are you now?"

Sandy followed her mother-in-law's lead. "About twenty-four."

"Look at you, still skinny as a rail with a slight bump and that radiant skin. I loved that part about being pregnant." Mary added, "Heck, I loved the big belly and every step of becoming a mother."

Sandy took a big sip of her coffee. "Besides the initial morning sickness, I've felt great."

"I don't remember being allowed to drink caffeine when I was pregnant," Mary quipped. "People would give you a stink eye even if you had a glass of wine. Of course, when my mother was pregnant with me no one batted a lash when she smoked a cigarette or drank a fifth of whiskey. Times are always changing."

Mary got up when the timer on the oven went off, pulled a fresh batch of oatmeal raisin cookies out, and placed them on the stove, the scent of cinnamon and sugar surging through the small kitchen as she dashed some salt onto them.

"Everything tastes better with a hint of salt," Sandy said, her belly rumbling.

"Oh my," Mary gushed, "someone's hungry. We'll let those sit for a minute, and then you can have as many as you want. Lord knows you need to start eating for another person."

"Thank you, ma'am."

"Now you call me Mary or Mom. Whatever you like, but no ma'am." His mother spoke with a Southeastern Pennsylvanian accent that Sandy knew her husband had tried to get rid of, preferring that people couldn't tell where he came from.

"Okay if I start with Mary?"

"That works." Her mother-in-law paused before asking, "Have you guys come up with any names?"

Sandy rolled her eyes by accident.

"Oh no," Mary sighed. "We already had one too many Jimmys and Jameses around here."

The two both roared in laughter as James snuck in. "What are you two laughing about?"

"None of your business," Mary insisted. "Now, take some of those cookies and let us finish our conversation. I'm sure your sister will be home soon and would love to see you."

James left like a small boy with a glass of milk and a plate of cookies, curious as to what the adults were talking about.

"Now, where were we?" Mary asked.

"*Jimmy.*"

"Oh yeah ... Don't name that child that. My son obsesses over his father, but I guess you already know that by now. Sometimes I wish they'd just come and tell us he's dead. At least then I'd stop thinking he's going to walk back in that door each and every day. In fact, someone from some woman from an Army task force called me the other day asking about Jimmy. I told him that my son had no luck and neither would they. If Jimmy wanted to go off the grid, he'd figure out a way and they'd never find him. He may have not finished college, but damn, that man was smart.

The conversation was one question away from getting personal. Sandy knew how to dig through someone's deep subconscious. "Can I ask you a question?"

Mary nodded but seemed hesitant.

"Do you honestly think your husband's still alive?"

"I'm not sure, dear." Mary suddenly got up to walk to the counter. "As they say in marriage until death do us part, but I haven't seen a death certificate. As shocked as I was the day it happened, I can't say I was surprised."

"But James said you were devastated."

"I was, but that's different. Jimmy had left us over and over, but that time I knew it was for good. He took his stuff – all of it. His best friend, Brian, who was also his boss, disappeared around the same time. I knew I would never hear from him again."

"James never told me what his father did after he retired from the Army."

Mary smiled, but it seemed timid. She turned her back to Sandy, washing dishes in the sink. "Jimmy never told me a damn thing either."

She vigorously scrubbed a bowl. "He was probably trying to save me from all the worrying."

"That's all he ever told you?" Sandy wished she could take it back already, practically interviewing the woman. The caffeine was kicking in and so was the baby. "You don't have to answer that."

Mary gazed out the kitchen window into the backyard. "One time he opened up a little more. I think it was the Fourth of July. Jimmy got a little drunk, as he always did when Brian was around, confessing he was part of a hostage unit in the Army, and that he would still do interrogations when they needed him. In hindsight, he was very good at getting people to talk." Mary stared into her eyes. "Kinda like you."

"I wasn't trying to pry." Sandy hands shook. "It's this annoying habit I get from my job."

Mary laughed. "That was supposed to be a compliment, dear. I'm told you're great at what you do. The truth is we didn't know what Jimmy did. All I know is he could've retired and got a normal job, but he kept leaving us – especially after James's sister, Heather, committed suicide. Every time he came back, his face got older and his soul wearier, saying that he felt dirty — that he needed to fix it. I don't claim to see someone's actual soul, but you would know if you saw it."

Sandy had seen it many times – with her grandma, and James, and every day with her patients. The drained expression on their faces as they saw death closing in on them from the rearview mirror.

Mary continued. "I'm sure you're curious to know why I've kept myself in this house for the last twenty years."

"That's your own choice," Sandy insisted. "I would never make any judgments."

"I wouldn't blame you if you did," Mary said, putting away dishes, fidgety. "Most people assume it was the virus that did this to me, but it was much more than that. I enjoyed those years. Jimmy was home for the most part. We were a family for once. No, the First Pandemic merely jumpstarted my condition."

"If you don't mind me asking, what turned it into a more permanent state?"

"Jimmy was about to leave at the end of '27 to start a new project with Brian. He said he couldn't tell me where, but that he'd be much closer if I needed him. I'd grown used to the seclusion, and when I asked Jimmy if the world was ever going to be a safe place, he gave me a reassuring answer that didn't match the expression on his face. Like it was going to get worse before it got better. And he was right. This is the only place I ever felt safe after that."

Sandy met her mother-in-law at the window to share a view of the backyard, knowing Mary was on the verge of opening up. James continually told her about the garden where he and his sisters grew flowers and vegetables. It was still there, a little less magical than his whimsical description.

"There are two ways to go crazy in this world," Mary said, still gazing outside. "You can shelter yourself away from the truth or run straight into it. I'm sure you can figure out that James is the latter of the two. You can't blame him, though. We've been through a lot in this little old house."

"James is done searching for his father." Sandy put her hand on Mary's shoulder to comfort her. "He's much more focused, especially with the baby on the way."

"That's good." Mary finally looked at her. "The way my husband hid his work from me only made my mind wander farther into this deep anxiety. I'm glad that James never found much on that bender of his. When he started asking all these questions, I mistakenly told a curious young man that it might lead into dangerous territory – an enticer for someone like my boy."

"He sure is a curious one.

As Sandy said that, the smoke alarm went off; the fumes were heavy from the second batch of cookies overcooking in the oven. Mary grabbed a broom and shut it off as James shouted from the second floor, "Don't burn the cookies!"

Sandy yelled back to him, "Don't worry ... *We're* okay." She wiped the tear that had fallen down the side of her cheek, glad she'd finally met the woman who gave James life. Her husband was a complicated subject and Mary was the only one who might've known him better than her. "Luckily," Sandy joked, "the only thing he really cares about is cookies for now."

Mary approached Sandy, embracing her. "He was lost before he found you," she said with a whimper in her voice. "So just promise me you won't ever let him go down that road again."

"I promise I won't ever let him do that."

CHAPTER 5

The rusty blue house hadn't changed since childhood, the front porch lined with bouquets of tulips and roses. A statue of the Virgin Mary adorned the yard. It had been almost eleven years since James had seen his father in the backyard, the same location that had triggered an angsty young man into adulthood – or whatever he called the last decade. His wife seemed excited to finally meet her mother-in-law, as she should be, but Sandy might've overlooked the fact that going to Pennsylvania could bring back sour memories.

James glanced around to see if anything had changed in the house that had smelled like cookies and coffee since the days his grandparents owned it. The frames with Pops's missing pictures were still hung, replaced with quotes from the Bible. *"May God bless this home and all who enter."* His father had erased his identity on that day ten years ago, making it nearly impossible for any agency to find him, especially with a war going on.

The Yamaha upright piano remained in the den. His father had bought it for all three of the kids, but they all knew it was really for James. He had written the beginning parts of his piece "Little Flower" on it after his sister's death. The finished version blew away the professors at his final review. On that day, he would officially find out he was going to graduate. It also happened to be the same day the war began and his father went missing. James never figured out if the two were related.

Peeking out onto the back porch, he remembered arriving home that day. His father's car had been parked on the lawn. The house was empty, but the doors were wide open as if a ghost had let him in. His father's attic office had been stripped of all its computers and electronics. Even the Alter World console was gone. When he opened the back door, all he could hear was his mother, Mary, sobbing like a manic child. Patricia held her, trying to calm her down. James had asked, "Where's Pops?" His tiny mother had turned away from the concrete patio and looked up at him with her bloodshot, soaked blue eyes. "He's gone," she had cried. "Your father left us, baby ... He finally left us for good."

For the past two days, James couldn't get the message out of his head. *The future is calling you, son.* The message didn't make sense the first time and now that it was the future, it still made no sense. He convinced himself it was only a glitch, knowing everyone in the house was adamantly opposed to any more searching for Pops.

As he grabbed the suitcase and headed up the stairs, the creaking of the wooden banister reminded him of the ghosts. Although Heather did her final deed in Center City, he always felt her presence in the house. Determined not to mess up the decent start to the weekend, James reminded himself of how excited his little sister was for ninety-nine percent of her short life. The same way he needed to act more often.

He followed an itch toward the attic on the third floor, remembering that hollow feeling that had overwhelmed him. Pops's office was closed. He wondered if Patricia and his mother had meant to keep it that way, the doorknob seemingly staring at him, inviting him to come in. He peeked in to find nothing except a bunch of mail thrown into the center, scattered and unorganized, dust building up along the corners as cobwebs hung from the ceiling fan.

"What are you doing?" Patricia shouted from behind, scaring the piss out of him.

Though his thirty-four-year-old sister seemed content, the wrinkles gave away a weariness that couldn't be masked. She wore her nurse scrubs and a baggy hoodie, hardly the popular fashionista anymore. In high school, she had been both homecoming queen and the valedictorian on her way to becoming whatever she'd wanted to be. She had since refused ample opportunities in the Interior, petrified that their mother wasn't fit to be alone. The only times James had seen her happy in the last ten years was at his wedding.

"Do you know about all these letters, Patty?"

"I know Mom likes to throw Pops's mail in here."

"Why doesn't she throw them away or burn them like most bitter ex-wives or widows?"

Patricia grabbed some of the mail and sorted through it. "Mom's changed over the last couple of years."

James knelt and helped his sister grab what she couldn't. "I was shocked when I found out she called Sandy and invited us to come. And today she seems content. She looks—"

"Happy," Patricia interrupted. "It's the new meds she's been taking."

"But she's always been on some form of antidepressant and they made her, well, you know, numb."

"Well, thanks to all those clever ads, they've made it seem acceptable for all these law-abiding citizens to take what we used to at the clubs."

James snickered. "Man, she almost beat my ass when she caught me with molly in high school. I should go right down there and tell her what a hypocrite she is."

His sister grabbed his shoulder. "You, sir, will do no such thing. This is the happiest she's been since we were kids, and no one's taking that away from me."

"From you?"

"Yes ... from me!"

James gazed into his sister's cold blue eyes. She had taken the brunt of it for years.

"I have a boyfriend," Patricia declared. "It's been a long time coming."

James held his sister's shoulder. "That's amazing, Patty," he said. "I'm sorry for leaving you here with Mom. You could've had a whole life, but stopped everything to be with her. All I wanted to do was run away."

Patricia stacked the mail into neat piles. "It's what I decided to do. You're too sensitive – always have been. I was never mad at you because you're a lot like him."

"Who?"

"Pops ... He was pretty fragile too."

"I never even saw the man cry."

The two sat on the empty wooden floor as Patricia put her arm around him. "When you were about ten or eleven, Dad came home a little different from before," she began, still with her Delco accent intact. "*Yous* guys all went to church and I think he must've thought he was alone. I heard him downstairs on the piano playing this beautiful piece. I was gonna tell him how pretty it was. I was halfway down the stairs when I saw him sobbing like it was the first time he had cried in his entire life."

James shook his head in disbelief. "What's wrong with our family, Patty?"

"Maybe we're cursed, but we're going to be okay, bro." Patricia then began singing. "*Where have all the soldiers gone? ... Long time passing ... Where have all the soldiers gone? ... Long time ago.*" Her voice echoed off the walls. "*They've gone to graveyards, every one ... Oh, when will they ever learn?*"

James remembered. "Pops was always that singing that stupid song? What did it mean anyways? What were we supposed to learn?"

"I don't know." She asked, "So, you still searching for the old man?"

"I have a feeling he's out there somewhere. Don't you ever feel the way I do?"

Patricia gazed down at him. "To be honest, I'm disappointed with him. It takes a selfish man to leave his family like that."

"That's why I want to know if there's more to it," he said. "I sometimes think he could've been running for his life to save us from trouble. I mean, Uncle Brian left too."

"Well, he didn't have a family."

"True," James sighed. "I sent Pops my final message two days ago, and oddly enough, I got the same message he sent me ten years ago. "

Patricia grabbed her brother from the floor and dragged him into her bedroom. It had been years since James had felt the telepathic sibling connection they'd had as kids, but when she reached for something high up in her closet, he knew it was important. Behind a pile of clothes was an old leather satchel.

"That's the bag he always had over his shoulder." James placed it in his hands. "He never let it out of his sight. I thought it was gone."

Patricia asked, "Do you remember the last message he sent to me?"

James nodded. "Something about finding the answers in the stars."

"Yeah well, he sent me that same message two days ago as well."

"So maybe it wasn't a glitch?"

"Glitch or no glitch, it made me realize the answer was in the stars?"

"What do you mean?"

"This bag was in your bedroom. There are all those glow-in-dark stickers on the ceiling, and that's right where that little storage space is located. It only took me ten years to figure that out."

"This is weird." James started to peek into the bag. "What's in here anyway?"

She checked to see if anyone was coming. "I don't know – some pictures, letters, and flash drives from his time working for whoever. It doesn't mean anything to me, but with all your research it might be helpful. Some of it seems pretty official, like government documents."

"Do you think I should still try to find him?" James was almost embarrassed he'd spent so much of his time doing so.

"You just want to know. I get it. I don't think you'll be happy until you find the answers." She paused. "Will you do me one favor, though?"

"Of course."

"Don't tell Mom or Sandy I gave that to you." She gave him a vicious stare. "They want you to move past this, and they're probably right. Don't let this journey to find Pops get the best of you like it did before, or else you might end up like him, or worse. Your baby and your wife are what you need to be concerned about."

James kissed his sister's forehead. "Thank you." He rushed to hide the satchel under some clothes in his suitcase, hoping it would get back home unnoticed, contemplating if he should leave it behind. It was so close to being over but he wouldn't quit until he saw the bones. Nonetheless, he kept the satchel, still wondering if he was the last person on earth who gave two shits about his father's unsolved disappearance.

CHAPTER 6

Using the rearview mirror, Adriana Diaz glanced at the wrinkles under her dark brown eyes, hardly focused on the two-lane highway she drove down. The day was too hot for May. The AC blew nothing but dust in the stick-shift sedan. Her sweaty armpits stained the gray buttoned-up shirt. Meanwhile, the partner she had met that morning slept peacefully, her head out the only window that opened. When Diaz passed the *"Welcome to Richmond"* sign, riddled with bullet holes and tagged with graffiti, it was a stark reminder that the city she was headed into had yet to recover from the Last War.

For the past five years, Diaz had been a special detective in an Army task force dedicated to locating "drifters" – uniformed members or military contractors who'd gone missing during the war's domestic conflicts. In most cases, it was for census and tax purposes, although there were many instances of sedition and fraud. This particular investigation, which had begun with a couple of red flags, involved three drifters who'd all disappeared a decade ago, including Diaz's former superior, Sergeant Jim Grady.

"Ronson … *Despierta!"* Diaz shouted, purposely waking up her partner with a heightened version of her Nuyorican accent. "We're almost there and you're sucking out all the cool air."

Martha Ronson, a southern hard-ass from DC, wiped the drool off her chin. The athletic fifty-four-year-old had a sassy bright white bob. Although her new partner was almost ten years older than her, Diaz found the insistently hetero married mother of four annoyingly sexy. It was Ronson's final hurrah before retirement, and even on the first day, it seemed like she was half-assing the assignment they had three weeks to complete.

Still groggy, Ronson asked, "Where are we?"

"Our destination." Diaz navigated through the potholed streets. They were in the former capital of Virginia to speak to the husband of Ellie Brown Ginsberg, one of the other drifters on their list. "You've been asleep for almost an hour while I've been driving this gas-guzzling piece of shit."

"I was getting some beauty rest," Ronson said in her cocky southern twang, scanning through the case files on her UniTab. Under her breath, she quipped, *"Lord knows you could use some."*

Hot and frustrated, Diaz pulled over to figure out directions. She half ignored the snarky comment and the sign in favor of the Light Keepers on the side of the road. She put her frizzy black hair up into a sleeker ponytail. The GPS insisted they go down a road blocked by two vandalized police cars, stripped for their parts years ago. Diaz found a detour and realized she'd hardly discussed a game plan with Ronson, who according to her military and law enforcement credentials, was once good at her job – the only thing they had in common besides preferring to be addressed by their last names.

Diaz asked, "Why do you think it took so long for the Army to investigate this one?"

"It got lost in one of the cyber attacks." Ronson had a condescending tone. "If we can't locate them this time around, then we declare them dead." She spat out the window. "No need to complicate things."

Taking a detour, Diaz argued, "Just because they weren't all soldiers like us doesn't mean they don't deserve a thorough investigation."

"C'mon, Diaz ... You know as well as I do that most of our drifters go flying off the radar for a reason. Maybe they all started that Light Keeper cult."

Diaz sighed. "This one drifter I found had killed his brother – a

Free Folk mercenary who also happened to be his child's godfather. No one ever wanted to call it what it really was — a civil war."
Coincidentally, there was a lifelike mural of three Free Folk men hanging from the empty concrete wall. It was captioned "*DEATH TO ALL THE FASCIST TRAITORS.*" Shaking her head, Diaz quipped, "It got real medieval up in here." The ropes were still hanging in case anyone forgot.

"Damn sure did," Ronson agreed. "And while these kids may have won the war, they had to witness the devil's wrath up close and personal." The dirty-mouthed yet devout Christian woman pointed out a couple sharing a needle at what was once a bus stop. "If we do find this sergeant of yours, don't be surprised to find him in a similar predicament."

"There's no way Grady turned to drugs."

"You never know." Ronson looked at her curiously. "What did he do in the Army?"

"When he left my unit he went on to train other units on ethical interrogation methods. Back when the rules still applied. I guess he joined this JTID after he retired – the same military contractor that connects all three of our drifters. All I could find out was that it was funded by the Army and decommissioned around the same time they all went missing." She had another thought. "What the hell do you think this JTID was up to anyway?"

Ronson rolled her eyes. "It's too early for so many damn questions, hun," she said as they entered the worst part of town. "Let's see what we can find and be grateful we didn't end up in a place like this."

The center of Richmond was ground zero for one of the largest domestic conflicts – one that had changed the course of the Last War. At the time they'd called it the Battle on Broad Street. Now, the remnants reminded Diaz of her first tour in Aleppo. A stretch of a college campus was reduced to rubble in the Free Folk's attempt to take over the state's capitol building. Disgusted, Ronson closed the only working window to block the stench of sewage runoff and avoid the toothless man offering them "the best heroin in Virginia."

Driving down the one clear stretch, Diaz sighed. "This is sad."

"It would've been a lot worse if the FF won that battle," Ronson reminded her. "With that momentum, they might have tried to take New York or DC next."

Diaz added, "It doesn't say much that we left it this way, though. Especially after those kids died for the New Civil Rights Act that wouldn't have passed without them."

Ronson sighed. "Meanwhile the KOA took all the credit and the EFI still hasn't gotten around to cleaning this mess up. Their Initiative may sound good on paper, but it's a slow process when it coincides with a war. Eighty percent of the country is still waiting to be upgraded."

"It's a big country."

When the car stopped, Ronson moaned, "Well, all I know is I'm gonna be pissed if I don't get to see my retirement because I was killed in this dump."

They pulled up in front of a three-story brick building, where windows were broken and doors were optional. A motley crew of drifters stood out front, a diverse mix of different ages, races, and genders dressed as rough as the city they lived in. Every town on the Outside was different, and while Diaz never wanted to patronize anyone by playing dress-up, the modern pantsuits they both picked that day screamed that they were from the Interior.

Diaz checked her UniTab. "I guess this is the place."

Putting on an N95 mask, Ronson said, "I don't want to catch anything from these mouth breathers."

"You can't do that. It's obvious enough that we're not from these parts, so the last thing we want to do is insult them."

Ronson hid the mask in her back pocket as they stepped out of the vehicle. "Your ass is mine if I catch something."

Diaz cracked her knuckles to calm her nerves. "Let's see what we can find."

An enormous man approached them. His arms were brick walls with protruding veins, his cheeks covered in permanently inked, black teardrops. "You ladies look lost," he said menacingly. "Hampton Roads is about two hundred miles east of here."

"We're not looking for any trouble." Diaz waved a badge as if it would make him trust her more. "We're here from the Lost Patriot Task Force looking for information on a man named Ian Ginsberg."

Seeming confused, the man said, "That dude killed himself three years ago." He turned to another person in the group. "Hey, Poe, didn't you used to date that dude?"

The woman he called Poe was at the far end of the steps, a red bandana wrapped around her mouth and a fitted cap worn backward. Before either of the detectives got a good look, the woman made a run for it. Diaz hadn't pursued a suspect in years, reluctantly chasing after the woman through the rugged streets of downtown.

The group cheered. "Don't let them piggies get you, Poe!"

The woman turned into an alleyway, but Ronson, who bragged about being a marathon runner, kept after the woman behind the building. She chased Poe through a parking lot overrun with tents. Diaz, feeling useless and out of shape, got a cramp and staggered behind as the chase continued.

On the street over, Poe zig-zagged around a burnt-out fire truck and used a broken bicycle as an obstacle to throw in Ronson's way.

Diaz trailed behind.

When Poe made her way up a fire escape, Ronson grabbed the woman and tackled her to the ground. The other pedestrians in the streets had scattered, thinking law enforcement agencies were staging a crackdown.

Finally, Diaz caught up, tired and out of breath.

"You have to stay in shape to catch these young kids," Ronson declared.

Poe picked herself up off the street. "I'm thirty-seven, bitch."

"Still a whole lot younger than me."

Diaz asked Poe, "Why'd you run?"

"I don't want to go to prison. They need me here."

Ronson seemed puzzled. "We just wanted to ask you about Ian Ginsberg and his wife – Ellie. I don't even think we have the authority to arrest anybody." She turned to Diaz. "Do we?"

Diaz shook her head no.

The woman finally relaxed, pulling down her bandana and taking off her baseball cap to smoke a cigarette. She had blondish-gray hair tied back in a ponytail and looked much older than her age. "Ian was married to her before she went missing. I don't even know if they were divorced when we dated, but he always reminded me of how badass Ellie was."

Diaz asked, "So why did Ian kill himself?"

"Don't know … Maybe the drugs? Maybe the endless searching for Ellie? Maybe he just died from a broken heart."

"Did he tell you what his ex-wife was involved in?"

"Some secret military project."

"The JTID?"

"Yeah, that was it."

Diaz asked, "And you think it had something to do with that?"

Taking a seat on the steps, Poe said, "Ellie came back to Richmond around the same time Ian was organizing the People's Front – the real heroes of this city – which must've been around 2032. She told Ian she'd be back soon. Then a week later she used a hidden cell phone to call him saying she'd been detained by some militia in Ohio. They were on a bus heading southbound through Kansas." Her voice was more subdued when she said, "That was the last time he heard from her."

Diaz plopped down beside her. "I'm guessing Ian didn't just let it go."

"Nope ... After they told him the JTID mysteriously disappeared, he drove up to Kansas and talked to every single agency in the area. He finally found a transit record of a bus accident that happened on Highway 35 on the same day. There weren't any names listed in the report and he thought it was a cover-up." Exhaling a huge cloud of smoke, the woman joked, "No offense, but y'all seem late to the search party."

"We're following orders," Ronson explained, watching her back the whole time. "Anyone else ever come poking around about this?"

"Maybe five years ago," Poe answered. "At that point, Ian and I were both heavy into the needle so I don't know how helpful we were."

"What department were they with?" Ronson asked. "The Army? The VA?"

Poe laughed. "No, it was some kid on tour with his band. Ian recognized his name and confronted him. He was searching for his father – Jimmy Something or other."

Excited, Diaz asked, "Jim Grady?"

"That sounds about right," said Poe. "When Ian told him that they were all dead, the kid stuck around for a night to get high with us. Ian told him not to waste his time."

Diaz followed up. "So I guess Ellie never came back home?"

"No, and when I met Ian here he was already drowning his pains away."

Diaz checked her UniTab to remember the name of the third drifter. "Did Ian ever mention a Quinn Baxter?"

"Doesn't ring a bell," Poe said. "There was Ellie and that Grady guy, and someone they called Suzi Q."

Confused, Diaz told her, "There's no one who goes by that in our case file."

Poe abruptly stood up and pulled out an old smartphone to show them. "I just remembered something. I'm not sure if you have this picture on record, but this is the three of them a couple of weeks before they went missing."

Diaz recognized Grady who, unlike his days in the Army, wore an ashy beard in the photo of them smiling, having not aged gracefully since she'd last seen him. On the other hand, Ginsberg looked the same as the photo in their case file – strong cheekbones, dark brown skin, and the same playful box braids as one of Diaz's ex-girlfriends. *Cute,* she thought. She glanced at the third person, unsure if it was Quinn Baxter or Suzi Q. Whoever it may be was tall and rail-thin with pink pigtails, and a pale face covered in so many tattoos it was unrecognizable. There were ink hearts around her pronounced rosy cheeks. An abstract daffodil on her forehead.

"This is very helpful," Diaz said.

"Don't get too caught up in this," Poe warned. "You two don't want to end up losing your shit like Ian."

"We're doing our job." Diaz winked. "And I'm pretty good at mine."

Poe grimaced. "So was Ian."

Ronson interrupted and asked, "What did Ian do, if you don't mind me asking?" She smirked. "I mean, besides a lot of heroin."

"Before Ian dedicated his life to activism he had been both a Navy Seal and a brilliant mathematician, so don't get too cocky out there on the road." Poe put the bandana over her mouth and nose. "I wouldn't want to catch anything from you two." She headed in the opposite direction they'd come from.

Diaz had always found her missing vets, but the woman only added to her suspicion that this particular investigation was stranger than most. Ronson wasn't going to make it any easier.

"Wipe that look off your face, Diaz."

"You could use a little more tact."

"You wouldn't have gotten any of that intel if I didn't catch her in the first place." Ronson kicked trash out of her way. "Where to next?"

Diaz checked their itinerary. "I guess we have to locate this Quinn Baxter – whoever she is. I think we need to go to Kansas to follow up on that accident."

"Have you tried getting a hold of Grady's family?"

"While you were sleeping I called his wife, Mary, asking about it," Diaz said. "She mentioned that her son had looked for him, and only found a dead end, which must've been here in Richmond." She paused to stretch her legs from the run. "I don't want to bother them anymore unless we run out of leads."

"I just want to get this over with," Ronson told her, picking up Poe's still-burning cigarette butt. "I survived three deployments, two deadly viruses, two bullshit wars, and a cheating husband." She took a big puff from it and put it out. "Lord help me if I don't make it through this mission."

CHAPTER 7

It was the Tuesday night before the competition James had been
prepping for all year, but the elephant keeping him awake at night was
the satchel his sister had handed him – quite literally a bag full of
secrets. He'd never rest until he figured out what was inside, so after
Sandy went to bed, he quietly plucked it out of his suitcase and brought
it to the office.

Inside his geeked-out man cave, he'd built a music laboratory
designed for inspirational moments. A huge thin-glass screen wrapped
around the desk like an IMAX theater. A five-octave keyboard collecting
dust from its lack of use. In the center of the screen was a 3D sonogram
– a little alien creature floating in an elliptical-shaped ectoplasm with an
unformulated skull. The images always frightened him until it was *his*
baby.

As James stared at the pictures of their little boy, reminded of the
dangerous potential the satchel could unleash, his UniTab buzzed like a
sign from God. It was Tomás, always calling him at the most random
times. When James cued the video call to his workstation, his friend's fat
head took over the eighty-inch panoramic screen.

Tomás grinned like a madman. "You excited about tomorrow?"

"I'm getting there," James sighed. "Why do you look like you're up
to trouble?"

"I have to go meet with that *friend* I was telling you about."

"You better be careful with those—" James stopped himself before
mentioning the Light Keepers, possibly incriminating them both if their
conversation was being scanned. "They're cracking down on that hard."

"I'm good, Mami," Tomás joked. "And what are you doing up so
late? I bet you're thinking about digging through that bag."

James shouldn't have told him. "What do you think I should do?"

"I've seen you come a long way in a short time. Sometimes it's best to let bygones be bygones."

"And what about you?"

"I'm taking care of my shit," Tomás said. "You're the one opening up the gates to hell."

Although James shrugged, he knew it was the truth.

Tomás continued. "I wanted to wish you good luck in the competition tomorrow. I'll be sitting in the front row with that beautiful wife of yours, watching you take home that first prize."

"We'll see."

"Have some faith in yourself, hermano." Tomás winked. "You'll find that light soon enough."

With those parting words, the screen went blank. James was alone again. The best idea would've been to follow Tomás's advice and hit the sack, but he needed to know what his father had hidden away.

He cleared his desk, opened the satchel, and pulled out the first item – a wrinkled polaroid. It was of Pops, probably in his mid-thirties, with a young female soldier. The two were posing with big grins and beers in some foreign city, his father dressed in the desert fatigues he remembered so well.

He pulled out another photo and recognized a man he hadn't seen in decades, posing with his father. He and his sisters called him Uncle Brian, but he wasn't related to them in any way. The super-fit, curly-haired man had lived next door to them when Pops was stationed in Germany. He loved to spoil them, not having any kids of his own. He was Pops's best friend, even though they'd always seemed like complete opposites. Brian had left around the same time as Pops. James's mother had told him she saw soldiers searching his house, which most likely meant his uncle had been killed in the war.

Next, James pulled out an op-ed Pops had printed out from the

New York Times about the Midwest Melee. It was from the leader of the US division of the Free Folk, the corrupt governor of Ohio who would later be hung.

"*You have left us with no choice but to take this country from within,*" he stated at the beginning of the famous piece that had escalated the conflict on home soil. "*We will join forces with our so-called enemy abroad, those of us who choose God over your so-called Great Upgrade.*" It was his manifesto, and with dozens of police units and Army brigades already secretly on the Free Folks' side, along with foreign aid from enemy countries, they'd staged a successful coup of the Ohio statehouse. They had their eyes set on other parts the country.

It ended with, "*Us Free Folk will rid the world of anyone who doesn't obey God's orders.*" Unfortunately, those orders came from fascist dictators who believed in the dismissal of global warming, which would end up biting them in the ass in more ways than one.

Sick of the slow pace, James finally dumped all the contents of the bag onto his desk: a dozen or so photos, printed documents, and five flash drives. Most of the photos were of his father in random countries with random strangers he had met along the way, until one caught his eye.

A man, maybe in his late thirties, with a receding hairline and dark brown skin posed in a wheelchair. He wore a Hawaiian shirt in a dimly lit factory filled with computers. The people behind him were strapped with wires as they ran on treadmills. He turned it over and there was a handwritten message.

"*Hello, my good sir. You were indeed correct about resurrecting such a place. When shall we expect your arrival? Your expertise would be greatly appreciated.*" It was signed: "*SRT. – The Retreat 2.0 – 02/2032.*"

It didn't look like much of a Retreat – more like a strange testing laboratory. While the initials, SRT, sounded familiar, it could've been anyone given his father's past. James threw the polaroid back in the pile, skimming through some of the documents. Most of them consisted of redacted text – the kind he'd only seen in CIA documentaries. There were several confidential files that mentioned major branches of the government but none mentioned Sergeant Jim Grady by name, so James wasn't sure how his father got hold of them. Underneath the mess, he found an envelope with a printed letter inside, sent from his Uncle Brian with no return address. It read:

"Jimmy, I'm leaving the Retreat. I've waited for you long enough. It's not my cup of tea, but it does have great market potential. I'll keep my money in for now. I'm starting my own company with funding from some high-profile donors. We could work together again as we did in the Army and the JTID. The profits from this will be ridiculous and we wouldn't have to be the pawns anymore. You can't keep running from me. I know I made a huge mistake, but that doesn't mean your hands are clean from this mess. The past will find you."

His uncle's harsh words had James shaken. *The past will find you?* As James suspected, whatever civilian jobs Pops had landed after the Army had been as unconventional as whatever he'd done in the service. There were government contracts, some strange warehouse, his long-lost uncle Brian, and a confidential project known as the JTID. The rabbit hole was only getting deeper as the first hour flew by, and he hadn't even gotten to the flash drives yet. At least the paper trails didn't risk finding their way into the Cloud's surveillance.

Although, the Free Folk may have dismissed science, they had convinced many intelligent hackers to work for them. After the Last War – most of which had been fought in backrooms via cyber attacks – the allies of the EFI had imposed heavy regulations on the net. The thought of plugging the outdated flash drives into his workstation, full of his father's clandestine activities, didn't sit well with him. Then again, the curious itch usually beat out his better judgment.

It certainly did that night.

Only one of the flash drives had a label. A random collection of numbers and letters that meant nothing to him – *J8y131Rd.MC.ML.xxx.* When he inserted the drive into his computer the entire screen went black and a series of primitive coding in white lettering began loading. It reminded him of the DOS interface he had learned about in a Computer History course. Two words blinked on the bottom left of the screen:

"ACCESS CODE?"

That simple question felt like a sign to stop the search. James was tired and Sandy would kill him if she knew what he was doing . It was never just the drugs she worried about. Before she'd come along, he hadn't cared if he got in trouble. Now the possibility of federal prison didn't seem as thrilling. Whatever was in that bag didn't belong in his hands. There was no way of guessing his father's access code anyway, hardly knowing the man with a million secrets.

In a moment of zen, James unplugged the flash drive and packed the items back into the satchel. He hid the bag in his closet and was halfway to bed when an absurd idea came to him. *What if the access code was right in front of me all along?* He tiptoed back to his office and found the labeled flash drive, wondering if those letters and numbers (*J8y131Rd.MC.ML.xxx*) were his father's password.

It sounded too easy until it worked.

"WELCOME TO AFANET: YOUR SECURE DATABASE."

The new network prompted a list of files, most with coded names: *ScorpionRex, Alpha Blue,* and *FA.Z2.* James thought it easiest to start with the directory labeled: *MESSAGES.* He realized how spoiled he was, cringing when he had to type out the command prompts on the antique OS. When he figured out how to open the directory, he found fifty or so messages all from the same man – SRT. The odd scientist from the photograph had sent dozens of memos. He started with the first one on the list.

"*The avatar is here waiting for you, my dear friend,*" the man said in the message dated four years ago. "*I shall keep mine eyes peeled for your response.*" For years this SRT sent the same dispatch in one way or another. "*Where are you?... When are you coming here, dear friend?... Why must you hide your self, Jaybird?*"

The files appeared to be sorted chronologically. He read the oldest message on the list after scrolling to the bottom. It was from the week before Pops disappeared – April 22, 2032. SRT wrote:

"*It's been a while, dear friend. We have finally completed the Void. Since that no-good business associate of yours is finally gone you should come to give it a tour in person. And as you suggested in our past correspondences, I vow to not let this fall into the wrong hands.*"

James added the Void to his new group of names he'd never heard of before, figuring that's what SRT was working on at the Retreat. If his father was the intended recipient then he'd never responded to the message board ... ever. It was quiet for years until he found another long message from five years ago.

SRT: "*If you're still out there, you know by now that I had to make a deal with the devil and sell the Void. I want you to know there's always a place for you in 'our world' – whatever they decide to call it. We saved your old username for you to access whenever you're ready to shine. Your anonymity will always remain safe with us.*"

There was one last message from only a couple of weeks ago.

SRT: "*Is that you, Jaybird? It seems as though you have found your avatar but now I can't locate you, my friend.*"

James's deep fascination with whatever the Void consisted of was interrupted by the sound of footsteps coming his way. He'd forgotten Sandy's new habit of waking up in the middle of the night to pee. He unplugged the flash drives, stuffed them in the satchel, threw it behind the desk, and improvised a song on the keyboard. He hit a sour chord right as she came in to check on him.

"That's pretty," Sandy joked, wiping her eyes. "I know your mind's wandering because of the competition, but when do you think you'll come to bed?"

"Give me ten minutes." James continued his charade as an impassioned songwriter. "I'm trying to figure out what comes next."

Sandy bought his little act and headed back to bed.

"Love you." He waited to hear the door slide shut.

James wasn't lying to her. He needed to figure out what came next after the Void was sold, beginning to sound more like a start-up company than a top-secret mission.

"Ginger – what's the Void?"

It seemed like a safe enough question to ask. The peppy AI woke right up and rambled off the definitions of the word. "Not valid or legally binding ... empty space ... having been dealt no cards in a particular suit."

James whispered, "Not that Void."

"Abyss, nothingness, vacuity ... *oblivion*?" Even Ginger was guessing in synonyms.

"Is there a company called the Void?"

"This might be helpful." The synth cued a link to an article on the computer screen, written five years ago and titled: "THE BIRTH OF B.C.I."

"We have seen the advancement of technology grow rapidly from day one of the 21st century. Forty years in, and well past the peak of Web 3 and 4, consumers are still left wondering what comes next after VR hit its stalemate. The metaverse is dead – at least the VR-based version we imagined two decades ago. Even Alter World couldn't survive after the war ended.

But is there something new on the horizon?

It seems as though the same anonymous entrepreneur who brought us Alter World was pouring all their equity into a new project called the Void. For five years, the start-up didn't make any crypto nor a single dollar, solely working toward a breakthrough that we have yet to see in our lifetime.

A fusion of the metaverse, VR, and a technology only previously theorized before – BRAIN COMPUTER INTERFACE.

On the day of this writing (March 3rd, 2038) that same start-up sold for a trillion dollars, a record-breaking deal in any industry. LucidiTech, a brand new subsidiary of Gupta Energy, bought the Void and says the investment is well worth it.

So what makes this BCI-based world different from our exhausted metaverses? If your pockets are deep enough, you'll soon see for yourself when Lucidity is publicly launched in the next few years."

James's head spun. *Is SRT the anonymous billionaire the article was referring to? Did my father have something to do with creating this huge system that everyone's talking about?* He already felt the effects of the melatonin pill, but as he reread the article, it was hard to blink, let alone fall asleep. He had an epiphany – a mind-blowing revelation.

It's not a game.

Calvin and Tomás weren't the first ones to tell him that. Pops had said it to his mother and the kids every time he'd defended his use of Alter World, and Lucidity was starting to sound awfully similar. If his father wasn't dead then he had to be somewhere, and there was no better place to hide than in a virtual metaverse. It seemed as though Pops had recently found the avatar waiting for him in Lucidity.

III

PART THREE

CHAPTER 8

It's only a silly competition, James reminded himself with his orchestra's performance only hours away. He'd tossed and turned all night thinking about his father being in Lucidity, excusing his unsettled focus that day in school as a consequence of not getting his usual six hours of sleep. The final bell rang, and he was about to leave school when Kyle passed by with a mischievous grin. His cocky student had been quiet all week. *Almost too quiet.* As an unwarranted suspicion set in, and with two hours until he had to be at the Lincoln Center, James headed to an NA meeting to fill the time.

It was an hour earlier than the one he usually attended, and not recognizing anyone was what he was counting on. The man running the meeting was a borderline cornball, but at least it wasn't Kalen Green. He didn't need her tough words getting into his head.

When he came out of PS-39 the dark clouds had lifted, and as he was about to cue an Automated, Kalen approached him, a dirty look on her face. He thought she was upset with him for not coming to *her* meeting, but it wasn't anger he saw in her sharock-colored irises.

"Tomás is dead," she said, her frown transforming into a grimace, head hanging low. "They found him in an alleyway this morning – an overdose."

"That's impossible."

"People relapse sometimes."

"Not Tomás." James shook his head in disbelief. "He had it figured it out."

Kalen pulled out a pack of slim cigarettes, handing one to him knowing he couldn't resist. "When's the last time you two talked?"

"Last night." He hit his first cancer stick in ages. "He bought front-row tickets as soon as they went on sale to make sure both he and my wife had the best seats in the house. He was more excited about life than ever."

"God damnit, he told you, didn't he?" When James nodded, she made sure her surroundings were clear. "Please keep this between us." She drew him in closer. "I was the one who sent Tomás to the Light Keepers."

James shook his head furiously. "That's why he's dead, isn't it? Like the news keeps saying – it's a fucking cult preying on people like me and Tomás." He grabbed another cigarette from his counselor, now chain-smoking. "Do you work for them?"

"I don't know if anybody works for them." Kalen took a deep hit from her skinny smoke. "Someone came to me many years ago, when I was in a dark state of affairs. They helped remove a great deal of clutter from my memories." She sighed. "I told Tomás not to talk about it, but he obviously told you."

James tried to hold back his tears. "We'd practically become brothers," he said. "He's supposed to be my baby's godfather. It may be their fault Tomás is dead, but I blame you for sending him to them like a goddamn guinea pig!"

"There's much more to it than that," she insisted. "Will you at least hear me out?"

"Fuck off!" He began walking away. "Don't contact me either."

"Where are you going?"

"To conduct a recital."

"And then what?"

"I'm gonna try to be a normal person living in a world that's just as cruel as it's always been."

~

None of his friends or family members had died since James had become sober. He normally would've headed into a bar and had a few drinks –

concert or not. There was a liquor store on the corner with a holographic advertisement for his favorite vodka in the window, the clear liquid poured over two ice cubes with a splash of soda and lime to finish it off. The automatic door slid open, luring him to come in, but James took a deep breath and continued. With another hour to kill, a long walk to the Lincoln Center would hopefully calm his nerves.

The Koch Bridge was crowded. After it'd snowed and rained for most of April everyone seemed excited to be out on a perfect seventy-five-degree day – everyone but James. Kids on hovering skateboards zipped by, bumping into him as he peered down at the passing East River, trying to forget about the conversation he'd had. The billboard on the Manhattan side of the river didn't help.

It was a large black-and-white image of an androgynous alien creature – the face of the Light Keepers, who ironically didn't have a face. In bold red letters, it read: *"Anyone with information please contact the FBI."* James knew someone. Who was Kalen Green to play God anyway? By the time James reached the other side of the bridge, his anger had only grown.

Right when he thought it couldn't get any worse, Sandy texted him from the hospital. *"Patient M is leaving us soon."* One of her favorites was about to die, and even though that was part of the job, it was the part she hated the most. Suffice to say, she wouldn't be attending the competition either.

Inside the Lincoln Center was a live hologram display of the legendary acts that had performed on the famous stage, making James more nauseous than he already was. He found a restroom, stumbled into a stall, and puked until the blood vessels in his eyes were bloodshot. Until every bit of golden mucus was flushed from his esophagus. He splashed some water on his face, as ready as he was ever going to be.

Backstage, his students stood huddled together in a corner, overwhelmed by the venue they were about to perform in. When James received word that they had five minutes until their turn, he headed over to his students for a pep talk. He needed it as much as they did.

"Tonight may be the one chance you get to perform on this glorious stage," he said as Calvin gave him a big smile. "I know we've had some differences in the past, but that's life." He looked over to Kyle, who nodded and seemed to be concentrating. "In the last week, you've stepped it up and now I know we have what it takes to win tonight."

If only for that one minute, James's students listened to him like a football coach before the big game. He brought them out to the stage and a cheering audience, mostly consisting of parents and the students' chaperones. Nonetheless, a sold-out Lincoln Center. He tried not to take notice of the two empty seats in the front row set aside for Sandy and Tomás.

As the orchestra ran through *Brandenburg Concerto No.3 in G major*, his students blazed through the Bach piece in perfect unison as if they were the New York Philharmonic. Despite the events of the day, James stayed calm during their performance, conducting the young masters like his hero Richard Strauss – calm and organized. He waved his left hand to guide them to the end. They followed along. It was perfection. After a five-second applause, James set them up for their more difficult piece

"Train Wreck" fell off the tracks right from the top. It was immediately flat, and then one by one the dominoes began to fall. James couldn't figure out where the mistakes were coming from. Someone was off time in the cello section. The brass section sounded out of tune. He saw Calvin take his eyes off his holographic sheet music, distracted by the cocky grin Kyle gave him. When the bully winked, James knew they were being sabotaged.

After an awkward applause, James bowed to the crowd and stormed off the stage. Behind the curtain most of his students seemed ashamed of themselves, shaking their heads in utter confusion. Calvin,

with his fists clenched, looked like he was about to punch someone.
When Kyle joined them wearing a sly smirk, the keyboardist he was good
friends with raised her brow, communicating their intended plan had
worked. That's when James lost it.

"What the hell did you do, Kyle?" he shouted, approaching the
student. "I know you botched this!"

Kyle put on his best poker face. "I don't know what you're talking
about, Mr. Grady."

James, turning beet-red, yelled, "I can't believe you and your little
minions would stoop so low as to undermine your fellow classmates to
prove a point to me."

"You can't prove that," Kyle snickered. "So what, maybe I did mess
up." With a fake whimper, he said, *"There was just so much pressure for
us to be perfect."*

"Don't you fucking lie to me!"

"You want the truth?" Kyle began. "The truth is you're an ex-drug
addict. I followed you to one of your sad little meetings one day. You're
just jealous of a bunch of high school kids so you favor the poor and
disenfranchised like Calvin here. We weren't going to win with that
weird-ass song anyway."

"You little son-of-a-bitch." James grabbed Kyle by his arms,
squeezing them tight. "Tell your classmates what you did!"

"Let go of me!"

"Tell them!"

"What the fuck's wrong with you, man?"

Without realizing it, James had lifted Kyle a foot off the ground,
while another student taped the incident on her Uni. Knowing he'd been
caught, James dropped the bully and addressed his orchestra.

"I know there are a lot of young minds in here who I've managed to
reach with the bit of wisdom I have." He spoke to his students and the
camera recording him. "I also know there's a lot of spoiled little shits in

here who'll never appreciate anything because they already have everything."

Everyone was silent except for Kyle. "You're so fired."

James bit his tongue and left before it got any worse. All he wanted to do was fall asleep next to his wife, but she was stuck at the hospital until late.

As soon as he got home he melted into an empty bed, more emotionally drained than he'd been in years.

CHAPTER 9

The next morning James entered Brighter Minds Charter with his head down, sunglasses on to hide the full extent of his tired puss, awaiting the inevitable consequences. It didn't matter how much of an asshole his student was, James should've handled it better, and would've if he hadn't just found out his best friend was dead. When a couple of his students from the orchestra passed by avoiding eye contact with him, he knew it was bad, and he'd only been in the school for five minutes when the principal, Ms. Sykes, summoned him to her office.

Mindy Sykes was only a few years older than him and always sympathetic to his struggle, hiring him even after some of the prominent parents had voiced their objection to his shadowy past. Sykes didn't care about his history and thought he was one of their finest instructors.

"Let me start by apologizing for my behavior last night," James said as soon as he sat down. "I was having a shitty day. It was uncalled for, and I acted out of line."

"I'm going to cut you off right there, Grady." Ms. Sykes summoned him into her office, her glasses hanging off her rosy nose, wearing a tight, unbuttoned blouse and always flirty. She closed the door with her UniTab and whispered, "Kyle is a spoiled little shit." She paused. "But his mother's on the city council, and she's a real piece of work herself. I don't know if either one of us wants to deal with the backlash of the politics in this particular school."

"So, what does that mean?"

Sykes showed him the footage of the performance on one of her screens. "Look, I know what Kyle and his minions did. Unfortunately, it'd be hard to prove and not worth the legal battle." She pulled a tab out of her desk and continued. "This is a resignation form effective as of today. You're going to sign it, and this should appease Ms. Gibbs. Think of it as a transfer package that gives you six months of severance pay. Plus, you won't have to deal with Kyle ever again."

"What about Calvin?" he asked. "How's he going to survive another year with that kid?"

Sykes grinned. "Calvin was the one who came to me this morning about their prank. He and his mother agreed that he could transfer to whatever school you ended up at, as long as it was in the district."

"This is all happening so fast." James scratched his beard. "Isn't there an easier way to solve this without these drastic measures?"

"Take it as a blessing in disguise, Grady. According to your records, you haven't had time off since you started here three years ago. You won't have to do the summer session, giving you plenty of time to take a much-needed vacation."

There was a reason James never took time off. As long as he was working, his routine was manageable. "Where would I even go?"

"You could check off some spots on your bucket list, or find an old friend to reconnect with." She smiled. "I just joined Lucidity, which is a bit expensive, but well worth the money."

Sitting across from Ms. Sykes, he thought about the clues he'd recently discovered. His now-former principal didn't realize she'd sparked a light bulb – a stealthy game plan for his summer off. Without school and the orchestra, he might have time to possibly reconnect with Pops in her recommended destination. On his way out of her office, James thanked Ms. Sykes for always having his back and asked for one last favor.

"Do you mind if I have a quick word with Calvin before I go?"

~

Brighter Minds, his first "real job," had left him with a bittersweet feeling as he sat in the orchestra room for the last time, waiting to speak with Calvin. The three years he'd spent there were full of memories, but he was relieved to start with a fresh slate. James was curious to know which school his student had in mind for his senior year, but also had questions about an unrelated matter.

"I apologize for last night," he said as soon as Calvin arrived. "Yesterday wasn't my day."

"You should be pissed," Calvin fumed. "We worked our asses off all year just for Kyle to undermine us all for one of his vendettas."

"Did he at least apologize to everyone?"

Calvin laughed. "He's not going to change his story, Mr. G. Every word out of his mouth is complete bullshit, including that lie about your drug use."

"Exactly." James was just glad he didn't have to run Calvin through his previous decade filled with substance abuse. "So, do you have a school in mind for your senior year?"

Calvin fiddled with a set of drums. "Don't worry about that right now. You got any big plans now that you're off for the summer?"

While his student practiced his pocket beat, James pondered an idea he wasn't sure how to say out loud. "I was thinking about joining Lucidity," he shouted over the pounding snare and kick drum, which immediately caused Calvin to end on a crash cymbal.

"You should totally join, Mr. G!"

James reminded him that the system wasn't free; that they had some savings, but not enough to throw away on an unnecessary extravagance. He said, "That's a lot of money to spend when you have a child on the way."

"There's a little secret that most people don't know about," Calvin explained. "The most expensive part is the DreamCatcher ... But if you cancel within a month they'll return the full deposit. They don't tell users about that, because most people are already lured in by then. The first two weeks are just for dealing with the side effects anyway."

"Side effects?"

"Don't worry about that, Mr. G. You tell me what you want to see and I'll lead you there. I am a guide after all." Calvin asked, "What are you looking to get out of Lucidity anyway?"

"I'm trying to find someone."

"Like a secret girlfriend?"

"No ... nothing like that."

"That's what half the users go in looking for." Calvin became more discreet. "I haven't tried that aspect out yet, but my guests tell me that it's better than real s-e-x." He whispered, "Ms. Sykes is in there, and she's not coming for the games."

"That's not what I'm looking for," James said, slightly appalled. "I'm trying to track someone down."

Crossing his arms, Calvin seemed hesitant. "With all due respect, that type of search is frowned upon in Lucidity. Most people go in to hide their identity. They don't want some stranger wandering around, trying to figure out who they are and who they know."

"All I need to know is that you're going to help me when I get to this Lucidity ..."

"You're in good hands," Calvin assured him. "I can introduce you to some Avis who might be able to help you, but you can't go asking too many questions. All the rules are in the manual, so make sure you go through that first." He seemed excited. "This whole system is gonna blow your mind, Mr. G."

Calvin was a freshman when James had started at the school, but had grown into an adult since then. His student was going to become the teacher.

"You don't have to call me Mr. G anymore."

"Then what should I call you?"

"James."

"Nah ... That sounds weird," Calvin cringed, heading back to class. "I don't know what your plan is, but you know I always got your back."

"I don't know what my plan is either."

"Hopefully you'll get your money's worth." Calvin headed out of the orchestra room. "Tell your wife that I'll make sure to keep you out of trouble."

While his student left laughing at what seemed like meaningless banter, James had the crippling thought that Sandy didn't know anything yet. She hadn't heard about Tomás's death or the outburst that had gotten him fired, and certainly wasn't going to understand his next agenda, meaning he had to come up with an actual plan.

~

Ever since James had plugged Pops's flash drives into his computer, it seemed like more drones were hovering above. On the walk home from school, he could've sworn he was being followed – that every stranger had an agenda against him. There was a man with a hoodie following him. *Why would he wear that on a hot sunny day?* he thought. The fact that Kalen Green, an admitted Light Keeper, had been attempting to reach him all morning didn't help with his paranoid notions. The FBI had made the consequences crystal clear.

When James got back to the condo he heard voices inside – a conversation muffled through the soundproof walls. He thought for sure Sandy was at the hospital, since she wasn't home when he'd left earlier. Out of some Catholic instinct, James made the sign of the cross, scanned his eye on the keypad, and entered the condo. He was bombarded as soon as he walked in.

"Why didn't you tell me about Tomás?" Sandy asked, her cheekbones stained with mascara, still in her pajamas. Kalen Green was on one of the large screens behind her on a video call with his wife. It felt like his counselor was in the room with them, so he stood in front of the screen to block the camera.

"What are you doing here, Kalen?"

"I was checking in on you."

"You have some nerve calling my wife after what you did to

Tomás."

Kalen pleaded, "There's more to it than that. Can you both meet me some time so I can tell you what happened?"

"You need to stay out of our lives!" James cued the synth, "Ginger, turn off all screens and cameras."

Wide-eyed, Sandy asked, "What the hell was that all about?"

"You heard her ... Tomás is dead!"

"And she wanted to see if you were doing okay. What's wrong with that?"

"Kalen was the one who got him killed," he explained. "She sent Tomás to the Light Keepers."

Sandy paced around the condo, taking in the severity of what James had told her. "Don't forget that she saved your life when you were in a rough spot."

"That's the only reason I'm not going to turn her in," James insisted, "but we need to keep our distance from her. The less we know, the better." He rubbed his beard and forehead. "We could go to prison for withholding this info."

"What about the memorial for Tomás?"

James shook his head no.

She nervously tapped her fingers on the kitchen counter. "Are you going to be okay?"

"I'm coming to grips with it."

"There's a process involved when your best friend dies, you know?"

With a straight face, James assured her, "There's nothing I can do but move on. That's what Tomás would want me to do."

"Is that why you're home so early?"

After Sandy had already heard the worst of the news, James told her about the competition, and how he had lashed out at Kyle. She didn't seem surprised to hear about the stunt. He told her about the deal Calvin and the principal had made, and how it was a blessing in disguise.

Sandy asked, "What are you going to do in the meantime?"

"I was thinking about trying out Lucidity."

She laughed until she realized he was serious. "Why would you want to do that? You don't even like video games."

The words were on the tip of his tongue – *It's not a game.* James wanted to tell her about the satchel and the messages from the billionaire, SRT, but that wasn't part of the deal he'd agreed to. They were both too tired for an argument, so he formulated a different sales pitch.

"Calvin keeps telling me to join Lucidity," he began, "and his mother wants me to keep an eye on him this summer, so what better way to kill two birds with one stone." Sandy seemed to be listening, so he continued. "There's a one-month trial period so it won't even cost us that much." He wasn't even sure if that was true, but it sounded good. He joked in his cranky old man impression, "I need to see if this *whatchamacallit* is going to warp his *young impressionable mind.*"

With an exhausted giggle, Sandy wrapped her arms around him. "I'll give you one month." She played with his scruffy beard. "I want you to be happy and I know Calvin would love it if he could see his old teacher in a new light." She paused and pointed to her belly. "Once that month is over I'm going to need you focused on this one."

James followed Sandy to the bedroom where she immediately fell into the mattress. The mascara wasn't fresh enough to be from finding out about Tomás. It turned out she'd cried herself to sleep in a spare room of the hospital after Patient M died. James lay down next to her, wishing he could tell her everything, but it seemed as though she had enough on her plate already.

"One month," he promised with a pinky exchange that felt wrong. He never thought she'd budge so easily.

CHAPTER 10

No one is going to die today, Sandy hesitated to think. She sat in her office on her first day back at the hospital after a six-day sabbatical.

Dealing with death was what she'd chosen to specialize in. She thought she had grown numb to it, but the circumstances of her last patient had caught her off guard, hitting a nerve that she hadn't felt in a while. After her emotional breakdown, the hospital had practically forced her to take a leave. She didn't have any patients on that Wednesday afternoon following her time off, which made getting the memory out of her mind difficult.

On the night of her husband's competition, Sandy had been leaving the hospital when Monica Klein had ended up back in the ICU. The doctors had been skeptical of the days she'd gone missing. They blamed the brain trauma on whatever holistic operation her family had led her to. Sandy had sat with the woman all night even though she was in a vegetative state. Early the next morning Monica had woken up for a few seconds, pointed to a television screen in the hallway, and died of a brain hemorrhage. When the medical doctors and nurses arrived, Sandy was in tears, a sign that it had become too personal. Doctors don't cry, she'd thought, blaming her reaction on exhaustion. It might have only been a coincidence, but the screen Monica had pointed to was airing a report on the Light Keepers. Sandy hadn't mentioned that in the report, knowing it would have every agency down her throat.

Now, with nothing left to do, she was about to head home when her UniTab alerted her to an impromptu mandatory meeting in the conference room. Her boss, Dr. Eugene Haskell, was head of the department of psychology and rarely called group meetings, so she knew it was important.

"Today I received a memo from the FBI," Dr Haskell said to the group. He was a short man with a trim beard, blemished apricot skin, and a preference to get straight to business. "They wanted me to give you all a briefing on the Light Keepers. From this day on, we're supposed to inform the agency if we suspect any of our patients are dealing with this criminal organization."

Interrupting, Sandy asked, "Doesn't that go against doctor-patient confidentiality?"

Dr Haskell shook his head. "It's highly unethical, but bear with me as this order comes from way above my pay grade." He handed out SYNCDIN glasses for them all to use and turned off the lights. "The reason I'm showing this to you is so that you can pick up on any signs or similar phrases a patient might use suggesting interaction with the Light Keepers."

When Sandy put on the glasses, a figure appeared on the opposite end of the glass touch-screen table – the Light Keeper. It was a slender avatar with the slight curves of a woman, which Sandy presumed it was. It illuminated in violet and blue arrays of electronic wires pulsing through her semi-translucent skin, reminding her of the nervous system images she'd studied in medical school. The hypnotic creature swaggered forward with her hands held together like a professional speaker, or a gentle preacher during a sermon. She didn't have any facial features but somehow seemed to be staring right into Sandy's eyes.

"Don't be afraid," the figure said with a soft and even-tempered voice. "You are living in an invisible monarchy of pre-determined possibilities, complacent to an automated existence. While the Last War might have come to an end, it will not be the last. Even though we cascade in a better direction, it's an illusion that will crash under its own archaic ways. Though the truth exists deep within, our minds continue to be manipulated by the ruthless puppeteers, forever on the hunt for the next resource to exploit."

The Light Keeper faced Sandy as if she were the intended audience. "This is why we hide in the shadows," the figure said with an unidentifiable accent. "We are dangerous to the system and their monopolies. If our history is of any accord, they intend to steal the light we've found and weaponize it, creating an existential threat as we've never seen."

The illuminated-glass avatar bent down into a downward-facing dog position, and took in a slow deep breath, exhaling the bad spirits from her lungs, its head resting in deep meditation.

"Don't be afraid," the figure said. They ended the pose and faced Sandy once again. "The Light Keepers are not the enemy, but they will do everything in their power to make us seem that way. We protect ourselves so that they can never manipulate our energy."

The figure reached out her hands, the electrons pulsating like a lightning storm to her fingertips. The figure tilted its head and leaned toward Sandy. The Light Keeper was about to say something when the image cut off and the lights came back on.

"All right, that's enough," Dr Haskell said, shaking his head in disgust. "That mumbo jumbo goes on forever, so I'll send you all the transcript of it."

Before anyone noticed, Sandy wiped a tear that had fallen down her cheek. Neither her eyes nor her thoughts had adjusted yet. The Light Keeper, or whoever it was, had her mesmerized. The rest of the team seemed unfazed as Dr Haskell went on about other matters. *They didn't see it as I did*, she thought. *She was staring right at me.* Sandy couldn't let it go, so she followed Dr Haskell out after the meeting.

"What is it, Grady?"

"Do we know what the Light Keepers are supposedly protecting?" she asked. "It was kind of vague."

Dr Haskell stopped in his tracks. "They're a goddamn cult killing people!" He tried not to raise his voice but was clearly furious with her.

"For all I know, it could be the gold at the end of the rainbow."

"But they've only been accused of a handful of deaths," she argued. "The news calls them a terrorist group, but they haven't taken responsibility for any of those deaths. It seems a bit rash, don't you think?"

Her boss sighed. "Sure – only a few have died so far, but you know how these groups escalate. The T-Theory cult started small until the mass suicide of 2031. Thousands of people died thinking they'd transition into the soul of King T of Terminus." He sighed. "It's our duty to find the signs so that never happens again, so if one of your patients uses the terminology heard in the Light Keepers' message, you need to let me know. The Feds aren't fucking around with this."

Even though it didn't sit well with her, Sandy agreed, making the turn toward her office when the conversation hit a stalemate. Dr Haskell was never much for debates, so it wouldn't help to pester him about it.

"Grady," he shouted as Sandy was about to slip into her office. "We're not finished yet."

Dr Haskell put on a gentler front as he walked her in a different direction, more humble when he wasn't acting as a bossy manager. He had four daughters of his own and sometimes treated Sandy as his fifth.

"How was your time off?" He used his sensitive-dad voice. "It looks like you got a little sun."

"I will have a *little son* in a few months," Sandy joked, knowing he loved a good pun.

She understood what Dr Haskell was getting at though, checking in to see if she was emotionally stable enough to handle her responsibilities. She thought about playing the pregnancy card, knowing he'd back off immediately with his wife in the back of his mind. She decided to save that for a later date.

"I got too close," she admitted. "Monica was this vibrant spirit. Even on her supposed deathbed, she was cracking jokes through the pain. We stayed in touch and became friends when she wasn't my patient anymore." She paused. "I'm not sure where that falls on the ethical scale."

"It happens to the best of us," he said. "Did Ms. Klein say anything to you before she died?"

"She was comatose the entire time, and before she came in that night, she just wanted to live life again and drink champagne at eleven in the morning."

Dr Haskell continued down the hall toward his office. "The FBI is investigating her family." He asked her to take a seat. "After she got better, did she tell you about her miracle cure?"

"Monica said her sister took her to Sedona and introduced her to a spiritual healer. She went on an ayahuasca retreat in the middle of the desert and met God, or at least that's what she told me."

"Nothing about the Light Keepers?"

"Nope."

Dr Haskell turned his computer screen toward her. It showed a video from the day Monica Klein had passed away, the angle clearly showing her pointing to the screen before going into cardiac arrest, her eyes focused on the FBI's public service announcement.

"I'm guessing that's not in your report," Dr Haskell huffed.

"Many people spasm before they die."

He replayed the video. "Ms. Klein reacted as soon as they mention the Light Keepers. She points directly to the screen where the sound is coming from with a look of terror."

"She was about to die!"

"And whose fault do you think that is, Grady? The Light Keepers are a suspect in the deaths of eleven people so far. Two of them happened to people using Lucidity. The other nine people were magically cured by the group, only to experience the lethal side effects afterward. Ms. Klein may have been number twelve."

Thirteen if they counted Tomás, Sandy thought.

"She never spoke of the group," she said. "But if you want me to put it in my report, I will."

Dr Haskell contemplated this. "It's not worth mentioning this time. Like you said, it was a natural reaction, and you've seen enough deaths to know better." He gazed out the window and added, "Next time I won't be so lenient, Sandy."

Sandy winced. "I don't know how comfortable I feel about turning my patients over as terrorist suspects."

"Do you want to get your ass in trouble with three weeks left until your maternity leave?" It was a rhetorical question. "They're trying to figure out who's in charge of the organization before anyone else has to die. Isn't that more ethical than allowing someone to get sucked into another merciless cult?"

Sandy was about to agree to disagree with Dr Haskell when an alarm on her UniTab went off, reminding her it was time to leave. James was installing Lucidity that afternoon and she had to be there as some kind of third-party participant. Meanwhile, her boss waited for a response.

"I trust your judgment, Dr Haskell, and I assure you that I will inform you if I notice any suspicious behavior in the future."

After her interrogation was over, she left the hospital, aiming to make it home before the unexpected storm began. Even though the sky was ready to drop out at any second, that wasn't what she was stressed out about. James was about to join Lucidity, a platform that hadn't been tested to her standards and was partially responsible for at least two deaths. In addition to terminally ill patients, the Light Keepers also seemed to target former drug addicts, including her husband's sponsor. If the cyber cult was the storm, James was the guy standing in the open field with a six-foot metal pole.

CHAPTER 11

After hardly sleeping the night before and anticipating the arrival of the DreamCatcher, James chugged a cup of decaf tea to psych him into feeling awake. They suggested he prohibit his caffeine use before going into Lucidity. That week he'd had a medical check-up and taken several psychological assessment exams in order to access the system. All the distractions made him forget about the fact that he'd been fired and his best friend had died. He'd spent some much-needed time with Sandy during their unexpected time off, but never confessed to her why he was joining. Calvin made it sound as if it were free, but the Gradys would still lose a nice chunk of his deposit and possibly destroy his marriage. *Nothing to worry about*, he sighed as the buzzer rang, faking a smile to get himself excited.

"I'm Nera, from LucidiTech," said the tiny woman in her early twenties, with trendy silver spectacles and tattoo sleeves on top of her tan complexion. The lackadaisical tone matched her fashionable mullet and subtle goth makeup. She chewed gum and fiddled with the lanyard around her neck as two self-driving suitcases and a large container followed behind with the hardware equipment. "Where should I set up?"

James led her to the office, cleansed to the guidelines of the Owner's Manual. *No exposed wires, papers, clutter, and space fit for the console necessary to run the system.* Nera pulled out a black chair from the large container they called the DreamCatcher, and although his student claimed it was worth a hundred thousand, it didn't look much different from any other gaming chair he'd seen before.

"This is where the magic happens," Nera said with a mischievous grin as she installed the device. According to her, the DreamCatcher was the most important factor for the existence of BCI, and therefore

Lucidity.

The butterflies in James's stomach emerged from their cocoon. "Is it as real as they say it is?"

"Didn't you go through the manual?"

"Some of it."

Nera chuckled. "I respect your approach. Most of the people I install for think they have it all figured out before they go in. They study the manual before the big day thinking they have an advantage. It leaves them with too many expectations and not enough of the *thrill*. You on the other hand are going in blind." She finished her inspection of the office. "This should be ... interesting?"

His stomach tightened. *Interesting for me or for her?* It had been gray all morning, but a storm was looming in the distance. A rumble of thunder crackled from miles away. The lightning appeared to be drawing closer.

James inquired, "What happens if we lose power while this machine is connected to my brain?"

Nera pointed to the black box she'd taken out of the largest container. "That's the backup generator. It has enough power to get you back to reality without any major side effects."

"I keep hearing about these side effects ... What exactly are we talking about?"

Nera rolled her eyes, seeming sick of his inquiries. "Jesus ... you're lucky we don't give you a pop quiz on the manual. I'll tell you all the details as soon as I install the system." She stepped away to take a peek at the rest of his condo. "Where's your third party?"

James checked his Uni for any new messages. "She should be here any minute. Do you use Lucidity?"

"That's why I got this job." Nera almost smiled for the first time. "I applied to be a guide, but they said I didn't have the right people skills. It's not my strong suit, in case you haven't noticed. They save the fireworks and confetti for when you get into the sectors of Lucidity." She drilled holes into walls and installed sensors around the room. "Luckily for you, I'm a damn good operator."

James had a million more questions for the young woman but left Nera alone when he heard Sandy come in, soaking wet from the storm that the sky had unleashed.

"Sorry I'm late," she said, "I got caught up in a meeting with Dr Haskell filling me in on my duties for when he goes on vacation."

James grabbed her coat. "You look like you've seen a ghost."

"I didn't expect this storm to come in so fast." Sandy noticed the large crate in her living room. "I guess Lucidity arrived along with it."

This must be a bad omen, James thought. Grabbing a towel, he helped her dry off. He jumped as the thunder shook their building. "Is this stupid?" he asked. "Tell me now and I'll send it back." Her eyes were full of rain and doubt. "Is there something I should know about?"

Sandy sighed. "In the meeting we had today, we discussed the Light Keepers' involvement in those Lucidity deaths, and I need to make sure you don't get sucked into that mess."

"Are you kidding me? If someone solicits that garbage to me, I'll turn them in myself." He almost forgot how mad he'd been. "Kalen's lucky I liked her."

After changing out of her wet clothes in the bedroom, Sandy continued. "If you're not worried about the Light Keepers, then why are you so skeptical of going into the system?" She fixed her hair. "I told you I'm not worried about the sex stuff. You're the most loyal man I know."

There were a dozen excuses he could give her. That it was the money or the time away or the side effects. He could blame it on the storm outside or the Light Keepers, but it would all be a lie told by *the most loyal man she knew*. It'd been driving him insane all week.

James blurted out, "I'm looking for my father inside Lucidity."

Sandy stared at him from the reflection in the mirror, her

backward gaze haunting, the silence tedious as she slowly approached him.

Nera interrupted, shouting from the office, "The system's all set whenever you two are ready!"

After asking the operator for more time, Sandy shut the door and squeezed the life out of James's hands.

"You can't go back on this path again." James could hear her try to control the anger in her voice. "Don't forget when I met you, you were this close to overdosing." Her index finger and thumb showed the tiny amount of space between James and death. "Who knows how many other times you almost got yourself killed? You were arrested in the middle of Kansas because you had a hunch. You got banned from Alter World, which I didn't even know was possible." She stared at the floor with her fists clenched. "We have a baby on the way, James. You can't go down that road again."

James looked at his wife, employing his impenetrable puppy dog eyes. "I'm just trying to be honest with you."

"You made a promise to me." She seemed to be forcing herself not to yell with Nera in the other room. "Did he finally send you that long-awaited message?"

"I found something else," he said. "Pops has an avatar in Lucidity."

Sandy's grip grew even tighter. "So, you're telling me that your saint of a father who hasn't found the time to contact you in ten years has managed to find a spot in this expensive metaverse. Meaning, if he is alive, he's an asshole who left his family and decided not to reach out to anyone." She sighed. "You already got your closure, babe."

James pulled his sore fingers away from hers. "I'll be good."

Sandy's nostrils flared, grinding her teeth to keep calm. "I'm going to be completely clear with you right now. I don't care what you decide to do, but if I see one sign of the old James – that hyper-sensitive drug addict who almost ruined his very important life – then I'm going to take myself and your son elsewhere. Your one month is now three weeks, so you better find some closure by then."

"I promise."

"Pinky promise me then!"

The gesture was a silly ritual, but Sandy took it as their ultimate test of loyalty. James crossed his little finger with hers, knowing he was the liability in their relationship.

When they walked into the office, Nera spun in the DreamCatcher like a child, seeming embarrassed when they caught her. "Okay, let's get serious here." She cued her UniTab. A small silver drone flew out of one of the suitcases and hovered around the room, scanning the environment with infrared light. "That's Eden," she said. "She'll be my guide out here and yours in the Cave. She's double-checking the perimeters for any other hazards."

"All scans clear," Eden said, her accent British-Indian. "This space is now functional for takeoff."

Nera instructed him to take a seat in the DreamCatcher. "Are you comfortable?"

"Extremely," he said, wishing he could fall asleep in it.

"You'll notice that there aren't very many buttons, but if you reach underneath your right armrest, you'll feel a tiny trigger. Go ahead and pull that." When James pulled it, his whole office was taken over by the system. A series of needle-thin thread wires attached to his temples and wrists. Nera continued, "You're going to feel the most minimal pinch as these wires connect to your veins. They'll monitor your heart rate, blood pressure, glycemic levels, etcetera, etcetera. This is how the system knows when to pull you out."

Sandy seemed alarmed. "Pull him out?"

Nera replied, "If he shows any signs of distress the safety protocol will immediately begin a low-stress ejection, limiting the adverse side effects. We'll test this all out during our initial run."

"So, what exactly do you need me for again?"

"The third party is required to observe the potential user's test and authorize their access to the system." Abandoning her professional veil, Nera joked, "It pretty much filters out all the weirdos. I mean, if you can't get anyone to vouch for you, then you might not be a good fit for Lucidity … Am I right?"

Wires as thin as spider silk dangled from his body. James caught a side-eye from Sandy, obviously still holding a warranted grudge. His wife paid close attention as Nera explained the process taking place. He only half-listened, lost in his thoughts. The rest was in one ear and out the other until James heard that he was only going to a testing simulation.

"So I don't get to go to Lucidity today?"

Nera chewed her gum in disdain. "Technically you will, but for today you'll be in what we call the Cave. I'll put you through some scenarios to learn how to control your senses and movement within Lucidity. A few of the tests may be uncomfortable." She smirked as if she enjoyed that part the most. "Eden will be there to guide you."

"I have a question," Sandy interrupted. "What if I need him to come out of Lucidity? Like if there's an issue with the baby."

"If you need your husband to depart from the system you can simply use the Lucidity app installed on your Uni." Nera was much nicer when she talked to Sandy. "Coming back into the real world is about a ten-minute recovery process." The operator gave Sandy a more serious grimace. "Never try to wake up anyone inside the system by unplugging the console."

The two women stood above him speaking like he wasn't in the room. Sandy asked, "What happens if I do, though?"

"Just don't," Nera quipped with a morbid grin. "As for you, James, unless you like the pain, I'd stay away from the Red Zones when you do get to Lucidity."

"Pain?" he asked.

"Duh," Nera chuckled. "It's what separates BCI from virtual reality, and the true reason roughly a third of people who sign up never make it to Lucidity. It's all in the consent form you both signed." She paused, more dramatic than usual. "You asked if it was real ... It's about as close as it gets."

Whatever fluids they were pumping into James's body made him simultaneously loopy and hyper-aware. He felt the pinch of the wires and reached for Sandy's hand. The operator reminded them the environment had to be sterilized to his senses, which meant no outside physical contact. His heart rate was on one of the dozen screens displaying his health indicators, but James was more fascinated by the pretty colors.

"Did you give me drugs?" he asked. Both the women giggled as if he'd missed some inside joke. His wrists tingled as his eyelids grew heavy. "I feel kinda ... wacky."

Nera stuck out her pierced tongue at him. "It's not drugs, man," she said in a stoner voice. "That's a little melatonin and serotonin cocktail we give you when necessary." She turned to Sandy. "It looks like we're ready for takeoff as soon as we get your consent."

An alert sounded on Sandy's UniTab. "What's this?"

"It's the final waiver," Nera explained. "Since you're the official third party, you get the final say on whether James goes into the system or not."

Sandy asked, "Are these Light Keepers a real threat to Lucidity?"

Nera sighed. "My boyfriend thinks it's a group of hackers with a vendetta against the company. The Void left some disgruntled hackers behind when they made the biggest deal in history. Out of our million users the only two deaths we've had occurred when avatars went off the grid, and as far as we know, no one has solicited for the group."

"So would your boyfriend say I was being paranoid?"

Nera fidgeted. "The news doesn't have as much to report since the war ended, so it makes sense that everybody gets a little unnerved when they see the word *terrorist* popping back up in the headlines. They don't mention that the two victims joined the system with ulterior motives to seek out the Keepers."

"So James is safe?"

"Trust me, he'll be fine."

As the system loaded, James waited for Sandy's approval. The operator emphasized the fact that his wife had the final say. She paused for a moment, contemplating something in her head. Once he found out pain was involved, he prayed one of them would pull the chord on the idiotic notion. He almost wanted her to say no, so he could move on.

"He's all yours." Sandy sealed the deal with her thumbprint. The expression on her face said, *I trust you, but don't fucking let me down.* Luckily, Nera was there to cut the tension.

"I'll have him home for dinner." She awkwardly laughed. "You ready for takeoff, James?"

"Try not to hurt me too much." The program finished loading as a loud burst of thunder shook their apartment. "You have a sadistic side."

"It's why I love this part the most." Nera raised her eyebrows to him, telling him to "take a deep breath."

James inhaled like he'd been saving it for an eternity. He stared up at Sandy, who gazed back at him like a mother watching her child being sent off to war. The roller coaster was already on its initial ascent.

"Now breathe out."

As the carbon dioxide poured out of his lungs, a bullet-like device shot into the back of his neck, his eyes practically popping out of his skull. Sandy gasped, clenching his arm like he was bleeding on the pavement. *What have I done?* His final thought before the room went blurry, a trembling sensation flowing to his forehead as it all went dark.

CHAPTER 12

It was pitch black.

James thought he was still in his office until a subtle radiance reflected off his own body, naked, with his arms resting on an uncomfortable wooden chair.

"Sandy?"

His voice echoed off the hidden wall, but no one answered. He could speak and see, the rest of his body held down by some invisible force.

"Nera?" he asked. "Is this the Cave?"

Again, no one answered. His fingers twitched, but that was the most he could muster. A chilly gust shot across his cold body, the scent reminding him of his month in the ICU – a floral hint to mask the sterile funk he despised. When an annoying buzzing approached him, James asked, "Is someone there?" It dashed around the dimly lit space in different locations, zipping past his ear like a confused dragonfly. It finally rested in a location out of his immobilized peripheral vision.

A familiar voice whispered, "Hello, James." Eden, the AI drone that he'd met in his office. "I'm right behind you." There was a tap on his shoulder, but no one was there.

It was the first movement he'd made.

"You're getting close," Eden hinted.

The synth kept taunting him to turn, but James remained an incapacitated prisoner trapped in the chair. "Eden ... tell them I'm stuck and I want out," he pleaded, feeling helpless. "This isn't what I signed up for."

When the humming stopped, an echo-less silence set in. "Eden? ... Hello?" The most soundproof space he'd ever been in drowned out his words like a muzzle. The more he tried to free himself, the more he sank into the ground, a thousand-pound weight on his chest. He heard the flow of the blood rushing through his veins, every organ running like a drunk factory worker. The lights went off in the simulation. His heart pounded, skipping long beats on the brink of madness.

"Get me the fuck out of here!"

He screamed it as loud as he could and it boomeranged right back to him, bellowing in his eardrums. The echoes returned, sobering him up from his mini panic attack. They couldn't hear him in the outside world, or could they? It felt cathartic to howl into the hollow chamber as the warm glow faded in, and an out-of-sight Eden came back buzzing.

"All you have to do is turn around," she said, so sweetly that James found it infuriating. The synth taunted him, tickling and poking him. The numbness wasn't like novocaine. No, her love taps were painful. He followed the frenzied pattern, impossible to keep up with even if he were mobile. It made an abrupt stop, hovering a foot from his nose.

Eden was a fucking *hummingbird*.

An especially abnormal one with a chic pattern on her three-inch body. Her wings were a blur, fluttering in front of him, cartoon eyes straight out of a vintage Disney film. The feathered creature stared at him in a human-like manner, analyzing his thoughts.

"If you don't want to find your father, then we can end this now," she said through her tiny beak.

Caught off-guard, James asked, "What'd you say?"

Eden giggled, flying closer. "I said, if you don't want *to go any farther* then we can end this now … The safe word is *eject*."

A panic set in as he fidgeted, trying to break loose of the invisible straps, a hallucination caused by the fluids Nera had pumped into his veins. He could've sworn Eden had said, "*to find your father*," but how would she know that? The only other explanation – it was a dream.

"This isn't real!"

The hummingbird came within two inches of his nose. "Then wake up, James!"

Clenching his fists, James used all his might to make one final push. The chair began to shake. He pushed himself up and the restraints holding him down smashed into a million glass pieces, the shimmering debris vanishing into dust. He attempted to catch his breath, panting with his palms to his knees as if he'd run an untrained marathon. Gazing around, he realized it wasn't a nightmare or a bad trip.

He was inside Lucidity.

Naked and barefoot, James tiptoed on the hard pebbles toward a distant silhouette, a reflection of himself in a waterfall that flowed upward against the laws of gravity. The walls of the cave illuminated at the tempo of the soft chamber music. He slid his fingers across every hair of his forearm, wondering if he was doing the same thing in the DreamCatcher. Either way, it all felt natural, standing nude in a mirror, judging his chubby gut and poor excuse of a health regimen. The kind shadows highlighted a couple of muscles he hadn't noticed in his ultra-violet existence.

When the buzzing returned, he covered himself, hiding his front side from the synth against the stones, his bare ass facing the cartoonish hummingbird.

Eden floated close by. "There's no need to be shy."

"Do you have something I can put on?"

"I'm not programmed to judge you," she insisted. "All I see is a bunch of zeros and ones."

"I must look so stupid from their perspective, swaying my arms around. Sandy's probably getting a big kick out of it."

"This isn't VR, James. They only know that you've made it to level six. If you want to experience Lucidity, you merely have to understand that you're already here."

James listened even though he was distracted by how precisely designed the hummingbird was, flickering its wings a thousand miles per hour. Even though he despised the erratic movement of flying creatures, he reached out to touch the 4D avatar, grabbing it in an ill-willed curiosity. Eden became erratic, struggling to escape his hands in a thousand directions, her tiny hollow bones squirming between his palms.

Throwing the bird in the air, James shouted, "What the fuck?"

Eden was real as day.

It hadn't dawned on him until that moment that he was walking on hard dirt, his feet already sore from the sharp cracks. Like a gleeful child, he began touching different parts of the cave. The waterfall was the same temperature as the ocean in Virginia Beach. The tangible boulders were rough like sandpaper.

The synth returned, unscathed from his assault. "Are you finally getting it?"

"This is wild."

"It's only the beginning, James."

The dirt changed to grass and the cave got brighter. James's naked self strolled through the soft blades, noticing his knees didn't ache and his carpal tunnel seemed non-existent. His glasses were gone, but he saw each stone of the cave in twenty-twenty vision, maybe even better.

"I haven't felt this young in a while," he said, slightly winded from his joyous escapade through the field, his genitals flapping. "I could use some underwear to keep everything in place, though."

Eden giggled. "We're getting to that now, but first we need to choose your avatar. "

James scoffed. "I don't need anything fancy."

"Well, you have a million options to choose from." Eden pointed to his reflection, half-naked in an empty simulated cave. "You can be an animated cartoon character or a hybrid animal." In the waterfall, James transformed into a rabbit standing upright. "There will be more to learn

THE SUN FOLLOWER

if we go in this direction."

He was hardly able to stand on his paws, falling to the ground, unable to keep his balance. "I want to be a human, if that's okay?"

"Many users go in as some version of themselves," Eden explained. "It all depends on what you're looking to find in one of our sectors. Since you've signed up for the premium package, you'll have more options to choose from. Keep in mind that comes out of the Lucies in your account."

James couldn't remember what plan he'd wound up choosing, signing up before Sandy could change her mind. After a week away from Pops's files, his bright idea now sounded foolish. He lay on his back, still in the form of the furry avatar, trying to figure out what the hell he was doing in Lucidity. Morphing back to human form, he wondered if his father would even recognize him after thirteen years.

He picked himself. "Can you make me younger?" Eden didn't answer, but his avatar changed in the mirror to around nineteen, skinny as a rail with his patented buzzcut. "Perfect."

"Remember the avatar you choose will be what you design your wardrobe around, so changing your base appearance is a big upgrade from this point on." Eden buzzed back around in front of him. "Are you okay with this avatar?"

James nodded.

"Moving on then." Eden zipped back away. "Let's get you all dressed up. You get one complimentary outfit and three more for fifty percent off." An array of options were shown all over the cave-like a catalog. Everything from modern to medieval – avant grade to glam and everything in between – flashed all around him. "Many of our users love to change their look every time they come in."

James continued sifting through the different wardrobes. "I just want a black hoodie, jeans, and some Doc Martens."

"Is that it?"

"That's it."

"Like this?" The exact outfit he asked for appeared on him. "That's quite boring if you ask me."

"I thought you weren't a judgy synth."

"It's your money," she huffed. "Besides, your lack of imagination will save us all a lot of time."

The synth's rude comments didn't bother him; he was already used to Ginger, his passive-aggressive home-bot. James glanced at himself in the mirror, the reflection of a handsome young man he hardly recognized. His mission in Lucidity didn't require fitting in with the other freaks. He didn't even know what his plan was exactly, or what this new world was all about yet.

"You'll need a name for your avatar," Eden reminded him. "Maybe something a bit more creative."

He remembered the storm coming in before entering and thought about the way he had felt for the last fifteen years. Starting a brave new course, stuck without any answers.

"Dark Cloud," he answered.

Nera checked the system. "Okay, you're all set. Enjoy your experience in Lucidity, Dark Cloud."

"So, I'm finished with my training?"

"Not quite," she snickered. "But you're on your own for the rest of it." The hummingbird flew away and the lights went out again.

After that, James went through a series of odd scenarios as part of some psychological assessment. They blasted a hyper-strobe into his eyes as an obnoxious noise blared. It was followed by keeping him in the pitch-black cave for ten minutes straight to see if he'd crack. It wasn't exactly a pleasant experience, but none of it deterred him enough to press the holographic *eject* prompt displayed a finger tap away.

When the cave transformed back to its original form it had a sweeter scent but had grown hot and muggy. James, roleplaying as Dark

Cloud now, realized the putrid scent was coming from him.

Covered in a thin coat of honey, he squished the sticky substance when he clenched fists, anticipating one final test. A tunnel that he hadn't noticed before was lit with an orange glow, a hissing sound growing from inside. It didn't sound like Eden. An intense pressure pulled him toward the tunnel, the noise swelling into a horrific screech.

"You've got to be fucking kidding me?"

During the first pandemic, while the adults were focused on viruses and politics, James had anxiously obsessed over another threat – murder hornets. Now, thousands of them surrounded him, an ungodly swarm he'd only pictured in nightmares, the silhouettes of their wretched antennas hovering over him in a menacing pattern.

"You can't hurt me!"

It didn't frighten off the hornets, their hisses only growing more aggressive, ready to attack at any moment. He dashed toward the tunnel that they'd come in from, hoping to escape. The flying demons built a wall, stinging him over and over on his way past them. He couldn't find the exit. He climbed up the rocks until there was nowhere left to go. Out of some primal instinct, he screamed at the top of his lungs, waiting for them to devour him.

"Aaaaghhh!"

The hornets retreated, leaving James hanging high up the cave wall, only holding on using the adhesive effect of the honey.

Jumping down, he twisted his ankle on the landing, his whole body swollen from the hornet stings. It was the pain Nera promised. He limped through the cave. Assuming his six-legged enemies were gone, he chalked it up to another test. The hissing faded back into the mix. James knew it wasn't over yet.

The swarm came together high above him, choreographing themselves into a sphere formation. They raged in a dizzying frenzy, a fireworks extravaganza transforming into one giant murder hornet. It stared at James with its almond-shaped, black-mirror eyes. Its distorted shrill splattered translucent slime all over him. He snuck backward, his feet still sticky from the honey, falling into a pit that seemed to morph out of nowhere. The large hornet swarmed above, slowly descending on him. Its hairy legs squirmed, attempting to wrap themselves around James's ribs. He shouted in agony.

The *eject* button popped up in front of him. Right as he was about to tap it, he noticed an opening high up in the Cave. It must've been a hundred feet above him. Using every ounce of adrenaline, he kicked the predator off and headed toward the light. He was halfway there before he realized he was flying, and as soon as he did, it all went pitch black again.

When the white noise faded out of James's earbuds, someone pulled the mask off. His vision was blurry for a few seconds, but he was back home. Nera stood over him with a tiny flashlight in her hands, blinding him with it. James tried to catch his breath, wondering what the hell just happened.

"You were lying to me the whole time," Nera said, checking his temperature and using a stethoscope on his chest.

James was still disoriented. "What are you talking about?"

The operator shrugged. "There's no way someone who pretends to be as aloof as you could score in the top ninety-seventh percentile, let alone fly in the Cave."

"I don't know what you're implying." James already had a small headache building. His own body felt unfamiliar. "Did I pass or not?"

"You're ready for Lucidity."

"It felt like I was going to die."

Nera giggled. "No one dies in the system."

She finished up with her physical exam, giving him a curious smile, and handing him a digital passport with his name printed: *Dark Cloud 20/20*. She turned to his wife before leaving the room. "He's all yours,

Sandy."

Sandy's eyes were glassy. "Are you all right?"

"She's mean!" He checked his body for the remnants of honey, his hands trembling as Nera left the room. "Never have I experienced anything so horrific in my life. Even when I tried to convince myself it wasn't real, it continued to warp my senses. Then those fucking bloodsuckers came into the picture and I wanted to throw up."

"Oh my god, I'm so sorry, babe." Sandy caressed his chin with that look of solace. "You can return it right now if you want. You don't need this stress."

James laughed, almost manically. "Are you kidding me?" He stood up from the DreamCatcher. "That was fucking amazing!"

IV
PART FOUR

<u>CHAPTER 13</u>

On a hot and muggy Wednesday morning, Diaz and her partner traveled throughout Kansas for the third day in a row, nothing but grass fields surrounding them for miles. With Ronson busy behind the wheel, Diaz pulled out her UniTab and viewed the black-and-white highway footage they'd retrieved a day earlier. She zoomed in on the video. A military double-decker bus approached. Smoke came from the windows of the bus. Then *BOOM* – it exploded right in the middle of the highway.

Dated *05/19/2032*, Diaz had played it over and over that morning.

"How many times are you going to watch that?" Ronson asked. "If our drifters were on that bus, then no one survived."

After their visit to Virginia, Ronson had gone home to take care of family issues and returned to the road more belligerent than before, claiming the video had all but closed the case. "One and one make two." It seemed as if Ronson was now using the investigation as an excuse to drink and get away from her unhappy marriage. Diaz ignored the comment, not ready to give up, using her own time back in Brooklyn to continue the investigation with her neighbor.

It turned out that Suzi-Q was a notorious hacker who'd infiltrated the Pentagon's Cyber Protection Unit. Interestingly enough, Suzi-Q had vanished around the same time Quinn Baxter – their third drifter – was arrested for malware. Now that the Q seemed to make sense, Diaz still hadn't figured out why the JTID needed a nineteen-year-old hacker. While explaining the intel to Ronson she might have left out the fact that her neighbor was somewhat of a hacker himself, who'd illegally pulled the files from the FBI's confidential archives to find out more about Quinn Baxter, leading them to where they were headed that day.

The smell of whiskey recycled through Ronson's sweat glands. "I thought we were going to Baxter's home," she said, trying to get a look past the vehicles ahead. "The coordinates you gave me are leading me to some place called the NCU Binary Mind Corporation." She gazed back at her GPS. "Where the hell did you get this intel from?"

"I have a guy at the NYPD," Diaz lied.

"Well, it sounds like something you got off AFAnet."

"What the hell is that?"

"It's what's left of the Dark Web. The Earth First Initiative got most of them hackers."

"No, that's not where I got it," Diaz said, "and also it's not that hard to find if you put in a little effort." Ronson, who had been a detective in DC before moving to the task force, rolled her eyes as Diaz continued. "Her twin brother Nick runs this place, and I'm hoping he knows something about his sister's disappearance."

"Everyone seems to be heading there," Ronson noticed. "Do you know what they do at the NCU, Miss Smarty Pants?"

Raising her nose, Diaz said, "As far as I know it's a research facility for BCI projects."

"Like what Lucidity uses?"

"I think so."

Ronson asked, "Would you ever go into Lucidity?"

"If I had the money I would," Diaz replied. "Maybe I'd meet someone in there. They say it's more real than life itself, and it's been a long time since I—"

"Okay, partner." Ronson gave her a dirty glance. "Spare me the details. Besides, you could easily find someone in real life if you tried a little harder. "

"But yesterday you said I was fat."

Ronson chuckled. "I said you didn't need to eat the whole damn box of cookies."

"Well, you don't have to get shit-faced every night either."

"Touché." Her partner seemed to realize that they had hardly moved. "Now this is why we need AVs everywhere because we humans can't drive for shit."

Fifteen minutes later, they finally pulled into the busy parking lot of the NCU Binary Mind Corporation. It was a large two-story building probably erected in the 1980s – bland with outdated architecture in what used to be a business campus. They were in the middle of Bumfuck, Kansas after all. Even so, there was a line that wrapped around the building, and judging by the license plates in the parking lot, some of them had traveled far to get there.

Diaz headed to where the line began. "I guess we have to wait a minute."

As usual, Ronson didn't seem to care for the rules, storming in past the disgruntled people who'd probably been waiting all morning. Reluctantly following along, Diaz was shocked to find a modern lobby awaiting them inside. Elevator Tech-Pop played as drones led people to different corridors. A holographic bubble showed an ultra-realistic dream landscape. One of the drones hovered above them with an orange spotlight on them as a receptionist with an annoying smile greeted them.

"How can I help you folks today?" The extremely pale woman asked with a slight Midwestern tinge.

Ronson replied, "We're here to see Nick Baxter."

"Do you have an appointment? Mr. Baxter's busy at the moment."

Ronson got in the woman's face, cocky and irritable. "Tell him it's about his sister who's been missing for ten years. Or do I need an appointment for that too?"

"No one's come to me about Quinn in ten years," a man said. He'd been standing behind them the whole time, shorter than the detectives, who were both around five-five. Diaz figured it must've been her brother, Nick Baxter, hardly disguising his baby face with a half-ass attempt at a beard.

Knowing her partner could be aggressive, Diaz took the lead. "When was the last time you saw your sister?"

Baxter twiddled his stubby fingers. "I haven't seen Quinn since she abandoned the JTID."

"So you're aware of this military contractor?"

With a smug laugh, Baxter replied, "The JTID is common knowledge in the world of BCI, but you won't find it on Seeker."

"And JTID stands for what?"

"Justifiable Technology-Based Interrogation Design." Baxter pretended to be out of breath. "The Army was using an early form of the tech to get intel out of their enemies. Of course, they had to rush the research when the war seemed imminent."

Shocked, Diaz asked, "They've had BCI for that long?"

Baxter nodded. "Even with all the innovations during the war, most thought BCI was decades away from a breakthrough, let alone going mainstream, but here we are."

"Seems irresponsible," said Ronson.

"Probably." Baxter was silent for a moment, before adding, "Of course, my sister gets busted hacking them and they force her into employment. Then she and a couple of others skipped out before their time was up."

"Do you think she stole some information from them?"

Baxter mocked her lack of knowledge. "The JTID already saw her as a criminal, so they immediately thought it was some espionage tactic when she went AWOL. Knowing my sister, and her alter ego, Suzi-Q, I wouldn't doubt if she sold out to the Free Folk. That's probably why she was killed in that bus accident."

"So you know about that too?"

"The Army came to me ten years ago to tell me my sister was dead." Baxter had his hands on his hips, looking over their badges. "That's why I'm curious to know why you're both here?"

Ronson interrupted, "That's not anywhere in our files. Do you know anything about Jim Grady or Ellie Ginsberg?"

"Jesus Christ, this is like déjà vu," he fumed. "Now unless you have some new discovery, I'd like to get back to running my operation."

Diaz glared over at her partner waiting for the *I told you so* look, but Ronson hadn't finished yet. "Mr. Baxter," she began, fluttering her lashes at the decently handsome younger gentleman, the same tactic she'd used in Kansas City to get the video. "I'm so curious about this BCI. Do you mind giving this old lady a tour of what you do here?"

"You don't look a day over thirty-five," he teased. Shooing away his assistant, who stood by like a robot. He led them both down one of the many corridors. "Let me show you what we do here at the NCU Binary Mind."

When Baxter's back was turned, Ronson pointed to her eyes with her index and middle fingers, and then in a circular motion. An old Army hand signal, indicating for Diaz to pick up on anything suspicious. The corridor was low-lit with laboratory-like observation rooms on both sides, each with ten people in DreamCatchers. Although Diaz had seen plenty of news reports and videos about Lucidity, it was mesmerizing to see them used in person.

The subjects were calm, and most of them wore a gentle grin, a mask to hide the light. It seemed peaceful enough. Baxter explained that the NCU Binary Mind was a non-profit working for multiple clients including LucidiTech and the EFI, among other big names.

Diaz asked, "Are these outsiders?"

Baxter shrugged. "These are *people,* detective. Do they live in the poorer areas of our society? Absolutely. We're creating jobs when that seems like an impossible feat." He led them farther down the hall. "LucidiTech found that their users were more receptive to human avatars compared to synths, so they came to us to fill that void. It's a win-win for everyone involved."

Diaz groaned. "It sounds as if you give them peasant jobs catering to the rich."

"I'm assuming you live in the Interior, right?" Baxter asked.

"I live in Brooklyn." Diaz dialed up her New York swagger. "Trust me, I don't like this new divide we created, but I can tell you that we've come a long way in the last twenty years."

"And yet you still called them outsiders? Tsk tsk."

As smug as Nick Baxter came off, he was right. Diaz had been judging them all along the road trip for reasons that would've seemed absurd when she was a kid. *Why? Because they didn't have solar-powered roads? AVs? Drones hovering to provide non-stop security?* She had never thought of herself as privileged until that moment.

Chortling like a giddy actress, Ronson joked, "My partner hasn't had her lunch yet, so she's getting a li'l *hangry*." She continued her game with Baxter. "I'm curious to hear exactly what a job in Lucidity entails."

"I can assure you they love what they do." He shunned Diaz, leading Ronson farther in. "Let me show you."

When Baxter wasn't paying attention, Ronson pointed out a restricted area with a green access light. Diaz slipped in undetected, ending up in a pitch-black corridor. She tiptoed through the darkness searching for an on-switch, feeling her way against the cold walls until she triggered a light to come on. Another observation room. Except in this one, the test subjects were topless women, no older than nineteen or twenty, wearing only adult diapers.

As she crept deeper in, a second room lit up behind her. The test subjects were built like athletes or soldiers with synth transplants, replacement body parts, and scorpion tattoos on their forearms, signifying they were all part of the Knights of Azrael – KOA for short.

Seeing them reminded Diaz of when the KOA had tried to recruit her, and although the privately funded global militia had ended up being the heroes of the war, she was glad that she'd turned down their offer.

The Knights had a mantra – *Destiny to the Mother*, which came off as indoctrinating.

Nick Baxter was running specific tests with these two different groups, which seemed ethically questionable, and judging by the soldiers' reactions, painful as well. They were screaming at the top of their lungs and convulsing in their DreamCatchers, only held in by the tight straps.

When the corridor went dark again, Diaz rushed back to where'd she come in. She felt around for a door but found a glass panel instead. It was at the other end of the restricted hallway. Right as she was about to turn around, a third observation room lit . It was worse than the other two combined. She counted.

One, two, three, four ...

There were five children, all connected to smaller versions of the strange DreamCatchers. Like lab rats.

All Diaz could think was, "What in the hell is going on in this place?"

CHAPTER 14

Diaz was horrified by the sight. They were so, so tiny, and even though their eyes were covered, she could tell they were scared. They shivered. The lights came back on, and the windows transformed into black mirrors. Baxter stormed down the hallway with Ronson following behind.

"What the hell are you doing down here?" he shouted.

Diaz barked a laugh. "I could ask you the same thing."

"The tour's over!" He forced them out. "Maybe the next time the Army comes, they'll give me some answers instead of rehashing shit I'm trying to put in the past."

"We're not from the Army," Ronson bragged, making sure everyone heard her. "We're from an Army task force called Lost Patriots."

Baxter huffed. "Get out!"

With a smile, Ronson whispered to Diaz, "They really do need to come up with a better name for us."

After Nick Baxter stormed off into another corridor, a drone shined a red beam down on the detectives in the bright lobby. "Please exit the facility," it commanded as everyone stared at them. Diaz rushed ahead of her partner, bowing her head in embarrassment.

"Where to next?" Ronson asked.

"It's over," Diaz shrugged. "One and one make two as you said. Nick Baxter only confirmed what we already speculated."

Exiting the strange facility, Ronson put her arm around Diaz. "I haven't known you for that long, but you don't seem like someone who gives up that easy. Our deadline isn't for another week."

"Why are you so interested all of a sudden?"

"Despite my reluctance early on, I'd like to make sure we find that sergeant of yours. I'm not going to leave one of our own behind."

"You just like being on the road with me," Diaz flirted with a poke to Ronson's nose. "There's nothing else to find."

"What did you see in that restricted area then?"

"Nothing that has anything to do with our case."

"I'm curious."

When Diaz told her of the naked women and the KOA soldiers, Ronson laughed. "That's the lack of sex talking," she joked. "He was showing us the rooms where the employees of Lucidity work. When Baxter realized you went down the restricted area, he told me it was the experimental research section."

"They were decked out like naked babies!"

"It's called science, Diaz. *Shit* literally happens during some of the experiments. And also, some people don't mind getting naked." She grinned. "I once posed nude for an art class in college."

Diaz stopped walking. "And what about the kids I saw?"

Ronson brows rose toward her widow's peak. "Baxter didn't say anything about no kids. Are you sure that's what you saw?"

Diaz kept walking ahead through the lines of people. "I don't even know anymore." She was still adjusting to the sunlight. "I'm glad us old folks both learned a little something about BCI, though." She turned to Ronson and asked, "Can we go home now?"

As they made their way through the parking lot, Ronson said, "You don't find it odd that all this ties back to brain-computer interface? I mean, your sergeant was involved in Lucidity a decade before most people knew it existed."

Diaz finally took a breath when it was clear of drones. "I guess it had something to do with his interrogation skills," she said. "It seemed like they were torturing some of those KOA soldiers but Grady was against that."

Their conversation got interrupted when a woman ran toward them screaming, "Excuse me!" It was the receptionist from the NCU. "Don't leave yet!" Terrified or lost, she glanced around, also checking if the drones were capturing her every move. She was out of breath from chasing them, perversely shaking when she handed a piece of paper to Diaz. "Mr. Baxter wanted me to give this to you."

"What is it?"

"Mr. Baxter said it was a flyer he found in his sister's jacket a couple of years ago," the woman told them. "Mr. Baxter doesn't know what it means, but Mr. Baxter thought it might help you find out what happened to Quinn."

Diaz hardly glanced at it. "We're already here, and free if he wants to give us any more information. I'd love to ask him more questions about those experiments he's running."

The receptionist passed a certain point in the parking lot, and it was as if she came out of a spell. Her entire body language transformed, straightening up her posture. "Do you have an appointment? Mr. Baxter's busy at the moment." She hurried back to the building before they could ask her any more questions.

"That was fucking weird." Ronson grabbed the piece of paper from Diaz's hands. She grinned after reading what it said. "He may have been a complete douchebag, and his assistant is most certainly a malfunctioning android, but I think Mr. Baxter might have given us our next lead."

Diaz shook her head. "It's some crumpled-up flyer meant for the trash."

Hopping in the passenger seat, Ronson started in with her stupid laugh that was both irritating and infectious. "Were you not listening to your buddy Poe in Richmond? She said the last phone call Ellie Ginsberg made was when they got detained in Ohio, exactly around the same date this flyer says." She sighed. "Jesus Christ, you're so damn hellbent on figuring this out that you're missing the clues right in front of you. Check out the address on this."

It was a flyer for an anti-war protest:

"The Rally to End All Violence – April 25, 2032, Lorain, Ohio."

At the bottom of the flyer was a handwritten message:

"Do not respond to this message in any way other than showing up. No cyber trails ... Burn after reading."

Ronson was right – it was a new lead.

"Don't you want to go home to your husband and retire?" Diaz asked.

"Who said he was part of my retirement plan? I'm down for the ride as long as it doesn't get too fucking twisted. This sergeant of yours was into some serious shit, like one of those true-crime mysteries I always wanted to work on."

"You were in IA for ten years," Diaz reminded her. "There must've been some interesting cases."

"My Internal Affairs unit made sweeping changes once we figured out most of our bad apples were already secretly supporting the FF. They didn't even know what hit them when they were the ones behind bars."

"Well, that's pretty awesome."

"True," Ronson gloated, "but this reminds me more of those podcasts about all the shit that goes down behind the scenes of new innovations." She added, "Do you know they still don't know who created AlterWorld? ... And the KOA is just run by some random guy named Wells – another anonymous CEO."

Diaz knew exactly what her partner was yammering on about. The freakish accidents, corporate cover-ups – *investigators who suspiciously went missing*. Whatever was going on at the NCU Binary was suspect, especially Baxter's assistant and the note she'd handed them. It felt like a call for help. Diaz smiled at Ronson, but inside her stomach was bubbling. They were running on fumes in the middle of Kansas working on a case that was going into dark territory. If her partner was looking for an exciting farewell tour, it seemed she was about to get her wish.

CHAPTER 15

Tiny wires penetrated his skin. An assortment of hormones kicked in. James lay back in the sleek DreamCatcher thinking about the tasks he hadn't completed with his new time off. Instead, he'd spent the week researching his father's folder. It seemed as though the anonymous billionaire, SRT, still held a ten percent share in the mega-corporation after his sale of the Void. That same man had promised his father an avatar in the new system, and James had spent a huge chunk of their bank account on that faint glimpse of finding that avatar.

It had been almost a week since his tutorial in the Cave. Nera had warned him of the fatigue that would follow his initial test run. James had slept more than usual. While awake his brain was foggy, his body was sore. Sandy didn't have any sympathy for the side effects, facetiously warning, *What could possibly go wrong?* The only thing easing her mind was knowing that Calvin was guiding him in Lucidity that night. With that, James put in his earbuds, placed the mask over his eyes, and braced for the bullet-like disposable chip to be blasted into his cortex.

~

James, or Dark Cloud, found himself on a long flimsy bridge that stood above a vast veil of puffy clouds. A clear night's sky surrounded him with a million stars and more colors than his mind imagined. Comets flew past him, so close it felt like he could touch them. When the fog disappeared, he saw the top half of a spherical glass dome. The bridge itself, made of wood and rope, swayed in the heavy winds that blew it from side to side. The spaces between each board were far and wide. No clear sight of any surface below. Focused on not looking down, he continued onward with his head up until finding a safe spot. The silhouettes of other avatars scurried up ahead on the slim pathway into the glass dome, but James stood frozen.

Was this another test?

From behind, a woman groaned, "You mind moving forward?"

Gripping the rope as if his life depended on it, James cautiously turned his head to peek at the avatar yelling at him. She wore a slimming astronaut suit, and through the helmet she had purple skin, a young face, and 3D green eyes popping out in contempt.

"You're wasting our time, honey," she said with a slow Nawlins' drawl.

"Is this part of the Welcome Facility?"

The woman had a big laugh. "This is the *waiting room*. When it's crowded in the Welcome Facility, this is their buffer to file us in at a reasonable pace." She approached him. "First time?"

"I've been through the Cave."

"Then you're not getting very far tonight, sweetie. My advice is to figure out which sector you want to visit next time you're in here."

James tried not to think about his fear of heights. "What's the most popular sector to find someone? I already know his username."

"This guy knows you're looking for him?"

"I'm not sure."

"Then you're a stalker." The woman shook her head in disdain. "It's best you just enjoy what this place has to offer instead of bringing in your personal life. Experiment a little bit, if you know what I mean."

"I'm not into the sex stuff." He immediately realized how judgmental it sounded. "Not that there's anything wrong with that."

The woman roared with laughter, nudging him forward. "You think I'd wear this outfit if I was that kind of avatar? Not everyone comes here for that, ya know."

"What do *you* come here for?"

"Lucidity is a good place to find yourself ... *Dark Cloud*. I suggest you do that instead of going around trying to find users who *ain't* looking to be found."

So busy yapping with the woman, James didn't realize he'd already made it to the entrance. When the door slid open, the astronaut slipped past him and vanished into the crowd. Maybe she was right about him being a stalker. But how many other users were looking for their missing father in the system? He wondered how she knew his username anyway, his thoughts disappearing when he stepped inside.

~

The Welcome Facility was like a transit hub on LSD, bombarded by the sound of chattering and the downbeat EDM blaring in the background. Hundreds of avatars of all walks of life and imagination meandered through the main level – a series of walkways that overlooked the massive space. James felt the breeze of a manga man run by him as a gorilla with sunglasses chased after him. Others like the manga man seemed to come in as some caricature of themselves, playing dress-up for the evening.

Through the top of the glass roof, James could still see the universe. When he looked over a rail on the inner edge, there was a strange portal at the bottom of the Facility, hundreds of feet below. Compared to Alter World, full of signs and billboards, the Facility's design was minimalist and ad-free. Beautiful tessellations had been etched into the platinum walls. It reminded him of the photos he'd seen of the Alhambra, shimmering when the shadows crossed and the light refracted off. Roman numerals lined the main floor like a clock, and James looked back and noticed the Twelve (XII) above the entrance he came in from.

To control his racing heart in the hectic facility, he stood motionless, using a breathing technique his father had once taught him: *Smell the dandelions, blow away the petals.* James convinced himself it was no different from Alter World, but then, when he wasn't paying attention, he slammed into someone and fell hard onto the marble floor. A pot-bellied one-eyed cartoon creature wearing an athletic jumpsuit and a gold chain stared down at him.

"Watch where you're going, Dark Cloud," the creature demanded, before heading off into the crowd with an entourage taunting James.

"Fucking rookie!"

Lucidity was hyper-real compared to the Cave. As soon as James picked himself up off the ground, the shadow of an ominous figure crept up from behind, its footsteps shaking the ground as it approached. James moved to the side to get out of the way, but the shadow followed.

A deep voice whispered, "How did you find me?"

James felt the breath of the words on the back of his neck. "I don't know," he said, his voice quivering. "It's my first time in here."

When he turned around a lion stood on its hind legs above him, grinning through its sharp teeth, thick wet saliva lining its gums, a freshly brushed golden mane. The beast had glowing cat eyes and wore a red sports jacket with a name tag: *Cali-Cal*.

"Hello, Dark Cloud."

"Calvin?"

The lion roared with laughter, grabbing his belly with his two paws. His voice changed to a familiar one. "Yes, sir."

"Damn it, Calvin. You scared the shit out of me."

Calvin, the lion, gave him a full walk around. "What's with the get-up, Dark Cloud? ... You look like you're ready to go to the Yards."

James gave him the I-don't-know-what-the-hell-you're-talking-about look.

Calvin said, "That's where all the vagrants hang out." The lion pointed across the facility. "It's right over there through the tenth sector. It's absolute anarchy. That's not what you're here for though, is it?"

"You know what I'm here for," James whispered. "I told you I'd be patient, but I'll go anywhere if I can find a clue and I don't have a lot of time."

Calvin put his strong furry arm around him. "Let's go for a tour, Mr. G. After all, it's much easier to find what you're looking for if you know your surroundings."

The first sector, only signified by a portal and a roman numeral one, was called Springfield, and according to Calvin it was "where the old people hang out." He said it was full of shops and small streets, designed by users who either did it for fun or to make long-term investments. "Real estate in Lucidity isn't cheap," Calvin explained. "The more popular simulations get moved to the front of each sector, and some sectors like five, seven, and nine are still unclaimed. The original creators designed it to be a walkable world, but I'm sure it won't be long before LucidiTech goes outside of the boundaries to give the people what they want."

As they moved on the tour, a group of avatars huddled around the second sector wearing different forms of hunting gear – modern flannels, camouflage, and outlandish tribal outfits. "This is the Eternal Forest," Calvin explained. "It looks like this group is playing a game of 'Wolf and Man' – basically, a kill or be killed version of manhunt."

James raised his brow. "I thought you said Lucidity isn't a game."

"The world outside isn't a game either, but we still have football, *Jeopardy*, and war, right?" Calvin added, "Actually, a majority of our users come in to socialize, never leaving the Facility. They hang out to show off their new outfits like teenagers at the mall. It's safer in here because you never have to worry about winding up in a Red Zone."

"My Lucidity operator warned me about those," James said. "Then she claimed that I cheated because I flew to the top of the Cave."

"That's impossible, Mr. G. They turn the gravity up in Lucidity, or else this whole place would be a Red Zone full of idiots flying into each other."

James didn't want to argue so he brushed it off as they moved on.

It was interesting to see Calvin as a ferocious lion wearing fancy kicks and more confidence than he'd ever had at school. Multiple users waved to the popular guide. Like music, he seemed to have already mastered Lucidity.

"The third sector is the Lucidity Sports Compound." Calvin seemed unenthused. "Pretty self-explanatory. They have stadiums, golf courses, tennis courts, blah, blah. It's fun if you're into that sorta thing, but in the three years I've known you, I don't think ever heard you mention sports."

"Hey, I used to play basketball until the first pandemic," James joked. "Maybe I'd like to see if I still have any skills without my shitty knee bothering me."

"Trust me," said Calvin, "it's not a video game and you can't fly in there either. You can make your avatars bigger and take away your injuries, but that won't make you any better if you don't have the skill. People want to become cartoons or robots but forget that their functionality changes with that option too. You know how many wasted hours I spent training to become a clumsy cat?"

"Then why'd you pick this avatar?"

"It's my guide get-up." Calvin grinned through his sharp teeth. "I have a different avatar for my private time. Speaking of which, how old are you in this version of yourself?"

"Nineteen or so."

"You were a good-looking dude, Mr. G. I guess dealing with a bunch of teenagers put some years on you."

James grimaced. "Don't you know you're supposed to flatter your elders? Besides, I'm sure after Kyle's little speech you've all figured out it wasn't my teaching that aged me."

"We all go through shit and you know I'd never hold that against you. It doesn't matter anyway because next year we're going to kick ass at a new school."

Calvin gave him a fist bump, or *paw bump*, as if they were in the same location. They were actually a good twenty miles from each other. James had to remind himself yet again that Lucidity was only a simulation.

Taking it all in, James said, "This place is wild, Calvin."

"I warned you." Calvin gave him a big lion smile that somehow looked like him and said, "Only now you're in my classroom, *James*."

"It does sound weird when you call me by my first name."

"Told you!" Calvin nudged him toward the next sector. "If you're only coming here for a month, then the Wonders is the place to go. There are tons of mind-bending attractions that give you the full experience."

James moaned. "I don't like theme parks."

"Do you like anything fun, Mr. G?"

When James was young, dumb, and on drugs he'd had plenty of adventures. It'd been a slow process finding a sense of purpose since his sobriety, but he knew he'd already answered Calvin with his silence.

"Lucidity's meant to be enjoyed." Calvin turned to James. "So, while you go on your personal *man-hunt*, make sure you take it in the entertainment that it has to offer."

Calvin seemed to get a message in his ear as his eyes wandered away like he was on a phone call. "Yeah, I'll be right there," he said to someone else, before glancing back at James. "Hold tight right here, Mr. G. I have to go take care of some business."

Calvin headed back to the front of the Facility, leaving James alone.

His nerves had calmed since meeting up with his student, who made the strange world seem ordinary. He eased into how it flowed, strolling to the inner edge of the walkway to take another peek below. The main floor wasn't the only attraction in the Welcome Facility. On a lower level at the opposite end, a huge crowd of avatars headed to an event, lights flashing from the direction of a roaring crowd chanting someone's name.

A generic version of C-3PO made its way over to James, standing uncomfortably close to him near the railing. A rusty aluminum droid made from a collection of random kitchen utensils and computer parts.

"You heading to the concert tonight?" It had a robotic voice, a stream of tiny green bulbs lighting when it talked. "Eleonora's performing tonight."

"Never heard of her."

The droid laughed. "You must be new then. Eleonora's huge in Lucidity, thus the reason it's so busy tonight. Usually, people come in according to which time zone they live in, but when she performs many people either miss work or skip sleep to come."

"*Wow.*" James was uninterested in small talk, his focus elsewhere.

On the bottom of the Welcome Facility, the floor was designed with larger, more colorful tessellations which led to a dodecahedron in the center – a name James oddly remembered from a stoned-out conversation he'd had in Kansas with a man obsessed with Greek geometrics. What at first appeared to be a circular portal actually had twelve sides and a pentagon at its heart. If the level he was on was a clock, as the roman numerals seemed to suggest, the portal below was the center wheel pivot running the dials. There was a way to get down there, but no one seemed interested.

"What's that?" James asked the robot, who luckily hadn't gotten his hint to scram. The droid, in full character mode, waddled over like a creaky piece of metal and gazed down at what he was pointing to.

"That's the Void."

James popped up from the glass railing. "I thought that was sold to Lucidity and they'd overhauled the technology to morph it into this place."

"The Void should've never made that deal." The droid whispered, "Lucidity may have commercialized BCI, but I'm not sure if they're ready to deal with this level of capacity."

"It seems pretty harmless to me. Plus I've got an awesome guide showing me around."

"Did your guide warn you that Lucidity's one glitch away from a full-on meltdown?" The android got uncomfortably close. "Imagine what some evil mind can do with access to this technology."

James eased away. "I think I'm gonna try to find my guide. I'm sure you're a nice enough, but I'm not here to wrap my head around those kinds of thoughts."

The android continued anyway. "That's interesting you say that, *Dark Cloud*, especially since you showed up in Lucidity dressed like an angsty street rebel. Meanwhile, I tell you about an event that's brought in the most traffic this place has ever had, and you're more captivated by that desolate mausoleum down there. What are you really searching for in here?"

"I'm trying to reconnect with an old friend."

"You're searching for more than that," said the droid. "Maybe you need a bright light to make those gloomy clouds disappear."

James asked, "Are you one of them?"

But when he looked back, the android was gone and his student had returned.

Calvin gazed around. "Who are you talking to, Mr. G?"

It was a good question, and with the avatar out of sight, James wasn't sure what to tell his student without sounding delusional. He peeked over the rafter to see if the droid had jumped, even though it was supposedly impossible to fly. In Lucidity, it was hard to tell what was real, imagined, or both.

Scratching his bare face where his beard should be, James asked, "You didn't see the avatar I was talking to?" Calvin shook his head no. "Is there an Eleonora who's having a big concert tonight?"

"Yeah, that's why it's so crowded."

James asked, "So, she does exist?"

"Yes but—"

"So I'm not going mad?"

Calvin sighed. "Did the avatar you were speaking with magically vanish?"

James gave the vicinity one last look around. "Apparently so."

An unnerving grimace flooded Calvin's feline mouth. "This is Cali Cal." He stepped away to reach out to someone. "We got a possible 977 over here between four and five." He paced around like it was a serious matter. "I repeat ... we got a 977 over here between four and five."

A tall blond man in a tuxedo swaggered over. He was handsome, almost too much so, obviously overcompensating in the fantasy world. "I'm Lance." The man firmly shook James's hand. "As head of security here in the Welcome Facility, I need to ask you a couple of questions."

"Am I in trouble?"

"We're on high security because of the Light Keepers threat, so we must take extra precautions," Lance said. "Were you using your Navigator when you met with this unknown avatar?"

"My what?"

Lance moaned. "You should always keep your Navigator on because you would've known it was a phantom. They wouldn't have an ID and you could contact us for assistance."

"I didn't know it was so serious."

"It's nothing, but the bigger Lucidity gets, the harder it is to secure." Lance's eyes narrowed. "So tell me what this avatar said to you?"

"It was telling me about the concert, and then they started getting a little weird and talking about meltdowns in Lucidity, and something about making my dark clouds drift away."

"Definitely a Light Keeper," Lance huffed, gazing around the Facility. "From now on when you're in new areas use your Navigator to keep track of who you're meeting with. We've had more of these phantoms hacking into the system lately, so I'm glad you let us know."

While Lance and Calvin had a private discussion, James wondered what he was missing. What the hell was a phantom, or this Navigator he should be using? In the corner of his eye, James noticed a neon-blue dot on both his right pinky and thumb. When he pressed the two together it accessed the Navigator – a holographic display showing all kinds of helpful info. As avatars passed by he could now see their usernames, finally realizing how everyone knew his. It also showed him how much time he had left.

Five minutes and counting.

Calvin approached, shaking his head and laughing. "I can't believe you've been in here this whole time without using your Navigator. I knew you didn't go through the manual."

"Did I get you in trouble?"

"No, but you almost got yourself into some." Calvin explained that the Light Keepers had made contact with other guests that night, too. Every day there were more reports of phantoms soliciting for the cult with the ability to vanish in an instant.

"Just like on the outside," Calvin said, "the Light Keepers are meticulous about keeping themselves off the radar."

"And when do I get to finish the rest of the tour?

"Once you get past sector six, Aurora, it gets too wild. A married man in your profession doesn't want anything to do with that side of the Facility."

"Well, what about the Void down there?"

"Trust me," said Calvin, "that's the last place you want to go. LucidiTech's about to shut it down because they think that's how these phantoms might be sneaking in. I think it's haunted." The seven-foot-tall lion seemed focused on the front entrance, which was more crowded than before. "I have to go, Mr. G, so do me one favor."

"And that is?"

"Don't do anything stupid." Calvin put his paw on James's

shoulder and looked at him with his ferocious yellow eyes. "Remember that I'm vouching for you."

Despite Calvin's warning, James couldn't get the Void out of his head. He wandered back over to the railing and gazed down onto the oddly shaped portal, remembering the wise words of the purple astronaut on the bridge. "*Figure out which sector you want to visit first.*" James had a pretty good idea of where that was going to be.

CHAPTER 16

In a dark room filled with shadows, an old man sat next to a dialysis machine that he no longer needed. He opened the Venetian blinds to let in the light, revealing the dust settling over the walls of junk. Piles upon piles of newspapers, books, and DVDs crowded his already tight apartment, and after losing some hundred-plus pounds in the last ten years, the PUBLIC ENEMY T-shirt he wore practically drowned him. The hoarder had lived in the same rent-controlled closet for sixty-two years, but moved like he was in his prime. It was phenomenal considering he was supposed to be dead months ago.

Sandy Grady sat across from the old man, Xavier Cortez, in her usual boring work attire – a beige sweater and blue dress pants – her reading glasses sliding down her nose. She scanned a stack of files that she held high in her lap. She'd been meeting with Patient X, as she called Xavier when speaking to James, for about eight months. That April, Xavier had visited Puerto Rico only to return with a massive tumor that had drastically shrunk down to a pebble-sized blip on an X-ray.

Sandy had spent most of her time reading articles on the Light Keepers, attempting to get a better understanding of their intent. The media referred to them – and occasionally *her* – as hackers, a cult, and more recently, terrorists. But what was the purpose of killing sick people? Some sort of revenge against Lucidity or the Earth First Initiative? Euthanasia?

For months the media had called them dangerous without an explanation why. In one of the articles, a top oncologist compared the Light Keepers' methods to taking a shot of adrenaline. *"It fills them with life for a moment until they die,"* the specialist claimed in the article. After Tomás and Monica's demise, she worried Xavier might have chosen a similar path. Sandy knew no one rehabilitated that fast.

"How are you feeling today?" she asked.

"Amazing, my true love." Xavier always flirted, usually slurred because of the drugs he was on. Now more healthy, he moved his favorite chair out of the way. "Will you dance with me?"

Sandy blushed. "It's a little early for that, but I'm glad to see you're doing so well."

"I'll tell you my secret, Dr Grady."

"Oh, and what's that?"

"You," he said with a big smile.

"I'm the secret, huh?"

"More like the reason I'm appreciating this second wind." His hips began to sway as if he had the music in his head. "Reading your book and answering the same questions you asked those dying patients made me appreciate my life. It doesn't flash in front of your eyes until you think you're at death's door." Xavier paused and held his hand out. "Now dance with me, Dr Grady."

Sandy sighed, sometimes forgetting she'd even written a book. She held out her hand, but Xavier rushed off to find something in the mess he called his *home furnishing*. Underneath a stack of Yellow Pages from the twentieth century, he found a dusty boombox. He had a tape cassette in his pocket ready to go. The upbeat music played as he took her hand, his feet surprisingly quick.

Xavier said, "Now we can do this."

Knowing his frisky hands, Sandy made sure to dance with him like he was her grandfather. "You never answered my question." He gave her a spin. "You only said that I helped you enjoy this second chance at life, but you never told me what made it happen in the first place."

Xavier changed the subject. "Did you ever wonder what society would be like if we didn't go in a certain direction?"

"I don't understand what you mean."

Xavier didn't stop salsa dancing as he spoke. "Like, what if we lost the Revolutionary War? Or if Alexander the Great never conquered all of Rome? When did we become so afraid of each other?" The old man stared into her eyes as the music cut in halftime. "What if the pacifists had become the popular leaders of our world? Maybe we would've looked at war as unnecessary, if not for our barbaric ancestors."

"Humans are instinctively in survival mode," she said, not ready for one of his endless debates. "I studied this for years."

"You know what I mean." Sweat beaded on Xavier's top lip. "You've been taught your whole life that violence is inevitable. In the last hundred or so years, our country has been in constant disputes, and we've become pre-conditioned to it. As a child, I lived through the Korean War and Vietnam. As a soldier, I fought in the Cold one."

"No one fought during the Cold War, Xavier."

"I was a spy, sweetie." He winked. "Anyway, then it was in Iraq, Afghanistan, Syria, Ukraine, Africa, Poland, Russia, Brazil, and the beat goes on. This cluster-fuck of world domination and imperialism almost had us annihilating ourselves in the Last War. Our entire modern civilization is addicted to the bloodshed of others."

"I suppose you're right," Sandy agreed. "But we're out of it for now."

Xavier laughed. "A brief time of peace before we're doomed to repeat the cycle. But for the first time in my eighty-five years of life, I'm awake, and it's extremely liberating. I've been bitter for too long and I wish people knew that the only thing that matters is the sun coming up in the sky, the only light we can rely on."

Sandy unplugged the boombox. "Are you saying what I think you're saying?"

Out of breath and clapping his hands as if she'd won a prize, Xavier took a seat in his favorite chair. "I was a dying man and now thanks to the Light Keepers I've lived an extra two months with many more to go."

"You obviously read enough newspapers to know that's illegal," Sandy said, sitting on a pile of them.

"Isn't your job to make my pain go away, or is it just to assist me with dying?" He refused to look at her. "I knew you were a fucking sheep like everyone else."

Sandy managed her sentiments, although she was on the verge of tears. "Xavier ... I have to release myself as your therapist. We have deemed the Light Keepers, or any matter relating to that name or organization, as a dangerous threat to your well-being." She whispered to him, "You have to keep this to yourself from now on."

"They're not the fucking bad guys," the old man screamed as if it were some absurd notion. "In the last fifteen years, I've been on every drug this planet has to offer. This is the first time I've been free from the side effects. I didn't know terrorists went around saving lives. In my culture, we call them our *ángeles guardianes*."

Sandy knew enough Spanish to understand. "Then why don't your *guardian angels* come out of the shadows?" She began to pack up her things. "Why won't they say who's in charge?"

Xavier stood next to the window, gazing at the streets below with a sly grin. "What if Einstein never handed over the codes to Oppenheimer and they never created an atomic bomb? Sometimes you have to keep a powerful tool out of the wrong hands." He shouted, "I am become Death, the destroyer of worlds!"

"We're done here." Sandy held back on telling him about the other incidents that had ended in death, not wanting to jinx him. "You're gonna get your ass in trouble."

"Too late for that," Xavier quipped.

Just then, there were three loud knocks at his front door. "Mr. Cortez," a woman yelled from outside. "This is the FBI! Open up the door or we will break it down!"

Sandy froze but managed to whisper, "How'd you know they were coming?"

"I saw them from the window," he said loud enough for them to hear in the hallway.

"Have you told anyone else what you told me?"

"You're the only one I trust." He gave her the gentlest hug. "I'm not going to tell them anything. Now open the door, my love, and tell that husband of yours that he's a very lucky man."

Five agents stormed in as she opened the door. The leader was a middle-aged female, with standard blue FBI jacket and silver aviators. "Both of you put your hands up and get against the wall," she yelled.

The other agents wore black masks, armed with rubber-bullet guns, hardly treating Xavier like a senior citizen. They threw him to the ground, placing him in handcuffs.

"Be careful," Sandy cried. "He's dying of cancer!"

The lead agent – Miller, according to her ID badge – spoke without any hesitation. "Mr. Xavier Cortez, you're under arrest for illegal communication with a known terrorist." The agent continued with her list of Rights as they dragged Cortez out of his apartment. "If you cooperate we will grant you counsel." As if they were tickling him, the old man giggled the entire time.

"*Lo llevaré a mi tumba,*" Xavier said to the stern-faced agent, who didn't seem to be familiar with Spanish.

Sandy knew what that meant too. *I'll take it to my grave.* With her belly up against the wall and her mind on the consequences, she silently wept. *I'm going to be in so much trouble for this.* The three armed agents fled with the old man, but Agent Miller and the other blue-coat stuck around to investigate his clutter-filled one-bedroom dig.

"You can turn around now." Agent Miller's shoulders were broad, and her voice deep and intimidating. She didn't seem in the mood for a polite conversation. "You want to tell me who you are or do I have to perform a body scan?"

"My name's Dr Sandy Grady." She wiped the tears from her cheeks. "I was here for my Friday morning session with Mr. Cortez. He insinuated he may have ties to the Light Keepers only minutes ago and I made him aware of the legal consequences."

"And you were going to come straight to the FBI afterward, I assume?"

"As soon as I left here," Sandy lied, unsure if his apartment was bugged the entire time.

The agent didn't seem satisfied. "We have evidence that some sort of therapist in the region has been sending people to the Light Keepers."

Do you mean Kalen Green? Sandy almost said it out loud, knowing exactly whom the agent was referring to. If there were any time to come clean, it was then. Xavier's words got in her head: *Sometimes you have to keep a powerful tool out of the wrong hands.* It was too early for the whole truth and she was already late for work.

"I assure you that's not me," Sandy insisted. "I believe the Light Keepers are using methods of pseudo-science, which has always been a pet peeve of mine. A very dangerous idea to spread to the masses."

"I see you've done your research." Miller poked around Xavier's piles, fixated on one particular piece of evidence. "And it seems like Mr. Cortez might've had a little obsession with you."

The agent had come across one of Xavier's twenty copies of Sandy's book, *Life at Death*. Miller scanned the back cover. As much as Sandy had argued with her publisher, they'd decided to go with the testimonials from her peers over her simple elevator pitch: *"The honest thoughts about life at the moment we realize it's ending."* One of her peers had called her the "doctor of death," and though it was meant as praise, her work was much deeper than that. It was about the joy of living.

"You know, you could be of great assistance to us." Agent Miller glanced through some of the chapters. "The Keepers seem to have targets on the patients you deal with."

Sandy tightened her loose-fitting top around her pouty stomach, which at times wasn't even noticeable. "I can't exactly do any undercover field operations."

Mortified, Agent Miller immediately told her to sit down and instructed the other agent to grab her some water. She cozied up next to Sandy on the worn-out leather couch with the book in her hand. "I still think you can help us, Dr Grady."

"How so?"

"Do what you do in this book." It sounded more like an order. "We've acquired a list of possible suspects who are in a hospice or close to that point. If Mr. Cortez is any indicator, they're more likely to spill the beans on their death bed."

"Mr. Cortez wasn't—" Sandy blurted out before muffling herself. It wasn't worth the discussion. "Do I have options?"

"I can take you in as a suspect or you can help us."

With hardly a good choice in the matter, Sandy reluctantly agreed to be an informant until her third trimester. Agent Miller briefed her on the terms that went against every ethical code she swore by – non-maleficence, fidelity, and integrity to name a few. *So long doctor-patient confidentiality.* She signed the NDA stating her operation wasn't to be discussed with anyone, including her husband.

"It's sensitive national security protocol," Miller reminded her, acting as if it should be taken as an honorable duty.

To make matters worse, they'd contacted Dr Haskell to let him know about the predicament and her new role with the FBI. Xavier's private session hadn't been approved by the hospital, and after the last conversation she'd had with Haskell, she was already on his shit list. Her only saving grace was that he was off for the next couple of weeks.

"What's going to happen to Xavier?" she asked before the agent let her go. "He's just an old dying man looking for any kind of hope."

"If he gives us some info, then we can cut a deal with him." Miller helped Sandy up from the sofa. "Otherwise, he goes to jail."

"He's not gonna talk."

"We'll see about that." The agent walked Sandy to the elevator, practically pushing her on. "Have a good day, Dr Grady."

CHAPTER 17

Early that Friday morning James woke up with a message on his UniTab. "*9AM sharp!*" It was Calvin reminding him of their field trip to the Wonders.

James had waited three days for his next green light to go into the system, growing impatient with his trial period running out. Using aggressive advertising, Lucidity urged him to upgrade his subscription before his rates went up, but Sandy wouldn't budge on their promise. With only two weeks left, he didn't have time to visit some virtual amusement park, so he decided to ditch Calvin and choose his own adventure.

~

Unlike his first time, the Welcome Facility wasn't crowded and he didn't have to stand in line on a rackety bridge to get in. The Navigator allowed him to get around without needing the help of others to guide him, which came in handy once he figured out how to use it. Not wanting to waste any of his precious time, James followed the holographic GPS and headed in the direction of the Void.

A moving walkway led him to the lower levels, far below the floor where the big concert was held, taking him to the very bottom, which was at least twenty stories down. When he gazed up at the main level, a few spectators watched him like an ant underneath a magnifying glass. There must've been thousands of users in the system and James was the only lost soul down in the basement of the Facility.

The gate to the Void was a three hundred and sixty-degree portal – one-half of a dodecahedron covered in black liquid-like mirrors. On the main level of the Welcome Facility, avatars disappeared into the sectors through the portals, but those gates had themes and guides around them to lead the way. There was no one down by the Void. *Maybe this ride's broken*, he thought, on the verge of changing his mind with Calvin probably looking for him. It was a cyber ghost town down there and the Navigator didn't help, only indicating it was the entrance to the Void. Before changing his mind, he exhaled and stepped into the portal.

~

On the other side, James found himself surrounded by a dense wall of fog forming a circle around him. The sunlight, something he'd yet to see in any of the simulations, was dimmed by an overcast sky. Rose petals were laid out on the ground in front of him. Bubbles floated in a horizontal line in a different direction. Then a dirt trail. Gold bricks. A shallow stream mimicked the Facility's blueprint. Twelve different paths led into the fog, but he was distracted by an alternative route – a trail of radiant blue smoke summoning him to an opening between two of the other paths. Although the Navigator indicated there weren't any other avatars around, he could've sworn he heard a faint chatter.

"Is someone there?" he asked.

No one responded. He'd lost sight of the blue smoke and any sense of direction. Engulfed by the fog so dense he couldn't see his feet, he used his hands as walking sticks, bumping into the walls like a Rumba running its random algorithm, leading him farther from the starting point. The distant voices now sounded like a sitcom audience.

"*Ha ha ha ha ha.*" And they weren't laughing with him. "*Ha ha ha ha ha.*"

When it got quiet again James heard someone running away, the trail of blue following the shadow like a carrot on a stick. A whiff of the smoke hit him like a forbidden substance. His skin began to burn. His legs grew numb. Overcome with drowsiness, he fell to his knees like every time he'd used the needle, sitting in silence for what felt like forever, waiting for the anxiety to go away.

Numb and mindless and waiting.

This isn't real, he finally told himself. *This is just a video game.*

The laughter started back up, antagonizing him from somewhere within the fog.

"Why are you doing this to me?" he screamed, frightened it would never end.

Someone ran past James, but the fog made it impossible to see them. There was a scuffle in front of him that sounded like someone was being attacked, but the laughter stopped. Several footsteps scurried away and it got silent. New steps were getting closer. His navigator didn't work. The predator stopped moving when it was about ten feet away from him.

A familiar voice said, "You don't have to be afraid."

"Pops?" asked James, still out of it from the vapor. "Is that you?"

There was a silence. The blue smoke appeared in the direction of his father's voice. "Don't give up your search," he said. "You have to be more careful, but you're getting closer."

James picked himself up and approached his father's voice, but couldn't find him in the fog. "Come home and tell us what happened," he pleaded. "We'll understand."

The shadow chuckled in the fog. "It's a bit more complicated than that, but I trust you'll figure out this riddle. When you do, I hope you'll forgive me."

"I don't know what that means."

"Just listen for the signal," said the voice that sounded exactly like Pops's. "You'll know when you hear it."

"Did you say *hear it?*" I asked. "What the hell does that mean?"

The shadow sprinted away.

James chased after the sound as fast as he could, trying to keep up with the shadow who kept making turns in obscure directions. The blue smoke lit the path. It didn't prevent him from running into some sort of barrier that knocked him on his ass. He got back up and continued his pursuit.

"Why are you running from us?" James screamed, losing the footsteps and all visibility again.

Gasping with his hands on his hips, he tried to catch his breath as the fog began to fade, glancing up at what was either the beginning or the end of an elaborate corn maze. The tall stalks were a pale green and the sky had hints of blue but was otherwise desaturated of any color. His heart skipped a beat when he noticed someone else was lurking in the center of the cornfield.

A young Korean girl, maybe twelve or thirteen years old, seemed to be out of breath herself. "I think you're lost." Her voice was calm. A four-foot-nothing avatar who wore a pair of jean-overalls. French braids highlighted her glitter star earrings. "You need to come with me right now."

"But you're so young." James looked around for anyone else. "What are you doing down here?"

The girl giggled. "Drink this and we'll get you back home."

She gave him a vial with a glowing violet liquid. Although skeptical, he swallowed the tasteless fluid, and then the colors blossomed throughout the domain he stood in. Beyond the cornfield, there was an asymmetric arch made of steel that towered over him like a Dali painting come to life. It was a massive structure, even compared to modern architecture, but not as surreal as the brief conversation he just had with his father.

"Did you see a man pass you on your way in?" James asked, blocking one of the synthetic suns with his hand to get a better view of her. "Were you one of the people laughing at me?"

The girl shrugged. "It sounds like you got a whiff of the blue smoke and were talking to that scarecrow over there." She pointed to a silhouette. "That's why I gave you that sobriety tonic, and the reason us drifters stay away from places like this."

"Drifters?" James pretended to listen to the young stranger as he checked down every entrance of the elaborate maze, pondering how he'd made his way through it amid the fog.

Grabbing James's hand, the girl led him down one of the many paths of the maze. Her name was Mimi, and she walked far ahead of him, explaining that drifters were people who had substance abuse or mental health issues in the real world. James thought it was what his father was. Between the Void and the blue smoke known to cause paranoid hallucinations, it was "a perfect storm for a relapse." Mimi had had a similar experience herself.

"But how'd you know I was an addict?" James followed her, confused about how a little girl had a drug problem in the first place.

"Calvin worried about you when you didn't show up to meet him today, and then our head of security noticed you sneaking around the Facility. I decided to track you down even though it's my day off. Calvin said he warned you about coming to the Void."

"I'm not a very good listener."

"Apparently not." She zig-zagged through the maze as James followed closely. "And you're lucky I have a photographic memory." She took a second to decide left or right before figuring out the correct way to go. "You mind if I ask who was following you? After I inhaled the blue, it was a childhood bully that haunted me."

"Are you saying that whole experience was all in my head?"

"I'm the only other avatar down here right now," she assured him, "but don't worry, you're awake now."

James didn't believe her and was beginning to think they were lost in an unsolvable puzzle. He cautiously followed his new friend, taking much longer to exit than it did to sprint to the middle of the cornfield.

He stopped and scratched his chin. "Do you know where we're going?"

"*Ohhh*, is your Navigator not working?"

"No, and it hasn't for a while."

"Do you know why?" She grew frustrated with finding her way out. "It's because you took us off the grid, Dark Cloud – *no man's land*. You're not supposed to be down here, not only because you're a drifter, but because it's off-limits to Lucidity users and personnel."

"I don't even understand what the Void is," he muttered, more lost than she was. "Is it one big fucking corn maze?"

Mimi giggled, telling him to imagine a factory the size of Texas, full of test simulations. "A creative nerd's dream workshop," she called it. The maze was a minuscule section of the Void, essentially a junkyard of unlimited ideas that had been discarded and stored in a massive recycling bin of data and coding. There was actually a small section designated for Lucidity users, but the blue smoke had caused him to wander far from that spot.

Mimi abruptly stopped when they hit a point. "We made it!" She hugged him. "I wasn't sure if we'd ever get out."

"But we're still in the maze."

"Check your navigator."

It was working again, kindly reminding him that he didn't have time left after being down there for almost six hours. "What are we supposed to do now?"

"Lucidity doesn't have any control off the grid, so I don't know." Mimi instructed him to begin the ejection process. Not chancing her own risk of getting stuck on the grid, she did the same. "It's rumored users have gotten stuck down here for hours." A sly dig at James's current predicament.

"I don't want Calvin to be in trouble because I made a stupid mistake." James set himself up for his departure. "He specifically told me not to come down here, probably trying to spare my feelings by not bringing up my addiction."

"Calvin's our best guide and alerted us to the situation," Mimi told him. "You on the other hand are gonna be in timeout for a week, locked out of your account until next Friday."

"An entire week?" James shook his head. "Will you tell Calvin I'm sorry?"

"You tell him that yourself." Mimi had her fists pinned to her ribs as if she meant it. "Come back next Friday when your suspension is over. Calvin can take you on that tour of the Wonders he was looking forward to, and then you can come to my birthday party. Meet some friends who will keep you out of trouble." She added, "If you take it slow you'll enjoy the system a lot more."

"You're pretty wise for your age." James watched his timer run down, still stuck in the maze. "How old are you going to be?"

"Dirty thirty."

"I guess you took a couple of years off your life as well."

"Now you figured it out."

James glanced back at the cornfield, the arch now far in the distance. Why did his father ask for forgiveness? *What had Pops gotten himself into? And more importantly, what signal was I supposed to hear?* None of it made sense. "I don't think it was blue smoke that made me hear what I heard out there."

"Stop thinking so much, Dark Cloud," Mimi teased in his final ten seconds. "I'm guessing that's why you ended up here in the first place. The demons aren't in the Void; they're all in your head."

V

PART FIVE

CHAPTER 18

Surrounded by skyscrapers and a damp humidity, weaving through a sidewalk full of business elites and delivery bots, Sandy made her way to the Innovation Academy in Lower Manhattan. That Tuesday afternoon she was meeting with other informants to cover intel regarding the Light Keepers, and according to Agent Miller, the FBI wanted everyone on the same page.

Since the arrest of Xavier Cortez, Sandy's list of patients had grown as her actual patience waned. Every hospital in the region referred anyone they deemed questionable to the Feds, who in turn sent them to the psychologist for an unwarranted interrogation. On top of that, she'd hardly seen James in over a week, yet to tell him that she was an undercover agent. According to the NDA she'd signed, that wasn't even allowed. The overtime was not only unhealthy for her marriage and pregnancy but also for the patients she coerced every day.

When she entered the lobby of the Innovation Academy there was a team of NYPD officers, a pack of dogs, and a squadron of drones floating close to the ceiling of the skyscraper's lobby, once home to a disgraced banking operation. With the Knights of Azrael lurking about, decked out in their scorpion-embroidered, full-body armor, Sandy figured there also must've been someone important visiting. Otherwise, it was an excessive amount of security presence, and an extreme amount of gear to be wearing amid the May heatwave.

The academy, funded by none other than LucidiTech, centered its curriculum on robotic process automation, quantum computing, and BCI – all alien languages to Sandy's classic Ivy League education. Although she was curious as to why the FBI was meeting at the academy, let alone in the main auditorium, the eye candy of the intricate hallway distracted her for the time being. Without any special lenses, a school of AR minnows swam with her in the direction she needed to go.

Inside the auditorium was anything but what Sandy expected. An actress she recognized wore a T-shirt that read, "*Put Out The Light*," and mingled with the governor of New York. Usher drones guided the huge crowd of law enforcement agents, business advisers, and influencers to their assigned seats. One of them led Sandy to her assigned seat, which happened to be right next to her new boss, Agent Miller.

"Isn't this crazy?" Miller seemed smitten, looking around in awe. "Thanks to you and some other leads, we might've made a huge breakthrough."

"That's great." Sandy faked a smile. "Is Xavier okay?" She'd been worried about him ever since the raid. "I tried to ask another agent about him, but they wouldn't tell me anything."

Miller sighed. "Unfortunately, Mr. Cortez died the same day we arrested him. Sometimes cancer goes away and then creeps right back in. These experiments the Light Keepers are doing can be extremely dangerous."

"I know cancer. I see it every day of my life. Xavier had just gotten an MRI showing me the tumors had shrunk."

"Do you want to see the body yourself?" Miller fiddled with her UniTab. "He suffered a massive brain aneurysm so harsh that his eyes bled out. I can probably pull up some photos if you'd like."

Before Sandy could process what the agent had told her, the lights dimmed and they were instructed to take their seats. When they announced the first speaker, LucidiTech's CEO Prishna Gupta, Sandy realized how exclusive the meeting was and why the security was so tight. The elegant woman walked on stage to a standing ovation, wearing a colorfully patterned modernized dress of her region. From behind the thick podium, she seemed tiny, but on the larger monitor, her strong long neck and fierce emerald irises could hypnotize any crowd.

"Thank you all for attending today." Ms. Gupta glowed underneath the spotlight, speaking with a mix of British and Indian dialects. It was exactly same voice as Eden, the synth from James's training session. "Lucidity was the dream of my father, Sanjay, who died seven years ago. I have longed to capture his elegancy, his ideas, and his virtues. Today, we are at odds with an enemy who wishes to tarnish the beautiful fifth dimension my father only once imagined."

Ms. Gupta was a master salesperson, giving a speech that reminded Sandy of corporate seminars and the Behavioral Economics course she'd taken. "Despite having a universal basic income, people need to feel productive in a society and we need to make it safe for them to do so. That is what Lucidity will soon do."

Even among other world leaders and influencers in attendance, it was obvious that Prishna Gupta was not only the richest but also the most powerful of them all. She had total control of the room. After a long dramatic pause, the CEO changed her tone.

"Make no mistake, we will find out where these terrorists are hiding. We will find every single one of them!" The crowd roared, standing as if they'd scored a touchdown. "We will collectively put out this dark light!"

With that, she handed the meeting over to the FBI director, Gerald Zin, a large Chinese-American man with a grayish-brown beard and a shirt that didn't hide the pit stains. He waved to the crowd still cheering for Ms. Gupta.

"Now, now," Zin said with a grin. "We still have a long way to go. As many of you in the agencies know, we got a great tip last week that led to the arrest of a man named Xavier Cortez."

Behind him, on a huge holographic screen, Xavier was smiling, showing off his missing teeth while drinking a beer in the optimized photo. When the director mentioned Xavier's death, Sandy pinched the webs between her fingers to refrain from crying.

Zin continued. "Thanks to one of our newest informants, who successfully led us to Cortez, our agency has received a healthy stream of new intelligence." He paused. "With that being said, let's give a round of applause to Dr Sandy Grady."

With a drone shining a spotlight down on her, Sandy had no choice but to get up and graciously accept the standing ovation. *I'm responsible for his death*, she thought as they cheered her on as a hero. She wasn't even supposed to have been at Xavier's apartment that morning. Gazing around the room, she noticed that her boss, Dr Haskell, was in attendance. Sandy thought he was on vacation but he must've been summoned to the meeting, which he wouldn't have been happy about. He gave her a suspicious grin.

As they returned to their seats, Director Zin continued. "Through Dr Grady's particular work, she's diagnosed at least two patients who confided in her that they went to seek the Light Keepers' guidance. This leads us at the agency to believe that this cult – this terrorist front – is targeting drug addicts, outsiders, and the terminally ill as guinea pigs for their deadly experiments."

Zin cued a huge portrait of a woman onto the screen behind him. A woman Sandy was quite familiar with. "This is Kalen Green," he said, "a self-titled life coach, drug therapist, and hospice adviser. We discovered that Mr. Cortez had contacted her to gain access to the Light Keepers. Strong intelligence suggests that Ms. Green is one of the group's top recruiters, and now our number one suspect." He looked around the room. "Thanks to all your hard work, we plan on having her in our custody by this afternoon." The whole room practically exploded, now as if they'd just won the Super Bowl.

Sandy reluctantly clapped along, but inside her heart dropped to her empty stomach. Two minutes ago they were cheering for her, and now there were only two degrees of separation between her and the FBI's most wanted suspect. Did they know Kalen was her husband's counselor for the last three years? When the baby kicked, Sandy knew it must've felt the emotional roller coaster she was riding.

Director Zin hushed the frenzy, gladly absorbing the fanfare directed his way. "Because of their highly secretive nature and their intelligence capability, there's still so much we need to learn about this complex threat." As his speech continued, Sandy spent the time going over the potential consequences of her and her husband's association with the woman. "We will bring in Kalen Green today, and find out every detail she knows," Zin told the audience, although it seemed like it was directed straight toward Sandy.

The meeting, which lasted no longer than twenty minutes, abruptly ended. There was no Q and A. No sharing of intel, only Zin reminding them all to sign another NDA on their way out.

"Now that must've felt pretty good," Miller said. Before Sandy could get a word in about Cortez, the agent began briefing her on the following week's agenda. Her first order was to take the weekend off and prepare herself for a heavier load of patients the following week. LucidiTech had put a hefty bonus in her bank account to make it worthwhile.

Meanwhile, Sandy looked over the room, searching for her actual boss. "Is Dr Haskell okay with all of this?" She wiped her clammy hands on her pants to dry them. "I feel like he's pissed off at me for getting him involved."

"This is a matter of National Security," said Miller. "It doesn't matter what he thinks. Besides, we need him in the know for when we lose you." She led Sandy out of the aisle. "In the meantime, I'd like you to lose the attitude."

"Just tell me your interrogation didn't have anything to do with his death?"

Miller laughed. "The Feds aren't in charge of that part of that process," she said. "Prishna Gupta is pulling every resource she has to play damage control. If the public knew how real the threat was to Lucidity – especially if they saw the photos of what the Light Keepers are capable of – her stocks would take a massive hit. They're banking on getting real intel out of this local woman." Director Zin waved Miller over and it seemed important. "Expect to see me in your office next week to go over your reports in person."

As Sandy made her way out of the meeting, a dozen or so of the attendees shook her hand in admiration. Whatever magic powers she possessed acted like a bug zapper on a hot summer's day, unintentionally luring innocent victims in. Even Ms. Gupta made her way over, tailed by two drones, a couple of Feds, her press team, and a KOA member.

"Thank you." Gupta gave her the Namaste gesture. "You seem to have a gift."

It was a blush-worthy moment that Sandy could never speak of. Even with all the goodwill toward her, something wasn't sitting right. She left the state-of-the-art skyscraper with an uneasy feeling, and still had to head to the hospital and deal with another long list of patients. But first, there was one more task she had to take care of.

CHAPTER 19

Deep in rough waters, under a black starless sky, James frantically paddled his arms, attempting to swim to a shore that kept drifting farther away. A brute riptide. A series of crashing waves, flinging him around in a dizzying manner until the beach disappeared. He wasn't alone. A girl screamed in the distance.

"Help!" she shouted. "I'm drowning!"

He followed the direction of her voice out deeper into the endless body of water, spotting her hands flailing in hysteria. Right as he was on the verge of reaching her, a wave at least fifty feet high came barreling at them both. He reached for the girl and had her hand, but lost his grip as he rode the trough upward and over the top of the crest. And before he came back down himself, it all went black.

Upon awaking, he found himself in a dark room, lying flat on his back, attached to a machine. A door opened. Two men came in wearing black goggles and lab coats. One of them filled a syringe from a glass vial, squirting the remnants onto the floor. On the other side of the cement wall in front of him, the girl was screaming again.

"Leave me alone!" He heard objects come crashing to the floor as the girl continued to put up a fight. "Get the fuck off me!"

Right as he kicked himself away from the one man, the other struck him in the arm with a syringe, and it all went black again.

Frazzled and sweaty, James then woke up on the floor of his bedroom, half of the comforter on the ground and the other half on the bed. Now he was truly awake. It was the same reoccurring dream that had begun in high school, haunted him in college, and finally faded away with a heavy amount of booze and heroin. The same dream he'd had the morning his father had disappeared. Although James never saw the little girl in the dream, he always assumed it was Heather, and that seemed to make sense because it was May 30th, the anniversary of her death.

Most of the psychologists James visited over the years, including his wife, concluded that he was subconsciously blaming himself for his sister's suicide. No matter what they told him, he always thought he could've done more to prevent it. Heather inspired him to embrace life, so he never understood why she took her own. Most doctors blamed it on her headaches that began in her short adolescence, putting her on every medication they could think of as a cure. Unfortunately, his sister had had more pain than any prescription could fill.

Still in his underwear, James asked, "Ginger ... what time is it?"

"It's almost five in the afternoon," the synth replied.

"Shit!"

It wasn't as if he were late to anything, but ever since his off-the-grid adventure to the Void, James had been sleeping for over twelve hours a night. He finally rose to his feet and headed into the kitchen to make a late breakfast. As usual, Sandy was off at the hospital putting in more time than ever before her long-awaited maternity leave.

James cued the synth. "Ginger, put on anything other than silence."

Of course it'd be the news, he thought.

A female reporter spoke, "Today, law enforcement agencies raided the home of a suspected Light Keeper, only to come up empty-handed."

Half-listening, James told his order to the kitchen AI. "Two eggs ... scrambled." A red and orange glow illuminated the surface as a separate machine cracked two eggs on top.

The reporter continued. "We spoke to Director Zin of the FBI to see what he had to say."

It cut to a press conference where a larger man stood behind a podium and said, "Her disappearance only implies that she is, indeed, a sly recruiter for the Light Keepers. We believe that we only missed her by a couple of hours."

The eggs on the surface flipped themselves as the glow began to dissolve, leaving James a perfect plate of scrambled eggs.

The man continued, "We want the public to know that the suspect could be armed and dangerous."

Now curious, James peeked at the split-screen. On one side there was aerial footage above a neighborhood, and on the other, the FBI director stared into the camera. With a serious tone, he stated, "If anybody has come into contact with the suspect or has any knowledge of her whereabouts, you should immediately contact a law enforcement agency. Again, her name is—"

A soft tone resonated through the condo, interrupting the report and cutting off all other media. It was Sandy. When he answered, she popped up on the screen embedded in the counter, sitting at the desk in her office.

"You're awake," Sandy said on the screen, giving him and his out-of-control beard a once-over. "Looks like you could use a shower too."

"I was getting to that." James fixed his hair. "Anything exciting going in your life?"

Sandy sighed. "I had an early meeting this morning and now I have to stay late again. The good news is I'll have the whole weekend off so we should take a trip to Montauk."

"But I already spent too much on the system."

Sandy shrugged. "Well, I need a vacation and it'll be our last one before the baby. Besides, I got a nice little bonus for all this overtime I'm doing."

"Since when does the hospital give unexpected bonuses?" But before Sandy could answer, he remembered the news report. "Did you see they almost caught one of those fucking Light Keepers today?"

Sandy was quiet for a moment, then said, "You don't have time to watch the news if you can't take care of yourself."

"You're starting to remind me of Pops – gone all the time and always worried about what I'm getting myself into. Are you working on a top-secret mission too?"

"*Nooo*," Sandy giggled. "We've merely had a recent influx of patients to deal with. This is only temporary ... Besides, you've been a worthless mess this week anyway. I know Nera warned us both of the side effects, but I want to make sure that's all it is."

"What are you asking me, Dr Grady?"

"I'm making sure you're not depressed," Sandy said. "You lost your job and your best friend, and I know that this day can bring up a series of emotions. Is there anything else I should know about?"

James hadn't told her about violating Lucidity's policies, or that his experience in the Void felt vividly close to a relapse. He'd even had withdrawal symptoms for a couple of days. She'd surely tell him to quit. If he told her about the dream she'd say he needed to get out of the house. The only problem was every time he did he could've sworn he was being followed. He was becoming as paranoid as his mother.

"I'm just tired." James brushed it all to the side, including his hair. "Let me book us a place in Montauk. We'll take a train out there on Saturday morning." He blew a kiss, sending cartoon hearts onto her screen. "It'll be good to get some actual time with you."

"Deal." Sandy playfully caught the hearts. "Now get your ass out of the house and get some sun on that pale white-boy skin, so you don't get burnt all weekend at the beach."

James agreed – even if it was another white lie – and let his wife get back to work, scraping down his eggs, which came out as salty as that day invariably felt every year. Out of instinct, he almost called Tomás for an impromptu meeting at their favorite diner, forgetting that he no longer had a sponsor. Forgetting that Tomás had died.

Meanwhile, Calvin was still upset with him for ghosting him for the personal tour he'd cleared his schedule for. And Calvin's mother, Loretta, was at him to give her an in-depth review of Lucidity, and its effect on a young brain. She had some concerns about her son's health, and possible future with the company.

"*It looked like he was dying in that Dream-contraption,*" Loretta had texted him, "*and I can't bear to lose him like his father.*"

"*It seems safe as far as I can tell,*" James had replied in one of the long messages back to his student's mother. It wasn't a complete lie. As long as he wasn't getting James out of trouble, Calvin's job seemed relatively harmless.

His mother called from her new UniTab, a contraption that she would've never used six months ago. She came on the screen, staring down at the camera, not knowing how to utilize the chat mode correctly.

She gave him an odd glance. "Aren't you supposed to be in school?"

"I took the day off," he lied. "Nice to hear from you too."

"I just wanted to see if you were doing okay because of the day, and all."

"It's never easy but I'm good … I'm surprised to hear from you."

"Well, Patricia was showing me how to utilize this Uni phone thing and showed me how to share this old video I found." She smiled. "I thought you'd like to see it."

James cued it to his largest screen. The footage was from Heather's fifth birthday party at the Linvilla Orchards.

In the video, Mary spoke from behind the camera phone. "Don't be scared of the goat, sweetie," she said to a seven-year-old James crying in a petting zoo. *See, I was cute once,* he thought.

Little Patricia taunted him. "They're not going to hurt you, *scaredy* pants."

"And what are you two doing?" his mother asked, panning to Heather and Pops.

Heather played in a garden. "I'm showing Daddy the sun followers." Her tiny voice was squeaky like a chirpy cartoon character.

"You mean the *sunflowers*," his mother laughed, correcting her pronunciation.

"No, Mommy." Heather pointed at the flower. "If you watch it closely for a long, long time it always tries to face the light. Without the sun then we wouldn't have life on this planet. That means I'd never have you or Daddy or James and Patty. We need to make sure that we're all sun followers and appreciate everything it creates." As the camera zoomed in on Pops, he had a bewildered expression, as if he could see some sort of higher power in Heather.

His mother cut off the video.

"Your father was blown away by that," she said, full of tears. "And it wasn't about Heather being his daughter; it was the way children had these innocent minds that they lost when they got older." She paused. "He called you all his sun followers after that." She looked up at James. "You're going to make a great dad, ya know. Your father was great before he let the world get to him."

"I remember," James said, holding back his tears, the sleeplessness making him emotional. "Hey, whatever happened to Uncle Brian?"

"What makes you ask that?"

"I just remembered that trip me, Heather, and Pops took to Virginia Beach that one summer, that's all."

"He wasn't your uncle, and your father and him had a falling out. I believe he died a decade ago." She paused. "Are you still searching for your father?"

"No."

"James Michael Grady?"

"I'm not."

"You have a baby on the way and a good job."

He hadn't told her about being fired. "I know, Ma. I was just having a memory of Heather on a fun trip. Probably one of the last times before all the headaches started."

"And the nightmares," his mother added.

"Nightmares?"

"Oh, James, just remember the good times." She seemed on the verge of crying again. "I'm gonna head to church now and maybe you should get out of the house yourself. Don't end up like me."

"Okay, Ma. Love you."

After his mother ended the call, James opened a picture of an eleven-year-old Heather, staring at him with her Bambi eyes and purple hair in pigtails. Little Flower was the nickname James had given Heather, but after the suicide, he thought he'd cursed her with it. *Flowers always die too soon.* Before the headaches and nightmares came, it was impossible to catch her without a smile. It seemed as though she was giving him one at that moment.

"Did I fail you?" he asked his dead sister out loud, still thinking about the recurring dream that had resurfaced.

It had been years, and yet every time it felt like a memory. That was impossible, of course. There was no tsunami. No mad scientists. There was only a little girl dealing with excruciating pain, and nothing he could do about it. That's what he told himself every year, although he had yet to believe it. He wondered if Lucidity was helping him or fucking up his brain even more. In fact, he was beginning to think the curse might be in his genes.

CHAPTER 20

Blinded by the sun, Adriana Diaz lay naked and uncovered in a posh hotel room, having a hard time remembering the night before. After another week-long delay in their operation, she and Marty Ronson had reconvened at a bar in downtown Cleveland, and considering her throbbing headache and blurred state of affairs, she could only assume it had ended in decadence.

"Wake up, partner," Ronson shouted, only wearing a bra herself. "It's already noon."

Diaz blushed. "Did we ... ?"

"Grow up, Adriana."

"It's just that you're married."

"Will you get dressed already?" said Ronson. "I just want to go to the location on the flyer, see if we can find anything, and get back here to close up this investigation."

Diaz only remembered bits and pieces after the first few drinks. Ronson had said something about leaving her husband, opening up about a lifelong conflict with her sexuality. While endearing the night before, Ronson had swiftly returned to her normal rude self that morning.

Brushing the one-night stand to the back of her mind, Diaz focused her attention on the most complex case she'd ever been on with the task force. Most of them lasted three days tops. In her time off, Diaz had checked in with the office in DC to update them on the investigation. Her superior seemed frazzled, telling her to report back when they were finished, and to keep their findings closed until then. Diaz hadn't mentioned the conversation to Ronson, even in her drunken stupor.

That afternoon they were heading to the location from the protest flyer, an abandoned mall in what used to be known as Lorain, only forty minutes from Cleveland, in their upgraded thirty-five-year-old Toyota Prius. Diaz let her partner drive so she could research the town on her UniTab. The most updated pictures she could find were fifteen years old, and it seemed like it had fallen on hard times well before the war ever began.

"I kinda miss these electric wires," Ronson said as soon as they crossed Cleveland's checkpoint onto route 90.

Diaz ignored her, not feeling quite as nostalgic, and pissed at her partner's dismissal of their one-night stand. The aftertaste of regurgitated vodka reminded her of the pounding migraine, but when she checked the glove compartment for an aspirin she found a handgun instead.

"What the hell is this?"

"I got that old *thang* in West Virginia," Ronson replied. "I've seen some people carrying them in Richmond and Kansas, so I got me one too."

"How did we get it through the checkpoints?"

"It's un-chipped."

"Holy shit," Diaz fumed. "You know how much trouble we could be in for having this?"

"I want to keep you safe." Ronson gave Diaz her puppy dog eyes. "You never know what we might run into out here."

"Don't give me that flirty bullshit."

"It's not like we're those savages from the Free Folk."

"These people don't know that," Diaz argued. "We're trying to get them to trust us, and having one of these is not going to help. We're way too close to where the Midwest Massacre happened – the fucking reason they created these new laws in the first place."

"Then just keep it in the glove compartment where I put it. Jesus Christ, no need to get your panties in a bunch."

"Oh, grow up," Diaz shouted. "Isn't that what you told me to do?"

Ronson never answered and they weren't speaking when they arrived in what was now called Serenity Lake, a town that was more vibrant than in the pictures. The old fast-food chains and other closed-down businesses had been restored into functioning artistic landmarks. There were floral decorations and strings of lights on the main street running parallel to Lake Erie, where a park filled with families and children gathered for a festival on a hot afternoon.

"Hello there," a pleasant voice greeted them. It was a young woman in purple-lensed tea shades, her skin a tawny-beige. Her curly hair went well past her waist. "Are you two visiting?"

Diaz stepped out of the vehicle. "Is it that obvious?"

The woman smiled. "I think it's safe to assume. Did you come for the Jamboree?"

"My wife and I heard about it." Ronson played up the charm in her undercover role. "We didn't buy any tickets though."

"That's okay, we have a different method of payment around here," Joy said. "You should come in if only to try the best locally brewed hybrid lager you've ever had."

Ronson's eyes lit up, never one to pass up a free drink. "I guess we can stay for a minute."

The woman named Joy led them past the free food and beverage stands, while the band jamming in the distance seemed to be the main attraction. There were colorful vapor trails, silently soaring through the blue sky.

"After the years of chaos, my people can't deal with fireworks," Joy explained, who, as Diaz soon found out, was the mayor of Serenity Lake. "I'm in charge of greeting the outsiders when they come."

Ronson winced. "But you're the ..." She paused before finishing her statement.

"*I'm* the outsider, right?" Joy smiled, suggesting, "I guess that's your perspective."

Curious of the strangers, the oddly dressed locals stared at the detectives. Joy knew the name of every one of them, telling the detectives a brief history of Serenity Lake, a ghost town all but abandoned at one point, coopted by a group of artists trying to escape the conflict before it even began. "After the war, the Earth First Initiative gave us the option to build a factory to be used for the Great Upgrade," she told them, "but we found another way to sustain our town."

She was such a delightful speaker that neither of the detectives had any idea they were being hustled. When they got back to their vehicle, three of her people were busy searching through it.

"We know you're not here visiting," Joy said, her arms crossed as a man handed her Ronson's gun. "And there is no Jamboree."

"Full disclosure," Diaz began, "we're from an Army task force attempting to find three missing people who worked within the branch. They were last spotted heading to this location." She handed the flyer to Joy. "Is there anything you can tell us?"

"How'd you get this?"

"We came across it in Kansas."

"This is from ten years ago, so my mother would know more about it." Joy signaled to the others. "She's at our farm at this exact address."

"A farm?" Diaz asked. "According to my research, it's an abandoned mall."

"We can take you there now and show you," Joy insisted to the detectives. "I'll even get your wife another beer for the road."

Now in the driver's seat, Diaz followed the bicycle caravan through Serenity Lake, pissed at her partner's irresponsibility. They barely made it up the road when the street lights began flashing. As if a silent fire alarm were set off, the townspeople immediately left the festival without packing up. The caravan stopped ahead of them and Joy jumped off her beach cruiser, marching toward the detectives' car in a hurry.

"The KOA is heading into town so you two need to be out of sight when they get here," she said. "Either they're coming to harass us again or they followed you two here."

"Now, why in the hell would they follow us?" Ronson laid on her accent thick as if she'd already had way too many. "We're not the problem here."

Joy rolled her eyes. "Go ahead of us to the farm. You'll get there a lot faster than us." She handed Diaz the flyer and handgun. "I trust that you'll give these to my mother when you arrive."

Diaz followed the thirty-mile-per-hour speed limit of Serenity Lake, cautiously aware of the people scurrying home. They weren't the only ones who didn't want to deal with the KOA, known to detain people for months.

The farm Joy spoke of was in fact a rundown shopping mall, now with a bright paint job, solar panels, and a glass dome for a roof. Diaz drove to the loading dock as ordered. There, a large garage door opened and a woman around the same age as the detectives emerged – tall and robust with a neon-green afro that added a couple more inches. Behind her was a group of people in the same neon-green lab jackets.

"Hand over the firearm." She was clearly unhappy to see the *outsiders*. "I can't believe you brought this into our peaceful sanctuary."

Diaz handed over Ronson's illegal pistol. "I'm guessing you're Joy's mother?"

"And I'm guessing you don't belong here."

"I'm sorry, ma'am."

"That weapon you brought may have put us all in harm's way," the woman warned. "Now let's get you two inside so we can have a little discussion."

As Diaz drove through a small dark tunnel following a drone, Ronson stuck her head out the window like a dog on the highway, practically drooling.

"You okay?"

Slurring her words, Ronson replied, "This sure is *intrestin'* farm they *gots* here."

It was indeed. Vertical rows of fruits and vegetables grew in both natural and artificial sunlight, cross-pollinating with the insects freely roaming. There were a few decks overlooking the arena-like facility, which once was a food court. Inside, everyone wore the neon green coats, the lights flashing the same as they did in town. A drone led Diaz to her intended parking spot where they were ordered out of the vehicle.

Ronson stumbled out of the passenger side, giggling herself into a frenzy. She yelled, "Hello Green Coats!"

The tall older woman met them in their vehicle. "It looks like your partner drank our Kool-Aid." She grinned. "That kicked in faster than normal."

"What'd you put in that lager?" Diaz asked.

The woman smirked. "It's a little truth serum – all-natural and allergen-free. Now, if you don't mind, I'd like to ask your wife some serious questions."

CHAPTER 21

Diaz sat quiet, watching as Ronson gazed at an overgrown summer squash as if she'd never seen one before. "Squash ... It's a funny word," she muttered. "*Ska-wash.*"

"My name's Skya," the woman said to Ronson, now distracted by a hypnotizing kaleidoscope of live butterflies. "You were sent here by my daughter."

"Joy obviously gets her good looks from you," Ronson blurted, struggling to keep her balance. "You're so pretty."

Skya showed her the flyer. "How'd you get ahold of this?"

Ronson lay down on the hood of the vehicle. "Some asshole named Nick Baxter," she said. "It had this address on it, so we followed it here. Honestly, I just wanted more time on the road with my partner." Her eyes grew heavy as she grinned. "Adriana is the prettiest woman in the whole ... wide ... world!"

"Okay, that's enough," Diaz shouted, held back by one of the green coats. "She's not in her right mind."

Skya showed the handgun to Ronson. "Did the Knights of Azrael send you?"

Ronson popped up from the hood as if she were possessed. "Fuck the KOA! I would never work with those barbarians." She shouted, "Go get 'em, green coats!" She passed out.

Diaz checked her partner's beating pulse. "Is she going to be okay?"

"We had to make sure you two weren't infiltrators," Skya said. "Your wife's gonna be fine. She'll wake up a little woozy in an hour or so."

"She's not my wife, and we're not infiltrators!"

"No shit, Sherlock," Skya laughed. "The fact that you both started by lying to us didn't help your case, though. That's why we needed to know that you could be trusted before taking you to a safer place."

"Are we in trouble because of the gun?"

Skya groaned. "I don't know yet, but if you had any affiliation with the KOA, your partner would've spilled the beans already. That concoction always works." She raised her eyebrows at Diaz. "And I guess you know how she feels about you now."

As helicopters buzzed over the farm, a romantic relationship was the last thing on Diaz's mind. The lights flashed with more urgency. Snoring loudly, Ronson slept comfortably on the slim hood of their Toyota while half of the "green coats," as Ronson called them, scurried away. The other fifty or so huddled around Diaz.

"We have to hide you down here," Skya told her. "They don't know about this area."

As the ground below Diaz began to sink, a substitute floor replaced what was above, lowering them and their rental into a basement much smaller than the farm. It seemed to be designated for lab experiments. A sizable green coat placed Ronson over his shoulder, waving at Diaz to follow him. When a whistle blew, the rest of the green coats scurried past Diaz toward an unexpected sight – an arsenal of guns she'd only seen in absurd action flicks.

Meanwhile, Skya fiddled with Ronson's pistol like it was the problem. "This thing isn't even loaded," she said. "Did your partner know what kind of risk she was putting you two in?"

"She wasn't going to hurt anybody." Diaz focused on the arsenal. "What about those?"

"A precautionary measure. The KOA likes to do surprise visits to make sure we're following protocol."

"Why? You got something to hide?"

"You don't get to ask the questions in my domain." Skya led the detective into a surveillance room. Green coats sat behind an operations board scanning through monitors from across Serenity Lake, including the interior of the farm. "Tell me more about these Army vets you're looking for."

"I don't think we have time for my stupid investigation right now."

"Give me their names," Skya insisted.

"Jim Grady, Ellie Brown Ginsberg, and Quinn Baxter." Diaz tried pulling up a file on her UniTab. "There's something wrong with this thing."

Skya pointed to the gadget. "That's not happening down here." She pulled the flyer out from between her breasts. "This town was created by a bunch of us drifters and hipsters, so we used these messages to stay covert when we weren't sure who the enemy was." She gave it closer a look. "I don't recognize any of the names you mentioned, but there was an incident around this date here, right as the war began." Skya sat behind one of the computers, oblivious to the KOA raiding her town. "Was one of your vets covered in tattoos?"

"Quinn Baxter," Diaz said. "She was a skinny thing with a pink mohawk."

Skya laughed. "That pretty much fits the description of half our population," she said. "But from what I remember, there was this tattooed girl and a middle-aged man who came here with Farah. They weren't even here a day before this militia came and took all three of them away." She tapped on her keyboard. "Give me a second, and I'll see if I can find the footage in our archives."

"Did you catch the name of this militia?"

"We were a bunch of hippies taking over a junkyard, attempting to find peace during a war. Every damn agency in the country was interested in our intentions." The live surveillance footage showed the KOA had made it inside the walls of the farm, rummaging through the crops to see if anyone was hiding. Skya sighed. "As you can see, some of them still are."

"What exactly are the Knights looking for?"

"Any excuse to shut us down." Skya pressed a key dramatically, bringing up a list. "Found it!" She got up to deal with her other problem, letting Diaz have her seat. "Let me know if you find anything interesting."

The woman had cued surveillance footage from high above a street corner, a rundown apartment building in the far background. Early in the morning, judging by the orange glow on the concrete. A military bus pulled in, blocking the left side of the screen as a group of masked men with guns stormed into the building.

There was a time stamp: *09:42am – 05/19/2032.*

Diaz noticed the same military plate number of the bus that had been obliterated on a Kansas highway. *626.* She peered at the screen for minutes until a few of the masked troops came around the back of the bus with Ellie Ginsberg in handcuffs, acting unusually cool for the situation, and boarding the bus. Quinn Baxter, AKA Suzi Q, dragged her captors on the bus with her until they tasered the tattooed woman into submission. Another minute passed before they brought around another hostage.

Jim Grady had aged since his days in the Army with Diaz, and the black eye didn't help. With a solemn expression, he stared at the concrete. But when his captor wasn't paying attention, he turned his back to the camera, flicked it off from within the handcuffs, and grinned before stepping onto the bus. Grady was always the jokester, she thought.

Maybe he didn't know he was about to die.

It began to dawn on Diaz that she was observing the same bus on the same day as their missing persons were never seen again. Checkmate. Her partner had figured it out a week ago, but Diaz had always hoped there'd be a happier ending. She needed proof they were on the bus and she could hardly contain the waterworks running down her face.

"That was the day they took Farah." Skya stood right behind the detective. "Do you recognize those other two people?"

Caught off-guard, Diaz wiped her face. "I'm confused. I still don't know who this Farah is?"

Skya rewound the video to a specific part. "That's her right there," she insisted. "She was the one who taught us how to build this farm."

Diaz insisted, "That's Ellie Brown Ginsberg!"

"But Farah wasn't in no damn army," Skya said. "She told us she was an agriculture engineer – a glorified farmer." Growing more frustrated, she pointed to the woman they were both referring to. "Do you know what happened to her?"

"I can only tell you that the bus didn't make it to its next stop."

Skya seemed lost for words as one of the green coats signaled over to her. "Give me one minute," she said. "Hopefully, my daughter can get these assholes to leave so we can finish this conversation."

All of the screens transitioned to a camera angle right above the KOA soldiers and the mayor of Serenity Lake. They stood in the middle of the indoor farm. The control room stayed silent as they listened in on the conversation.

The leader of the KOA had a steel mask over the bottom of his face. "Where's your mother?" He had a synthetic growl, was a solid foot taller than Joy, and more intimidating with twenty-some soldiers surrounding him. "Are your people hiding again?"

"We don't like to be bullied around here," said Joy, "so when I know you savages are coming, I send my people to their homes." The mayor opened her arms to point out the crops his soldiers had destroyed. "You've had enough fun for one day."

The man got in Joy's face. "I know you guys are up to something here," he said. "We had reports of unusual traffic in the area – the kind that's highly frowned upon." He gave his soldiers a signal, leading them back to the exit. "We'll be back soon enough."

"Thanks for wasting our time," Joy muttered, signaling a peace sign to one of the cameras.

Back in the control room, the lights stopped flashing as everyone breathed a collective sigh of relief. Diaz, on pins and needles, prayed they wouldn't be found, her partner passed out on a couch with no clue of what she might've caused. The real leader of Serenity Lake acted serene, as if nothing had happened.

"Close call." Skya examined the paused video clip and zoomed in on Ginsberg. "So you're telling me Farah's dead?"

"I think so," Diaz replied. "My partner and I saw the footage in Kansas when this same bus was hit by an explosive."

Skya paced the room, scratching her chin. "I just got a message from her a couple of weeks ago saying she was going to return to show us some new innovations. Farah must've figured her way out of that mess and made it back to her family. "

"That's impossible." Diaz turned her chair toward the woman. "Her husband hasn't seen her since this incident, assuming we're both talking about the same person."

Skya seemed bewildered, taking one last glimpse of Ginsberg before turning to Diaz. "Why are you searching for her now if this happened in '32?"

Diaz didn't have an answer for the woman, her head throbbing again. She'd never found any aspirin. *Why did the Army wait so long and why did her commander tell them to keep their mouths shut about the investigation?* One of the green coats pulled the car around as another one gently placed a sleeping Ronson in the passenger seat.

Skya handed over the keys but confiscated the gun. "Are you sure you two know what you're doing?"

"I don't know anything anymore," Diaz confessed.

"You might be in over your head." Before walking away, Skya said,

"I have a feeling you'll find what you need to know and when you do, you'll realize that we were on the same side all along."

One of the green coats, a teenage girl, opened the car door for her. "She must trust you," she said as the bigger gentleman placed Ronson upright in the passenger seat. "No outsiders are ever allowed down here."

Diaz waited for twenty minutes with her unconscious partner to go back up to the main level of the farm. The people were out and about again, waving to Diaz on her way out of town. Back on the highway, she finally noticed the wires Ronson had mentioned and wished it were simpler times again, even though such a time never existed in her lifetime.

When they got to the checkpoint, Ronson finally woke up. "What happened?"

"Case closed," Diaz admitted. "Looks like you were right."

A groggy Ronson squinted as they approached Cleveland. "Good," she said, closing her eyes again. "I can't wait to get back home to my husband." Obviously, Ronson had never cared about her or the investigation.

Frustrated with her partner, Diaz never mentioned that they'd have to rendezvous again in DC to go over the investigation with their superior. She'd write the report declaring Ginsberg, Baxter, and Grady officially deceased, but that wasn't the end of the investigation for her. *It was never a missing person case*, Diaz thought. It was a clear-cut triple homicide, war crime or not, and she intended on finding out what happened.

VI

PART SIX

CHAPTER 22

The main level of the Welcome Facility was busier than James had ever seen it. As he was heading toward the fourth sector, a cluster of glitter-covered, drag queens half his size handed him a flyer. "Come meet us in NuAmsterdam, you big rebel." They blew sparkly dust on James before moving on. Although the flyer felt like a thin piece of paper, it was animated with men. women, and anyone in between – naked and sweaty – gyrating in a lavish mansion.

"Don't look so intrigued," Calvin said, creeping up on him as usual. His student's alternate avatar was a doppelgänger of the kid he knew in the real world. He sported tie-dye jeans, shiny red kicks, and a slanted box-cut instead of his usual fade. "The eighth sector is intriguing and all, but not really appropriate for an expectant father with a wife at home."

"You know what I'm trying to do here." James forced the flyer into his student's hands. "And I'm running out of time."

"You need to lay off that idea." Calvin discarded it into thin air. "You don't want another repeat of your last visit here."

"Are you going to give me shit all night?"

Calvin scratched his chin and grimaced, but couldn't contain his I'm-only-fucking-with-you smile. "We're good, Mr. G." He gave him a fist bump. "Friday nights are more lively anyway."

James always drilled his orchestras on being punctual, so Calvin had every right to be upset with him for missing his scheduled tour. He was even late that night, procrastinating on whether or not to go into the system. He didn't want to spend another week in a Lucidity-induced fog but figured his student would keep him out of trouble.

"Thanks for sending Mimi to rescue me." James bowed his head. "That was pretty stupid of me."

"I told you the Void is haunted." Calvin moved on. "No need to dwell on it."

When they reached the portal, only designated by a "*IV*" overhead, James gazed at the inverted reflection of a menacing black-and-white version of Dark Cloud.

Calvin asked, "You ready for this?"

James shook his head no, his butterflies turning to goosebumps, but before he could change his mind, his student pushed him through.

~

Inside the fourth sector, a huge arch with fluorescent letters greeted them: *THE WONDERS*. James immediately found himself in a hectic parade procession, where all the oddest avatars from the Welcome Facility seemed to have gathered. The DJ was a ten-foot-tall machine, a body made from speakers and sub-woofers, blasting a thumping trance beat that shook the ground. A group of TV-headed figures performed some choreographed ritual around him. It was hot and crowded and weird. The swaying spectators bumped into James. The vertigo-inducing strobes began to kickstart an epileptic seizure.

Calvin pulled him off to the side right in time, screaming over the music, "Didn't I tell you it was wild?"

James nodded, pretending like he wasn't about to hyperventilate as enormous animated floats marched past the crossroad. "These are all avatars?"

"Technically yeah, but half of them are synths keeping the festivities lively. No human can keep up this energy all the time."

James remembered he could use his Navigator to identify his surroundings and to tell who was real and who was a synth – or what they called NPCs in AlterWorld. Nudging his student to go somewhere quieter, he asked, "Is this all the Wonders has to offer?"

Calvin didn't reply, but judging by the mischievous look in his eyes he had another place in mind. They left the parade and headed deeper into the Wonders, rushing through a street filled with classic carnival-style games for those nostalgic for the pre-G era. As they got farther in, the entertainment seemed to get more intense, his Navigator warning him that he was in a Red Zone. There was probably a good explanation for it in the manual, which he still hadn't given any time to. Although driving was supposedly prohibited in Lucidity, there was a version of bumper cars that involved deadly crashes at high velocities.

Witnessing a fiery wreck, James asked, "Those aren't real users, are they?" The teenager was far ahead of him. "Calvin, where are you taking me?"

Before his student had a chance to answer, a creepy old-timey clown caught James's attention. It had black eyeballs, a vampire's smile, a raggedy polka-dot costume, and a miniature top hat. The clown jumped at people passing by. Most users made blatant attempts to avoid his pathway, but James, captivated by the hideous creature, accidentally made eye contact.

"What are you looking at, you anti-war whiner?" the clown shouted with a deep vindictive voice. "You want to challenge me?"

The clown stood in front of a game called SPHERE, obviously waiting for a contender. In an area below them, two avatars flung illuminated balls at each other in a one-on-one match. Spectators cheered, gawking at the contestants. James kept his eyes on the current match, attempting to understand the logistics of the intense form of dodgeball.

"You don't want to challenge Mr. Maurice," Calvin warned him. "He's always trying to goad fresh meat into playing him."

"Why is this so popular?"

"It's in a Red Zone. It comes with higher consequences than those kiddie games we passed."

"I thought you brought me here so I could *experience the Wonders*."

"Not against him," Calvin urged. "He always wins, and I was looking forward to taking you to Mimi's party later."

"So why can't we do both?"

Maurice interrupted. "Hey, dip shit ... Are you going to play me or what?"

A crowd started to form, waiting to see if Dark Cloud would accept the challenge, exchanging verbal bets in anticipation. Judging by the small talk, his odds were pretty slim, but a few users were rooting for him to beat the reigning champion.

"Come on, you fucking pussy," the clown ranted. "You come in here all brooding like you got some sort of daddy issues." Realizing he'd struck a chord with James's reaction, the clown went further. "Use some of that angst on me, ya snowflake."

Calvin huffed, "Don't do it, Mr. G."

The crowd chanted otherwise.

"Fuck it," James said, his adrenaline rushing. He turned to the circus freak. "You're on, Bozo."

When James threw his hand in the ring everyone cheered. Everyone except for Calvin, who paced behind him scoping out the arena. It all seemed cut and dry to James. Don't get hit by the sphere. Use the blockades for protection. With the match only a minute from starting, the avatars filled the seats of the coliseum-like stadium while an announcer hyped up the match. "Are you ready to *Spheeerrre*?" The crowd roared when they announced Mr. Maurice, but had a mixed reaction of laughter and hoots for Dark Cloud.

In a corner designated for the players, Calvin asked, "You understand how this works, right?"

James smiled and waved at the spectators above. "I was king of dodgeball in the alleyways of Germany," he said.

"That makes me feel so much better." Calvin gave him some simple instructions. "Don't try to catch anything Maurice throws at you and stay behind the barricades for as long as you can. This blood-thirsty crowd's gonna hate you for it, but that's usually how he kills his opponent."

As the timer hit the thirty-second mark, James asked, "What do you mean by *kills*?"

"I hope you don't have plans for the weekend," Calvin sneered. "I don't think you did your homework on what a Red Zone means."

"Then why'd you bring me here?"

"So we could bet some of *your* money on the clown you're now about to go against!"

"Oh."

The Jumbotron floating above the rink read: *Dark Cloud 2020 vs. Mr. Maurice.* James had missed the end of the last game but noticed one of the players wasn't around anymore. With his trip to Montauk the next morning and his last Lucidity hangover still lingering, the stakes began to feel high. His only glimmer of hope was that some people had bet on him. Calvin disregarded the slim odds.

"People like to bet on the underdog, hoping they might win big on a tiny wager." The timer ran down. "Unfortunately for you, nobody's ever beat this asshole."

Two glowing spheres rested in a circle on both sides. When the whistle blew, the clown sprinted to pick up his ball. James staggered seconds behind to grab his. Calvin shouted from the sidelines, "Hide behind the barricades!" Aimlessly standing with the ball in his hand, James raced for the protection of the walls. Before he found cover, the clown nailed him in the top corner of his back.

"Motherfucker!"

It felt like he'd been shot. He bought time behind the barricade to deal with the pain. Maurice fired shots thinning out his only protection. The crowd booed and heckled. Calvin covered his eyes from the sidelines. James thought it'd be over if he simply let the game clock run out. The buzzer sounded. The the timer was reset. Another round to go.

During the short break, Calvin called him over. "You survived longer than I expected, but you won't be able to do that in the second half. All your barriers will be gone, so I hope you know how to run faster than whatever that was." He added, "Don't let him catch one of your spheres."

"Why's that?"

"Because you'll be paralyzed for five seconds, and it'll be much more painful than that shot to your back."

Before James could comprehend the bleak notion, the buzzer sounded and round two was underway. There was nowhere to hide as sure as his student warned. James sprinted around like a frantic turkey, dodging Mr. Maurice's bullets. After losing his breath, he rested as the clown raced for one of the spheres. Standing like a deer in headlights, James gave up. He waited for the onslaught. With a menacing grin, the clown wound his arm back and chucked it at him. The sphere came at James unusually slow and he caught it only inches from his face.

The crowd gasped.

A buzzer sounded. A five-second timer came on the Jumbotron. Mr. Maurice stood frozen near the halfway line – an easy target for James. The seconds clicked. His first shot was off. The crowd booed. With one second to go, he chucked it as hard as he could and hit him in the middle of the forehead. The clown fell to his knees, bled from the wound, and disappeared.

It was alarmingly silent for a solid three seconds. Then, as if everyone had figured out what happened, they collectively erupted into a deafening howl.

"Holy shit, Mr. G!" Calvin shouted as he left the arena with his new fans lining up to introduce themselves. "How'd you do that?"

"I don't know ... I'm just wondering why he lobbed it so slow on that last shot?"

"Are you kidding me?" Calvin gave him a baffled look. "He usually lets the rookies off easy, but he wanted to kill you for some reason."

His student was right. When they showed the instant replay on the Jumbotron it was as if James had caught a bolt of lightning, clocked at one hundred and eighty miles per hour. Even in slow motion, it wasn't anything like he remembered.

"There must've been a glitch."

Calvin grinned. "Who cares? You just won me a ton of Lucies."

"You put your money on me?"

"As I said, some people bet on the underdogs." Calvin's grin was as big as ever. "I didn't believe it when you said you flew in the Cave, but maybe you do have special powers in Lucidity, Mr. G."

CHAPTER 23

Later in the Wonders, James headed into a quaint lounge lit by hundreds of candles and a bohemian aroma – some mixture of vanilla-stained oak and patchouli. Calvin had brought him there through a secret alleyway that only a selected group of guides knew about. The calm vibe was a nice change of pace from the rest of the Wonders. His swollen back still throbbed from the Sphere match as he redirected his mind to the music.

On a small stage with a red-sequined curtain, the oddest trio he'd ever seen performed on it. The trumpeter – a four-foot, three-hundred-pound bullfrog – laid a melody over the sprawling guitars of an extraterrestrial beatnik. Finishing off the trio was a lanky figure wearing red spandex over its body, tapping out a minimalist drum beat on a set of hovering pads.

"Synths, I presume?"

"They're real musicians, Mr. G, and they're so good I've been too intimidated to jam with them."

Intrigued, both by the fact that one could play an instrument in Lucidity, and that his student thought this particular band was that honed, James listened with a critical ear. There were subtle nuances that only a music geek could explain – pristine technique and time signature changes that only functioned in a mathematical pattern.

When James thought it couldn't get any better, a lovely blue elf-like woman came from backstage, adding rich soulful vocals. Her pointy ears stuck out through the serpentine beehive of shiny white tresses. The way the spotlight caught her dress made it translucent, but she didn't seem to mind, and neither did the mesmerized audience. Luckily for James, his student dragged him away before the hypnotizing siren cast a spell on him, too.

"That was Eleonora," Calvin told him. "She's doing a surprise performance for Mimi."

"The same Eleonora who had that huge concert on the lower level last week?"

"Yep ... Our Mimi knows everyone."

In the back corner of the lounge, a motley crew of characters mingled around Mimi, the birthday girl with a silver tiara and a crooked grin. An Egyptian hookah floated around the table, producing a green skunky fog, and for the second time, James had to remember Mimi was not the little girl she posed as.

"Nice to see you again, Cloud," Mimi shouted from across the table.

As soon James saw her, it reminded him of his time in the Void. A realization hit him like a brick. He snuck around the table. "When we were in the corn maze last week you said something about a scarecrow."

"Yeah, it was some prop hanging in the middle of the field." She got up out of her seat. "Why do you ask?"

"Oh, no reason."

No reason except that James now knew that he wasn't imagining things anymore. It was only Pops's favorite character from his favorite movie, *The Wizard of OZ*. The scarecrow had to be the avatar his father would use. Not to mention that Pops specifically said to listen for a signal. Of course, at the moment those were only hunches or hallucinations, so James kept them to himself.

Mimi walked him back around to the popular end of the table. "So, are you staying out of trouble, Cloud?"

Calvin answered. "He just beat Mr. Maurice in Sphere!"

"Thank God someone finally beat that bullying clown," one of the guests remarked. It was the same astronaut woman he'd met on the bridge, only more wasted than before. "You deserve a hit from the Maestro for that."

Mimi intervened before James had to explain his addiction. "This is Space Angel," she said. "She claims to be much older than us all, but I don't believe her. Her goal's to visit every sector in Lucidity, and I'm going to make sure she does." Mimi giggled. "And this is her first time trying the Maestro."

James shook Space Angel's hand. "We met on the bridge," he reminded her. "I was the guy too chicken shit to move forward."

"Oh right!" Space Angel's deep south twang came out as she told the story of his first night in the system. "This boy was like a dead possum on that rackety thang." He felt the same way that night, still trying to figure out how he'd caught the sphere. When she asked for an explanation, he simply told them all it was beginner's luck. Without her helmet on, the purple-skinned woman, who might have been slightly stoned, gave him an endearing grin. "I told you there's no need to go around searching for missing loved ones when there's so much else to explore."

Calvin pulled James to the side. "I told you not to go around asking about this person you're looking for." He folded his arms. "Space Angel knows people at the IA and I'm trying to make a good impression with her. I don't need you acting suspiciously." Frustrated, he asked, "Who are you looking for anyway?"

"My father."

"But he's dead. Like ten years ago, right?"

"It's a long story, Calvin, but I think I already found him once."

As his student processed the absurd comment, the enchanting Eleonora interrupted, seeming unimpressed with James. "Who the hell is this?"

"This my buddy, Dark Cloud." Calvin's voice cracked. "He's new in here."

Glancing at James, Eleonora rolled her eyes. "Mandatory dance party in one minute," she told them. "And that means you too, emo-boy."

As Eleonora dragged everyone into the middle of the room, the band delivered an even funkier set. Mimi and Calvin exhibited their beatboxing skills, sparking a battle in the center of the dancefloor. Space Angel showed everyone an old move called "the Floss." Every avatar in the lounge joined in the festivities except for James, who stood off sulking in a corner.

After the initial high of the Sphere match and his new discovery wore off, his guilty conscience began to set in. *This isn't what I'm supposed to be doing here,* James told himself, thinking of his pregnant wife at home. The ridiculous thought of finding his father's avatar already began to sound ludicrous. Of course there had been a fake scarecrow in a fake cornfield. He was two seconds away from an Irish goodbye when Eleonora grabbed his hand and pulled him onto the dance floor.

"There are no wallflowers allowed in my club!" She swayed her hips to the beat, dissecting him with her wide ocean eyes. Every movement was salacious. "I can help you," she whispered, creeping closer to him.

"I'm a married man! You're very beautiful and all, but I'm not interested."

Eleonora laughed so hard that she almost cried. "*I meant*, I can help you find your father."

"How do you know about that?"

"I have good ears." She pointed to her elf tips. "Now dance, motherfucker!" She pushed him toward a space in the pulsating crowd. With no other choice than to follow the sassy woman's lead, he let go of his inhibitions and matched her movements. Before long, she had dragged him back to the quieter corner.

With everyone half gazing at the two, including Calvin, James asked, "What do you want with me?"

Taking the lead, Eleonora twirled James. "I'm intrigued. Lucidity hasn't been around nearly as long as your father's been missing, and yet here you are searching for him." She did have good ears. "What makes you so sure he's in here?"

As they continued dancing, James made sure to filter his next words. "Let's just say my father might've had a friend who helped create this entire world, and this friend claimed to have left him an avatar to use. I thought I'd found him ... The only problem is I don't how to find him again."

From the expression on her face, Eleonora seemed genuinely interested. "Well then, let's just say that I have a friend who might be able to help you."

"Who?"

"I'll need to give him some personal information for this to work."

"Calvin told me not to talk to anyone about this," James said, pulling away from her.

Eleonora strengthened her grip, not letting him go. "Relax." She smiled at the others who noticed his hasty reaction. "This is one hundred percent up to you, Cloud. If you want to remain anonymous – so be it. But I can't help you without that info."

"And why should I trust you?"

With her index finger to her sultry blue lips and one hand to her curvy hips, she posed. "I'm *thee* Eleonora," she said, "not some asshole hacker trying to scam you out of your money. The question is, do you want my help or not?"

With his student preoccupied, James nodded yes, whispering to her his father's name and the Jaybird avatar he hoped to find, already feeling like he'd said too much. He even mentioned the scarecrow, although he said it was a long shot. "Keep this between us."

Eleonora nodded. "I hope we can find something, and for your sake, let's hope your father wasn't another one of those traitors."

"What do you mean?"

"You know that most of those who went, quote unquote, 'missing'

around that time did so because they were involved with the coward ass
Free Folk, right?"

That thought had never crossed James's mind until that moment.
Maybe he didn't want it to.

With an awkward smile, Eleonora continued. "Either way, I hope it
helps you find some closure." She made a date for them to meet again in
Lucidity and kissed him on the forehead. "The clouds always clear after a
huge downpour."

James didn't know what that meant but it sounded lovely coming
from her. When he turned around, Calvin was standing right behind
him.

"What was that all about? I always took you for a shy guy, but in
one night you've managed to take down Mr. Maurice and dance with the
sexiest woman on the planet."

"She's okay."

"*Psssh*! Eleonora's a goddess." Calvin checked to see if the elf
woman was in sight. "But she loves drama and has been known to roll
with questionable crowds."

"We were actually talking about getting you up on that stage,"
James lied. "She said we should both come jam with the band."

Calvin seemed to enjoy that notion. "You're surprising me tonight,
Mr. G."

"Sometimes I surprise myself too."

Not wanting to disappoint, James led his student to the stage and
found a key-tar that none of the other musicians were using, pointing out
a violin to Calvin who already had his eyes set on a Djembe. They hopped
on stage and added their twist to the Electro-Funk song. All of a sudden
the ceiling opened up, a storm cloud appeared, and heavy rain poured
down into the lounge. No one seemed to care about getting soaked,
reveling in the music and the atmosphere as the party continued.

James wasn't sure about the mysterious woman he'd given way too much information to, but Eleonora had captured his imagination that night. From a soundboard on the side of the stage, she winked at James. She was the one making it rain. His night in the Wonders had given him his first legitimate clue about Pops's possible whereabouts. It had also turned out to be one of the most exhilarating times he'd had in ages.

CHAPTER 24

Coasting swiftly along on a Mag-Train, James caught a brief glimpse of the outside parts of Sussex County, Long Island. The high-speed railways were planned all along the highways of the United States, but so far they were only used to get from one huge metropolitan region to another, or in this case, for a quick Saturday morning ride to Montauk.

While Sandy slept on his shoulder, the night in the Wonders lingered in his mind. He had thought about giving up the search for his father until he met Eleonora, who planted a seed of hope. In the past, when he began to figure out answers, he'd always sabotage his mission with drugs and alcohol, never ready to face the reality that Pops might be a con artist, a traitor, or a dead man. Would knowing that give him any closure? It also didn't sit well with him that the last time he'd fallen off the wagon was in the same town they were headed to.

There, on his honeymoon four years ago, James had taken a long walk on a dark road and come across a store with his name on it – *Liquor*. After Sandy's parents found out James used to be an addict, they never looked at him the same. Wallowing in self-pity, he bought himself a bottle of vodka and stumbled onto the sands of Lake Montauk. A group stood around a fire pit speaking about politics, God, and the nature of the planet. James half-remembered rambling on about *how nothing mattered* and how they were *wasting their time trying to save themselves*, forgetting how alcohol could turn him into a belligerent fool. That's when a kind woman named Kalen Green walked him back to his motel, where he slept it off and had been sober ever since.

When the train got to the end of Long Island, Sandy dashed out of her seat, excited to be out of the hospital for the weekend. James had been aware from the beginning of their relationship that her career demanded the hours. Hell, she'd been in her eighth year of school when they met. His wife desperately needed a vacation and he wasn't going to ruin it with any of his own petty issues.

An AV Carrier stored their luggage for the day as they headed straight to the beach. Even pregnant Sandy came for the activities, renting a surfboard as soon as they arrived. James, pretending not to be exhausted, hid his yawn from her and covered his pale flabby body in sunscreen, his first time out of the condo in what felt like weeks. With the calming sound of the ocean, he put aside the anxiety of being followed by the boogeymen for the weekend, considering it might all be in his head anyway.

Sandy polished the longboard. "How was the party last night? You were still in the system when I went to bed."

"It's hard to explain." James sat up from his beach chair. "I know it's only a simulation, but last night I felt like I was there."

"Technically, a simulation is a real experience. The human mind stores it as a memory along with other real-life experiences."

"When you put it that way ..."

James gave her a censored version of the Wonders, making sure he didn't bring up his Sphere match or the private dance and discussion with Eleonora. Sandy nodded like he was an insane person speaking about an alien planet he'd visited. It sounded like that to him, too.

He reminded her, "You told me to have a good time, so I did."

"It sounds like it." Sandy pulled off her beach cover-up, hardly showing. "Still, something about this technology doesn't sit right with me." She sighed. "Red Zones and end games ... A sex sector they call NuAmsterdam."

"How do you know all this?"

"I heard the way my colleagues were talking about it at that conference in Atlanta," she said. "I hope you told Calvin not to fool around with those Red Zones because the ejections can cause horrible side effects."

With a dumbfounded smile, James nodded. According to everyone at Mimi's party, he must've been lucky to beat Mr. Maurice, and would've never agreed to the match had he known it could ruin their weekend away. He still didn't know how he'd caught the sphere, and maybe it was psychosomatic, but his back still hurt from being pegged by the clown.

Sandy flexed her muscles and forced the baby bump to show. "We're on a beach and we're going to forget about everything else for now." She lifted the longboard up above her head. "What's the point of vacation if we can't vacate from reality for a little while?"

There were hardly any waves, but James was curious. "Are you sure you should be surfing this far along in your pregnancy?"

"This is a paddle board, silly."

When he realized that Sandy wouldn't do anything as dumb as him, he made sure not to tell her of his next plan. He had pretty much insinuated that he was over the search for his father a few days earlier. There was no need to ruin Sandy's last vacation before they had a child.

~

After a long day of sun, they headed back to their motel on the eastern side of Montauk, an outsider town now called Snug Harbor. They rode in a taxi cab past an abandoned house spray-painted with the words, "*INTERIORS NOT WELCOME.*" James had almost forgotten there was an actual person up front until the driver greeted them.

"Where ya guys be from, eh?" the young man asked.

He couldn't be much older than one of James's students. His accent was somewhere between Caribbean, Irish, and teenage sarcasm. His light skin was covered in freckles, his curly hair standing high due to the headband he wore. James waited for his extroverted wife to answer, but between the sun and their seafood dinner, Sandy had dozed off.

"We're from the city," James replied, "but my wife used to work at the motel we're staying at."

"Don't pay attention to *dem* signs," he said. "The locals here use scare tactics to keep what we have left. Unlike most outside districts, Snug Harbor had a chance to modernize with the first round of the Great Upgrade. We voted against it because we knew it would be followed by gentrification. We didn't think they'd put up these borders to make us feel *inferior* to the *Interiors* if you catch my breeze."

"That's always bothered me too," James insisted. "It used to be so simple."

The kid laughed. "It's never been simple." He peered at James through the rearview mirror. "You look familiar," he said. "Have we met before?"

"I don't think so," James replied. "Did you ever attend the Brighter Minds Charter School?"

"Nah … that sounds fancy, though."

"Well, what's your name?"

"Anthony."

James introduced himself as they pulled into the Inn. "Well, Anthony, thanks for not giving us a hard time," adding, "Technically, I'm an outsider too."

"All I care about is that you're a good human." Anthony parked the car. "Would you like me to bring the luggage to your suite … sir?"

James wasn't oblivious to the kid's smart-ass comment. "I can handle it."

The Harbor Inn was hardly a luxury hotel, about as charming as it was dusty, which hadn't changed much since the day it was built eighty-odd years ago. Adorning the oak-paneled walls were framed portraits of windjammers and fishermen on the local docks. The furniture was dated and musty. Sandy yawned as they entered the same room they stayed in on their honeymoon, half asleep from her cat nap in the taxi.

"It's been such a hectic week at work," she said.

James lay sunburnt on the bed. "Whatever happened to patient X?" He gazed at the noisy ceiling fan. "Last time you mentioned him, you said he'd miraculously gone into remission."

Crashing next to him, she sighed, "I'm tired and stuffed from our dinner, babe. I don't want to talk about work."

"Did he?"

"Can we just watch something?" She turned on a box television with a clunky remote. "This room always reminds me of my childhood, but I didn't realize how bad the picture quality was back then."

Dropping his cross-examination, James stole the remote and began flipping through the channels. Most of the stations aired classic TV shows and movies, but it did have a few modern feeds in a low-quality HD form, including one of the news channels.

"Tonight, the search for a possible Light Keeper continues," an anchor reported. "Although the FBI failed to obtain the suspect during the raid on Wednesday, they managed to find an unchipped handgun in the suspect's home. Authorities speculate the underground cult may be arming themselves for a widespread attack. They hinted at bringing in the KOA to locate their top suspect, Kalen Green."

A photo of his ex-counselor popped up on the screen and James burst out of bed. "Did you know about this?"

"She's just a suspect." Sandy casually fiddled with her UniTab. "Why do you care anyway? She's not your therapist anymore."

"I told you she was sending people to that cult!"

Groaning, Sandy sat up on the bed. "I knew this raid was going to happen."

"What do you mean?"

"The reason I've been so busy is that patient X – Xavier – got busted when I was at his apartment. The FBI got involved and I had no choice but to become an informant." She paused, nervously scratching her head. "I'm not even supposed to tell anybody, but I'm sick of lying to you."

"I knew you've been up to something." As furious as James was, it was difficult to be upset with her. "I haven't been upfront with you either," he admitted. "That woman I met, Eleonora, might know someone who can help me find Pops."

"The elf goddess with the voice of an angel?" she said, repeating his vivid description of Lucidity's own pop star. "Are you sure she doesn't have an ulterior motive?"

"Jesus Christ, Sandy, you know me better than that, and you said I had a month."

"Meaning, you have one week left," she rebutted.

"Whatever, you just told me you're working for the goddamn FBI."

"It's not like they're putting me in the field," Sandy huffed. "They're forcing me to take the patients, who insist on telling me the very private details of their lives, not knowing I'm supposed to hand in detailed reports to the agent in charge." James could see she was on the verge of tears as she lay back down and buried her head in the pillows. "I feel like a fraud."

"I'm sorry." James combed his hand through her hair to calm her down. "That goes against everything you believe in." As the news report continued, he asked, "How much trouble is Kalen in any way?"

"She was recruiting for a presumed terrorist group."

"I tried to warn her."

"She'll be fine." Sandy closed her eyes, her voice fading. "Now get some rest."

When his wife fell asleep, James grabbed a hidden pack of cigarettes and snuck out of the room. One more secret. He walked toward Lake Montauk, past the same liquor store that had tempted him once before. As always, the thought crossed his mind. He took a deep breath and moved on. A chilly breeze reminded him it wasn't quite summer yet, and that life could get bitter and cold in an instant. He hadn't thought about people secretly following him until ...

"You mind if I bum one of those?"

It was the same kid who'd driven them to the Inn, Anthony. Out of the car, he was much taller than James imagined, adding a couple of years to the age he'd first presumed. He gave Anthony a smoke, not minding someone to help him find his way.

"These things will kill you," James joked. "Isn't there a little beach around here?"

"I can show ya round if you don't mind the company," the kid told him. "It can be a bit tricky to find it in the dark." The young man gave him history lessons on the way. "The Black and the Irish came out to Montauk because no one else wanted to travel this far. While the better-offs discovered Jones Beach and the rest of the Hamptons, we found our peace at the End of the World."

"I didn't know that."

Anthony explained, "*Ya* see, they had a lot in common at the turn of the twentieth century. Of course, the powers-*dat*-be always making sure to divide us – race, gender, religion, residency, and so on. All so we don't see what's happening."

"Well, what's happening?"

"A propaganda campaign," he insisted as they reached the tiny shore between them and the water.

"This world can get pretty fucking petty," James lamented. "Even as they tell us we're past all the bullshit, we're being separated into these new classes – this interior-outsider crap – and these same corporations are still in charge."

Stopping, Anthony turned around to get a better look at James in the moonlight. "Now I remember where I met you," he said. "You were that drunk guy my mother had to walk home some years ago." He came closer. "Did someone send you?"

"Send me?" James looked at him. "I'm just here on vacation with my wife."

Anthony scoped out the perimeter even though there wasn't a soul around, chain-smoking his second cigarette. He fidgeted through a smartphone and showed James a message. It read: "*You need to leave – ASAP.*" The email was from an unknown sender on a server that hadn't been used in a decade.

"That was from you, yeah?" Anthony said, "We've been waiting to hear from someone."

James took a step back. "I don't want anything to do with your bullshit cult, man."

Flustered, Anthony thanked him for the smoke and scurried away, leaving James all alone on the quiet beach. Kalen Green, his old friend and now the most wanted person in the country, was hiding out in Montauk with her son.

On the walk back to the Harbor Inn, James tried to put some pieces of a larger puzzle together, but it didn't make sense. He smoked the cigarette until it burnt his fingers, suddenly not cold anymore. He kept coming back to the only possible explanation, hoping it was only one of his delusional theories.

James stormed into their motel room and turned on the light. "Was it you?" he asked. "Were you the one who warned Kalen to flee?"

Half asleep, Sandy got up to grab a bottle of water, taking a sip to moisten her lips. "Kalen saved your life, babe." She lay back down on the bed, closed her eyes, and said, "So I decided to save hers."

VII
PART SEVEN

CHAPTER 25

On a gray Monday morning, Sandy made her way to the hospital in an AV Cruiser, zipping past the construction that never seemed to end. After a couple of days in a quiet beach town, the Upper Eastside felt busy and loud, but it was the noise in her head causing a spike in her blood pressure. While she'd convinced James there wasn't anything to be worried about, that was far from the truth. Sending Kalen Green an email on the day of the raid was a felony – plain and simple – and she'd already had enough ties to the suspect to make any idiot suspicious. Her only intention was to get her husband out of the condo to unwind, forgetting that he'd first met Kalen in Montauk. With a few minutes to spare, Sandy cued a recent news story pertaining to the Light Keepers.

"Over the weekend, Barney Maxx gave a rare press conference," a reporter said over clips of the White House lawn. "The president signed off on an emergency order granting the KOA government clearance to join forces with the FBI and Homeland Security in their hunt for the terrorist cult. A first since the war ended. Not surprisingly, the Bill didn't go through Congress without some strong opposition."

The screen cut to a muted clip of an older Black woman talking on the floor of the Capitol as the anchor continued. "Colleen Harding – the senator from Louisiana, who also acts as the US ambassador for the CTE – claimed the real threat lies somewhere deep in the Lucidity system itself. In the emergency hearing she said, and I quote, 'The KOA are nothing but a bunch of dangerous damn foot soldiers.' She went on to say how their imprudent methods would only make the situation more volatile."

Sandy cut off the feed, knowing that her mess had only become worse with the KOA now involved. As she entered the hospital, the deafening silence reminded her that Agent Miller was coming in for an impromptu assessment of her undercover work. Sandy convinced herself the Feds were on to her little game. The agent had messaged her the day before to make sure she'd be there for the meeting as if they'd had the arrest planned already.

All of a sudden she felt nauseous, as though everyone were staring at her. She wasn't sure if it was pregnancy or anxiety, but something made its way up her throat as she hustled into a bathroom. She found a toilet and puked out her entire breakfast. "I just want this to be over," she whispered to herself, dry-heaving out the rest before realizing she hadn't shut the stall's door.

Agent Miller stared at her in the mirror. "You okay in there?"

Sandy cleared her throat, heading to the sink to run cold water over her face. "Pregnancy's a bitch," she groaned. "Do you have any kids?"

"Twins," Miller replied. "You get a whiff of hard-boiled eggs? That used to disgust me when those two were on the way."

Sandy gargled some water and spit it out. "After a nice weekend away I didn't realize the hospital's stench of cleanliness could be so putrid." She squeezed her shaking hands. "So, what's this surprise meeting about?"

"Surprise?" The agent laughed. "It's a routine checkup we do with all of our assets." A first for that new upgraded term, *asset*.

When they left the bathroom, Agent Miller went into evaluation mode, interrogating Sandy about the potential suspects the Feds had sent her way. "The agency needs a win." She hoped the doctor of death could work her magic once again. "I'm gonna go through your notes, but off record is there anyone who lines up with the Light Keeper's MO?"

"It takes time for people to open up during therapy," Sandy reminded the pesky agent. "They have to *trust you first*."

Although it was a dig at the Fed's lax policy on ethics, Agent Miller was too serious to pick up on the sarcasm. She kept it brief, giving Sandy a list of the next round of "patients," and telling her which ones to pay extra close attention to. Even though there were more than before, the agent promised that her time as an informant/ asset was over at the end of the week. "Keep up the good work," she said before leaving to meet with another lowly informant.

With a huge sigh of relief, Sandy headed to her office, put some food back in her stomach, and rushed through patients like a speed dating app. Standard routine as of late. As much as it didn't sit right, she hoped to find another suspect to keep Kalen off the Feds' radar, therefore saving her own ass in the process. Ten hours later, and she had come to the end of her list of patients.

She recorded as a vThere were no breakthroughs today."

Then her UniTab buzzed, alerting her to a last-minute appointment. It wasn't a video call or a SYNCDIN session, but an actual person coming into the office. Sandy hadn't had one of those in weeks. Grabbing a bag of dried chickpeas from the break room, she read over the patient's file:

Name: Mahoe. Age: 54. Gender: Non-Binary. Occupation: Monk?

The patient wasn't in hospice condition yet, but had stage four pancreatic cancer that would play out like a cruel death sentence. Whoever it was, they weren't on the FBI's list of suspicious characters.

When Sandy returned to her office, a giant figure stood waiting for her, causing her to almost choke on her half-chewed snack. The stranger with a six-foot heavy-set frame had a dark honey complexion and beautifully wrinkled lips locked in despondency. Their eyes were dark and foreboding. They wore a bright long dress with a hypnotizing pattern that matched their one earring.

Sandy cautiously closed the door behind her. "You must be Mahoe." She kept reading their file, remembering the cancer. "I wish we could've met on better terms."

Mahoe didn't speak, observing the doctor's credentials and memorabilia, towering high enough to see the shelves Sandy hadn't dusted in months. Behind framed photos of her wedding in Rhode Island, there were a few copies of her book, and for another five minutes, the mystery patient flipped through the pages without a word.

"My *New York Times* best seller," she joked, knowing most of the printed copies sat on the shelves of college libraries. There was no response from the monk. "The new East River Sanctuary is only a few blocks from here. It's a beautiful day and an Automated could get us there in a few minutes." When they didn't respond again, she grew agitated. "Whatever it takes to make you feel comfortable."

Out of nowhere, the Intruder Alarm went off in the building. It hadn't been deployed since the war – a time when it wasn't unheard of for a rogue Free Folk supporter to launch a surprise attack. Mahoe grinned and summoned her toward the exit stairs although it was the opposite of protocol. With the lights flashing and her heart racing, Sandy followed Mahoe down thirteen flights to the outside of the hospital.

Without any explanation, the monk led her up York Avenue with their arms resting behind their back in a calm manner. As curious as Sandy was cautious, she followed along, matching the wise Mahoe's silence and firm posture.

When they made a right on 71st Street, Sandy asked, "Can you tell me where we're going?"

Mahoe never broke character on the sweaty, and extremely nerve-racking, fifteen-minute expedition to the same spot Sandy had suggested in the first place.

The East River Sanctuary was built on top of the FDR Parkway, designed for meditation and reflection. It was lined with bushes of tulips, art installations, and a glass sound barrier to block out the city's noise. The after-work crowd made it busy, but there was hardly a peep besides the wind chimes and the library-worthy conversations. It was the perfect place for Mahoe, who seemed captivated by a fountain.

Sandy approached the red-flag candidate with the utmost amount of tact, used to dealing with patients who'd lost their way after being diagnosed with a terminal illness. "Why did we leave with the alarm going off?" She used her lowest voice. "We're supposed to stay put." When she got nothing but another grin, she finally lost it. "Is this one of your annoying monk superpowers? Because it's really not amusing me anymore!"

Suddenly, Mahoe began cackling in a deep yet fake-sounding monotone.

"*Hah hah hah ... Hah hah hah.*"

People rose from their yoga mats to see what the commotion was about as Sandy dragged the monk away to a more desolate spot.

"Silence is so vital, Dr Grady," Mahoe said – robotic and zen at the same time. "It allows us to reconnect with our subconscious mind."

"So you do talk?" When everyone stopped paying attention to them, she asked, "What happened to your vow of silence?"

"I'm not a monk." Mahoe rested next to the pool of water. "That was one of my Jedi mind tricks. Since I live a celibate lifestyle I used it as a joke in the encrypted file we uploaded into your planner. Most of the other stuff is true, though."

Growing weary – and wary – of the stranger, Sandy whispered, "Is this some kind of test?"

"Why would you say that, Sandy?" They smirked. "Or should I call you FBI Agent Grady?"

As many patients as she'd seen over her short career, this one was the toughest one to read. *Is Mahoe an agent too?* Since becoming an informant, she'd never had a chance to thoroughly dive into her patient's history anymore. Her work had become abysmal. Now sitting in the park, she had no idea who she was dealing with, and because it would be suspicious and rude to use her UniTab, Sandy slyly whispered into her earbud, "*Ginger* ... call Dr Haskell."

When her synth didn't respond, Mahoe chuckled. "We had our people set off the alarm and disable security, covering the tracks of our meeting today. Neither of your bosses will ever know about this."

"You're not a Fed, are you?"

"Nope."

"So what makes you think I'm not going to turn you in as soon as this is over?"

Mahoe placed their arm around her shoulder. "Because last Tuesday you warned a mutual friend of ours to flee, and I'm pretty sure the FBI frowns on aiding and abetting a terrorist suspect. Luckily, our team covered up any connection between you and Ms. Green."

Sandy scratched her head. "What about my husband? He must be on their list."

"You mean because of the *anonymous* meetings he attends?" Mahoe assured her, "We can keep all that hidden if you give us the intel we need. I know it may sound like coercion, but we prefer to call it an insurance policy."

Sandy felt like she might throw up again. "I'm listening."

"Your office is bugged," Mahoe told her matter-of-factly. "That's why I wanted to get you away from the hospital without a word. We're not sure if it's the Feds, but it must be someone that knows you're working with them. Someone in your office?"

"Or someone like you?"

"I assure you, it's not us." Mahoe dipped a hand in the water and splashed it on their face. "I don't think anyway."

"And by us – you do mean the Light Keepers, right?" Mahoe didn't answer with words, but their brows raised. "Look, I'm glad that Kalen got away," Sandy continued, "but that was a one-time get-out-of-jail-free card. I don't know what your little cult is trying to pull off and I don't care to be associated with it." Sandy got up and stormed away, shouting over shoulder, "Leave me alone or I will turn you in!"

"Dr Grady ... Wait!" The monk was persistent, leering at the onlookers growing agitated by the distracting pair. "You used intel acquired at a classified meeting," they reminded her in a calm manner. "If you truly want to help people like you write in your book, then this is a cause worth fighting for. Otherwise, it could be unsatisfactory to you in the short-run, and worse for everyone at the end of the day."

"All I can tell you is that every agency in the world is on the hunt for you." She paused. "What else would you like to know?"

"Just find out who the mole is," Mahoe said. "We need to know so they don't stop us."

"Stop you from doing what?"

Mahoe didn't respond.

Instead, the enigmatic figure walked back toward the city, leaving Sandy with a whole new set of worries. Thirty minutes earlier she had been on her way out the door, only a week away from a long maternity leave. Now it had only gotten worse. Essentially, she'd become a double agent on the wrong side of the law. Her office was bugged and there was some mole she was to identify. Cradling her ever-growing belly, she whispered, "What the hell has your mommy gotten herself involved in?"

CHAPTER 26

As soon as James entered the Welcome Facility, there was a message on his navigator: "*Meet me in front of the Eighth sector.*" It was from Eleonora, but he wasn't even sure how to respond, never making it that deep into the manual. He was still nervous about the electrical storm about to begin before he entered the system. On his way to his destination, he passed by the infamous tenth sector known as the Yards, where a rowdy pack of vigilante avatars prepped for some kind of battle simulation. As always, Dark Cloud sported his black hoodie and patented insecurity – a perfect candidate for the group of vagabonds waiting to go in. An oversized creature akin to an ogre stared at him in a blood-thirsty manner, but James snuck by before any words were exchanged, realizing the eighth sector was far worse than the Yards.

NuAmsterdam, or as his wife called it, *the sex sector*, was one of the places he'd promised to never visit. The users congregating around the portal were decked out for some sort of wild Halloween orgy in sci-fi porn, side-eyeing his boring and uninspired avatar skin. Uneasy with Eleonora's meet-up spot, James was about to ditch his date when someone tapped him on the shoulder.

"James?"

It was Nera, his operator from the Lucidity. Besides the camouflage bodysuit, the shaved head, and the war paint under her eyes, Nera's avatar looked similar enough to the woman who'd set up his DreamCatcher. It was hard to tell where she was heading on the forbidden side of the Facility – the Yards or NuAmsterdam?

Stumbling to find the words, James said, "Cool outfit."

"Thanks and you look ... less old," Nera responded, awkward like a sarcastic teenager. "What are you doing over here?"

"I think I've gone the wrong way." James walked over to the railing to get away from the risqué crowd. "This whole side is much more cavalier."

Nera followed. "I'd invite you to the Yards for our Tuesday night Battle Royale, but your wife made it crystal clear to me she didn't want you going in the Red Zones." She sighed. "Kind of a shame, though – you could be a real asset with those numbers you put up in the Cave."

"I still don't know what that means."

"Never mind, Dark Cloud," she said with a shrug. Her screen name was Nera-Mind and now he understood the pun. "I'm not going to peer pressure anyone. I keep telling my boyfriend I'm not coming to the Yards anymore, but as you can see, I'm addicted." She, too, prepped herself for the rumble she was about to get into, stretching her hamstrings on the railing. "How is that kickass wife of yours, by the way? I had fun chit-chatting with her while you were in the Cave and told her to call me if she needed any help."

Before James could answer, he caught a glimpse over Nera's shoulder. Eleonora strutted toward him in an avant-garde burlesque ensemble. A tight-fitting violet corset accentuated her blue breasts while the bottom quarter of a long floral dress only hid the lower part of her legs. Glowing butterflies and adoring fans surrounded her. They cleared a path for her like royalty as she strolled into James's conversation.

"You ready to go, Cloud?" Eleonora turned to a star-struck Nera. "I'm sorry I have to steal him from you, but we're kind of on a time crunch."

As the diva dragged James away, Nera gave him a most peculiar grin, both envious and alarmed. Everyone seemed curious about the odd couple – exactly what Sandy was worried about. Earlier that afternoon she'd come home to seduce him, stripping down to nothing but her newly gained tan lines. The rumors about Lucidity would make any partner nervous, and Eleonora's company had already made him look like a liar and a cheat. He only hoped Nera wouldn't tell her, seeing as they'd become besties.

James asked Eleonora, "Why are you taking me in here?"

"This is the only way to get to Simon."

"Who the hell is Simon?"

Eleonora clenched his hand and dragged him into the portal. "You'll find out soon enough."

~

Inside NuAmsterdam, a grimy house track blasted in a dystopian industrial area. It reminded James of some of the shadowy places his band had toured on the underground circuit during the War. Below a dusk-colored sky, a wide array of costumed avatars danced and flirted in the promiscuous sector, but it was much tamer than Sandy's wild imagination made it out to be. At best it was a PG-13 movie with some partial nudity. In the corner, a neon sign read: *"No sex allowed in the Plaza … Get a fantasy room, you pervs."*

James accompanied Eleonora like a one-man entourage, concerned with the optics of his tour guide. People stopped making out with each other to gawk at her, but no one approached. Using his Navigator, it said, *"DO NOT DISTURB,"* in a warning sign above her head. Eleonora graciously blew kisses to the fans, hand-signaling heart signs over her chest. The one creeper who made the mistake of getting too close was escorted away by security.

"Unlike the real world, nothing in here is without consent," Eleonora told him. "If someone's stalking or intimidating you, you can report it immediately." She groaned. "Or at least that's the way it's supposed to be."

James asked, "Is it not that safe anymore?"

"Let's just say Lucidity's getting lax with their policies and Simon isn't happy with the way they're running the show anymore."

"So the guy I'm meeting is some sort of geeky fanboy of the

system? ... *Great.*"

Eleonora walked beside James for the first time as they made their way out of the plaza. "I'm sure he'll explain everything when we get there."

James glanced around. "To be honest, NuAmsterdam doesn't seem that bad."

"*Ohhh*, Cloud," she giggled, "the Plaza is just how they suck you in. Before long you're participating in orgies and cheating on that wife of yours. Trust me, it can be tempting even for the most committed souls."

"I mean, the sex can't feel that real," he scoffed. "Not that I care anyway."

"All I can tell you is that the real deal is never the same afterward."

Not going into detail, Eleonora switched to a less flashy outfit – leather spandex, and a black veil to hide her identity – leading him into what reminded him of the grittier version of Times Square. Scantily clad barkers promoted shops and clubs with names like Nutty Buddies and Raw Dogs. It wasn't exactly a brothel, although silent business transactions were certainly being made, and as far he understood, that was all legal and consensual. A huge crowd formed around a standard male avatar fornicating with a synth humanoid overly endowed with the best of both genders. The "No Sex in Public" rule was definitely off the table as voyeurs too shy to participate themselves, but not enough to keep their hard-ons in their pants, cheered on the exhibitionists.

James gazed up at the statue-sized blowup doll. "Why do I have to meet Simon in this sector?"

Eleonora giggled. "To be honest with you, I had to make an appearance in the Plaza so I'd thought I'd kill two birds with one stone." She took a detour down a quieter walkway. "His spot is off the grid so we'll have to lay low from here on out."

"I was already kicked out for going off the grid." He continued to trail her, reluctant nonetheless. "Plus, I told my wife that I wouldn't go into any Red Zones."

Eleonora rolled her eyes. "Did you make that pact before or after you became the rumored champion of Sphere? You won't get ejected." She dragged James inside a vintage cinema house when no one was paying attention. According to the marquee, "*DEEP THROAT starring Linda Lovelace*" was the main attraction. "We just have to make sure no one follows us." She headed into the lobby. "It's an exact replica of the Harem Theatre that once existed on West 42nd Street." Passing by the posters of old peep shows, they made their way down the empty aisles to the front of the stage. The porn playing on the projector screen had a scene full of hairy penises penetrating hairy vaginas and more. When James asked where everyone was, she told him "no one cares to watch when they can live out their fantasies right inside here." Beckoning him with her index finger, Eleonora lured him over to the movie screen before disappearing inside what appeared to be another portal.

As James followed like a fool, a force held him back from going in – a prompt asking if he approved the purchase. The admission to the Harem cost 50,000 Lucies, which according to the one part of the manual he checked out, was about half that in dollars and came directly out of his deposit. He'd hardly spent anything so far and intended on keeping it that way. Just as he was about to bail on Eleonora, over her and this unnecessary detour he'd gone on, she returned through the screen.

"Sorry," she said, granting James access. "I forgot how much it cost so I went ahead and took care of it for you."

"That's way too generous to spend on someone you barely know."

"Not to gloat, but that ten-minute walk through the Plaza paid me four times as much as it cost me to get you in here."

When James came out the other end it was like a film noir, everything in black-and-white including himself. Smoke poured out from the sewer's manholes as female synths walked the streets in fur coats and mini-skirts. The fire escapes were full of half-naked avatars. A collective of moans bounced off the alleyway. Eleonora didn't seem interested in the seductive environment, hurrying ahead of him instead.

Meanwhile, a disco ball shining through a fogged-up window mesmerized James, a mustached man pressing a pair of naked breasts against the glass. The woman appeared through the steam, along with three others, staring directly at James. "Ms. Sykes?" he shouted. She nodded, waving for him to come in. Everyone had warned him people were cheating in Lucidity, but to see his former principal – married with three children – shocked him.

"Stop playing around." Eleonora grabbed his hand, pulling him down alleyway after alleyway that finally ended in a brick wall. His Navigator was inoperable and they had taken so many turns that he didn't know how to get back.

"Hey, it's me," Eleonora whispered, but it wasn't directed at James. "Can I get some service here?" Whoever she was talking to didn't answer. "The entrance is around here somewhere." She touched certain bricks in a neurotic manner.

"This is a dead-end and there's no one else here!"

As soon as James shouted it, two shadows approached them, almost transparent besides the red light of the alleyway reflecting off their shadows. A closer look revealed the oversized rectangular goggles they both wore, a fish-eyed reflection of the surroundings. When one of them got close it wasn't Dark Cloud he saw, but the same James Grady who'd left his pregnant wife for a stupid game. A small guard stood in front of him with a scanner as the larger guard circled.

With a shrill and raspy voice, the smaller guard asked, "Who's the kid affiliated with, Elle?"

"He's just my friend," Eleonora answered, obviously familiar with the strange character. "Simon's expecting us and you know how anal he is about his time."

"We've had some security issues lately," the smaller guard continued. "Yesterday there was another incident involving phantoms in Lucidity. Those teenage technophiles are doing everything they can to disrupt the system and word on the streets is that Feds are poking around in here."

"I assure you he's not affiliated with either of those groups."

The other guard finally finished their scan. "The kid's clean," she said in a much more pleasant tone. "You're both free to go through."

With that, Eleonora gave her supposed guard friend a fierce scowl. "This way, Cloud," she huffed. "You're going to love the Retreat." When she stepped through the brick wall, it bent like a raindrop in a puddle, but that wasn't the matter boggling his mind.

"The Retreat?" James asked, remembering the photo he'd found in his father's bag.

But the guards were gone and so was Eleonora. With no idea of where it led, he stepped through the brick wall.

CHAPTER 27

On the other side of the alleyways of NuAmsterdam was a sunny tropical paradise, surrounded by palm trees and lavish flower-filled gardens. At least two dozen guests donned high-fashion face coverings. By some protocol, a domino mask and sunglasses had been automatically added to James's avatar as well. Through the sculpted bushes, there was a white sand beach in the distance, but the rowdy pack of sunset masqueraders seemed more interested in Eleonora's late arrival. She wore the same outfit she originally had on, only with a violet silk bandana covering her matching lips. For a few seconds, James forgot where he was, enthralled by the surroundings of the exclusive soiree. A message popped up on his navigator that he couldn't open.

He interrupted the masquerade. "Why isn't this working?"

Eleonora pulled him away from the other guests, who seemed appalled by his disruptive behavior. It didn't help that his avatar's skin didn't quite fit the atmosphere. "You need to slow your roll, Cloud."

"I think my wife might be trying to contact me."

Eleonora seemed perturbed, her arms crossed. "Your Navigator's not going to operate in here," she said. "I encourage you to go and see what Simon has to say. I didn't get you this far for you to give up now."

The people continued giving James ugly grimaces. "What's their deal?"

Eleonora grinned. "They're just jealous that Simon's giving you fifteen minutes of his time. It's very rare." She pointed to a man standing alone next to the shore. "He's waiting for you now."

Following Eleonora's instructions, James walked down a flight of stairs to get to the beach. The man he presumed to be Simon skipped rocks over the tide, staring off into the endless ocean. He had dark brown skin that sparkled with beams of light off his bald scalp, his back muscles bulging through the white silky shirt that went past his knees. When the man turned around, James recognized him from one of the polaroids in Pops's satchel, almost positive that it was SRT – the creator of the Void.

"What doth thou thinketh of my humble abode?" Simon queried in an overdone Shakespearean accent. "It's a spectacular view that one doth admire."

"It's breathtaking." James hid his anxiety about being off the grid without his Navigator. "Eleonora said you'd be able to help me find someone in Lucidity."

"*You're not in Lucidity anymore,*" Simon said, now in a high-pitched impression of Belinda the Good Witch. "You can take off those shoes, my boy. We're going to take a little walk."

Listening to his host, James slipped off his Doc Marten's and dug his feet into the sand, picking up a handful and letting the breeze drag the tiny stones out of his palm. Every detail was so lifelike, and the man dawdling toward the ocean was presumably the person who'd created it all.

"I was just at the beach last weekend." James kicked the water. "But this is something else. I can't even imagine how much time it must've taken to figure out the complexities of these simulations." He gazed at the dinosaur-sized rainbow dolphins frolicking in the ocean. "I'm guessing the S stands for Simon?"

"I assumed you might know who I was." Simon transitioned into a more serious tone. "I'd prefer to stay undoxxed, though." James nodded as the man added, "I'm curious to know how you came across your father's AFANET key?"

Making an effort to keep it short, James told him a five-minute version of his ten-year journey to find his old man. "My sister found this bag hidden in our attic and turned it over to me," he said. "I found the polaroid you sent him asking him to come to the Retreat, but it certainly didn't look like this."

Simon chuckled. "This is a replica of the version your father helped me design in Alter World – with a few added dimensions, of course. It was our little escape during some of the worst times." Simon had met Jaybird in Alter World years ago, never mentioning he was the creator. For years Simon had listened to Pops's concepts of how to make it better, and they'd become good friends who agreed to keep their private lives anonymous. "One day Jaybird told me he'd come across this technology that would revolutionize everything and I revealed who I was to him with no response."

Gazing around the heavenly masterpiece, James balked at the idea. "Not to shit on my dad, but I don't think he had the capability to build this. He always told me his coding skills were average at best."

Standing in the low tide Simon went on to explain that in the late twenties, "Jaybird was recruited into a private government contractor testing an early version of BCI." They recruited his father for his interrogation skills, but he became close friends with the unnamed engineers who were beginning to realize the existential threat of their creation.

"So do you know where my father is now?"

"I've been tracking Jaybird's movement from the last month since he showed up and it's been in and out. You were the only one who came close to him one day in the Void. Then he disappeared again."

"Is his avatar a scarecrow?"

Simon nodded.

James's eyes shot open. "So that was my father?"

"Now, now. There's still more to explain." Simon checked out his surrounding like he was being tricked. "You were the one person searching for him and no one else knew that avatar existed except for me. Are you working with someone else, James?"

James chuckled. "I barely know how to use my own avatar."

Simon crossed his arms, giving a suspicious grin. "That's not what it says on your Lucidity History Record."

"You tracked all my movement?"

"Precisely." Simon went on to tell James how he still had access to the security protocol in Lucidity. "This is not normal behavior for a rookie." The man knew every zone James had visited in his accumulated nineteen hours in the system. Everything he'd done there. The Sphere match and his suspension for ending up off the grid in a corn maze. It ended when he asked, "How exactly did you know Jaybird would be there in the Void that day?"

All James remembered was going on a hunch, inhaling the blue smoke, chasing shadows, and waking up with Mimi rescuing him. A psychedelic nightmare that had taken him a day to recover from. "I thought he'd be in the Void because that was the only spot you mentioned in the cables. He was the one who found me, though."

"I don't think that's him, James, but because of you, that's how I figured out your father's identity." Simon abruptly paused and began sobbing. "I had a feeling he was dead, but I didn't want to believe it."

"What are you talking about?" James asked. "The fucking scarecrow had his exact voice. It was him."

Simon shook his head no. "I'm well aware of what you're speaking of, but he never came and neither did the rest of them. People have been hacking avatars and they must know his identity here. But I don't think they know it in the real world. "

"I don't understand."

"Your father was an important person." He paused with a tear running down his face. "I hate to be the bearer of bad news, but according to public records he was killed ten years ago in a roadside bombing." He pointed to Eleonora in the distance. "I only found out myself when she came to me a few days ago and told me about you."

James shook his head. "The Army and whatever dummy

corporation he worked for both told my family that my father skipped town. A lot of people were doing that when the War began."

"Oddly enough," Simon clarified, "the investigation into your father's whereabouts was only recently discovered by an Army task force." He paced around as James remained silent. "What did your family do with all the money?"

"What money?"

Simon seemed confused. "One of the four working on the project, Brian – the only one I ever met – came to the Retreat to make a deal on their behalf. They practically handed me a treasure map, so in return, they were all given substantial compensation."

James recalled the message from the files. "You mean Uncle Brian?"

Simon nodded. "I think that's him. Is there any way you can find him?"

"I haven't seen him since I was like fourteen or so, and my mother told me was dead."

"That might be true," Simon groaned, hanging his head low. "I'm sorry, my boy." He kicked the inch-deep water in some deep contemplation. "I think the man we've both been looking for is dead."

James stood in the sun of the most peaceful paradise he'd ever been to and felt nothing. He didn't know if it was relief or shock, and only snapped out of the daze when his Navigator buzzed again. "I have to go." He rushed back up the beach, almost at the stairs when an out-of-breath Simon caught up with him.

"Wait!"

"I have to go see if my wife's okay," James insisted.

"Don't you want to know what happened to your father? Because I sure as hell do."

"I'm done," James yelled, making his way up the stairs. "You can go find him using all the money and resources you have, but I can't do this anymore."

Simon trailed close behind. "If you're truly finished with this search, then you should go home and destroy those files you have. They could be very dangerous in the wrong hands." He took a deep breath. "I never met your father in person, but you should know that in our world he was a hero."

James furrowed his brow at the comment, storming through the chic masquerade, bumping into whomever got in his way. The conversations had already halted when they noticed him being chased by the host of the party.

Eleonora rushed to stop him. "Where are you going, Cloud?"

James brushed past her, too, waiting for his Navigator to come back on. "You could've told me my father was dead." He turned to the gawking spectators and ripped off his mask. "I hope you're all enjoying your little party. Just know that some people paid for it with their life."

Simon caught up. "There's so much more to explain."

"Oh yeah, what was his fucking life worth to you?" James shouted. "Or was he collateral damage for your trillion-dollar deal?"

"Calm down, James!"

"No ... tell me how much it costs to pay him off?"

"I didn't pay him off."

"How much?"

Simon's nostrils flared, some pent-up energy ready to explode. "Fifty billion dollars," he yelled, "and I'd like to know why they never got it and why your family never saw a dime." When Simon realized they had everyone's attention, he whispered to James, "Keep those files safe or destroy them." He rushed back toward his private beach, covering his face as Eleonora chased after him.

Besides the sound of the gentle waves crashing onto the simulated shore, it was dead silent in the garden for a moment. The guests began gossiping with one another, discreetly staring at James as if he were someone important. Before he could contemplate any of it, another alert went off on his Navigator.

Confused and broken-hearted, James stepped through the portal, and back into the black-and-white alleyway. When his Navigator was operational again, he prompted the ejection process to begin. *At least I'll get home quick*, he thought, reveling in his last moment inside Lucidity. It was an impressive world, but his search was over.

"Rest in peace, Pops ... I hope it was worth it."

CHAPTER 28

At the DC office for the Lost Patriots task force, Diaz and Ronson had a
meeting with their supervisor, Mario Vazquez, who had put off the case
debriefing after Ohio, stating that he was "sorting out internal matters" –
whatever that meant. When they arrived, he had a grim frown, taking the
detectives into his office and closing the blinds.

"We were hacked," Vasquez told them when they were all seated.
He was a middle-aged, mustached man who took his job less seriously
than Ronson. "I thought I got these orders from my higher-ups but they
knew nothing of it." The Army intended on brushing the investigation
under the rug, still under fire for the Midwest Melee during the War.
Vasquez ordered them to hand over their reports and to keep their
findings under wraps, probably under scrutiny for letting them slip
through.

"That case was closed years ago, but the file must've vanished when
we updated our system." Vasquez joked, "Sounds like you had a wild
goose chase through the outside." With that, he let them go, giving them
one last task together.

Before her train back to Brooklyn, Diaz met up with Ronson for
coffee, her mind racing with more questions. "Why would some hacker
give us that specific case? And don't you find that our road trip took us to
some pretty precarious locations?" She never asked Vasquez any of those
questions, so her partner got the full brunt after a few espressos. "And
why was Ian Ginsberg or the Gradys never told, while Nick Baxter was?"

"That'll all be taken care of tonight," Ronson reminded her. "Can't
we just celebrate the fact that I'm retiring?"

Since Ohio, they'd spoken many times, and Ronson had finally
broken through her tough outer layer, admitting she had strong feelings

for Diaz. Ronson had a whole plan for the two of them, including a trip around the world sans combat gear and pesky investigations. She told Diaz, "We could have a peaceful life from here on out."

But as far as Diaz was concerned the case had only begun, and when she told Ronson about the copies of the reports she'd made, and the private investigation she had planned, her partner seemed less than thrilled.

"What in God's name are you thinking?" Ronson got up out of her seat, straining herself not to make a scene. "I've been doing this shit my whole life, Adriana. Let the kids fight their battles and let us heal our wounds for a change."

"Isn't finding the answers the first step to healing?"

"That journey will never end." Ronson kissed her. "I hope you've come to your senses before I see you later tonight."

"And what if I can't?"

With glassy eyes, Ronson said, "You can either give up the witch hunt or forget about any chance of this relationship panning out."

~

With Ronson's parting words in her mind, Diaz took the MagTrain back to New York. Arriving home, she slumped onto the couch in her modernized pre-war apartment, physically tired and mentally drained. Her bags were unpacked in the hallway, reminding her of the scattered road trip with Ronson, never realizing her partner was that serious about them until the spiel at the coffee shop. She wanted to let it go and crawl into bed with an imaginary version of Ronson, but there was a knock on the door.

It was Dan, her neighbor and new partner in the investigation. He was a coder for SYNCDIN by day, and a borderline illegal hacker by night. Even with Diaz's access to government files, Dan somehow always managed to dig a bit deeper.

He knocked again, "I know you're in there, Diaz."

The lanky Brit had recently become obsessed with an old show called *Friends* and adored how the characters stopped by neighbors' apartments without warning. Understanding personal boundaries was sometimes difficult for Dan, who had been diagnosed with ASD. When she let him in he had a maddening grin, which meant he'd found something.

"We need to have a chat about Ellie Brown Ginsberg," Dan said in his proper English accent, pale and barefooted with his distinct schnoz focused on a UniTab; his sandy blonde hair spiked high and messy like he hadn't slept in days. Judging by his BO, he hadn't showered either.

"What about Ginsberg?" Diaz made a cup of coffee to keep up with him. "We couldn't find that much personal information about her."

"That's because Ellie Brown didn't exist until the year 2024," Dan said, "which is around the same time a woman named Farah Sylvain went missing in Haiti – a woman who matches the facial identity of Ms. Brown." Dan showed him the two side by side on his UniTab. While younger in one, it was the same woman from the Army's file.

"So she changed her name?" Diaz shrugged, "That's not unheard of."

"It is when she's claiming to be a neuroscientist in one place and agricultural engineer in another, especially for a homeschooled twenty-three-year-old from an impoverished country."

"Not everyone is private schooled their whole life," Diaz said.

"That's not what I meant." Dan picked up the SYNCDIN glasses off her table, offering her a pair. "Let me show you."

"I can hardly do IRL right now, and you expect me to do AR?"

"Suit yourself," Dan said, his hands and fingers constantly in motion while speaking. "Let's forget about Farah for now and focus on Ellie Brown, the ghost who went to MIT and was recruited by JTID after she created the first controlled BCI space called *a room*."

Diaz mused, "A room?"

Seeming to stare into an empty space, Dan sighed. "It's specifically what Lucidity now uses on a grander scale." He explained what Ellie Brown had envisioned was more or less like Ayahuasca used for therapeutic value, but billionaires and defense contractors were more interested in its market potential and weaponization. "The Void used this technology to integrate VR and the Metaverse with BCI, which is what made it worth a trillion dollars." Dan said, "Which I'm sure she never saw a dime of."

Diaz had a hard time concentrating on her long-winded neighbor, distracted by the thought of Ronson's tantrum earlier that day. Dan went on a side tangent about corporate greed, and the complex nature of the technology, which she hardly understood. Maybe Ronson was right and she was too old for this shit?

Dan continued. "I don't think you comprehend how massive this is." He stood up, flailing his long arms, pointing to things Diaz couldn't see. "They had you searching about for Suzi-Q for fuck's sake, and with a tad bit of my help, you may have gotten a bit closer to solving every nerd's speculation that she was murdered. The woman you call Ginsberg created BCI, even though it was never credited to her, and I'm still not sure who this Grady chum was, but he was wrapped up in quite a fascinating ordeal to be alongside those two ladies."

"He's dead, Dan," she reminded him. "They're all dead now."

"Of course – *very tragic* – but it has to make you wonder how two detectives on a small task force got put on this particular case?"

"Because I'm a damn good investigator!"

"Of course, I just mean it seems like a matter the more technologically inclined might deal with."

"Well, it's never too late to teach an old dog new tricks." Diaz knew he was right, asking, "Even with your help, do you think I'm in over my head?"

For the first time, Dan seemed stumped. "The origin of BCI is blurry since it all seemed to happen amid the war, and suspiciously at a defense contractor run by the Army." He thought for a moment. "What I find most curious is that specific branch had a third of their domestic personnel detract to the Free Folk." He paused. "It makes you wonder if there's some correlation between BCI and the War."

"So what you're saying is *yes*, I'm in way over my fucking head ... And all this so those some rich assholes can go play in Lucidity?"

"That's only my theory," Dan sighed. "All I know is my girlfriend is obsessed with this OS. I keep telling her something terrible's going to happen one day – that it needs more time and testing before bringing it to the masses. So what does she do?" he said. "She gets one of those bloody DreamCatchers installed right in my living room."

"You're an Alpha who sounds a lot like one of us old ass Gen-Zers," Diaz teased, getting a rise out of an agitating him. "My Puerto Rican mother used to say, *Them automated cars are gonna kill us all, baby girl.* But after I drove all those days on the outside, trust me, AVs are the better alternative."

Dan mused at her point. "My parents are both dead so I don't know what they would say," he said, matter-of-factly. "But I'm all in for assisting you on this investigation, which reminds me of the Manhattan Project."

"That's not making me feel any better." An alarm went off on her UniTab reminding Diaz to get ready. "Ronson's picking me up in a half an hour. Can we talk about this later?"

"That's fine." He was still dabbling his fingers in the air on his way out. "I have to go hang out with my girlfriend before she logs in anyway."

"You have a girlfriend, huh?" Diaz walked him out. "I guess that's why I haven't seen you as much."

"I guess the same applies to you," Dan said with an awkward wink. "I'll let you know if I figure anything else out."

~

An hour later, Diaz stood underneath a bus stop in the pouring rain, waiting for her partner to arrive. The forecast had called for an intense storm to rip through the northeast like a wildfire. She wore her Army Class-A uniform, which was much tighter than the last time she'd worn it over a decade ago. *Ronson was right about the cookies,* Diaz thought as her partner pulled up in an AV-Cruiser.

"Why in God's name are you sitting out here in the rain?" Ronson asked with a window rolled down, also in uniform. "The app tells you the exact second I'd arrive." She gazed back at the building she was supposed to move into. "And why are you still living in this twentieth-century dump?"

Diaz hopped in, beating the monsoon. "Nice to see you too. It's called a pre-War apartment and I think it has a lot of charm."

"I've never heard of this pre-War period you speak of," Ronson remarked. "Besides, your apartment isn't a historical landmark; it's just an excuse for you being a cheap skate."

Diaz tried to hold back her laughter, but she knew her partner had her pinned. "You're such a dick." She cracked up so hard that she snorted, making both of them chuckle like two kids with an inside joke. Once the ice was broken, her partner scooted over and held her hand.

"I'll live wherever you want." Ronson held Diaz's hand, staring into her eyes . "Even if it is in that shit-hole." She paused. "I'm sure you've had some time to think about what you said this morning."

Diaz giggled, "That was the caffeine talking."

"Thank God," Ronson admitted, before getting a phone call on her UniTab. "It's my kid, so I gotta take this."

Diaz nodded, always forgetting that her partner – *her romantic partner* – had four children from her previous marriage. Diaz had planned on having some of her own but got caught up in her career. She imagined what it would be like to be the cool stepmother – holidays and vacations with a real family – until she was distracted by her own

UniTab. It was a new message from Dan.

"*Farah Sylvain lived with her aunt in Richmond for three years!*"

Noticing Ronson wasn't paying attention, Diaz replied: "*So?*"

"*Her aunt was head of neurology at VCU, and you'll never guess what her main focus was.*"

"*Brain-Computer Interface?*"

"*Precisely.*"

"*Okay?*"

"*Okay?... Richmond!... BCI!????*"

Diaz noticed Ronson wrapping it up with her daughter, playing coy and holding her hand. She didn't have much time, typing: "*Is that it?*"

Dan didn't reply, the ellipsis staggering like all the times her ex-girlfriends had ghosted her. Diaz tapped on the seat cushion, knowing she'd have to hide her UniTab at any second. Dan wrote back:

"*Her aunt sold a patent to the JTID, and guess what? She was killed in a car accident a week later.*"

Diaz stared at the message, putting the pieces to the jigsaw puzzle together in her head. She'd always wondered about Ellie's ties to Virginia's ex-capital city, and Dan's last message brought up so many new inquiries.

"What ya reading?" Ronson asked as soon as she got off her call.

Diaz hid her UniTab. "Oh, it's nothing ... My neighbor's obsessed with that old show, *Friends*, and I made the mistake of pretending to like it too. Now he keeps sending me clips."

Ronson pretended to gag. "Can they retire that show to the trash, already?"

"So, we do have something in common," Diaz laughed, trying to forget about what she'd read.

"I guess so."

A sour vinegar taste rose into her esophagus as they zipped around corners through the torrential weather. She tended to get car sick and

Dan's new intel wasn't helping to calm the Chinese takeout rumbling in her stomach. Ronson went on and on about their future while she pretended to listen.

"We can start in Portugal and Spain and then go farther east." The vehicle made an abrupt stop when someone jumped out into the road. Ronson was unfazed, asking, "Doesn't that sound nice?"

Not able to hold it in any longer, Diaz prompted a screen to release an aluminum bag and threw up the veggie dumplings eaten too fast. With her eyes sweating and full of twinkling stars, she tossed the bag into a handy trash receptacle.

"Well, at least now I know what you think of our future together," Ronson said with a pout.

"It's not you, Marty."

Ronson pulled away. "It's that goddamn case, isn't it?"

"Someone murdered them."

"If you keep following this case, you're going to end up dead too. Who knows what fucked up rabbit hole these hackers sent us down? That lazy ass president of ours is now talking about bringing in the KOA to find the Light Keepers, and for all we know, it was them who infiltrated the Army and our little task force."

"Doesn't it make you the least bit curious?"

Not willing to look at her any longer, Ronson replied, "Don't expect me to come to your funeral."

"I'm sorry, Marty," Diaz said as the Automated arrived at their destination, "I can't put my blinders on just yet."

"Fine," Ronson groaned. "Let's just take care of the task at hand, and then we can part ways."

CHAPTER 29

With a storm raging outside, Sandy paced between the kitchen and the office of their condo, sipping on a half glass of pinot noir to calm her nerves. She worried that the intensifying lightning would cause a power outage. While James lay in the DreamCatcher, she imagined a death row electrocution like she'd seen in school. She recalled Nera's assurance that the backup generator would prevent any brain damage, but every blast of thunder made her second guess any absolute.

Sandy was well aware of her husband's planned rendezvous with the mysterious Eleonora, who according to a Lucidity gossip site had used the system to gain her fortune and popularity. She couldn't figure out why this Eleonora was helping out James of all people. But caught in her own spiderweb of lies, it grew harder for her to criticize her husband's search. With that thought, she finished her tiny amount of wine, waiting for the thunderstorm to end and James to be done.

When her door buzzer rang, Sandy practically jumped out of her slippers. The screens showed two women in military uniform in her lobby, requesting approval to come up. She had a feeling her aiding and abetting a wanted terrorist had finally caught up to her. Between Kalen and Mahoe, the fake monk she'd yet to tell James about, she was in deep with the Light Keepers.

"Who is it?" Sandy asked through the touch screen.

"We're detectives from the United States Army," said one of the women. "This is the Grady residence, correct?"

"It is ..." she answered. "What's this about?"

"We wanted to talk to your husband about his father, Jim Grady."

Sandy buzzed them in, relieved they weren't there for her, but now concerned for a different reason. *This can't be good*, she thought. She used the Lucidity app on her UniTab to wake up James, but her message was immediately returned: *"The user is not active in Lucidity."* She tried again and got the same result. When the soldiers knocked on her front door, Sandy hid the bottle of wine and wiped the slight purple stain from her upper lip before opening up.

"Hello, ma'am," the taller woman began in a southern accent. "I'm Detective Ronson and this is Detective Diaz, and like I said we're here on behalf of the United States Army. May we have a word with your husband?"

"Give me one second." Sandy signaled to the detectives that she'd be right back.

In the office, James was still passed out in the DreamCatcher, but his numbers had spiked since she'd last checked on him. Sandy shot a message to Nera in the hopes of her assistance, but it was also returned with an auto-response: *"Sorry I'm not available,"* it said. *"Doin' my thing in Lucidity at the moment."* Sick of lying, Sandy decided to tell the truth for once.

Sandy returned to the living room. "My husband's in Lucidity right now and I don't know how to get him out." The two detectives understood.

Ronson seemed preoccupied with her UniTab. "We can wait a few minutes."

At first, Sandy didn't understand why they were there until she saw the grimace on Detective Diaz's face – a somber expression she recognized from her years of bereavement counseling.

"Please tell me what's going on?"

Detective Ronson said, "We should wait for your husband, Dr Grady."

"I'm a clinical psychologist so it may be easier if I know what to expect."

The detectives gazed at each other and Detective Diaz sighed, addressing her more formally. "The Secretary of the Army has asked us to wish her deepest regret that your father-in-law, former Sergeant Jim Grady, was killed in direct action as a result of the Last War."

Hearing the news felt like being shot in the chest. James was going to be devastated, Sandy thought, already anticipating his reaction. There was never a perfect euphemism for the situation so she braced herself for a long night ahead, already in the reconstruction phase, trying to skip ahead a few steps to stay ahead of her husband's emotions. Caught up in her thoughts, Sandy didn't realize her light brown skin had turned completely white.

"Are you feeling okay?" Detective Diaz asked. "Maybe you'd like to sit down?"

When Sandy excused herself to check on her husband's vitals, Detective Diaz followed close behind. The two women stood over James, motionless in the DreamCatcher, the top half of his head covered by the visor. The detective, seeming uncomfortable in her uniform, gazed around the room at all the components of Lucidity.

"How does he like the system?" she asked, obviously trying to deflect from the seriousness of the situation. "I've been thinking about checking it out myself."

Sandy tried to hold back the tears. "I don't know how I'm going to tell him," she murmured. "James was obsessed with his father."

Diaz pulled Sandy farther into the office and out of her partner's sight, whispering, "I remember the emails Grady used to get from his kids. They called him Pops, right?"

"You knew James's father?"

The detective nodded. "I was with Sergeant Grady for almost five years," she said. "We called him BlueJay in our unit, but since I never had a dad, I always considered him my Pops too." The detective's shoulders hung low, her eyes glassy. "I never got a chance to tell him that."

"I'm sure James would love to hear some stories," Sandy told the detective, comforted by the presence of someone who wasn't a stranger anymore. "But if you're thinking about investing in Lucidity, be wary of the many glitches." She showed the detective the app. "This Emergency message system doesn't seem to work, so I don't know if I'll be able to get him out anytime soon."

Out of the corner of her eye, Sandy noticed the satchel at the far end of her husband's desk. She had glanced at the redacted cables and top-secret zip drives a couple of times – they were confidential and hardly the topic she wanted to discuss with the two military officials in her home. When Diaz was distracted, Sandy hid the leather bag in the closet, but turning back around she realized the detective had found something else.

"Holy shit!" Diaz showed Sandy a polaroid that was on the floor. "This was my twenty-first birthday. Sergeant Grady knew I was missing my friends and family back home so he threw me a party." The woman had aged but her smile was the same. "This is so random."

After the week Sandy was having, nothing seemed random anymore. "James is searching for his father in Lucidity." She forgot that wine, or at least the psychosomatic effect of it, acted as a truth serum. She grabbed the satchel back out of the closet and dropped it down on the desk. "This is the only thing Jim Grady left behind for his kids."

Detective Diaz glanced over the contents of the folder, pulling out a couple of the redacted reports. "This is some serious shit in here," she whispered. "When did you get this?"

"Maybe like a month ago. I don't want James to be in any trouble, though."

Diaz assured her that nobody was getting turned in and that she'd spent the last three weeks on the outside searching for Sandy's father-in-law and two others. She told her, "I know your husband was searching for him because we ran across someone who'd met him along the way."

"I guess James always suspected foul play," Sandy sighed. "But why are you here instead of at his mother's house?"

Diaz explained the formal death notification for James was her idea, only sanctioned by the Army at her request. "As far as I know, the service officers were sent to Ms. Grady's house this morning, but she wouldn't come to the door. Which is why we are handing over the flag and death certificate to his son."

Sandy smirked. "That sounds like Mary, but there's one thing I don't understand."

"What is it?"

"You said Jim Grady was killed in the Last War, but according to my knowledge he'd retired well before that began."

"I think my sergeant – your father-in-law – was more mixed up in government affairs after his time in the Army than when he was in." Diaz pointed out James. "And your husband might not be far off in his hunch about Lucidity, since much of our investigation has centered on BCI."

From the living room, Ronson shouted, "Everything okay in there?" With her footsteps heading toward the office, Sandy grabbed the stack of files off the desk and hid them in the closet. When Ronson came in, she said, "Let me know if Adriana is asking too many questions."

"Your partner has been nothing but helpful." Sandy closed the closet door. "We were waiting to see if my husband was coming out anytime soon."

Ronson stared at James in the DreamCatcher. "Can't you just unplug the damn thing? That's what I did when my kids would get sucked into one of their video games."

"I'm afraid it doesn't work that way." Sandy checked on her husband's vitals. His heart rate was above normal so she sent one last message: *Please come home.* Again, it came back with the same response. "It may be best if I tell him myself. The ejection process is like waking up from a dream. In my field, we refer to it as a reverie or a hypnagogic state, and the side effects of Lucidity can make them much worse."

Ronson smacked her lips, boasting, "I told my partner there was something off about this system." She composed herself, returning to a more formal tone. "Please send your husband our condolences."

"Thank you." Sandy walked the detectives out. Detective Ronson, despite her southern charm, seemed eager to get the hell out of there, while Diaz kept a good distance behind.

"This isn't over yet," Diaz whispered when her partner was out the door. "Grady was a good man, and I know that man adored his family, so whatever happened to him was not by his choice." She sent a message to Sandy's Uni. "That's my contact information for when you're ready to talk some more."

"And you're sure he's dead?" Sandy asked.

Diaz grabbed her umbrella and nodded. "I saw it with my own two eyes."

When the detectives left, Sandy felt like she'd been hit by an emotional hurricane. Her mind picked up the rubble as the real storm grew to its finale – golf ball-sized hail beating on the panoramic windows. After hours of thunder, she'd grown used to the storm noise, but when she turned around and saw James, who'd entered as silent as a ghost, Sandy almost pissed her pants.

"Damn, you scared me," she shrieked, her hand on her chest.

"Are you okay?" James curiously peered around the condo. "You kept sending me messages and then I thought I heard voices on my transition back home."

"Do you want to have a seat on the couch?"

"I've been sitting for the last four hours."

"Right."

"What is it?"

"There were two detectives here from the Army who confirmed

that your father ..." Sandy paused, trying to finish her sentence without any emotion. "They said that your father did in fact die ten years ago."

"I know."

James now took a seat on the couch, sounding relieved as Sandy stood over him, fixing his messy hair that needed a trim. His eyes gazed at the wall. "And I know what you're thinking," he continued. "You're probably trying to figure out what stage of grief I'm in, but I've been in acceptance of this inevitable for a long time." He pulled Sandy in and wrapped his arms around her to kiss the top of her head. "I'll tell you everything in the morning – as soon as I cancel Lucidity."

James stood up and headed to bed, clearly having figured out some revelation in that same system.

When the storm outside eased off, the condo seemed incredibly quiet, leaving Sandy with nothing but thoughts racing through her mind. She stared at the detective's contact information, more interested than ever in the father-in-law she'd never met. James had found his closure – or at least made a giant head start in that direction – as soon as Sandy was finally understanding the allure of Jim Grady.

VIII
PART EIGHT

CHAPTER 30

James woke up cold and damp, gasping for oxygen in their queen-sized bed.

For a week straight he'd had the same nightmare of the drowning girl and the tsunami wave, always ending in him being injected with a syringe. At some point, he thought he'd get lucid, that he'd know it wasn't real and be able to change the circumstances, but they always came as the same two-for-one-special like a movie he'd seen a thousand times. The waves in the ocean were pixelated, he remembered. There were thick wires suction-cupped to his skin in the basement laboratory. Too surreal to be a vivid memory.

In a foggy haze, James picked himself up out of bed, rinsed the night sweats off in the shower and forced himself to get dressed. On days like those, he'd usually call his sponsor, who'd give him practical wisdom on interpreting wild dreams and other nonsense. But Tomás was dead, and now, according to the death certificate sitting on their dinner table, so was Pops.

The last month had been a series of surreal incidences. James desperately wanted to discuss it with Sandy but she had an unexpected meeting with her *friends* – their codeword for the Feds. With the search over, he couldn't figure out what to do with his idle time. There was only one friend left to turn to.

"Good morning, Ginger," he said.

"It's close to two in the afternoon." She never reciprocated the love, always quick to point out his human error. "What can I assist you with?"

"I'm trying to figure out what I should do today?"

"Well, James, judging by your sleep scores and blood pressure, exercise would be good for you." She sighed. "It *is* seventy-eight and sunny – the perfect day to go outside for a run."

It irked him when Ginger gave him healthy options as if Sandy had reprogrammed her, and even though Lucidity suggested an exercise regimen to make up for the fatigue, he'd yet to follow through. He stared down at his stomach, which was growing at the same rate as his pregnant wife's, and decided to heed his synth's suggestion. Yearning for the fresh air and a change of perspective, he pulled out the skateboard Pops gave to him as a kid and took it for a spin.

The streets of western Queens hustled with people, either taking advantage of the ideal spring weather or cleaning up after the devastating storm. He rode up Vernon Boulevard, and distracted by the music in his ears, ended up three miles from home in Astoria Park. The salty air emanating from the East River reminded him of the artificial paradise Simon had named the Retreat, and the million other questions he'd never asked the trillionaire.

As he rode past a group of school children, he caught a whiff of the sparklers their teacher must've handed out. The scent of sulfur and charcoal reminded him of summer, or more precisely, one particular 4th of July.

James was twelve years old or so, and Pops was home that year – the scent of fireworks and burnt cheeseburgers in the backyard. His mother was scrambling to maintain the grill as his sisters ran through the house with sparklers. Mary yelled, "Will you girls bring those outside?" Ignoring the chaos, young James sat in the den reading his book on the fundamentals of chess.

"Since when did you become interested in that?" his father asked, standing in the doorway with his usual Bullet Rye on the rocks. He'd had a bit more than usual that afternoon. "You never seemed to care when your old man suggested it."

"My history teacher said it's the game of life," James told Pops, who stumbled in and studied the pieces left on the shallow oak coffee table.

Pops pointed to the king and queen that had set up the checkmate. "That's the billionaire and the bureaucrat," he began. "All the other pieces represent the social hierarchy, and the board itself is the world that those two drunkenly trample over to get whatever they fancy."

"So, my teacher was right?" James wasn't sure what his father was getting at, more worried about his first pube coming in than some existential crisis – another new concept he had learned about.

"This is a goddamn strategy session for war," Pops said. "The game we pawns play is right on that shelf over there."

Pops had never sounded so grim, his eyelids swinging low onto his upper cheeks, pointing to a dusty board game that hadn't been pulled out from its cardboard container in years. *CHUTES AND LADDERS.* He unfolded the plastic board, a colorful cartoon trail lined with poorly drawn boys and girls in precarious situations.

"Imagine this game on a grander scale," his father mumbled. "We all start down here." He pointed to the first spot, a little girl gardening. "We try to get to that one-hundredth spot and win that blue ribbon." Pops pointed to a boy who'd broken a window. "We work and fight and get knocked back down because in life there are a lot more chutes than ladders."

Twelve-year-old James was over halfway to the finish line when he landed on one chute after the next. His father never landed on one, methodically flicking the arrow the entire game.

James yelled, "You're cheating!"

Pops laughed as he sucked down the rest of his bourbon in one sip. "Son, there's nothing in the rules about how to flick the arrow," he argued. "If the system's broken, then it's your job to fix that fucking system."

"So what's the difference between this and chess?"

"Who said there was a difference?" Pops laughed, already drunk by three in the afternoon. "Life is a war and we're all fucking screwed unless we find a new strategy. Your only job in this world, James, is to leave it in a better place than it was." He sighed and shook his head. "Or at least that's what I romanticized."

The memory was so vivid, and although not the best one of Pops – agitated and tired – it was an accurate representation of how his father had been from then until the day he disappeared. James felt himself becoming that way too, surprised he even noticed the children laughing and playing in the park. After weeks of being too paranoid to leave his condo by himself, convinced there was a hooded man following him, he had an epiphany of how to end all the nonsense for good.

Too impatient and out of shape to skate back home, James summoned an Automated, and in less than ten minutes he was back in his condo, preparing to cancel Lucidity and burn the satchel Pops had left behind. With those two enablers out of his life, he could move on. There was only one problem. James didn't know where he'd put the satchel.

From what he could remember, it was sitting on the corner of his desk – but now it was gone. In a panicked frenzy, he began checking every corner of his condo. He rummaged through the closets. Checked underneath the beds and inside the pantries. He even tried the freezer in case he'd put it there while sleepwalking, which had happened several times during his spout of recurring dreams. It didn't matter what James planned on doing next because all the files – the same ones Simon warned could be treacherous in the wrong hands – were nowhere to be found.

CHAPTER 31

After stepping off a train in Bushwick, Sandy followed the GPS on her UniTab to an aging brick apartment complex. One of the few structures left from the twentieth century that hadn't been fully renovated. It was her first of two stops before actually heading to the hospital that day. She walked up five flights of stairs, a task she hadn't accomplished in forever, and knocked on an unfamiliar door. In her arms she carried the satchel Jim Grady left behind.

Detective Diaz opened up. "Hello, Dr Grady," she said, glancing around the hallway and seeming confused. "I didn't expect to see you today."

"I'm sorry if I'm interrupting anything," Sandy said. "Your address was in the contact info you gave me and I felt like this was a sensitive matter that needed to be handled in person."

"Of course." Diaz invited Sandy in. Her apartment was more modern than its exterior implied and so was the detective herself. She had welcoming dimples and a gentle demeanor, now in workout clothes rather than a military uniform. "Some tea, Dr Grady?" Diaz asked.

"No, thanks, and you can call me Sandy if you'd like."

Heading to the kitchen, Diaz smiled. "My real name's Adriana, but I prefer Diaz." She brought out her cup of steaming tea. "The only people who call me by my first name are my angry ex-lovers and my mother."

"So, like the partner I met last night ... *Ronson*?"

Diaz took a seat and nodded. "I forgot you're a psychologist. Did you figure that out using your psychoanalysis skills? "

"Well, she called you Adriana and I'm pretty she's not your mother ... So what happened between you two?"

"I decided to keep working on this case."

Hearing the detective's words made Sandy second-guess her agenda. "Maybe I should take a step back myself," she said. "I all but forced my husband to give up his investigation."

Diaz eyed the satchel. "So then what made you change your mind?"

"My husband spent ten years searching for his father and he deserves some answers. She added, "And now I'm curious myself."

"Then I guess we're in business."

"I guess so."

"You do understand that I'm not working for the Army or the task force anymore?" Diaz said. "They sent us to find out if Sergeant Grady was dead or not, but I'm trying to figure out who killed him." When Sandy asked if it was a murder, the detective said the circumstances leading up to their deaths seemed pre-meditated – how they'd been forced onto a bus by an unknown black ops group that was hard to identify during that chaotic period. "They were sent on that bus to die."

"So, can I trust you with these?" Sandy placed the satchel on a coffee table in the middle of Diaz's living room. "Like I said last night, I'm not exactly sure what's on all these old flash drives and papers, and I kinda want them out of my home. I don't even need to know what the JTID is and I'm not sure I want to find out."

Sandy heard a toilet flush and a young man stepped out of the bathroom. "Justifiable Technology-based Interrogation Design," he said in a British accent. He was thin, oddly dressed, and carried a portable SYNCDIN device. "It's where this BCI all started, or so we thought." His bright green eyes scrambled through invisible files she couldn't see, never glancing at her once as he rambled on about the history of the group, adding that Jim Grady played some intricate role for the military contractor. "It was quite hard digging up any information on the group, but I believe they stole the coding from a neuroscientist in Richmond."

Diaz cleared her throat. "This is my neighbor, Dan – kind of a hacker for historical records and other useless information."

"First off, there's no such thing as useless information." Dan pulled off the glasses and gazed at Sandy before looking away. "Furthermore, knowing our history is key to not repeating our previous mistakes."

When the young man finished, Diaz signaled to Sandy to come in the kitchen, whispering, "Dan's a freelance coder who works for some of the biggest corporations – UniCorp and SYNCDIN to name a few – but he does some info-mining on the side."

"Isn't that illegal?"

"Yeah, but sometimes we have to break the rules to find what we're looking for." Diaz finished her tea and added, "That's why he's been so helpful with this investigation."

Dan had snuck into the kitchen, uninvited. "And what I do is only half illegal."

"This is a serious situation," Sandy told him. "My father-in-law went missing ten years ago and my husband almost died looking for him. He went as far as to search for him in Lucidity."

"Brilliant!" the young man shouted. "What an interesting scenario!"

"An interesting scenario?" Sandy said. "His father's dead!"

Diaz shook her head, covering her face as if her neighbor had made the same mistake before. "Speaking of learning from the past ..."

"Oh right," Dan said. "I apologize, ma'am. I'm simply curious to know why your husband would be searching for him in Lucidity?"

"I think it had something to do with this." Sandy looked through the satchel, pulling out a document her husband had written on, circled with a highlight marker reading: "*J8Y19B1RdM.LXxx*." "That's the avatar he's searching for."

Taking the piece of paper, Dan was quiet for a moment, clearly deep in thought. "I'll have to ask my girlfriend for her help, but I may have an idea on how to locate him in the system, or at the very least, where this particular avatar is hiding."

"My husband already tried that," Sandy insisted. "He's been using the system for almost a month."

Dan smirked. "Trust me, there are better ways to find things as long as you don't ask too many questions."

Doubtful, Sandy turned to Diaz, who admitted, "Like it or not, Dan usually finds what he's looking for. Isn't that what James deserves?"

Sandy pushed the satchel toward Diaz and the strange young man, symbolically giving up ownership. "Here's a question for you." Sandy now addressed Dan. "What are your thoughts on Lucidity?"

"The potential benefits of BCI could be astronomical if used justly," Dan said, "but the fact that they're using the technology to build this massive metaverse is extremely irresponsible." Still focused on the username, he added, "Of course, my girlfriend thinks it's the best thing that's happened since sliced bread."

"My husband quit the system this morning. I know he made some friends in there, but I'd rather not worry about it anymore."

Dan barked a laugh. "Lucky for you." He began poking through the satchel and his eyes lit up. "This is a gold mine!" He pulled out zip drives and confidential cables. "You sure you don't mind if I have a look at this?"

"It's all yours," Sandy said. "I have to meet with the Feds after this, so I planned on leaving it all here anyway."

Her next stop that morning was at the FBI headquarters in Manhattan at the request of Agent Miller, but without thinking, Sandy had unintentionally outed herself to the two.

Dan stepped back, now analyzing her every move. Even Diaz seemed caught off-guard by her admission.

"I'm just a lowly informant," Sandy explained. "Unless you're a Light Keeper, this satchel has nothing to do with the case I'm part of." She didn't know what the Feds wanted with her but she assured them,

"This has nothing to do with either of you."

The young man was about to leave when Diaz shouted, "Dan, wait!" The detective held up the satchel to him. "I know you're curious."

"But I've already said too much." Dan was already halfway out the door. "Why should I trust you, Dr Grady?"

Sandy stood up and approached him. She pleaded, "For the same reason I'm putting this confidential information into the hands of a detective I barely know and a stranger I only met ten minutes ago."

"The Army or my task force can't find out about these continuing investigations," Diaz insisted.

Sandy turned to Diaz. "Do you think I'm going to turn you in? I'm stuck here in this duplicitous position where I seem to be lying to everyone including my husband. I want to find the answers like the both of you."

While the two strangers now huddled in a corner trying to decide how to handle the precarious situation Sandy had put them in, an alarm went off on her UniTab, reminding her of the meeting she had to leave for. If they didn't take the folder, she wasn't sure what to do with it.

Diaz stepped forward. "Jim Grady was a good father who got mixed up in a bad mess," she said. "If they killed him, it was because he knew what they were doing was wrong."

"Seems like you've been searching for him for a while now too."

Diaz shook her head. "I guess not long enough."

CHAPTER 32

A half an hour later, Sandy checked in at the FBI headquarters in midtown Manhattan. Despite the fact she'd never been there before, it seemed unusually hectic for a Wednesday afternoon. Everyone scurried around in a dizzying scene of choreographed commotion as if something big were going down. With one minute left until the debriefing, she hurried through the floor traffic that ran like a neighborhood without stop signs. She wiped the sweat off her chest, took a second to compose herself, and entered the conference room where the informants were supposed to meet. She was told there'd be a small group of five or ten others, but when she arrived it was only her.

She received a message from Agent Miller: "*Have a seat and we'll be right there.*"

Sandy complied, sifting through her detailed reports, trying to figure out what the agent might be interested in. She'd taken a more rushed approach with the patients the Feds sent her, now subconsciously leading them into incriminating themselves. She remembered Mahoe coming into the hospital two days earlier, dragging her out during a false intruder warning, and blackmailing her for FBI intel.

It almost felt like a dream, but it wasn't. They must've been on to her. With that migraine-inducing thought running through Sandy's head, Agent Miller came in with the director of the FBI, Gerald Zin, following right behind. *Well shit*, Sandy thought. She'd been warned that he only visited New York for important matters, and she found herself gripping the arms of the chair to hide her shaky hands.

"Nice to see you again, Dr Grady." Zin had a business-like tone, a five o'clock shadow, and a damp unbuttoned shirt, fidgeting on a device like a typical Xer without a clue. He gave it to Miller to figure out. With a sly smile, the agent pulled up a picture of Kalen Green on a hologram receiver. The image of his husband's counselor spun in a three-hundred-and-sixty-degree profile like a Baroque bust statue. Zin asked, "Care to explain why you never told us that you had ties to this suspect?"

Pretending to act coy, Sandy said, "She was my husband's counselor at the NA meetings – anonymous being the keyword. He was devastated when he found out she was part of this cult."

Cracking his knuckles, Zin asked, "And when were you going to tell us this?"

"Today," she declared, her grip on the chair growing tighter. "I thought it'd be best to go over with everyone else around."

After slamming his fist on the table, Zin attempted to control his temper. "Dr Grady, Kalen Green is at the top of our suspect list and you didn't think to mention that important piece of information as soon as you found out?"

"Well, I—"

Before letting Sandy answer, Zin rambled on about how "every second was important in catching the Light Keepers," hinting that the agency had gotten wind of some sort of attack. He'd come from California, more specifically the American LucidiTech headquarters, to meet with her. "So, I assume your husband met Ms. Green at one of her meetings here in the city?"

"It was actually in Montauk." Sandy already wished she'd lied again. "He had a slip in his sobriety and was lucky to have run into her that night."

Zin seemed to have an epiphany, barking orders at the agent. "Miller, go see if the suspect has any other ties to Montauk," he demanded. "That's one of the few places that hasn't come up yet." He turned back toward Sandy. "That woman got around like a groupie at an EDM festival, if you know what I mean?"

More concerned with keeping her own hands clean, Sandy laughed along at his cringe-worthy comment. She watched Agent Miller address the other agents about the Montauk revelation through the windows of the conference room. They all marched back to their desks with a new mission, now at an even crazier pace than when Sandy came in. Meanwhile, Director Zin remained silent, either pissed off at her or contemplating his next action.

"I don't understand what's going on." Sandy straightened her posture. "Am I in trouble?"

Zin crossed his arms before speaking. "I wish you would have given us this information earlier. We have intel that leads us to believe that the Light Keepers meet outside of the system or in an underground spot within Lucidity to cover all their tracks. I'm not sure if your husband stumbled onto an NA meeting or a covert planning session." He wondered, "Did he mention the other attendees when he met Kalen in Montauk?"

In hindsight, what James stumbled onto that night at the beach hadn't sounded like a meeting to Sandy. Her husband didn't remember much, but he'd told her of a bonfire and some deep philosophical conversations in progress. Of course, there was no need to mention that to the director of the FBI.

"My husband, pushed over the edge by his new in-laws, was pretty hammered when he met Kalen," Sandy admitted. "All I know is she talked him off a cliff and he hasn't fallen off the wagon since. I guess her compassion is what makes her so alluring."

"And also what makes her so fucking dangerous," Zin countered, now up and pacing the room. "Miller told you what happens to their victims."

"So, was Xavier Cortez a victim or a suspect?" Sandy asked, still angry about the old man's sudden death. "Because it seems like the people you're calling Light Keepers are the ones who keep dying."

"Let me tell you something, Dr Grady." Zin got up in her face.

"We've had our eyes on the Light Keepers for a few years now, and sure, most of their messages sound like the typical enlightenment bullshit, but what's frightening is how they've mobilized under our radar." His breath was far worse than the rotten onion stench of his armpits. "In case you don't remember, there was also that little movement called the Free Folk, which most people disregarded for years, claiming it was only the Russians and their allies until they began corrupting our own citizens." With a fierce grimace, he added, "Their followers, too, became the victims when they died in that unnecessary war. They ended up losing to two things they didn't believe in – science and reason."

He was right, Sandy thought. When the Second Pandemic of the 21st century hit, a virus spread from a thawed-out saber-toothed tiger, and everyone in the world was told to stay inside for a couple of weeks. Calling it a hoax and ignoring emergency protocol, the Free Folk ended up killing half of their soldiers by ignoring the warnings. It was the second time they didn't heed the scientists' warnings. Once the virus was eradicated, the KOA swooped in and forced their surrender.

Pulling Zin's foot out of her mouth, Sandy said, "I guess I never thought about that way."

"I guess you didn't."

Agent Miller rushed back into the room frantic, only gone for a matter of minutes. "She has a son who lives in Snug Harbor." She tried to catch her breath. "It's the fringe town on the outside of Montauk."

"I know where Snug Harbor is," Zin huffed, his cheeks still flush. "There's no way she could make it through one of our checkpoints."

"Sir, our security firewalls haven't been bulletproof lately," Miller reminded him. "We should authorize a SWAT team."

"Do you mind if I give the fucking orders?" Zin shouted. "You may be in charge here in New York, but I still get the final say, and in case you don't recall, a raid means we'd have to bring in the KOA."

"You're right," Miller agreed, bowing her head to him. "We don't need those black-op assholes involved."

Zin took a sip of water. "I'd prefer we have a chance to capture Ms. Green on our own rather than the way they do things."

"That's a great idea, sir."

"Now go get the team up to speed and find out if she's even in Snug Harbor before you come at me with any more of that SWAT team bullshit."

Sandy, perched low in her chair after witnessing Miller get a taste of Zin's halitosis, also realized how high up on the food chain Miller was. Now alone with the man who'd been all over the news lately, her palms callused from gripping the chair so tight, she asked, "Is there anything else?"

"Actually, yeah." Zin twiddled his fingers with an idea. "See if you can pick your husband's brain more about the night he met Kalen." Right before she was about to leave, he whistled. "Make it subtle ... We don't need anyone else to know how serious this is." With that, he shooed her away, already on another call.

Sandy left, dashing to the closest restroom, feeling like she'd held her breath for a good ten minutes, every day anticipating her arrest. She found her only privacy in a toilet stall once again, the perfect space for her to finally exhale. When Sandy was about to leave, someone barged into the bathroom and she froze.

"I need to see if anyone's in here," Agent Miller said, speaking to someone on her UniTab, thinking she was alone.

Not wanting to draw attention to herself, Sandy kept quiet in the closed stall, which appeared to be vacant since the door remained unlocked. The agent walked lightly, her short heels clicking on the porcelain tiles.

"Aright, the coast is clear," Miller said as if she were on a discreet call. "It looks like Kalen's probably hiding out in Snug Harbor." She paused to listen to whoever was on the other side of the conversation as

Sandy held in a sneeze. Miller laughed. "Friday sounds perfect ... It's time to make this shit finally happen." The agent's heels clicked again on the floor and she was gone.

Sandy waited almost ten minutes before peeking out of the stall to see if it was clear, making a swift exit. On the main floor, everyone was back behind their desks, presumably mining clues to figure out where Kalen was. The Feds were getting warm even as Agent Miller seemed to be plotting her actions with someone else.

CHAPTER 33

It was dark and cold. James lay in a fetal position, half awake under a fortress of blankets and pillows, thinking about the dream he couldn't seem to shake. In the new version of it that morning, when he heard the little girl drowning in the distance, her scream was louder than before. When he saved her, he kept going higher and higher over the colossal wave, flying through it. They seemed to be getting away. He recalled soaring through the puffy clouds, but as always, the two of them ended up back in the laboratory and the dream ended in the same misfortune. Still exhausted, he was about to fall back asleep when a melody forced him to pull the covers off his head.

"*Happy birthday to you,*" Sandy sang with a better-than-average voice she always shied away from. She sat beside him holding a cupcake with a candle in it, finishing, "*Happy birthday to you!*"

"Is it really my birthday?" James shielded his bloodshot eyes from the bright room, blowing out the tiny flame to be nice.

"Babe, it's June 9th." Sandy placed her fist up to his mouth like it was a microphone. "You're thirty-two years old, Mr. Gemini." She used her deepest voice. "*What are your thoughts on going into this next period of life?*"

Pulling the covers over his head, he groaned. "No comment."

"It's time to wake up, old man." She ripped them back off, leaving him half-naked, covered in sweat and goosebumps. "Did you have the dream again?"

Blushing, James nodded. "Got any more advice on how to stop them?" he asked. "Nothing's working."

"They'll go away as soon as all this stress clears." Sandy handed him a towel. "We'll start with this whole day of fun I have planned for you if that's okay?"

James nodded again, forcing a smile. "I'll adhere to the good doctor's orders."

After a hectic week, he finally had a chance to tell her about Simon, kindly leaving out the gratuitous details of NuAmsterdam and the fact that Simon was an anonymous trillionaire.

Meanwhile, Sandy had handed over his father's satchel. "Diaz will take care of it from here on out," she'd told him the day before. "By next week we'll both be out of this rabbit hole."

While initially upset, James had realized it was best if he had no say in the matter. As long as the files remained in their condo he'd keep digging until those goddamned bones were found. They'd made plans to tell his mother and sister in person. It was well past time for Jim Grady to receive a proper burial.

Still lying in bed, James said, "Today is the first day of the rest of my life."

"Oh yeah?" Sandy quipped, already getting ready for their day.

"That's right." James got up and pulled her back onto the bed. "Pops always used that quote." He gazed at the wall, remembering the worst day of his life. "My father said you can let the inevitable experiences of your past get you down, or simply realize that you get another morning to live. Those who die don't get to do that anymore, so never take that luxury for granted."

Sandy gripped his hands tight like she now understood. "Apparently, your father was a very profound man."

"I'm done with that, though." James hopped out of bed and shouted, "Today is the first day of the rest of *both* of our lives!"

As much as he repeated it back to Sandy and himself, it couldn't dilute the dark cloud lingering over him, or that wretched feeling he had once again. His wife had helped the most wanted person in the world escape. He had put compromising flash drives into the Cloud during a period of heightened cyber-security. He found out that the AFANET he'd been accessing was basically the dark web. Meanwhile, an optimistic Sandy said they'd be out of the rabbit hole by next week. That still felt light-years away to him.

As they left their building that morning, on a walk to one of Sandy's surprise destinations, James's paranoia set back in. He had the sensation that someone followed them. He bent down, pretending to tie his shoe, and turned his neck to get a peek behind. Sure enough, a man in a hoodie crept in the distance, dodging James's eye contact. The man hid his face with a mask and sunglasses, which wasn't unheard of, but it was way too warm for a sweatshirt. Catching up with his wife, James chalked it up to his tendency to sabotage the calmer days. *It's all in your head*, he thought. When James turned around again, the man was gone.

Sandy had led him to one of his favorite spots in the city, the Court Square Diner. It rested underneath the subway tracks of LIC and reminded James of a New York that once existed. He hadn't been there since his last meet-up with Tomás, and it had been renovated since. When they entered, a drone host sat them in a booth. Holographic menus popped up in front of them. Although it still had that same scent of bacon, pancakes, and coffee, the size of the staff had dropped drastically. His wife was in awe of the updates. James wasn't a fan.

"This is great," he lied, hiding his cringe, sifting the menu to tap in his order. "What else do you have planned?"

Sandy's eyes lit up. "We're going to take the Lux-ferry to Manhattan, hit Central Park before the shadows take over, and check out this Electro-Jazz band I think you'll like. But first I wanted you to start the day off with your favorite breakfast sandwich ... What's it called again?"

Before James could answer, another surprise awaited him. "Georgie!" he shouted as a slim older gentleman approached. The man had gray bushy brows, a crooked smile, and the nice kind of wrinkles

James hoped to have one day. Georgie had been a server for sixty-plus years and loved every moment of it.

James said, "I thought for sure they fired you with all the changes they made around here."

"I own place now," the man explained in a thick Greek accent. "I save up all my money, buy diner, and upgrade to new system. Now my only job is to talk to the customers. But don't you worry, James, we still have the Queens heart attack."

James frowned. "I ordered a salad."

Pulling out his temperature scanner, Georgie asked, "Are you coming down with a new virus?" He checked his forehead. "Nope, you are like cold *angoúr*."

James pointed to Sandy. "I have to think about the future now."

The man nodded. "We are always fearful of what is to come, but we must focus on the present." Georgie smiled. "As my *pappoús* always say – *today is first day of rest of life*."

As the giddy old man left to greet some other guests, James felt the universe speaking to him over the darker energy he'd felt that morning. Georgie was right. He had to let the anxiety go and appreciate the present.

Observing him like one of her patients, Sandy insisted, "Besides the sleep issues, you're smiling a lot more since you joined Lucidity."

This has to be some sort of reverse psychology, James thought, before answering, "It's not real."

"Those avatars aren't fake, James. You know Calvin and Nera, and even that Eleonora you met is someone who exists in the real world."

Before she could finish her point, Georgie came out carrying a smaller version of the Queens Heart Attack – bacon, sausage, eggs, and potatoes in a hoagie roll, or a sub as they called it there. "I bring out half of sandwich so you can eat a small portion without becoming fat man."

James didn't have the heart to tell the old man that he hardly touched meat anymore, and right as he forced his first bite, a series of beeps flooded the diner.

BEEP... BEEP ... BEEEEEP ...

A National Emergency Alert had been issued. Georgie and the other patrons had their eyes pinned on one of the many new screens. Sandy, on the other hand, seemed preoccupied with a conversation in her ear.

"What's going on?" Sandy asked whoever she was talking to, listening for a reply. "But I don't understand." She asked Georgie to turn the volume up.

On every screen, Gerald Zin of the FBI spoke from a podium. "This morning, the Light Keepers released a new video to the public which we can only assume is a threat. We have spent months attempting to bring down this anonymous front. This dangerous organization is attempting to bring chaos to the peace we've maintained for almost five years now."

A reporter interrupted. "Is it true that you are gearing up a strategy with the Knights of Azrael?"

The FBI director seemed angered by the unsolicited question, unable to hide his dramatic sigh. "We are working with Lucid-Tech, the CTE, government officials from around the globe, and even the president has been on the phone to make sure this ends without any bloodshed." He rolled his eyes. "And yes, if the situation escalates, the KOA has been brought up to speed."

Zin shot down any further questions, continuing, more serious than ever. "We don't know the intentions of the Light Keepers or the full extent of who its members are. They could be a few underground hackers or as many as millions ready to violently flash-mob the American people. Let us not forget the T-Theory cult, or the enemies of the Last War who shall not be named, and how many of us were affected by those atrocities."

He took a deep serious breath. "We are asking everyone to go about their daily routines but to report any unusual behavior or discrepancies. You will notice more drones and safety officers in prime locations. Our main goal is to keep the peace."

Since it seemed like they'd been repeating the same thing since February, James paid no mind to the report until Sandy stared at him as if she had devastating news.

"What is it?" he asked.

"I have to go to work."

"Today?"

"Right now," Sandy sighed, keeping her voice low. "My *friends* need me to assist them with the search."

"I know you don't have a choice, but twice in three days seems unusual."

"I'll only be gone for a couple of hours." Sandy took a bite from her omelet and a quick sip from her coffee. "There's a special guest meeting you here in a couple of minutes anyway, and you know Georgie isn't going to let you out the door without a long conversation. You'll probably still be here by the time I'm done."

"I told you the Light Keepers are just trying to start some shit."

Sandy checked her UniTab, obviously annoyed with the Feds. "This doesn't seem like their MO."

James held her hands. "Should I be worried?"

Sandy grinned. "Only that you're going to eat the other half of that sandwich Georgie has in the kitchen." She gave him a kiss, grabbed her bag, and rushed out the door.

Taking a bite from his sandwich, James whispered to himself, "*Happy birthday to me.*"

CHAPTER 34

After a sweaty and cathartic jog in the heat, Diaz returned home that Friday at noon with more energy than she'd had in weeks. Her unsanctioned investigation continued even as Ronson's ultimatum weighed heavy on her conscious. Dan had taken the satchel Sandy Grady had given her, dissecting it like the best forensic pathologist in the business. It had been two days since she'd heard from her neighbor, and with her endorphins on high from the run, an impatient Diaz went up to Dan's apartment to check in.

Dan answered with a bad Italian accent, "How you doin'?" He wore boxer briefs and a stained T-shirt. "I was about to come down and confer with you." He raced to the bathroom. "Sorry, I haven't taken a piss in hours."

Inside Dan's apartment, a DreamCatcher had been installed in the middle of the living room. Outdated gadgets were scattered on his kitchen countertop alongside a plethora of stacked-up dirty dishes. Diaz was usually envious of how organized the young man was, but that day it was a mess. She tiptoed through to make sure she didn't step on anything, stumbling onto what was most likely causing her neighbor's unusual behavior. On Dan's largest screen was a digital crazy wall with hundreds of files, photos, and codes connected by zig-zagging colored lines.

When Dan came out of the bathroom, Diaz asked, "I thought your girlfriend moved in?"

"She did, but after we got into a heated argument, she spent the last two nights at one of her mate's flats."

"Probably because you installed this ugly contraption right in the middle of the living room."

Dan smirked. "Are you kidding me? She's a bloody employee of LucidiTech. She's pissed because I haven't paid attention to her since Dr Grady gave me that folder. It's scintillating!"

"I guess that explains this." Diaz pointed to the complex string theory on his wall. As a detective for the last ten years, she was used to seeing elaborate crime boards, but her neighbor's chaotic ensemble was dizzying. She could tell he hadn't slept in days. "Did you find anything on that NCU Binary I told you about?"

"It doesn't exist." Dan observed the board he'd created from afar. "LucidiTech never uses any third-party contractors or builds outside of the Interior." Using his UniTab, he zoomed in on the live satellite feed of the NCU Binary facility that Ronson and she supposedly visited. There wasn't a single car in the parking lot of the abandoned business complex. According to Dan's research, Nick Baxter was a low-level pot farmer. "It must've been hard to live in the shadow of Suzi-Q ... Like Monica Gellar must've felt with her genius brother Ross."

Diaz huffed, not only because she never thought Ross was actually a genius, but because Dan's intel had to be wrong. "And what about Ginsberg's aunt?" She pointed to her name on the board. "Do you think someone killed her for her BCI codes?"

"Well, yes and no," Dan replied. "I believe the accident wasn't an accident, but Ginsberg's aunt – we'll call her that for clarity – didn't create BCI." He stepped over an ancient iMac to get closer to the digital crazy board on the wall. "It's all in here."

"What does all this scribble have to do with the case?"

"Everything!" Dan enlarged a portion showing the elaborate coding with indecipherable letters, numbers, and symbols. "I like to consider myself an intelligent individual, but this QPL is alien to me." He tapped a finger against his chin. "I can't even figure out what kind of quantum OS is needed to run it. However, I do know how to read most of it."

Overwhelmed by the complexity, Diaz shrugged and said, "So what does this have to do with Ginsberg's aunt?"

"Let me show you." Dan scrolled over to a certain portion of the board that was a bit more decipherable, using alphabetic letters Diaz recognized. "So Ginsberg's aunt was named Roseline Baptiste, decent enough as neurology professor, but no genius." He zoomed even closer than before and it read: "*F%5S*7*." Dan explained, "This is where Farah Sylvain signed the origin of this code in 2020 – F-five, S-seven ... Farah buried her initials in the original coding."

"So what are you saying?"

Dan took a deep breath. "Farah knew someone might steal this from her, maybe even her aunt. This was her way of hiding her digital signature, so no matter where it went she would have ownership over it."

"Wait a minute," Diaz said. "Let me wrap my high school mind around this theory. So, what you're saying is that Farah changed her name to Ellie Ginsberg, went to MIT, and got recruited by the JTID, just so she could steal back her coding."

"You're more clever than you think," Dan joked. "Your vets may have stolen these from the JTID, which makes sense because Suzi-Q was notorious for that." The way her neighbor said it, he sounded in awe of the hacker, boasting about her like a famous revolutionary. "If Ellie Ginsberg is as gifted as I believe her to be, then Suzi Q and her could've been phenomenal together."

"Or dangerous." Diaz turned to her neighbor. "Did you find the picture of Suzi-Q we got in Richmond?"

"For fucks sake, you have a photograph of her?" Dan searched for it in his database. "Even when I figured out her real identity I couldn't find any images. It was like her history had been erased."

Pulling up the file from her UniTab, Diaz cued it to the screen. "That's her on the right." She pointed out the woman with the pink mohawk and tattooed face. "It's from 2032."

"It's absolutely mind-blowing how young she was when she

disappeared." Dan cropped the photo to fill the entire wall. "She could've been the GOAT."

Diaz had seen the photo a hundred times, but with it blown up large it all became clear to her. The dimple on Suzi-Q's chin. The crooked smile. The mole grazing her cheek in the middle of the heart tattoo. At that moment, Diaz realized she'd met her before.

"Holy shit!"

Dan jumped back. "Are you all right?"

"Quinn Baxter is alive!" Diaz's eyes grew wide. "She was the receptionist at the NCU Binary."

Dan scratched the patchy scruff on his chin. "You mean like that Tupac fellow?"

"Apparently." Diaz laughed at the '90s hip hop conspiracy theory. "I knew we missed something."

Dan sighed in relief. "At least I know I'm not going crazy now." He highlighted another part of the board. "I don't think she's the only one from your group who may be alive." He brought up a simple map of moving dots. "I traced the name Dr Grady gave me and found out that Jaybird character was indeed an avatar in Lucidity. Then I sent Nera in to search for him in a sector called the Void."

"Who's Nera?"

Dan mischievously raised his brows. "My girlfriend and your new neighbor."

Right as he said it, the front door slid open and a young woman came in with cloth shopping bags. "I see you're still at it." She was a small package with hip glasses, tattoos, and a mullet like all the kids of Dan's generation. The detective didn't believe his girlfriend was real until that moment.

"Nera, Diaz ... Diaz, Nera," Dan said, introducing the two. "Will you tell Diaz what you saw in Lucidity, my love?"

Before explaining, Nera rolled her eyes. "Danny sent me to find this Jaybird avatar and I ended up in some foggy corn maze. I was tripped out on this blue smoke, got super lost, and almost got suspended for going off the grid." She sat down in the DreamCatcher, finally taking a breath to relax. "I could've missed my group battle today."

"Are you really going in?" Dan seemed alarmed. "There was chatter about a Light Keeper threat on the telly this morning and you've gone in every day since you took your stay-cation."

"You're the one who sent me in yesterday." She spun in the high-tech chair. "And when I'm here you're obsessed with this case you won't tell me about. I'm not going to be your errand-runner because you're too afraid to join Lucidity."

"I don't trust it," Dan warned. "It's going to mess up that beautiful mind of yours."

"Are you kidding me, Danny?" She swung her arms open in front of his crazy board. "This is what's fucking up yours!"

As Dan pestered Nera about the side effects of her time in a sector called the Yards, she reminded him that he almost got fired for digging through confidential files. Meanwhile, Diaz meditated on her new development. *How is Suzi-Q alive?* Unless something had happened in the two-hour gap, her vets were passengers in that highway explosion.

Seeming annoyed, Nera addressed Diaz. "Look, I get that you want to find the truth, but you're digging into dangerous and illegal territory." She made her way to the bedroom. "Also, some woman followed me into the building looking for you. By the look on her face, I'd say she's in the same predicament as I am."

"Then I have to go," Diaz said, rushing out of the apartment.

Dan suggested, "We should tell Dr Grady about her father-in-law."

"Who else do you think is waiting for me downstairs?"

Diaz raced down the hallway, figuring out what she was going to say to Dr Grady. It seemed as though everyone in the building was getting themselves involved in a dangerous situation. She came down the stairs expecting her liaison. Instead, she found Marty Ronson in her hallway with a bouquet of roses, wearing a short summer dress and red lipstick.

Diaz's heart dropped into her stomach. "What are you doing here?"

"I've only been retired for two days and I'm already bored." Ronson's smile turned to a frown. "I can't get that investigation out of my mind. Like we missed one crucial detail."

"We did. Suzi-Q was the receptionist in Kansas and I don't think she's the only one still alive."

"Stop it right there!" Ronson put her finger on Diaz's lips. "The official word is that our MIAs are RIP. Whatever operation you have going on here needs to end. Security is way too high with the Light Keeper threat this morning."

"So, there was another message today?"

"Yes, and the Feds are taking this seriously."

"But you said you were bored and missed a minor detail."

Ronson dangled the flowers in her face. "I'm bored because I don't get to hang with you anymore." Her twang was on high. "And the thang I missed was not realizing how much I missed your dumb little face."

"You're so sweet," Diaz said wryly.

"You know what I mean."

Missing all the signs because of her unhealthy obsession, Diaz glimpsed herself self in the mirror, a filthy wreck that needed a shower. "Can I show you one thing?" She remembered a filter app that would digitally remove the tattoos from Suzi-Q's face. "Tell me you don't see it." It was a spitting image of Baxter's secretary.

"Holy shit!" Ronson paced the hallway to figure out some puzzle in her head. "But if that was Quinn Baxter, then why did she send us to Ohio to look for … *her?*" She folded her arms and bit her lips. "It doesn't make any fucking sense."

"And there's a possibility Jim Grady's alive as well."

"We saw the videos, Adriana. They all died on that bus!"

"The woman we spoke to the other night, his daughter-in-law, Sandy Grady, gave me a valuable lead," Diaz said. "Which reminds me that I should call her and let her know what we found."

"Jesus Christ, you got her wrapped up in this too?" Ronson sighed. "What the hell kind of trouble are you trying to cause?"

Diaz took her partner's hands and gazed longingly into her prairie green eyes, kissing her doubtful lips. "I do like you, Marty, and if this case drives you away, then it's not worth it anymore." She paused. "You say the word and I'm done."

"Well, goddamn it, Adriana," Ronson blushed. "Your passion is the reason I fell for you in the first place."

"So, you're in?" Diaz asked, inviting Ronson into her twentieth-century dump for the first time, her physical and emotional heart on the verge of being in sync for once. It was a double-barrel question waiting for a shotgun reply.

"Why not?" Ronson dropped the roses and pulled Diaz in by the hips. "Retirement's gonna be lame and depressing without you."

<u>CHAPTER 35</u>

Sitting by himself in the diner, James took another bite of the Queens Heart Attack, stress eating with his eyes glued to the news. Luckily, Georgie was always a nice distraction with a peppy spirit and a million stories. That was, until the owner mentioned Tomás.

"Where's he been? ... Mr. Tomás was the one who suggest I make this leap of faith." Right as James was about to tell him the bad news he got an alert on his UniTab. Georgie said, "That's your student, Calvin." A pair of SYNCDIN lenses popped out from the booth. When James put them on a true-to-life hologram Calvin sat opposite him. The old man was so excited about his upgrade that he sent Calvin the famous sandwich at Sandy's request. "It's *like he's in diner with* us!"

"Happy Birthday, Mr. G!" Calvin greeted him as if he were right there in the booth with him, his mouth already half full. "What are you – like, forty now?"

James chuckled. "Wait until I call you when you turn thirty-two."

"I'll still be younger than you."

James didn't laugh, but only because he'd caught a glimpse of the hooded man again, lurking on a corner outside of the diner. Whoever it was kept making brief eye contact. Finally, the man crossed the street and headed toward the E- Metro Line.

"What are you looking at, Mr. G?" Calvin asked. "I only have it set on AR mode."

"I have something I need to take care of, Calvin. How about I hit you up in a few?"

"I have to go into Lucidity soon, but I wouldn't recommend coming in today. Space Angel warned me something was going to happen."

"You mean that astronaut I keep running into?"

Signaling to him to come in closer, Calvin whispered, "She's more important than I thought – like some undercover boss or something."

"Then why are you going in today?"

"I can't miss my shift right now." Calvin put on the cockiest of grins. "My performance score is on fire!"

"Well, I'm done with Lucidity," James huffed. "In fact, I'm canceling my subscription the next chance I get."

"Did you ever find your father?"

"He's dead, Calvin."

"Oh damn!" The teenager almost choked on his sandwich. "I'm sorry, Mr. G."

"I was wasting my time all along."

James caught the hooded man once more, luring him toward the stairs of the train, literally waving him over. "I apologize, Calvin, but I really do have to run." He cut off the SYNCDIN call, took another bite of his Queens Heart Attack, and thanked Georgie, intent on finding the mysterious stranger who'd been following him all morning, and quite possibly for weeks now.

Besides the buzzing of extra drones, the Metro E platform was quieter than most Fridays. The tourist attraction lay underneath the Express – the more practical way to get around. When a high-speed flew by overhead it led James's eyes to the other platform, straight to the man in the hoodie.

From across the tracks, James yelled, "Why are you following me?"

When the stranger waved for him to come over, James rushed up and down the steps of the station, out of breath by the time he reached the other side, pointing to the sky. "I can alert one of these drones that you're stalking me."

The man didn't bother responding, pulling down his hoodie. Long black locks fell past his shoulders. When he removed his sunglasses and mask, James realized it wasn't a man at all, but someone he knew from Lucidity.

"Eleonora?"

Even without the blue skin, elf ears, and wild makeup, James recognized her androgynous cheekbones and slim nose. It was odd to see her as a dressed-down human being, especially after she pulled up her sleeves and revealed her two synthetic arms.

"Hello, Dark Cloud." Eleonora had a frail rasp that sounded nothing like her avatar counterpart. It seemed painful to speak. "It's about time I got you alone."

James asked, "What are you doing here?"

"Simon wanted me to pass on a message to you." She paced a bit, clearing her throat. "He kinda went digging through those files your father left and he found something you should see."

"Did someone break into my goddamn house?"

"Um, Simon created Alter World and the Void, so I'm pretty sure he knows his way around a backdoor firewall into your private home computer."

"What the fuck?" James lowered his voice when the few other strap hangers took notice. "Isn't that ... *illegal?*"

"First off, don't shoot the messenger." Eleonora held up her metallic hands. "Secondly, whatever your father was hanging on to must've been pretty fucking important because Simon begged me to find you. He knows I hate going out in public."

James remembered all the other times he'd seen the hooded man. "You've been following for weeks, haven't you?"

"What are you talking about, Cloud?"

"Then who was that?" ... Oh, never mind that now. Simon is just some gazillionaire who can't be bother with us peasants. He sits on some beautiful island all day, whether it's in Lucidity or the real world, and you're just one of his errand bitches."

Visibly upset by his comment, Eleonora pulled her hair up and put it in a bun, showing him another machine on her neck. "Our buddy Simon funded the project that saved millions of people like me from living in agony. This artificial thyroid is just one of his many accomplishments, and because of it, I'll soon be able to sing in the real world again." She paused to compose herself. "Go home and check those files your father left behind ... *like right now!*"

When an N train headed back home pulled into the station, James jumped on. "I don't have them anymore because he told me to destroy them." He asked, "And why should I trust you anyway?"

Eleonora stared deep into his soul. "You spent ten years searching for your father. You can't quit right when you're about to get to the end of the tunnel."

"I found the end, and there wasn't any light," he said as the doors closed and the train left the station.

When James got home, his office glowed from the morning sun, illuminating the dust bunnies drifting through the clutter. Even without Pops's files scattered around, it was a stark reminder of what a wreck he'd been for the last month. He checked his computer for viruses and any messages Simon might've sent him, but there weren't any of either. He noticed one of the flash drives blinking, still connected to the computer. Evidently, Sandy hadn't taken everything.

James opened the digital folder, bringing him back to the illegal AFANet database he'd pored over since he'd found the files. "*You have 1 new message.*" His eyes lit up, having never seen the network in live-action, knowing it must've been from Simon.

It read: "*Hello, James.*"

He scrolled down the black screen for more, but that was the extent of it.

"Hello?" James yelled it at the computer, figuring Simon must've hacked his way into the camera system too. "I know you're watching me."

His synth Ginger chimed in. "The program you're using restricts voice activation so you may have to make prompts with the keyboard."

It couldn't have been more obvious. He typed *"Hello"* and sent it out into the AFAnet, which he'd always assumed was only a collection of data. There was a ping.

"Still there, Dark Cloud?"

"Simon?"

"It's me, my boy."

"Why did you send Eleonora to find me today?"

"Someone is accessing your father's avatar again and I wanted to know if it was you."

James furiously typed in capital letters: *"I TOLD YOU I WAS DONE!"*

Simon replied, *"I had to check, but more importantly, there's a message your father tried to send me that for some reason never made it through. It might make more sense to you. Sorry for digging through your comp. An old habit of mine."*

Simon sent a link that James clicked, leading him to a plethora of unsent drafts in a folder that he'd never checked before.

Simon wrote, *"Check the one dated 1/15/2032."*

It led James to a video.

In a dimly lit bunker or basement, Pops recorded a message. He had a full beard, grayer than ever, and a sling on one of his arms. "I hate that we're meeting this way, but we've had to lay low for a while." His pupils were black as he addressed Simon through the camera. "We're in danger and you may be too. For years, the JTID has been running secret projects behind our backs. Those fuckers were using children – including two of my own – to test out archaic simulations hardly ready for an adult's brain to handle."

Pops held up a photo James hadn't seen in forever. It was from

their vacation to Virginia Beach in 2022 – Uncle Brian posed with him
and Heather and the bass they'd caught in the Atlantic Ocean.

"My best friend betrayed me and now my baby girl is dead," his
father cried. There was a loud explosion that shook the camera, but Pops
went on unfazed. "As you can see, there's a war going on above us so we
don't know how long we'll be holding up here. If anything happens to
me, you should know my name is—" The video started to glitch and cut
off.

James typed back to Simon: "*What did Brian do to us and why
don't I remember any of it?*"

"*I don't know, James.*"

Breathless and bewildered, James stared at a blank screen for what
felt like hours. There was never an explanation for Heather's suicide, but
her terrible migraines had started after that trip. All he remembered was
the beach. His memory was blank, but he did have one more question for
Simon.

"*Is the Jaybird avatar still in Aurora right now?*"

"*James, it's not who you think it is.*"

"*Is the avatar still in Aurora???*"

There was a long pause as James tapped on his desk.

"*Yes … And I think it wants you to find them. I must warn you
that Lucidity is not safe right now, and that avatar is most likely a
hacker.*"

A Lucidity ad popped up on the screen blinking:

"*YOU HAVE ELEVEN HOURS AND TWENTY-SEVEN MINUTES
TO RENEW YOUR SUBSCRIPTION.*"

James knew exactly what he was going to do, the images of
Heather and his son's sonogram reminding him why. He took a seat in
the DreamCatcher, a strange sense of déjà vu flooding his veins, a gut
feeling telling him to go as he hit the power button to the generator,
activating what would hopefully be his final journey into the system.

CHAPTER 36

With her plans for James's birthday ruined, Sandy rode into midtown hoping for a short meeting with the Feds. It didn't appear as though the Light Keepers were going away anytime soon, and her only saving grace was the baby boy in her womb. The traffic was unusually slow due to emergency checkpoints set up all over the city, so Sandy used the time to check out what the cult had released.

In the new video, and after witnessing her through the SYNCDIN lenses, the figure didn't seem as captivating. "Today, we will no longer tolerate the corrupt system that we find ourselves living in," the figure said in a more threatening tone than in her previous recordings. "As the witch hunt continues to shut down our truth, we have only become stronger and more mobilized. They have already killed some of our own and now it's our turn for vengeance." The figure pointed at the screen, warning, "No one should feel safe today." Their messages usually consisted of enlightened spiels about becoming better human beings, but this was dark. "Our love will burn these cities down."

As Sandy's Automated got close to the FBI's Manhattan headquarters she received a text from an unknown server: "*Meet me around the corner at the coffee shop. Make sure no one follows you.*"

The normally hustling midtown was eerily quiet for such a beautiful day, and with the extra drones floating above, Sandy wondered if the message was from Mahoe, or a trap to catch her in her unwanted role as a double agent. Whoever it was had made the text disappear before she could read it again. Busy contemplating her next move, Sandy didn't even notice Agent Miller standing right in front of her the whole time.

The agent asked, "You waiting for someone?"

Caught off-guard, Sandy threw on her most pleasant smile. "Don't you love this time of year?"

"Snap out of it, Grady! The director sent me out here to prep you."

"Over at the coffee shop?"

"What are you talking about?"

"Never mind."

Miller rushed Sandy back to the building. "The director is curious to see if you can get some answers from Kalen when we bring her in, but first they want an assessment of that message from the Keepers. There are some big-time players in the office today, so security's gonna be extra tight. "

Hurrying along, Sandy asked, "Exactly how long am I supposed to be here for?"

"Indefinitely. I don't have a say in the matter at this point."

In the outdoor concourse of the skyscraper, a crowd of reporters and curious citizens milled around, and judging by the size of the otherwise empty city, someone influential was coming in that day. When Sandy pulled out her UniTab to call James, it was taken from her.

"I have to seize this from you," Miller said. "Like I said, security's high."

Sandy chuckled out of combined anger, fear, and annoyance. "It's my husband's birthday, goddammit! I've done everything you guys asked me to, so the least you can do is let me tell him I won't be home for a while."

Miller handed the device back. "Tell him you have a patient who's dying." She whispered, "And lose the attitude, Grady. We all have other places we'd rather be."

The agent went through security and left Sandy with her UniTab, about to buzz her husband for the second time when she accidentally answered a call from Diaz.

"It's not a good time," she told the detective. "I'm with *my friends*."

"This won't be long," Diaz assured her. "I was going to tell you that we found that avatar you were searching for. And get this, Dr Grady, we may have discovered—"

Before the detective could finish, the UniTab was ripped from Sandy's hands again, this time by a rather aggressive member of the KOA. The asshole was tall, wearing a black beret and a self-righteous grin, confiscating it along with the others. "It's time to catch up with your superior agent!"

Sandy never got a chance to call her husband, holding in her tears as she rode the elevator up with Miller.

One more week, she told herself.

The FBI's Manhattan Headquarters bustled with sweat and nerves, and it didn't help that the Knights lingered around, armed with AR-15s. The tech team argued in a sealed-off think-tank, while the field agents gathered in a break room that Agent Miller headed toward. Sandy tagged along, but when the agent noticed her shadow she pointed Sandy to the notorious situation room.

"You'll be in there with the big dogs." Miller led her inside it. "Don't start with that emotional bullshit you've been giving me and Zin, though ... Tell *him* what you know."

"Him?" Sandy asked as the door shut behind her.

There were only two other people in the room with the red light. A woman, maybe forty or so, sat at one end of a long oval-shaped table. She had an impeccable jawline and dark brown skin, and her poker-faced demeanor matched her serious suit and tie. Sandy recognized her. *An actress or an influencer maybe?*

There was Director Zin, who gave her a warm greeting for once. "Dr Grady, thank you for coming in today. I hope it wasn't any inconvenience."

Sandy grinned. "I'm always available."

Zin went on, not recognizing her sarcasm. "This is Olivia Kane –

LucidiTech's CTO."

When Ms. Kane stood up, she was taller than Sandy imagined, giving her a fierce handshake and inviting her to take a seat in the middle of them.

"It's pleasure to meet you, Dr Grady," Kane began, kind yet straightforward. "We understand this topic is close to home which is why we want to know your opinion on this latest threat, from a personal and psychological perspective?"

Before Sandy could respond, Zin said, "Of course, that's a question we'll ask as soon as our other guest arrives. And just to warn you, Dr Grady, he can be quite abrasive."

"Who's *he*?"

Ms. Kane shrugged. "He's the asshole slash CEO slash commander of the KOA, who we only know as Wells. But without saying too much, we need his help in this matter."

The overhead lights dimmed and a screen facing the three switched on. With his back turned to them, the man named Wells smoked a cigar in a dark room, whistling an eerie tune, a synthetic wrist and bushy brunette curls sticking up over the back of his chair.

"Let's make this quick, *Mrs.* Grady." He had a deep auto-tuned snarl and tapped his smoky fingers on the armrest. "Some have suggested that Kalen Green is the voice of the Light Keepers." He seemed bored. "What are your thoughts on that, hun?"

"First off, it's Dr Grady, thank you." Sandy was both nervous and agitated by his outdated, and blatantly misogynistic, use of *i*. "And secondly, I don't know who this particular voice belongs to, but I'd say they may be manic or schizophrenic. Every message before today was more philosophical and peaceful, but this one was—"

"A threat of violence!"

"I was going to say erratic, Mr. Wells – like someone else had taken over it, or her, or whatever the Light Keepers are."

"That's a cute theory." Wells snickered and addressed the other attendees. "Tell me again why I'm wasting my time with some no-name psychologist when we have a terrorist who's plotting a violent attack?"

"Excuse me, but I wasn't finished speaking yet," Sandy said. "The Feds won't even give me Xavier Cortez's autopsy report which I'm usually granted access to."

Wells raised his hand, cigar burning. "To be clear, Mr. Cortez died in the KOA's custody, which was much nicer than anything the government could provide."

Sandy furrowed her brows. "How was it the Light Keepers' fault if he died in your hands?"

Wells prompted surveillance footage onto a screen. "Let's take a gander at what happened to your old friend on that fateful day."

Dressed in one of his many Wu-Tang hoodies in the video, Xavier danced with the drone trailing him around a posh hotel suite, a jacuzzi bubbling in the background. Then, out of nowhere, Xavier began shaking horrendously as if he was having a seizure. He stared at the camera with a cartoonish cheese, his nose bleeding. His eyeballs expanded like balloons that were about to pop, and when they did, the drone's camera lens was covered in red.

Sandy gasped.

As the video continued from a different angle, the old man's body lay face-first on the wooden floor, an endless puddle rushing out of his head.

Wells turned off the video. "Now aren't you glad you know what happened to Mr. Cortez?"

Besides Sandy, no one else seemed shocked. "What the hell was that?"

"Unfortunately no one wants to show that because they think it may disturb too many people," Wells replied. "For some of the Keepers' victims, it's even more intense, but it always seems to end with a massive brain hemorrhage like nothing we've seen before." The screen showed a warehouse filled with guns, explosives, and ammo as Wells continued, "Now imagine what the Light Keepers intend on doing in the real world after stealing these and making that threat today."

"I don't understand," Sandy said, horrified at the sight.

Wells shrugged. "Through their underground network, using an old dark web server called AFANet, they managed to smuggle four cargo loads of weapons intended for disposal last month." He cautioned, his tone kinder now, "I understand it may be frightening to see my people walking around armed, but we have to be ready for their attack."

Zin begrudgingly added, "We think it will be in one of the interior cities, New York being on top of that list, and that Ms. Green is coordinating it all from Snug Harbor."

"I've only met her a couple of times," Sandy said, "but I know she wouldn't harm a fly, let alone incite this type of attack. "

"Sorry to burst your bubble, Dr Grady," Wells replied, "but we recently found out she had strong ties to some extremely radical groups in her younger days."

"What about Lucidity?" Sandy asked. "Is that safe?"

Kane finally chimed in, assuring her, "As of an hour ago, all our safety protocols are intact, and besides a couple of those annoying phantoms, we haven't had any issues."

"Phantoms?"

Wells interrupted. "You've heard enough! If we need you to give Green a therapy session, we'll call you." He turned his chair a bit, revealing the right side of his face – a synthetic eye and a horrible scar on his cheek. "Grady's Irish – is that your married name?"

"Alright, Wells, you've made your point," Olivia Kane said, cutting the feed and turning the light back on. She turned to Sandy. "Let's get you out of here."

Sandy left the situation room, attempting to wipe the images from her mind, relieved they were sending her home. A tall agent led Sandy in the opposite direction of the elevator. "Director Zin told me to keep you here until we bring in the suspect," he said, standing outside a room with a sign that read DETAINEES.

"What the hell is this?" Sandy asked. "I'm an informant. An asset!"

"Relax." The tall agent pushed her in, locking the door behind her. He continued through an intercom. "This will be over soon enough."

It wasn't exactly a prison cell, but Sandy was in a communication quarantine. Grabbing a bottle of water from the fridge, she noticed a young man freely using his UniTab.

"They didn't take that from you when you went through security?" she asked.

The young man didn't answer, bobbing his head to the music in his earbuds. He had short dreadlocks, a tech-chic mustache, and a carefree demeanor. *At least someone's having a good day*, Sandy thought, taking a seat to rest her head on the table.

"Stay like that, Dr Grady," the young man whispered as she was about to close her eyes. Sandy played along, pretending to sleep for a good ten seconds. "Okay, that's good enough."

She lifted her head. "What the hell is going on?"

The young man checked through the glass. "I put the surveillance feed on a loop in here."

"And how do you know my name?"

"I sent you the message this morning, but you never came to the coffee shop." Mahoe sent me to check in with you."

"*Check in*?" Sandy chuckled, appalled by his casualness. "I was just in a room with the FBI, LucidTech, and the KOA. My commanding agent is the mole Mahoe was tracking, and now I'm being detained in a room alongside some unknown stranger working for the same people the whole fucking world is after." She took a deep breath to slow her heart rate. "They're going after Kalen today, so you need to tell whoever you work for to call off any attack."

"We're not the enemy," the man argued.

Disgusted, Sandy shook her head. "I almost believed that until I saw what happens to your victims."

"I wish I had the time to explain." He changed the subject. "So, you think Agent Miller is the mole?"

"The other day, I heard her in a secret conversation," Sandy told him. "She mentioned something was going to happen today. Are you sure she's not with you?"

"Not as far as I know."

Sandy regarded him for a beat. "Why am I talking to you anyway? I don't trust a word coming out of your mouth. Did the Feds arrest you when they found you lurking around their headquarters?"

"I'm an asset like you," he said, winking. "And don't forget, we never forced you to help us."

"That was my mistake," Sandy said with a shrug. "That was before I thought the Light Keepers were actual terrorists, plotting violent attacks on our cities."

The young man laughed. "This whole thing is only a distraction for what's really going down," he warned. "It's all going to happen in the system. It's so vulnerable right now. "

"What do you mean by the system?" Sandy asked. "As in Lucidity?"

When the young man noticed someone approaching, he hid the UniTab without a chance to reply as the woman opened the door and said, "Dante, they'd like to see you now." As he left the room, he gave Sandy a cocky smile when the woman wasn't paying attention. He pointed to the floor near her feet.

When they were gone, Sandy found the UniTab underneath the table. She didn't know how he'd gotten it past security, or if Dante's deep fake was still being executed, but she used it as her only chance to get hold of James and make sure he didn't go into Lucidity.

X
PART TEN

CHAPTER 37

Hopped up on caffeine and emotions, James strapped himself into the DreamCatcher, tears lingering around his baggy eyelids, Eleonora's words and the cause of Heather's death weighing heavily on him. Had he come to the end of the tunnel? The paper-thin wires were injected into his arm, releasing the sleepy chemical concoction. He melted into the comfortable contraption, his eyes about to shut when Sandy sent him a voice message.

"Hey, babe, I hope you're having a great birthday." Her voice began to distort. "I don't *thinnk younuu shhooulld—*"

Prompted to put on his mask and earbuds, James counted down in slow motion as well, "Fiiive ... Fooooour ... Thrrreeeeeee ... Twooo ..."

He braced himself for the chip injection.

~

In one moment Sandy was talking, and in the next James found himself in the Welcome Facility. The entrance transitions were normally smooth, but this one felt like he was blasted out of hyper-speed. It didn't help that it was extremely busy for a weekday afternoon. As he stumbled his way to the sixth sector, through the odd characters and the loud chatter, James bumped into a familiar face.

"Are you okay, Cloud?" Mimi asked, wearing a red sports jacket like Calvin's. "You seem lost."

"I didn't know you were a guide."

"I'm the head guide." Mimi attempted to deepen her nasal voice. "They have me at the Twelve today as part of my suspension for missing a shift last week. I stayed up a little too late for my birthday." She gazed up at him. "Do you know where you're going?"

James continued past the girl. "Don't you have something better to do than pester me?"

Mimi shrugged. "It's busy in here because everyone stayed home, afraid there'd be some flash mob attack or even worse – a bombing. It reminds me of when Alter World got busy during the peak of the war."

James remembered what Calvin had told him in the diner. "You know Space Angel, right?" Mimi nodded and he asked, "Did she tell you anything?"

Mimi seemed apprehensive. "I only know her because she's obsessed with Calvin. I think she works for LucidiTech, meaning your student will be theirs soon enough." She looked at him with narrowed eyes and said, "I hope you're not going to the Void. It's been closed ever since they found a bunch of paths that take you off the grid – like the one that led to the maze I found you in."

With no time, he lied, "Yeah, none of that trip made any sense."

"Does any of this make sense, Cloud? ... Lucidity is a fantasy world – *with some restrictions*. I bet you don't even remember what you look like in here anymore."

James followed Mimi to a bridge that ran from the second sector to the center of the Facility. Hidden mirrors lined the railings. He caught a glimpse of himself, almost forgetting that his avatar was a younger version of himself – brooding and buzz-cut.

Mimi stood behind him. "That's you, Dark Cloud. Do you even remember why you chose this avatar?"

"I wanted someone to recognize me because I've gotten old since he's seen me. In here, my face isn't pudgy, my gray hairs are gone, and there's not a scar on my chin."

"I'm sure you don't look that much different now."

"I'd show you if I could."

Mimi tapped a button on her Navigator. "All you have to do is turn off your filters." On the walkway, she was a little girl, but in the mirror, he saw a woman – tall and thick with bulging biceps that she flexed for him. "My avatar lets me live out the little girl I was never able to because I was stuck in a boy's body."

It all made sense to James now.

Mimi showed him how to do it. "And *voila* – there you are."

James gazed at the same man he'd seen in the mirror that morning, deciding he'd remain that way for his visit, sick of running from his own identity. "How old do you think I am now?"

Blowing a pink gum bubble, Mimi rolled her eyes. "All that matters is how old you feel. Now I have to work to do, so don't get yourself into too much shit, Cloud." She pointed across the Facility. "Calvin's over there by the Wonders if you want to say hi to him."

Once Mimi left, James crossed the sky bridge back onto the main circle between the second and third sectors. Passing by, James began picking up bits and pieces about the Light Keepers' threat.

"I heard they were going after Bangalore," a woman dressed for a hiking expedition speculated.

A gorilla in a baseball uniform argued, "Are you buying this bullshit?"

A gecko in racing gear asked a brute, bearded man, "Do you think we're safe in here right now?"

The bearded man replied, "This is the best place to be."

Closer to the Wonders, James noticed Cali-Cal back in his lion skin, entertaining a group congregated around him. James remembered telling him that he was never coming back, but it was too late.

Calvin shouted, "Mr. G, I thought you quit Lucidity." He gave him an odd look. "And I see you decided to turn off all your filters."

James made up a story. "It's the last day of my trial run and I had a couple of hours to spare after Sandy got called in. I'm also sick of running around pretending to be someone I'm not."

"Well, you picked the wrong day." Calvin led him to a spot near the railing, gazing around the busy facility. "You ever get the feeling in your gut that tells you something bad is gonna happen?"

Although James knew the feeling well, he assured him, "I heard this is the safest place to be."

"Something's off, though."

"That's Space Angel getting in your head."

Calvin sighed. "Trust me, she knows way more than either of us." He turned to James. "Where do you plan on going anyway? I thought the whole point of you joining the system was to find your father."

"Might as well get my money's worth, so I was going to check out Aurora."

"By yourself?" Calvin shook his head. "People get lost on the streets of Aurora."

"I read about it online," James lied. "They said it was ... *gleaming.*" Hip gen-Beta slang meaning "cool."

Calvin stepped back, crossing his furry arms. "There's something up with you, Mr. G. You couldn't even spare a few minutes to hang out with me this morning, which is not like you."

"Something came up. It's been a crazy morning."

Calvin, fidgeting with his hands and scanning him up and down, asked, "You promise you're not using drugs again?"

"No, Calvin!"

"Okay, give me a sec."

In the middle of a bustling crowd, Calvin met with the head of security, Lance, giving James a skeptical grimace as the two spoke. They seemed to be arguing until Calvin turned on his charm and made the man laugh. It ended when they shook hands.

The lion came back to James with a full-fanged smile, boasting, "Looks like I'm coming with you. You wanna tell me what's really going on? Lance said you have a couple of red flags and that you met up with Eleonora near NuAmsterdam on Tuesday night."

"We bumped into each other."

"*Mm hmm* ... You two were getting pretty heavy at Mimi's party."

"Get your mind out of the gutter, Cali Cal."

As much as James wanted to come clean, there wasn't time to tell him about the confidential files or the fact that his father might've helped design the simulation they were standing in. Like his trip to the Void, it wouldn't make sense anyway.

James headed toward the sixth sector. "You coming with me or not?"

"Actually, Lance wants me to go in because one of the guides is missing in Aurora." Calvin rushed ahead of him to lead the way. "I told you there's been some weird shit happening today. You know who else I saw heading toward the Yards?"

"Who's that?"

"Kyle ... Apparently, he joined last week for his eighteenth birthday. I told him the same thing I told you but he didn't listen."

"I'm sure we'll all be fine, Calvin ... *including that little shit.*"

"Whatever you say, Mr. G."

When they arrived at the portal, James asked, "Don't I get a tour guide's introduction to the great Aurora?"

"I thought you read all about it?"

He nodded. "Right." He strolled through the black mirror.

On the other end of the portal, James found himself on a high-tech jet ski, gazing at the skyline of an immaculate metropolis from across a calm body of water. The dusk sky reflected off the rolling waves. Glass skyscrapers seemingly collided on top of one another, but in a way that somehow connected them.

Aurora reminded James of an MC Escher drawing, a mathematical illusion that he'd noticed throughout Lucidity, with a swift rising tower in the center so tall and massive that he couldn't tell where it ended. A triangular edifice with two arches appeared to be the entrance in from the water.

There were ferries, boats, and other forms of aquatic transportation to get there, but Calvin now in his normal teenage skin, seemed to have chosen the jet skis himself. "Welcome to Aurora." He sat on one of his own. "You ever been lucky enough to ride one of these in real life?"

"At my uncle's beach house ..." James remembered the summer he'd visited Virginia and the reason he was supposed to be there in the first place. According to his Navigator, he had less than six hours, and it seemed like a million acres of virtual real estate in front of him. "There must be a quicker way?"

"Just follow me." Calvin led him toward the entry on the jet ski while giving a brief history of the sixth sector in his ear. "A master engineer named Yo bought the real estate for most of Aurora – obviously a genius or savant who decided who could build on their land." As they got closer, James noticed the impressive attention to detail in the intrinsic connection between every structure. They rode in a canal running through many of the skyscrapers – all with the name of different designers or companies branded on them – and pulled into a dock. "In case you're wondering, Yo was also the main architect of Alter World."

"Who?"

"Yo."

"What's up?"

"That's their name, Mr. G ... YO!"

"Ohhh," James said, getting out and taking in the spectacular park where a dozen fountains spit complex patterns, like a piazza out of some futuristic version of Venice, Italy. He asked, "Where's this guide you're looking for?"

"According to my coordinates, she's supposed to be right here." Calvin seemed confused as he spoke to someone in his ear. "Hyun-Joo's nowhere to be found, Lance." Calvin listened. "No, I'm right where it says." He looked even more bewildered, asking Lance, "Are you freaking serious?"

James looked at him. "Is something wrong?"

"I told you that you picked the wrong day, Mr. G."

A woman spoke from an intercom in the sky. Everyone stopped what they were doing. "Attention all, we will be shutting down Lucidity in order to make some necessary upgrades." Her voice echoed throughout the buildings. "We are kindly asking everyone to leave immediately to avoid the forced departure that will happen in exactly one hour. We apologize to our users, but we hope this will only make your next experience more memorable."

When the woman finished a bell began to ring, humming the A note that all church bells chimed – the same four hundred and forty-hertz tone that his orchestra used to tune their instruments. All James could hear was, "A ... A ... A ..." every five seconds or so, at about seventy-two BPM. Although most of the view was obstructed by the skyscrapers surrounding them, a blue light pulsating to the sound of the bell seemed to come from the tall structure James had noticed on his way in.

RING!

A song began to play through the same loudspeaker, a familiar A-minor piece that he'd written himself.

Little Flower.

James gazed at the pulsating sky. "Where's that coming from?"

RING!

"It's called the Peak." Calvin covered his ears. "All I can hear is that stupid bell, though, and according to our evacuation protocol, I'm supposed to stay until there are about fifteen minutes left to make sure everyone gets out safe."

As the song continued, heavily reverberating and slower with dragged-out notes, James asked, "You don't recognize this from your freshman year?"

"Yeah, yeah …" Calvin shrugged, keeping his eye out for the missing guide. "I remember your lesson on the church bells. You said the strike tone is an aural perception – an illusion in a magic trick or something like that."

"I'm talking about the actual fucking music, Calvin!" James pointed to the sky. "You don't hear 'Little Flower' playing?"

RING!

Frustrated and confused, Calvin groaned, "I don't know what's going on with you, but it's time to leave."

"The lady in the sky said we still have an hour."

"That's because they don't want everyone to panic." Calvin had his finger up ready to press a button on his Navigator. "I have the authority to force your ejection."

RING!

"Please don't," James pleaded, already gaining distance from Calvin, walking away and hoping his student wouldn't terminate the short amount of time he had left. *This has to be the signal,* he thought to himself.

While most of the Lucidity users were voluntarily disappearing, heeding the evacuation warning, Calvin shook his head in disappointment. He let James go with a cautious nod.

"Thank you, Calvin. I promise I'll explain it all later."

CHAPTER 38

Back at the FBI headquarters in Manhattan, Sandy woke up to a commotion after dozing off in the detainment room. Two men, a Knight and an FBI tech agent, were at each other's throats, arguing about something she couldn't make out through the thick glass. According to the clock, she'd only been asleep for twenty minutes, although it felt like hours. The door slid open and Agent Miller stormed in.

"Wake up, Grady. You can go home now."

"What the hell is going on?" Sandy yawned. "Why are they fighting?"

"Difference of opinions." Miller forcibly helped her up. "Now let's go."

"You're still going to bring Kalen in, right?"

"That all depends on how she handles herself right now," the agent insisted, leading her out. "We thought you'd be a good asset in getting Ms. Green to talk, but I guess Zin reconsidered, figuring you might be too emotionally attached. Now go spend this time with your husband." The agent turned her back, making sure to get the last word in. "I wouldn't want to ruin his birthday celebration."

After leaving the headquarters, Sandy cued an Automatic and headed back to their condo, Dante's last words lingering like the scent of rotten fish: *It's all going to happen in the system.* That was the real threat, she thought, hoping James had gotten her message to stay out of Lucidity. According to her security system, he'd gone back home, but for some reason wasn't responding to her calls or messages. When her app didn't work, she buzzed Nera, hoping to get more clarity. The operator didn't answer either. Stuck in another traffic jam due to the ongoing checkpoints, she cued the news trying to figure out what Agent Miller wasn't telling her.

A headline appeared on the screen: "*Light Keepers Suspect Located in New York As Feds Warn Of Hostage Situation.*" From the drone footage, Sandy counted at least ten agents on the ground, armed in riot gear, waiting for their next command. They only had rubber bullet guns when they came for Xavier, she remembered. When the baby started kicking, Sandy took a deep breath to calm both of their nerves. "Don't worry, Mama's gonna get us home soon enough." She reached out to Adriana Diaz, remembering the detective had made some discovery.

"What is it, Dr Grady?" Diaz asked through a video feed, Ronson in the background lying in bed with her. "I'm a little busy at the moment."

Sandy reminded the detective, "You mentioned the avatar with the screen name I gave you."

Diaz told her that it had been stagnant for years and it recently went untraceable, disappearing from the radar Dan had access to. She seemed to recall something. "I left my jacket in his apartment so I'll go up there and let him explain." The detective switched the feed over so she could use her POV-Lenses. "He knows way more than I do."

Watching the detective's movements through the screen of her Automated, Sandy asked, "What else did you find in the intel I handed over?"

Diaz chuckled. "I didn't think you wanted to be involved anymore." She made her way up to her neighbor's apartment via the stairs. "If you're so curious maybe you should come over and discuss it with us in person."

Sandy gazed at the line of Automateds waiting to get through the Midtown tunnel. "I have to get home and make sure my husband isn't in Lucidity."

"I thought he quit."

"I'm pretty sure he did, but I can't get hold of him and I don't where else he'd be." Sandy explained, "I heard the system is highly vulnerable right now."

"Maybe Dan's girlfriend, Nera, can help you," Diaz said. "I think she has a job at Lucidity."

"Nera?" Sandy's eyes lit up. "Little thing with glasses and tattoos?"

"That's her!"

"That's my husband's operator," Sandy said. "I've been trying to get a hold of her too."

"Her and Dan were fighting earlier, but I'm pretty sure they made up," Diaz said. "They might be doing the same thing my partner and I were doing ... *wink wink*." She laughed, walking through a hallway. "To tell you the truth, when Dan told me he had a girlfriend, I didn't even believe him."

Sandy closed in on the checkpoint in her Automated. "Well, I hope Nera's not in Lucidity either."

"I don't understand why you're so worried." Diaz buzzed a door to one of the apartments. "With everything going on today it seems like the safest place to be." When Dan finally answered, his skin was a pale white and his hands were shaking. Diaz asked, "What's wrong?"

The young man was speechless, letting Diaz in and leading her to a DreamCatcher in the middle of the apartment. When Diaz circled the device to get a better view, Sandy saw that it was Nera, her head tilted back. Blood poured out from her eyes down to her cold blue lips. Just like Xavier Cortez.

"Nera's dead," Dan said, his own lips uncontrollably quivering.

In shock, Sandy covered her mouth. She went through the checkpoint, temporarily shutting off her screen as an officer on foot scanned the inside of her Automated. She smiled at him as he waved her through to the entrance of the tunnel. When Sandy changed the screen back to Diaz's feed, she was checking Nera's pulse – two fingers to her neck artery.

Speaking to Dan, Diaz said, "I thought you were gonna spend the rest of the day with her."

"I was!" Dan seemed furious with himself. "I simply needed a little more time to figure out this code, so she went into Lucidity for her tournament in the Yards." A tear formed in his eye as he stared into the glasses Diaz used. "Who are you talking to?"

"I'm so sorry for your loss, Dan," Sandy said from the Automated, speaking to him through Diaz's UniTab. "I knew Nera. She set up my husband's DreamCatcher."

Dan stared at Sandy through the camera. "Well, for your sake I hope he's not in Lucidity today."

"I hope so too, Dan."

"I told her it was going to kill her."

"This wasn't Lucidity's fault." Sandy furiously shook her head. "This was the Light Keepers' doing."

"Are you sure, Dr Grady?" asked Diaz.

"Trust me."

"Have no doubt, I will find out who did this to her." Dan placed his hand over Diaz's camera and cut off the visuals. "Now if you don't mind, I have to take care of my dead girlfriend."

Five minutes later, when the Automated let Sandy out in front of her building, she blew through the lobby like a tornado, knocking over a couple of her neighbors in the process. The elevator seemed brutally slow. She stormed into an empty living room, rushed to James's office, and found him in the DreamCatcher – alive – but with vitals much higher than normal. A timer counted down on one of the screens.

"50 MINUTES UNTIL SHUTDOWN!"

Sandy recalled the comment Diaz's partner had made a couple of nights earlier: *"Can't you just unplug the damn thing?"* It was hard to imagine that it had been Nera who'd told her to never do that, the same woman who'd said, *"No one dies in Lucidity."* It appeared as though Lucidity was shutting down with James inside it. There was nothing left to do but wait – a familiar predicament that she hoped never to experience again.

CHAPTER 39

James frantically sprinted through Aurora, following the sound of the bell.

RING!

The song had faded away. The bell hadn't. He found himself stuck at a crossroads at the end of the elaborate park called Twelve Points. Only three of the mystery portals seemed to be heading in the direction of the Peak, so he played a quick game of *eeny, meeny, miny, moe,* and landed on the middle one. "And ... you ... are ... it."

RING!

On the other end of the mystery portal, was a simulation of a Brooklyn block party. Synth children splashed around in fire hydrants as pre-programmed adults waited to challenge avatars on the basketball court. James figured the warnings and the bells didn't matter to them. When he asked for directions, a little boy pointed to another portal.

The voice in the sky warned, "Fifty minutes until shutdown."

RING!

The bell became louder and closer.

Jumping through the portal, James found himself on a cobblestone road with horse-drawn carriages. A man smoking a pipe approached him in a top hat and slim-fitted pantaloons – ignoring the loud church bell, the blinking sky, and the stench of shit that completed the zone's historical accuracy. "*Ça fait longtemps, dis donc.*" He blew a puff of tobacco smoke in the air, the only scent that wasn't disgusting.

RING!

"Can you tell me how to get to the Peak?" James asked. "To where that bell is coming from?"

The short man spat on the ground, yelling in a French accent, "You Americans are so rude even after we save your asses." After the synth's overdramatic spiel, he gave James a cigarette, directions, and some unfriendly advice. "Maybe you should go back to the place you came from." Although it was probably part of the synth's script, it felt like a warning with the chimes growing louder.

RING!

"Forty-five minutes until shutdown ... Please evacuate now!"

RING!

As soon as James ran in and out of the portal, his avatar changed into a hybrid 2D-3D anime character. There was a reflection of himself in the broken glass window of an arcade, alone on a questionable side street in the same design. There were hiragana tags on the brick walls. The men, both real and synth, were too fixated on a dice game and in no mood to give directions. He was running out of time.

"Thirty-nine minutes until shutdown!"

A souped-up silver Kawasaki pulled up next to James, driven by a silver helmeted avatar that couldn't be identified. They signaled him to get on. James jumped on the back and held on tight.

"Take me to the Peak!"

RING!

With a zero-to-eighty kick-start, the anonymous biker whipped around objects at the last possible second, the bells getting louder. They swerved through narrow alleyways. The bike caught air and hit the concrete hard. They made a sharp left into a blinding tunnel, full of disorienting curves and slopes.

James yelled, "You're going too fast!"

RING!

The biker didn't listen and shifted into a higher gear. A hundred miles per hour. When James thought they would crash into a wall, they whipped down like a roller coaster. He closed his eyes and clenched onto the stunt driver, bracing for a crash once he heard the screeching brakes. He flew face forward onto the hard desert-like pavement, his forearms taking most of the brunt force. He stared up at the biker, who stared back down at him on the ground. The bell rang louder than before.

RINGGG!

"Who are you?"

RINGGG!

The biker pointed to a place behind them and then rode off, leaving a dust trail in James's face. Now back in his normal 3D avatar, he pushed himself off the ground, sore and nauseous from the ride. He was underneath the most massive antenna he'd ever seen. The biker was pointing to the place where the lights and the bell were all coming from.

The Peak.

"Thirty-six minutes until shutdown ... Please evacuate now!"

The Peak seemed to be connected by six glowing beams, all unevenly spaced in asymmetrical curves at least a thousand feet apart from one another. As far as his eyes could see there was nothing else around for miles. Aurora had disappeared, along with the unknown avatar who'd left him somewhere between the beams and the center of the giant structure.

RINGGG!

Every five seconds the sonic boom of the bell sent chills up his spine, hard to ignore from underneath the structure that seemed to flow toward the universe.

RINGGG!

In the center, there was a blue spotlight pulsating to the rhythm and a silhouette of the only other soul around. When James got close enough, he realized who it was.

"Calvin, what are you doing here?"

RINGGG!

Calvin covered his ears, circling to find a better viewpoint. "The guide I was looking for – Hyun-Jo – is supposed to be right here," he said, caught up in troubleshooting his Navigator problems, looking at James with wide, earnest eyes. "All of Lucidity is in a Red Zone and there have been dozens of reports of phantoms in every sector."

RINGGG!

The teenager giggled – his laugh high-pitched, crazy and off-putting. "Oh yeah, and to make matters worse, no one can locate our head of security, Lance."

RINGGG!

"Relax," James said, although the bell made it hard. "Maybe he didn't feel like waiting until the fifteen-minute mark. I didn't realize Lucidity hired you to be their security guard too."

RINGGG!

Calvin paced around. "It's hard to tell what my role is lately."

"Why are you being so paranoid? You died in a Red Zone and came to class the next day."

"How would you know that?"

"Lucky guess."

RINGGG!

Calvin eyed him like an angry detective. "Why are you here anyway?" His hands were behind his back. "And why do you want to stay in Lucidity so bad?"

"I told you I had to follow the song."

RINGGG!

"There's no music playing, Mr. G. Just that fucking bell!" Calvin yelled. "The system's been compromised!"

Then the bell finally stopped ringing. It became eerily quiet, a synthetic breeze blowing from the direction they came from.

"I'm getting us out of here before that bell starts up again."

Just as Calvin was about to eject them from the system, they both heard someone screaming in the distance, sprinting toward them like they were being chased by the devil. Now that the synthetic sun had set, it was hard to see anything but the shadow urgently approached. When it got close enough, James could see that it was Lance speeding toward them. He kept checking behind him, but there wasn't anyone else around for miles.

"Calvin!" Lance shouted. "Get the fuck outta here and go to the Peak!"

When Lance was about a hundred feet away he was lifted into the sky. Seconds later, he came plummeting to the ground at a high speed. Every bone in his body smashed on impact, shattering blood and guts everywhere.

Calvin's eyes froze wide open. "I don't understand. We're already at the Peak." He tried to contact someone. "Mimi ... Are you still in Lucidity?"

No one answered.

As Calvin worked on his Navigator, James wandered into the blue circumference of the spotlight. There was an elaborate coding on the semi-opaque walls that only radiated when the bell rang, now only heard at an elevator volume on an invisible lo-fi speaker.

"I think we're supposed to be inside here," James said.

Calvin rushed over to the edge of the circle, more focused on other matters. "I can't communicate with anyone because we're off the grid." His head propped up. "I think we're surrounded by phantoms too."

James heard it. Distorted shrieks coming from multiple directions and getting closer by the second.

Calvin grabbed his hand, bowed his head in prayer, and exhaled deeply. "It was a pleasure knowing you, Mr. G."

"It's just a game, Calvin." James smiled, pretending to be brave. "Just like I said before."

"Don't you get it? *This* is the attack the Light Keepers were planning."

The noises were getting closer and more disorienting. When James realized Calvin's theory was probably right, he yanked him into the circle, barricading himself around the teen. A wave of noise swelled toward them like a squadron of fighter jets in attack mode. He calculated how close they were and counted down in his head.

Three ... two ... one ...

James clenched every muscle in his body and threw his arms out in front of Calvin. Like a machine-gun drumroll, the phantoms collided into the blue light one after the other, unable to penetrate whatever forcefield surrounded them. They were stuck lurking outside like rabid, invisible zombies.

James relaxed his body.

Calvin untucked himself from the ball he'd curled himself into, clearly stunned to be alive. He pressed his hand against the glass. "This is a fucking barrier."

As the distorted shrills of the phantoms faded, 'Little Flower' played inside the circle, humming in an AM radio quality. Calvin's eyes grew wide trying to figure out where it was coming from.

"I hear it now," he exclaimed. "It's the piece we did my freshman year." The safe space they were in began to ascend like an elevator. It was hard to tell if Calvin was relieved or petrified. "What the fuck is going on, Mr. G?"

"I don't know," James said, "but I think this is where we're supposed to be."

CHAPTER 40

Surrounded by the translucent blue light, James and his student continued up toward the Peak as if they were being summoned onto a UFO. His feet were planted on a surface as transparent as the phantoms, terrified that if he moved in any direction he'd fall off. With less than thirty minutes until the system shut down, the ride seemed sluggish compared to most of Lucidity's attractions.

To distract himself, James listened to the rendition of 'Little Flower,' noticing an error he only made during one particular performance – a recording of his final music exam at New Paltz. One he didn't know existed. It only made what was happening even more peculiar.

Calvin, who was more accustomed to Lucidity, didn't seem as fazed by the invisible elevator. "We're safe for now." He poked around to find the boundaries of the portal. "You can move around if you like."

James gazed upward. "Where are we going?"

"I have no idea."

Still wary, James tapped the front of his boot down a few inches in front of him and heard the tinker of thick glass. He took a couple of baby steps to test Calvin's theory, gazing at the entirety of Lucidity from a bird's eye view, the twelve sectors expanding out of a vast blank space where he thought the Welcome Facility was supposed to be. Now he understood what his student meant when he called it real estate. As they rose to higher altitudes of the complex metaverse, the five beams of the Peak blurred into the rest of the simulated universe. A billion lights that went on forever.

When a chill set in the space, James dug his hands into the pockets of his hoodie to warm them up and came across the cigarette the

Frenchman had given him. He chewed on the filter to calm his nerves, but when he inhaled, the flimsy cancer stick lit itself. It didn't taste much like tobacco but was exactly what he needed.

Calvin huffed, seeming repulsed. "Seriously, what's going with you?"

"It's not a real cigarette." James blew a red circle into the blue light to get a violet effect. "I just wanted to see what it tastes like."

"What's happening right now is very fucking real!" Calvin paced around the tight space. "I don't understand why you're acting so casual about it."

"Do you think I'm okay with all of this?"

"I'm not so sure," Calvin said, his eyes narrowed. "We did catch you with a Light Keeper the first night you were in here and, not to be rude, but you do kind of fit their profile." The teenager got closer to him. "How do I know you're not one of them?"

"Seriously?" James threw the cigarette down. "My best friend is dead because of those motherfuckers. I don't know what's going in here, but trust me, Calvin, I'm not a Light Keeper."

"But you're still looking for your father in here, correct?"

"I was told his avatar was in Aurora."

"By who?"

James sighed. "Eleonora came to see me this morning, but it's not what you think. She's been helping me track down his avatar, and knew someone who could help me. With everything going on, though, I wouldn't be surprised if it was another glitch."

"You're telling me you met Eleonora in real life?"

"Briefly."

"Be real, Mr. G." His student gave him a sly grin. "What's she look like?"

"Get your head out of the gutter, Calvin."

"Look, I get it." Calvin gazed down as they flew through thick white clouds. "I still remember the day the soldiers came to my door and told my mom the news, but you don't see me wasting my life away trying to figure out how my father died." There was a slight whimper in his voice. "That kind of thinking would drive anyone crazy."

"I know it doesn't make any sense."

"And yet here you are." Calvin shook his head. "You do know what Einstein said about insanity?"

"I was supposed to listen for a signal. Do you have a better explanation as to why that song was playing?" James took a seat in the middle of the space portal. "It's what led me to this elevator, which happened to save both of us from those invisible bastards."

Calvin groaned. "I know there's someone else you're secretly working with too."

"Oh yeah, who's that?"

"My mother. She must've witnessed my forced ejection the night I was killed in a Red Zone."

James nodded. "That's why she came to me in the first place. She's worried about you like any mother would be, and if it makes you feel any better, I told her she had nothing to fear."

"I'm not so sure about that anymore."

"Everything's going to be okay," James assured him. "We'll be back in our homes soon enough. We can meet up and talk about what school you want to go to." He grinned, trying to have some faith in own his words. "There's one in Harlem that's both in need of a lead violinist and a music instructor."

"About that ..." Calvin shied away to his own section of the portal. "I start at the Innovation Academy this fall. That's what I was going to tell you this morning before you went chasing after Eleonora. I have to think about my future and I don't think it's going to be in music anymore." He stared up to where they were heading, a frightened look on his young face. "That's if we make it out of here alive today."

The portal began to ascend much faster. James stood back up, positioning himself to stay balanced as it shook like an earthquake. Calvin gripped his arm and closed his eyes as they headed toward a blinding white light.

James shut his eyes tight, grinding his molars, hoping he'd be back home any minute now as the speed rose. "I'm sorry I got you into this mess."

When the ride came to an unexpected stop, a wall of darkness surrounded them, reminding James of the pitch-black cave. It quickly disappeared and the temperature fell. Ice chips pelted him like tiny needles. A squall of snow made it almost impossible to see anything besides some sort of fire in the distance, electric-blue flames blazing in a narrow upward spiral. A fervent gust of wind blew him into something hard. He ricocheted to the ground. Silky white sand cushioned his fall. He stood up slowly, staring at the palm tree he'd run into and the many others nearby.

The top of the Peak was an odd sector indeed.

James headed toward the fire, his boots sinking deep with every stride. There was a scattering of footsteps behind him, but when he turned around no one was there. That logic didn't seem to matter anymore. The phantoms could be encircling them for all he knew.

He whispered, "Calvin?"

When his student didn't answer, James climbed a small dune to get a better view of the bonfire. The silhouettes of at least twenty figures stood in a circle. One of them, much taller than the rest, guided them in some sort of seance. Out of the corner of his eye, James saw Calvin running toward him, trying to fight his way up the snow and sand.

"Mr. G! It's right behind you!"

But before James could turn around, he was put in a tight chokehold – one metal arm around his throat, and another attempting to cover his face.

In a synthetic-sounding voice, it asked, "Who are you?"

Two other strangers tackled Calvin to the ground, and right as James was about to pass out, he was thrown face-first back into the sand.

"I asked you a question."

James rolled over to find a fierce robotic man standing over him. It was less than five feet tall but with its steel muscles and green glowing eyes, quite intimidating.

"My name's Dark Cloud."

It forced James to stand up and walk to the shore. "You're not supposed to be up here."

Where there was supposed to be a body of water was cut away by a tectonic plate, leading back down the same distance he and Calvin had come up from. The ridiculously strong avatar lifted him by the back of his hoodie, holding him over the edge.

"Who sent you here today?"

James's feet tingled, dangling over the space. He closed his eyes to protect them from the snow blanketing his face, not knowing how to answer with his heart racing as fast as it was. *This isn't real*, he thought. They had traveled up so high with a thousand miles between him and the surface of Lucidity.

"Just don't hurt Calvin!" James stared down to his death. "It's my fault he's here."

There was a whistle, a signal of some sort. James was put back on the ground. He turned around and saw his student with Space Angel, her helmet off and her hair down, wearing a straight face as she spoke with Calvin, seeming unaffected by the blizzard conditions.

"I apologize for that." Space Angel addressed James now, sending the angry android back to the bonfire. "XYXO can be a bit harsh, but with today's circumstances you can understand why. So, why are you here?"

They walked toward the light of the fire, and James was starting to get used to the cold. "I was trying to find my father," he told her.

With a groan, Space Angel said, "What's his username?"

"It's Jaybird 1983, but it's spelled differently."

"Never heard of him."

"Eleonora sent me to some guy named Simon. He said my father was dead, but then he sent her back to tell me his avatar was in Aurora."

"Simon ... as in SRT?"

"You know him?"

"Yes," Space Angel sighed again. "He's one of the only few who could pull off what's happening in the system today." She stepped back, seeming more suspicious of James now. "Who the hell is your father anyway? For all I know, he might be one of them damn phantoms!"

"He's not!" Of course, judging by his circumstances, James wasn't sure if that was true anymore.

"Mm hmm." Space Angel rolled her eyes. "Seems like it's been crazy in Lucidity ever since you've arrived." She began leading him and Calvin toward the fire pit.

As James approached, he noticed that the twenty or so other avatars were meditating, standing with their eyes closed and their palms out in front of them toward the fire. A couple of them were elf creatures, and some were animals and cartoonish figures like he'd seen elsewhere in Lucidity. None of them looked like actual people, though, which made James think he'd made the wrong decision by turning off his filter.

"That's Yo," Space Angel whispered to Calvin, pointing out the tall avatar James had noticed before. "They called us here to protect the Void until this nightmare is over."

"Silence," Yo intimated in a harsh whisper that made the flames angry.

The tall alien-like creature made its way around the fire, approaching Space Angel. Yo had these almond-shaped black pupils that slanted up, an oversized forehead, and delicate lips. They wore an elegant robe made of chocolate silk. "We have to stay quiet so we can hear the slightest sounds," Yo whispered in a monotone voice like it was aloof to the danger. Pulling out an odd pocket watch, they showed it counting down from the twelve-minute mark, only then noticing James for the first time. "Who's this?"

Space Angel replied, "Simon sent him ... says he's looking for some Jaybird fella that's supposedly his father."

Yo analyzed James for a few seconds, then made their way back to the center, grabbing the attention of the others by snapping their fingers. "Ten minutes," Yo said in their lowest voice. "Listen closely, it's not over yet." Everyone closed their eyes.

Most adhered to the apparent leader. Everyone except for XYXO, who seemed to still be homed in on James. He closed his eyes to not seem suspicious, only hoping to make it back home. James heard something other than the wind. A radio static coming from two separate directions and getting louder and closer. One was coming in from behind them, and the other one was speeding right toward Yo.

James screamed, "Phantoms!"

But it was too late.

The giant avatar, Yo, was jerked from the ground and dragged into the sky. Everyone scattered to find protection. The second phantom flew over them with a horrible shriek. James lost track of his student, more focused on Yo's trajectory high above him. Their four arms seemed trapped, and their mouth was forced shut as they beelined back down toward the ground level of Lucidity. James sprinted toward the shore to follow Yo, inches away from falling off the edge when someone yanked him backward.

"What the hell are you doing?" Calvin asked, his hand clenched to the back of the hoodie. "You can't catch them."

"If those phantoms can fly, then I can too." James tracked Yo's descent, his adrenaline rushing. "I've done it before."

"I told you that won't work in here. Besides, all the firewalls of Lucidity have been compromised. "

"Meaning?"

"That the Red Zones are now the dead zones," Calvin exclaimed. "And all of the sectors are in the red, including the ones off the grid. This is not the time to test out your theory."

"I got this."

James glanced down, and in that split second, remembered the dream that didn't quite feel like a dream anymore. He turned away from Calvin and jumped off the edge of the Peak, unsure if he was flying or falling, soaring down much faster than they'd come up. His radar was locked on Yo, who kept getting farther away. The simulated universe surrounded him, fake stars and galaxies. The top of the Peak receded in the distance. *This isn't real*, he told himself, knowing it was already too late to turn back.

Twisting his body into a diving position, James now headed face first with one arm toward the ground like a superhero. The aero-dynamics seemed to make him plunge faster. He gained ground on Yo, almost hitting one of the massive beams, which the phantom seemed to dodge with the precision of a trained pilot.

James, on the other hand, didn't have any control. He found himself back in the clouds they'd passed through earlier, making it impossible to see anything but doubt. *Is this what happened to Heather?* When he passed through the thick fog, the surface of Lucidity came into sight. *Did she think she could fly?* He was within arm's length of Yo when the phantom made a sporadic one-eighty and ascended upward.

Yo and the phantom were both gone again.

James continued to plummet into a dead zone, every instant of his life dashing through his head. He remembered that feeling of lying in an alleyway about to die, thinking about every mistake he'd ever made. He pictured Sandy's hazel irises gazing at him like an angel, his unborn child in the crib he'd yet to assemble. The skyscrapers of Aurora were drawing near, but he had to get back home. He had a future to create.

The air in Lucidity seemed less dense than water, but James imagined it as the deepest ocean. With one massive butterfly stroke, he mimicked the swimming maneuver and rocketed himself up. He was halfway back up through the clouds when he realized what was happening.

"I'm fucking flying!"

James continued the motion and picked up speed, catching a glimpse of Yo up ahead of him. He pushed as hard as he could, using every ounce of energy his mind could conjure up. When he caught up to the phantom, Yo reached out one of their hands to him, using the other three to wrestle themselves away. When Yo came loose, James caught the rather heavy avatar and pulled them back toward the top. He spiraled around the steel beam, but the phantom shadowed his moves. Its distorted shrill drew near. Yo lifted their leg and kicked the invisible predator in a vulnerable spot. As the static faded away, James followed the blinking blue light back to the top of the Peak.

"Why did you save me?" Yo asked. "You know we could've died right there?"

"So it's true?" James landed back onto the snow-covered beach. "I thought Calvin was just trying to scare me."

Yo shook their head. "You and I are only alive because you somehow knew how to fly in the system. If we make it out of here alive, I'll help you find your father, whoever he is." Yo approached the other avatars. "For now, I need to make sure all my friends are safe"

As James followed the leader, the Peak seemed at peace, everyone gathering around a fire bot quite as bright as before. He hadn't taken a count of how many other avatars were up there but noticed two who weren't. Space Angel and Calvin. He checked all around but there was no sign of either of them. XYXO approached alongside Yo, both their heads hanging low. Yo wouldn't make eye contact and the android's body language was unnervingly glum.

"Where's Calvin?" James checked near where they'd come in from. "I have to get him home." There was silence. "Tell me he's okay!"

No one replied.

James saw a shadow coming over one of the sand hills. It took his eyes some time to focus, dizziness coming over him. He had the thought of explaining to Loretta what had happened to her son.

"I'm alright, Mr. G." Sure enough, it was Calvin, but judging by the look on his face, something else was wrong. "They took Space Angel." He began crying. "I was holding her hand and then she was ripped away from me. I tried to do what you did, but I couldn't hold on."

Yo kicked the snow. "Fuuckkk!" He turned to Calvin. "It's not your fault."

James didn't know what the intentions of the group were, but Space Angel must've been important because even after falling to the ground Yo never seemed that rattled.

Yo approached the group, who stood in horror, declaring, "For what it's worth, Space Angel would be glad we accomplished our mission today. I'm not sure of what to expect on our journey back home." Yo checked their pocket watch and guided them into a corpse pose that would supposedly lessen the blow. "Be safe everyone."

James walked back over to the edge, choosing not to listen to Yo's advice, curiously gazing down as Lucidity went dark, one sector at a time. Even the millions of stars above him burned out like dying candles. An unnerving shadow drifted over. He didn't know if he'd see his wife again or ever meet his unborn child. If it was a dream, then it was the part where he was supposed to wake up.

And right on cue, all the lights went out, including the ones inside his own head.

XI

PART ELEVEN

CHAPTER 41

An excruciating headache gripped him. A tiny amount of light poked through, blinding him like a solar eclipse. James remembered leaving the system, spiraling through some wormhole, trapped in solitary confinement for what felt like months. *Is this hell?* He'd never believed in such a torturous afterlife. Not until that moment.

"Babe?" a woman asked.

It sounded like Sandy but was most likely his imagination again. The agony wasn't only in his head, but in every muscle, joint, and bone throughout his body.

"Mr. G," another voice said. "You awake?"

A dream, James thought when he heard Calvin, only a few thoughts floating through his normally busy mind. A numbness paralyzed him like his time in the Cave. When he regained the feeling in his stomach and esophagus, the acid rose to the top of his throat, and with no control over his body, he wasn't sure what would happen next.

"You might want to grab a bucket," an unfamiliar third voice suggested. "And do it fast!"

James strained to open his eyes against a force opposing the motion, the voices growing more coherent. "Hurry up!" The loud noise and commotion only worsened his migraine, and after finding the strength to stand up, a rippling effect pulsated through his body. His stomach rumbled like a thunderstorm, and when he burped it wasn't exactly a burp, but an arsenal of projectile vomit.

Now fully awake, James found himself back in his office.

Sandy rushed in with a trash can seconds too late.

A man wearing a LucidiTech shirt stood in front of him covered in puke.

Calvin dry heaved in a corner, his hands clenched to his knees.

The voices were real.

"Does somebody want to tell me what the hell is going on?" James yelled, his voice strained. The clock on his screen said it was only half past three, which made sense with the sun still high in the sky. He turned to Sandy. "When did you get back home?"

"Yesterday," she said. "Now go sit down."

"I'll feel better in a minute," James insisted. "We can finish your plans for my birthday."

"Didn't you hear me? Your birthday was yesterday, babe. Now go sit down while I get this man cleaned up."

James was escorted out of the office by Calvin, who used a shirt to cover his nose from the foul smell James assumed was the puke. Sandy led the LucidiTech man he'd drenched to the bathroom in the hallway.

"What are you doing here?" James asked, sitting down on the living room couch. "Is everyone okay?"

"Slow down, Mr. G." Calvin pulled out a syringe from a LucidiTech-labeled first-aid kit. "Sam said you'd need this once you finally woke up."

"Who's Sam?"

"Just hold still." Calvin stuck the needle in his arm.

It reminded James of shooting heroin. But it felt more like the adrenaline they'd shot into his heart when he'd overdosed, the liquid flowing through his body. "Did this happen to you too?"

"I felt like shit when I came out of the system yesterday." Calvin put the needle in a bag. "Luckily, Teddy always has these energy drinks that he swears kills his many hangovers. It's the only thing that asshole has ever been good for." He checked to see if anyone was around, and began whispering, "I buzzed you this morning and your wife answered, asking me a ton of questions about what happened in Lucidity. When Dr G told me you still hadn't woken up, I had to come and see if you were okay."

"But why did it take so long for me to come down? I thought we both went through the same process."

"You flew in the system yesterday," Calvin reminded him. "I don't know what kind of mind power that takes, but it must've drained you. You're lucky to be alive."

"What are you talking about?"

"It wasn't just us!"

Calvin cued the headlines on the large screen in his living room, split between the four major news feeds. James couldn't believe what had happened while he was asleep.

One screen read, *"SLAUGHTER IN THE SYSTEM,"* while another said, *"DEADLIEST CYBER ATTACK EVER LEAVES OVER A THOUSAND LUCIDITY USERS DEAD."* The dramatic footage trailed someone wheeled out in a body bag as a man followed behind, uncontrollably sobbing. A third headline declared: *"KNIGHTS OF AZRAEL CLAIM DEATH TOLL MAY HAVE BEEN MUCH HIGHER HAD THEY NOT STEPPED IN,"* with aerial footage of a house surrounded by a security force and intelligence agents.

"By all logical sense you should be dead," Calvin insisted. "A computer virus is responsible for the meltdown. The Light Keepers hacked the system from a backdoor and shut down the security protocol."

"Do you know what happened to Kyle? Is he okay?"

"I told him to not to go into the Yards."

"Jesus, he was a pain, but I never wished him dead." James sighed. "And your friend Lance?"

Calvin bowed his head and shook it. "I spoke with his husband earlier today. If you would've hit the ground, that would be you too."

The thought made James feel sick.

Sandy barged into the living room, cueing Ginger to turn off the screens. "He needs to rest, Calvin."

"I wanted to know what happened yesterday." James noticed how exhausted she was, the shadows looming around her eyes reminding him of the first time they met. When he attempted to comfort her, she pushed him away. "What's wrong?"

"You smell ... bad."

As soon as Sandy said it, he caught a whiff of the horrible scent coming from his pants. He'd apparently soiled his underwear during his twenty-four-hour sleep period.

"Let's get you cleaned up," she said from a safe distance.

After discarding every piece of clothing into a trash chute, James took a long shower. He came out of the bathroom feeling fresher than ever, but Sandy's hands trembled, still not okay from whatever stress he had put her through.

"What's wrong?" he asked.

She cued a file from her UniTab, telling him, "There's something you need to see."

The main screen in their bedroom aired drone footage of a small house resting on the shore. As it flew closer, an armed team in riot gear surrounded the location with their assault rifles drawn and ready to fire, the caption on the screen reading, "*KNIGHTS OF AZRAEL CLOSING IN ON CATCHING SUSPECTED LEADER OF THE LIGHT KEEPERS.*" His ex-counselor, Kalen Green, stepped onto the front porch with her hands in the air, seeming calm, as if she'd expected the raid.

James asked, "Is this live?"

"This is a recording from yesterday."

He was relieved to see Kalen giving herself up without a fight. At one point, she even grinned at the drone hovering over her. Then, out of nowhere, a young man ran out of the door with his hands behind his back – her son, Anthony – and in some grand gesture, pulled his hands out and waved two peace signs in the air. Kalen seemed caught off-guard by her son's actions, putting her body in front of him as three shots were fired into her chest. The KOA didn't stop, taking down Anthony as well. As the blood poured onto the cement, the video cut off, claiming technical difficulties.

"Is Kalen dead?"

Sandy nodded. "I'm sorry."

James walked to the bedroom speechless, having not witnessed such a grizzly scene since the War ended. "I guess they had their reasons." He brushed his teeth, noticing Sandy in the mirror, staring at him intently. "What?"

"How can you be so heartless?"

"Over a thousand people died in Lucidity yesterday and I witnessed it. I'm lucky I didn't end up dead in my DreamCatcher too. I've been telling you Kalen was dangerous ever since she got Tomás killed. You may have helped save her, but it was only a matter of time before the authorities got to her."

"There's more to it than that." Sandy told him about her trip to the FBI headquarters, meeting an informant who'd predicted the attack. It seemed to James as though she was defending the terrorists.

"I almost died because of those light-keeping assholes." James grew irritated with her. "Why can't you understand that?"

A knock on their bedroom door interrupted them. Sam, the LucidiTech operator, thanked Sandy for letting him use the shower and giving him a change of clothes. James didn't make eye contact with the man upon leaving, embarrassed by what had happened. He then remembered that his student patiently waited in the living room.

"I should go, too," Calvin said, rushing to grab his backpack. "And, Mr. G, I'm sorry about giving you so much shit yesterday. I'm glad you're okay." He clearly didn't want to be the third wheel in the matter. He was halfway out the front door when something on the ground caught his attention.

James asked, "What is it?"

"Someone slid this under your door," Calvin replied. "I didn't think printed flyers were legal in the city anymore."

James glanced over the glossy folded menu his student handed him, the name, "*NAFISSA*," printed in the middle of a yellow circle. Underneath in smaller print, it said "*Malian-French Fusion*." In the Interior, wasteful advertising like that had been banned since the Earth-First Initiative's first round passed. Even odder was that the restaurant, located in Philadelphia, was at least a hundred miles away. There was a message written in thick black ink.

"*Dark Cloud ... If you're curious to know more, join us for dinner tonight. The reservation is for five pm. Please bring Calvin and your wife along. Your attendance is the only necessary response to this message. No cyber tracks. No paper trails. Burn after reading – Yo*"

James felt Sandy staring at him from out of the corner of his eye. The peculiar avatar he'd saved the day before had somehow found him in the real world. The second time in two days that had happened.

Calvin snatched the flyer back. "How'd they know I'd be here?"

Sandy peeked over the teenager's shoulder to read the cryptic message. "And who's this ... Yo?"

"Yo was this avatar we met at this off-the-grid sector called the Peak." Calvin told the story with dramatic hand gestures. "This majestic four-armed alien-like creature was abducted by a phantom. Then Mr. G jumped off a ledge that was at least ten miles high, soared to the bottom to save Yo, and flew back up with them in his arms like he was a freakin' superhero."

James turned to his wife, realizing Sandy had never experienced Lucidity. She wouldn't understand half of what Calvin was saying. Even when he heard his student's account of what had unfolded, it sounded insane. Oddly enough, Sandy didn't seem fazed.

"We should go," she said.

James was ready to throw the piece of paper in the trash. "What if it's a trap?"

Sandy laughed. "Since when has that ever stopped you? Besides, I'm mentioned on that piece of paper, too, so I'd like to know what the hell is going on."

"What about Calvin? I can't take him a hundred miles from home without his mother's permission."

Calvin gave him a cunning grin, the same one he had every time he'd outsmarted his teacher. "Well, I could tell my mother that you almost got me killed yesterday. You could also explain to her why she has to keep her three jobs because you might've ruined my chances of getting into the Innovation Academy."

James didn't have a rebuttal, secretly knowing Loretta didn't care if Calvin got into the IA or not. She was more concerned with his health.

Calvin continued. "Or we could figure out what happened to Lance, Space Angel, and your Pops."

James had unintentionally brought two of his favorite people down the same path of destruction he'd been on for ten years. Sandy and Calvin were both sucked into his search in some way or another. They weren't going to budge, and at the end of the day, he too was curious as hell to know what Yo had to say.

"It looks like we're gonna take a little road trip then."

CHAPTER 42

Philadelphia, with its still subtle skyline, hadn't expanded into the 'burbs the way New York City had. James cruised in an Automated on I-95 with Sandy and Calvin, remembering the time he'd run away as a kid. He'd skateboarded to Center City during the First Pandemic, disregarding his mom's rule to stay inside. His anti-authority inclinations had always gotten him into trouble, but this afternoon James feared the stakes were higher than ever. He hid his nervousness from the other passengers. A random thought popped into his head.

"How come Nera wasn't there today? She's supposed to be my operator in case anything ever happens in the system."

Sandy looked at him quietly before saying, "Nera died yesterday, babe. She was using Lucidity and got caught up in some sector called the Yards."

All of it suddenly it became even more real. En route to some secret location, James had been half asleep. It hadn't sunk in until the moment that Nera, Kyle, Lance, Kalen, and Anthony were all dead, either killed by the Light Keepers or killed because they were part of them. It took all his might to control his temper, holding back both his tears and a fit of rage.

"Do you still think the Light Keepers are innocent?" he asked Sandy, who peered out the window ignoring him. "Didn't think so."

Calvin broke up the thick tension inside the AV Traveler. "The president's going to speak about the attack." He cued the speech onto the screen. "I wanna hear what he has to say."

President Barney Max, the former CEO of FutureFone and creator of the UniTab, was an eccentric man who wore odd glasses and funky polka-dot suits. He was usually peppy and optimistic. Even the folks from places waiting for the Upgrade applauded the Basic Income Bill his administration had quickly pushed through after the War. But as the president approached the podium, he too wore a grim frown.

"What happened yesterday was a travesty," the president began in his raspy voice, with James and his fellow passengers' eyes glued to the screen. "A vicious cyber attack unlike one we've seen in years. The terrorist group known as the Light Keepers attempted to dismantle the peace we've grown accustomed to. Our only saving grace was the intelligence agencies who came together to thwart any further actions in yesterday's events."

The president pointed out some of the people standing behind him. "LucidiTech's CEO Prishna Gupta had the foresight to shut down Lucidity before matters got out of control." The woman bowed her head. "Director Zin and his team of Feds were the ones who uncovered the terrorists' plot a few days ago." The FBI's front man folded his arms like an angry mannequin as the president continued. "And although the CEO of the Knights of Azrael couldn't be here today, he assured me his team followed protocol to apprehend Kalen Green in a peaceful manner."

"That's bullshit," Sandy said, breaking the silence.

James didn't know what she was talking about, but his wife wasn't the only one who disagreed. In DC, protesters stormed into the press conference to disrupt his speech. Director Zin stood up out of his seat. He took control of the microphone and demanded they all be arrested for supporting the terrorist.

After the commotion, Maxx seemed frazzled but carried on. "I understand some people may be upset by Ms. Green's death, but it was the right course of action," the president said, his eyes watering as the camera zoomed in for a close-up. "I, too, lost someone yesterday. This morning I received confirmation that Senator Colleen Harding – our ambassador to the CTE, and my dear friend – was one of the victims of the cyber attack. She was a huge fan of Lucidity, and even though I advised against her going into the system because of her high-level profile, she convinced me it was important to understand the technology."

The president tried to compose himself before finishing his statement. "Senator Harding claimed her identity would never be compromised, but she may have been a target of the Light Keepers." He added, "I knew Colleen as Cece, but I'm told her avatar in Lucidity was called Space Angel. If you ever had the good fortune to meet her, you would agree that we truly lost an angel yesterday."

As the Automated flew down the highway on the east side of Philly, James turned off the screens. "Did you know about this?" he asked Calvin.

Calvin shook his head no, seeming shocked by the president's speech. "We were there! We need to tell somebody what we saw, Mr. G."

James had dismissed Space Angel since they'd first met on the bridge, never taking her words seriously, now remembering her last ones to him: *"Seems like it's been crazy in Lucidity ever since you've arrived."* That was after she'd insinuated his father was a Light Keeper. If Space Angel was this prominent government figure, then who was this Yo she'd been quite acquainted with?

"Babe?" Sandy caressed his arm. "Are you okay?"

"Maybe we should go back home." James looked up at her. "I don't know if I'm up for this today."

"It's a little too late for that," she said as the Automated came to a stop. "We're already here."

The sign above the restaurant's doors read *NAFISSA* in the same font as the flyer. James half-expected a warehouse in the middle of nowhere, too afraid to search for the address on Seeker. People stood outside on the sunny afternoon, waiting to get a table at what seemed like a popular eatery. The crowd seemed melancholy. They probably hoped to drown out the devastating attack by eating their feelings away.

As James made his way to the entrance, his paranoia subsided knowing the meeting was in public.

The crowded restaurant was beautiful inside with a less-than-subtle theme of yellow floral arrangements. Water lilies, sunflowers, and begonias were painted on the wall in the same color. James was more taken by the aroma of meat, warm spices, and another scent he couldn't quite place. After clearing his stomach hours earlier, and not eating for almost a day, he hoped to at least get a free meal out of the ordeal.

"We have a reservation," James said to the host, an older woman with dark skin and a colorful head wrap that matched her even brighter smile. "A five o'clock with Yo, I believe?"

"And what is your name?" She had a soft tone and what was most likely a Malian or west African accent.

"James Grady."

"Of course." The woman led him and his party of three to a private room in the back. "You're a little early, but the other guests will arrive soon." She walked him through the busy establishment. "You met my son yesterday, Amadou. I believe he goes by XYXO in the system."

James grinned as he recalled his initial introduction to the android avatar. "He's a strong one."

The woman opened the double doors of a private room in the back. "My son says you're a hero, so let us reward you and your family with a delicious meal."

Before James could thank her, the doors closed. The woman was gone, along with Sandy and Calvin, who'd both made detours to the restroom. He loitered alone in the dining room, observing the long table set for twelve. A pita-like flatbread was set out as an appetizer, and since he was starving, he took a piece.

Halfway through his first bite, a hidden back entrance slid open. A young man entered in a wheelchair. "Ngome," he said, speaking through a computer. "It's good on its own, but better if you dip it in the peanut sauce." He joked, "Who the hell sent you here today?"

"XYXO?"

The young man struggled to smile. XYXO, or Amadou, was evidently stricken with the same disease as the scientist, Stephen Hawking. The technology for treating TBI had come a long way since his death twenty-odd years ago. Now translating inner thoughts into speech patterns was almost seamless.

"I'm probably not what you were expecting." Amadou wheeled around, observing him. "You on the other hand look the same as the man I met yesterday, but I bet you can't fly in here."

"Stop teasing him, Amadou," a voice said in a deep calming voice. They were speaking through a large screen in the center of the room. The androgynous person had tan wrinkled skin and yellow eyes. "Let's make our special guest feels at home. Judging by the look on his face, I'm sure he's already been through enough today."

"Yo?"

"In the flesh," they said. "I'm delighted you and the others could make it."

"Where are the people I came with?" James approached the screen. "They should've been in here by now."

"The lines for the bathroom get long on a busy Saturday," Yo said. "While we wait for them, you could tell me more about this Jaybird project you mentioned yesterday?"

James fumed. "He's not a project! He's my goddamn father. I'd also like to know how you had such a specific invite list before I answer any of your questions."

Yo grinned. "I wasn't sure how to break the ice, but I assumed you were eager for answers. So why not skip the small talk?"

James peeked at his UniTab, noticing it was past five. None of the other guests had arrived. Calvin and Sandy were still missing, too. He began to think that he'd been set up, and crept back to the entrance of the small dining room. The door slid open and Sandy came in as James was about to escape.

"Hello, Mahoe," Sandy said, staring at the person James knew as Yo.

Yo grinned. "I was just getting to know your husband, Dr Grady. After all, he did save my life yesterday."

"What the hell is going on, Sandy?" James rubbed his forehead, about to lose it, confronting the screen with Yo on it. "Tell me exactly what's going on here?"

"We are merely here to protect a project that has the potential to bring healing and peace to the world," Yo replied. "In the wrong hands, though, this technology could be disastrous. If project Jaybird has something to do with your father, then he may very well have helped create this movement."

"What movement are you talking about?"

"We're the Light Keepers, James."

James tried using his UniTab's emergency distress signal, but the device was disabled. Two other guests arrived through the camouflaged back entrance and they weren't as friendly as Yo. James made a run for it but was blocked by a larger woman at the main entrance.

James stood in front of Sandy to protect her. "She's pregnant," he said. "If you truly are good people then you'll let us go."

Yo smiled at him. "We're not here to harm any of you."

"Help!" James screamed, hoping that someone in the restaurant would save them as he squirmed to find an exit. "Help!" The large woman put her hand over his mouth to shut him up as a familiar face stepped into the room – a person he'd never expected to see again. James started to think the whole day had been one long dream as the ghost from the afterlife approached him.

"No, you're not dreaming," the man said, pinching the sensitive fat of his arm. "But we do need to talk."

"Tomás?"

A white gas poured out of the vents and filled the room. When James tried to escape, Sandy stood in front of him. She wore a small gas mask to cover her face from the fumes. The strangers surrounding him wore them too. His supposedly dead sponsor covered his mouth and nose with a cloth napkin. "What the fuck is going on?" James held his breath. He became woozy from the fumes. *This isn't real*, he thought before fainting into a stranger's arms.

CHAPTER 43

The space was cool and damp, brightly lit by overhead lamps with a dozen DreamCatchers in a circle, including the one James found himself in. They didn't look or feel like LucidiTech's model. He got up to observe the rest of the room, some sort of test lab, surrounded by nothing but walls of black mirrors. In the reflection he noticed Sandy standing behind him like a ghost in grayscale. He backed away from the ominous version of her and toward the pale image of himself.

"Where are we?" he asked but she didn't answer. "What the fuck is going on, Sandy?"

She inched closer. "Relax, babe."

"Relax?" James slowly laughed himself into a maddening fit. He separated himself even farther from her, his back against the mirror now. "If this is real, then I was just gassed as you stood by and watched." His blood boiled. "If this is fucking real, then you've gotten our whole family into bed with a known terrorist." He turned around and stared into the dark reflection, attempting to see through his own shadow. "Please tell me you're not helping these Light Keepers. Just tell me I'm still dreaming. "

Sandy took a slow deep breath. "This is real," she said. "We needed to get you somewhere so you could let it all out without causing a commotion."

James rubbed his forehead like a sander, so much so as of late that his skin felt blistered. "What day is it *now*?"

"It's still the same Saturday, babe. You were only out for about half an hour."

The whole day she'd known exactly where they were headed, never batting an eye about the anonymous invitation or his story about phantoms and flying. He should've known when she wasn't fazed by any matters that day.

James wasn't usually claustrophobic, but the air felt thick and suffocating. He fell to his knees, asking, "Where did they take me?"

Sandy caressed his face. "We're in a safe place right below the restaurant."

"I thought we both decided to put an end to this madness before the baby comes." He stared up at her calm expression. "I thought I was the erratic one."

"Turns out you were on to something all along." Sandy eased her grip, nudging him to stand. "I was only continuing what you started ten years ago."

James stretched. "I'm trying to be calm about this, but none of what you're saying makes sense. I told you I had to end this search for my own sanity and sobriety."

"Why did you go in yesterday?"

James told her how Eleonora had followed him, passing on the message from the unheard-of trillionaire with one last day before the promise was over. "Yesterday my curiosity almost killed me for the second time."

"But you didn't die. You ended up saving Mahoe with whatever you did in Lucidity." Sandy stared into his eyes. "You're a hero to them."

"I don't want to be part of this. Also, what the hell does my father have to do with the Light Keepers." James paced around the arcane basement. "They're fucking terrorists."

"For the last time, they're not responsible for the cyber attack."

"Did the FBI confirm this theory of yours?" James asked as Sandy tried caressing him. "Is that what Barney Maxx said to the entire world today?"

"Babe, you don't understand."

He pulled back from her. "No, the president said it was the Light

Keepers. You brought us right into their goddamn hideout. You saw how
well that went for Kalen." A thought struck him. "What'd they do with
Calvin?"

A screen lit up on the black mirror, surveillance footage of the
dining room he was kidnapped in. Calvin ate, laughing with Yo, or, as
Sandy called them, Mahoe.

"Was Calvin in on this, too?"

"No."

"Even worse! My student's future is on the line if we get busted
with these terrorists."

An intercom came on and someone cleared their throat into the
microphone. "We're not the terrorists, James," the familiar voice said
through the speakers. "We never were."

The black mirror lit up and there was a shadow standing behind it.
As James got closer, he realized it was Tomás, his signature gap-tooth
grin cheesing through the glass. James began banging his fists on the
seemingly unbreakable mirror.

"Why don't you face me like a man?"

Tomás laughed. "Because I know how much you wanna punch me
in the face. I get that you feel deceived, hermano, but we're only taking
precautions. As Mahoe said, we're not going to harm anyone."

James didn't know whether to laugh or cry or yell. "I thought you
were dead," he sobbed. "Kalen said you'd relapsed and I was devastated.
Why would she tell me such an awful lie?"

"It's just like that crafty Irish woman to give you a lesson in tough
love as the reason for my death. There's a lot more to it than that,
though."

It turned out Tomás had been hiding out in Philadelphia for weeks.
He'd been staying in a room in the basement they were in. Kalen had
sent him there after growing paranoid that FBI were on to her. She cut
off most ties with the group and told Tomás to flee, fearing he may be on

their radar, too.

"Kalen sacrificed her life to keep us protected in the real world," Tomás said, stepping out of the control room. He eased in to hug James. "Unfortunately, we weren't as lucky in the system."

With his best friend's arms wrapped around him, James tried to understand the story. "But the news said the Light Keepers were responsible for taking Space Angel's life. I witnessed it myself, Tee."

Tomás pulled away and crossed his arms. "I guess you're not hearing the words coming out of your own mouth. When you met Space Angel on the Peak, *which group* was she working with?"

It sounded like a riddle coming out of his sponsor's mouth, but the answer was right in front of him all along. "She was working with you guys … The Light Keepers didn't kill all those people." He shouted, "It was those fucking phantoms!"

"And it's about time." Tomás giggled like a hyena. "If you would've figured that out thirty minutes ago we wouldn't have gassed you. It was a group of hackers known only as the Incubi. They've been attempting to destroy our reputation for years to obtain our technology. The more they tarnish our name, the more they sway public opinion against us."

"For what, though? What exactly do these hackers want from you guys?"

"Remember when I told you that the Light Keepers changed my life?" Tomás held his arms high and wide to show off the damp space. "Well, they did it right here in this treatment facility." He pointed to a DreamCatcher. "Here, we don't use these to go into Lucidity; we use them to go into the mind and fix factors even medical science can't treat. It's a process called Phase One that goes through our memories, and after I was treated, I decided to help administer it to others who need it. Amadou has already made huge progress, as you can see."

"If it's so great," James asked, "then why wouldn't you share it with the world?"

"Good question," Mahoe said, strolling in from a door that didn't exist before. Mahoe was tall and tan, wearing a long black dress, heading straight toward James and kissing his forehead. "I never thanked you for saving my life." Mahoe signaled for Sandy and Tomás to give them some space. They agreed and left together. "If you would've listened to me yesterday, your journey home would've been much smoother."

James investigated the wall. He couldn't figure out where the exit was. "Whether your intentions are good or not doesn't matter right now," he insisted. "I don't want my student to have any part in this. Your group is being tracked by every government agency including a violent KOA."

Mahoe smirked. "Fun fact – with the right tricks you can also be off the grid in the real world."

"But why Calvin?" James investigated the odd DreamCatchers. "It's my fault that he keeps getting dragged into these dangerous places. He just got accepted into this Innovation Academy, and although I have my qualms about that decision, I'm pretty sure his heart's set on going there next year."

"Which is exactly why we need him," Mahoe said. "Space Angel ... Colleen – or Cece as I knew her – had high hopes for your student before her unfortunate passing. She thinks, or at least she thought, he was the future – one of the brightest souls we've ever seen."

"Have you met Calvin's mother?" James asked. "She's not gonna let her boy be part of a terrorist group, and neither will I. You need to leave him and my family out of this mess you've created."

"Calm yourself, young one." Mahoe's arms rested behind their back, contemplating a thought like a wise monk. "We have people everywhere, hidden within every institution. Not only is Calvin one of the brightest we've ever seen, but he thinks with his heart. And his psychological exam for the IA only proved that further. Calvin believes in what we're doing here, Dark Cloud." Mahoe placed their hand on

James's shoulder. "We were wondering when you might get on board. It seems we can use your help."

"I'm not here to be brainwashed." James eased away. "And I don't want you to ever contact us again. Now, how the hell do I get out of here?" He stormed to the mirror where the exit was. "This has nothing to do with my father anyway."

"You mean Jim Grady?" Mahoe cued a file from a primitive tab. A screen prompted the mirror in front of him. It was the handwritten note he had left on his desk at home. His father's screen name, "*J8y131Rd.MC.ML.xxx.*" Mahoe pulled out his father's satchel that'd been sitting in the corner the whole time.

"Where did you get that from?"

"Some good people were looking after it."

"The detective Sandy's been working with?" James asked. "Is she part of this too?"

"Not until yesterday she wasn't," Mahoe said. "Detective Diaz and her partner didn't know it, but they'd stumbled into our main facility in Ohio a couple of weeks ago, which first put them on our radar."

"There's more of these places?"

"As I said, our main facility is in Ohio. That's where my good friend Skya and I first received the original codes from the Light Keepers." Mahoe explained that the detectives had also found a man named Nick Baxter. With that intel, they'd put the pieces together that the NCU Binary Lab was short for the *eN-Cu-Bi*, but that the man and his facility had vanished like the Phantoms they controlled. "If Quinn Baxter's twin brother is half as smart as her, we have ourselves a huge problem. The case they were assigned had them trying to locate your father and two women who all worked for an Army contractor called the JTID."

"Yes, I remember seeing those letters in my brief research," James checked if the satchel had been damaged. "But as far as I understand they found out my father was dead."

"Unfortunately, all three of them are no longer with us." Mahoe smiled. "*But* ... it turns out the case wasn't given to them by the Army, and what they were investigating was our origin, which we didn't even know until this very day."

James scratched his beard. "I'm confused."

"You see, this Ellie Brown Ginsberg AKA Farah Sylvain was the creator of the first functional BCI. Along with a teenage genius named Quinn Baxter, they came up with the coding at the JTID. When the two of them realized its potential, both good and existentially evil, they knew they had to keep it safe. Especially with Free Folk gaining access to the JTID. Your father, recruited for his profound interrogation skills, risked his life to help those two smuggle it out from under them ten years ago."

"Are you saying my father wasn't part of the Free Folk?"

"I'm telling you that he was a Light Keeper who died trying to protect the coding from them. We didn't know it then, but they're the reason we have Phase One. Despite everything that's being reported about us, we've already saved hundreds of lives using it."

"It sounds like these defectors of the JTID are behind this Incubi?"

"Exactly!" Mahoe's voice raised for the first time that day. "When Diaz got farther into their facility, she even found out they were using children for these deadly experiments."

"Children?"

Mahoe sighed. "Isn't that messed up?"

James took a seat in one of the DreamCatchers. It all made sense and nothing made sense at all. He'd always thought it was a dream within a dream, or what one sleep doctor called a "false awakening." But it wasn't. It was a simulation – a vivid memory of the experiment Brian and the JTID had performed on Heather and him.

Mahoe asked, "Are you okay, James?"

"Actually no, I'm not." He stood back up. "But at least now the strange abilities I had in Lucidity make sense. I now remember how I learned to fly in the system."

CHAPTER 44

James explained the best he could that he was part of his Uncle Brian's experiments and that both Brian and his father had worked for JTID. When Mahoe told him what the organization did, the memory became clear. Heather was in a swimming simulation but she was drowning. It felt so real and then he awoke to her screaming in another room. "I remember now that Brian's people used a more archaic system – headsets and vibrations suits instead of the complex BCI of Lucidity or the Light Keepers." Until then, the needles they were injected with must've made them forget everything, but Heather was never the same after that. How could she be if the JTID was accustomed to using the technology for interrogation purposes?

"I'm sorry he did that to you and your sister." Mahoe paced the room, seemingly deep in thought. "But it explains why those phantoms can fly. They have been using this technology to train people, using every method they can to force us to hand over Phase One. By making us seem like a terrorist front, they used the FBI or the KOA to do their dirty work. The Incubi already have too much power and if they get a hold of Phase One, who knows what evil they will use it for."

"I can't believe they would do that to us ... to kids."

"Nor can I," Mahoe sighed. "Do you know this Brian's last name?"

"It was Collins, but I'm pretty sure he's dead. At least that's what my mother claims."

Mahoe listened to someone in their ear. "It was confirmed he is deceased? ... Okay." Someone else was watching them, maybe even from behind the black mirrors. The tall figure turned back to James. "My team has already researched all the intel in that satchel when Diaz and the other two arrived yesterday, and it turns out your mother's right."

"Good. He deserves to be dead." James asked, "Is Detective Diaz here right now?"

Mahoe grinned. "She is, and she's dying to meet you."

A few seconds later, the door slid open again and a woman with black hair and a tan complexion came in with a huge smile, approaching James like they were long-lost pals. "You look so much like your father. It's uncanny."

"I guess I'll take that as a compliment," James said shyly.

The woman who went by Diaz sighed. "You should know that your father loved you guys very much. He told me so many stories about your family that I felt like I was a part of it. Sergeant Grady picked me up when I was ready to give up with these little Zen-like metaphors and that silly folk song he would always sing."

James remembered too. He sang, *"Where have all the soldiers gone? ... Long time passing."*

Diaz continued when he stopped. *"Where have all the flowers gone? Long time ago ... Young girls have picked them, everyone ... Oh, when will they ever learn?"*

James hadn't heard that verse, but it was the same melody. They stopped and stared at each other before the refrain.

They both sang in an improvised harmony. *"Oh, when will they ... ever ... learn?"*

James grinned, not even trying to hide the salty tears dripping off his chin. "What does that song mean anyway?"

Diaz frowned. "Now that I think about it, he may have been talking about himself. Like whatever he was doing would eventually get him killed."

James reiterated, "When *will* we ever learn?"

Diaz lowered her head and looked over to Mahoe, who nodded to go ahead with whatever she had to say. "Speaking of that, I need to show you something." She cued a series of videos onto the screen. It showed

Pops getting on the bus in Ohio, and that same bus being blown to pieces in Kansas.

While bittersweet, at least James now knew where the *goddamn bones* were scattered. He addressed Mahoe. "What about my father's avatar being activated in the system yesterday? That's why I was there in Aurora."

Mahoe sighed. "Lucidity was compromised and the Incubi were using avatars that had been scrapped in the Void for years. That wasn't your father, James, but I'm concerned that they picked your father's avatar out of the thousands down there in order to figure out his true identity. Maybe they were trying to see if it would lure anyone in."

"That's what SRT said too."

Mahoe laughed. "Good old Simon. Just so you know, he is on our side. Shit, he's the reason we exist in the first place. It appears that he's still being hesitant, but has obvious reasons to hide his ties to us."

"But what about my song that was playing?" James asked. "Calvin heard it too."

Mahoe seemed perplexed for the first time. "You may think I'm going to give you all the answers, but the reason I invited everyone here was to put some of the pieces together. Truth be told, I can't explain everything, and right now we're having trouble communicating with our other hubs."

It dawned on James that his original question was never answered by Mahoe, who might have conned him with a smoke-and-mirrors tactic. "So why aren't we telling everyone about this Phase One?"

Mahoe chuckled to himself. "Are you familiar with the Reconstruction Era?"

"History wasn't my strong point in school."

"Well, after the Last War, much like the supposedly Civil one we had two centuries ago, there were those throughout our government who supported the Free Folk's agenda much like the Confederates. They have since pledged oaths and passed necessary bills as an act of atonement for their treasonous behavior." Mahoe shook their head in disgust. "Colleen Harding knew that this Amnesty agreement was all bullshit. She was trying to pinpoint the individuals involved in the next coup." They stared down with their yellow eyes. "There are still traitors who walk the floors of Congress, speak into the president's ears, and sit among the EFI and the CTE." Mahoe grinned. "And that, young one, is why we have to keep Phase One hidden for now."

While processing Mahoe's words, James stared down at the tessellations of the basement laboratory's floor shimmering from the overhead lights, but he wasn't trying to distract himself this time. It all made sense now.

"So what's your plan?" he asked Mahoe.

Diaz stood quiet, seeming curious as well.

Mahoe cued the door open, revealing a set of stairs hidden behind the black mirrors. "I thought we could discuss that over the dinner I promised the both of you."

The stairs led to an elevator and James figured out he was far deeper below street level than he thought. He followed Diaz and Mahoe onto the storage elevator, and when the doors closed there was an awkward silence. He stared up at Mahoe, reminded of his misadventure in Lucidity.

"Why do you call yourself Yo in the system?" James asked. "Does it mean something in a different language? Is it spiritual?"

Mahoe laughed. "It's like, Yo ... what's up?"

James was both amused and bewildered by the fascinating character.

He was overwhelmed by the scent of onions as they entered the banquet room. It wasn't the odor he associated with sweaty armpits or teary eyes. It was savory with hints of lemon zest, vinegar, and herbs. There were others, but he only recognized his wife, Calvin, Adriana Diaz,

Tomas, and Amadou. When Sam entered, James took his seat at the table to hide his face.

Sandy sat down next to him. "Do you understand now?"

"It doesn't explain everything, but I get it." He held her hand. "I'm sorry for not trusting you."

"I didn't believe them until they proved it to me either."

"There's more, though." James started to explain to her about the dreams but she stopped him.

"I was watching, babe." Her eyes watered. "I'm so sorry."

"I just hope they're not lying to us."

"You still think that?"

"I always need more proof."

Sandy nodded as Calvin grabbed the chair next to him. His student said, "I thought Lucidity was wild, but this is crazy, right?"

James asked him, "What's your mother going to think?"

"Please don't tell her. All I ever wanted to do was help others, and right now, I'm not sure she would understand what we're doing here." Calvin gave him the most intense gaze before his lip curled in sarcasm. "Have you told *your mother* about this?"

James pounded his student's fist. "We got this, Calvin."

"Of course we do, Mr. G."

Everyone took their seat at the table set for twelve. The others peered over at him with curious grins and there was one chair unoccupied. The appetizers were already finished, but dinner hadn't been served yet. Mahoe picked up a glass and tapped it with a spoon.

Mahoe began. "James, I'm sure you already know some of us here, but I'd like to introduce you to a couple of others who helped out at this particular care center." They stood over two of the unfamiliar people – a tall blonde woman and a light-skinned Black man, both probably in their mid-twenties. "This is Dante and Charlotte, who will act as your intermediaries in New York." He pointed over to Sam. "And of course, you've met Sam, one of our operators on the inside."

Mahoe moved over to two others, a middle-aged woman with a white bob and a young lanky kid. "This is Diaz's partner and girlfriend, Marty Ronson, hesitant like you, but has since come around." They moved over to the young man. "And this is Dan, whose girlfriend was an innocent bystander in the attack on us." Mahoe turned to James. "I'm told she was your operator, Nera."

James bowed his head to the young man. "I'm sorry," he said. "I didn't know her well, but she had a real sass that I admired."

Dan gave him a slight grin. "I loved the way she yelled at me too."

His honest comment broke the ice with some much-needed laughter, but it was also a solemn reminder of why they'd gathered in the first place. For a brief moment they had forgotten that over a thousand people had died the day before, including many of their friends and family.

Tomás cleared his throat to speak. "To our new Light Keepers, let me remind you this is *not* a cult." He stared directly at James. "You can leave here today and do as you feel. There is no sacred oath or penalty of death for ratting us out. We trust you and that is all we have so I hope you feel the same way."

"Tomás is right," Mahoe said. "We brought you here because we trust you. Today we mourn for those we've lost and push ourselves toward our original goal – helping people get better." Mahoe paused, choking up. "Yesterday was the biggest threat we've ever had. Thanks to Kalen and Colleen's sacrifice it was diverted, but not in the way we'd planned."

Mahoe clenched their fist to their heart. "We have not killed anyone with our technology, but they have killed us. Colleen was going to tell the world – and more importantly the CTE – the truth. They must've figured out she was working with us, which is why we must lay low for a while until this blows over. Then we will figure out who these Incubi assholes are and expose them."

Calvin raised his hand like he was in class, waiting to speak until Mahoe called on him.

"Yes, Calvin?"

"Since this is Phase One – does that mean there is a Phase Two and so on?"

"I'm sure the three original Light Keepers intended on creating more phases to the Sun Follower, but all we ever received was the first one."

James turned to Sandy and she seemed as stunned as him. He had shown her the video of Heather his mother sent him. "The Sun Follower?" He asked Mahoe, "Is that really the name of the program?"

"It is," Mahoe replied. "And that's why we are the Light Keepers protecting it. Does that name mean something to you?"

"It does."

Sandy gripped his hand, giving him a smile. She whispered, "How's that for proof your father was part of this?"

The hairs on the back of James' neck raised toward the ceiling, a warm sensation gripping his body. He realized it was never his story at all. It was Sandy's and Adriana Diaz's. It was Calvin's, who was considered *the one*, or at least who they called the future of the movement. It was about Kalen Green and Tomás leading them to Mahoe, and the woman in charge named Skya. There were thousands of people out there, hiding in the shadows to keep it protected. It was Quinn Baxter and Farah Sylvain's story. And Jim Grady had made sure it never went to a darker side like the Free Folk or the Incubi. No … He made sure it always went toward the light – a Sun Follower in his own regard.

In that instance, James realized it wasn't about him at all, but it *was* personal now.

James looked at them and said, "There's still one more person who deserves to know the truth."

XII

PART TWELVE

CHAPTER 45

It had been a week since Adriana Diaz was in Philadelphia, joining what was supposedly the most illegal cult in the world. For the first few days she waited for authorities to come knocking on her door, but like Mahoe promised they were safe for the time being. On the news, Prishna Gupta assured the public that Lucidity would reopen again when they fixed all the bugs, reminding everyone, "We didn't ban the airplanes after their involvement in an attack." While there was a ton of backlash over the way Kalen Green and her son were murdered, the president insisted it was the only way to stop the attack. Diaz wanted to scream to the world that it was a lie, knowing Kalen Green didn't even have a DreamCatcher in her Montauk home, let alone the capability to pull off what was now referred to as the June 9th Attack.

Oddly enough, Marty Ronson had embraced becoming a Light Keeper, insisting that they were being wrongly crucified like Jesus Christ himself. The Southern Baptist woman loved a good savior story, reminding Diaz that all they had to do was keep a secret, ready to put the past behind her and start the retirement she'd been promised.

On that Saturday, Diaz and her partner arrived at JFK with only a few suitcases, having booked a trip to Portugal, Spain, and New Korea, surrounded by PSAs about the dangerous Light Keepers – "*PUT OUT THE LIGHT.*" Diaz grew paranoid about getting flagged at the security checkpoint, but there weren't any issues besides the one bothering her all week.

Diaz asked, "Do you think we should've told them about Quinn Baxter?"

Ronson snorted. "We used some cheap filter. I didn't think it was a strong enough lead."

"I need to stop thinking about the bullshit and enjoy life for a while."

"You're damn right," Ronson said. "It's been a week and no one's come looking for us so far. Now, Mama needs some R and R if you know what I mean."

"Now boarding for Lisbon at Gate B23," a woman said on the loudspeaker.

Ronson asked, "You ready for this?"

"I'm ready," said Diaz, her UniTab buzzing. "It's Dan ... Should I answer?"

"Make sure the kid is okay before we get on this airplane for six hours." Ronson sighed, "If I'd lost you, I'd be devastated."

"Aw ... you do like me."

"Just answer the damn call."

Diaz answered. "Everything okay, Dan?"

"You need to see something," Dan said, hyper and way too close to his camera. "That deputy from the Kansas Highway Patrol slipped an encrypted message into the video he gave you." Diaz's UniTab buzzed. "I sent it to you."

In the video, the cameraman hid behind what appeared to be a barn, zooming in on the same black military bus from their investigation, stopping in the middle of the highway at a point north of where the explosion happened. She could see the mile marker in the background.

The unseen man narrated the events with a slow Kansas drawl. "This goddamn bus was *justa* cruising down the highway and all of a sudden it put on its brakes." He panned around but there was nothing else for miles. "I hid when I heard gunshots coming from inside."

As the footage continued, a couple of members of the militia scurried out, wounded from a scuffle, falling to the ground. A man and a woman got off the bus holding each other's hands, and when two more soldiers attempted to chase them, the same man shot them both in the knees.

"Holy shit!" the cameraman commented, zooming in closer to the action.

That's when Diaz recognized the two runners.

Jim Grady and Ellie Ginsberg were getting away from their captors. Grady had a nasty gash in his midsection. The cameraman panned back over to the bus as Quinn Baxter, with her easy-to-recognize tattoos and pink hair, tried to flee. A soldier twice her size jumped off the bus and tackled the tiny Baxter, her head slamming into the concrete. The loud crack was picked up from a hundred feet away.

The cameraman gasped. "Oh my goodness." He filmed Grady and Ginsberg stumbling into a dense cornfield and they disappeared.

Someone off-camera shouted, "Hey!"

When the cameraman panned back to the bus, the large soldier was marching toward him, his face mangled somewhere in the incident. One of his eyes was gouged out, and a syringe hung from his bleeding neck. The footage got blurry as the camera was thrown into the distance before the video cut off.

"What the fuck was that?" Diaz asked. "Should we tell James about this?"

Ronson had peered over her shoulder to watch. "From the looks of it, Grady probably died a couple of hours later. There wasn't any help or a hospital for at least a hundred miles. There's no reason to get James's hopes up for nothing."

Diaz, her heart pounding, asked, "What about Suzi Q? Maybe that *was* her in Kansas?"

"Didn't you hear her head hit the ground?" Ronson took Diaz's hands in hers. "Nothing's changed, Adriana, only they all died in different ways than we first assumed. That militia probably blew up the bus to hide the evidence. We already went over all of this," she argued.

"You need to give it a rest."

"We have to stay. We can do this vacation another time." Diaz watched a replay of the video, wondering where that bus was heading. "Is this the right time to go galivanting across the world anyway?" She paused. "I mean, for all we know another attack could happen at any time."

Diaz noticed Ronson hadn't said a word the entire time. She looked up from her UniTab and the other passengers were staring at her. At first, Diaz thought it was because she had said too much, but when she turned around, her partner was on one knee with a ring in her hands.

Ronson asked, "Will you marry me?" She paused for a second. "I mean, as soon as I finalize the divorce from my husband?"

As everyone awaited an answer, Diaz thought about the last month and a half. When she'd met Ronson there was a spark and an immediate attraction, but that had recently turned into fireworks. It had been so long since she'd felt loved and could give the same back, and it had only taken a deranged investigation to hash itself out.

"Why not?" Diaz kissed her new fiancée to the cheers of strangers. "I can't believe you chose to propose in the airport."

Ronson shrugged. "Well, I was going to do it in Spain – at somewhere super stinkin' romantic – but I didn't think you'd go unless I did it right now."

"You already know me so well."

"So, are you going to get on this damn plane or what?"

"Smash it, neighbor," Dan chimed in, his voice coming from her UniTab. Diaz had almost forgotten he was still on a call. He said, "I'll let our intermediaries know what you two figured out as soon as I can make contact with them."

Diaz stared at the young man, who'd been through the wringer in the last week. "Are you going to be okay?"

Dan smiled at them through the screen. "I have my sister here, so she'll keep me out of trouble. But trust me when I tell you, we will find out who killed Nera." He waved to both of them. "Now get on that bloody plane."

Diaz stepped back into the line to board the flight with her new fiancée, and although she had a million questions, those would have to be answered on another day. When they got back to the States, there would be another investigation, and the stakes would be greater than before. That didn't matter as Diaz stepped on the plane, knowing she had someone to do it all with.

CHAPTER 46

At the hospital, Sandy Grady packed up a few items from her desk, anticipating her nine-month maternity leave.

The week following the June 9th Attack had been the calmest seven days of her entire pregnancy. At her checkup the day before, the doctor had confirmed her blood pressure was finally back to normal, and that both she and the baby were in good health – the only two words she needed to hear after the turbulence of the last three weeks.

On the day of the attack, Sandy had received some unexpected help while James was comatose in the DreamCatcher. It turned out that Sam, the Lucidity operator that her husband had doused with vomit, was also a Light Keeper sent by Mahoe. He explained everything to her that James would learn later that same day. Sam had left the restaurant menu under the door for someone to find, but not before telling Sandy how they were trying to protect a specific type of technology that could save millions of lives. Sandy went on to tell Diaz, Ronson, and Dan, knowing they would be allies after Nera's death.

At first, the story sounded like one of Xavier Cortez's conspiracy theories, who'd always said that every innovation was militarized before the public even knew it existed, forever quoting Oppenheimer with his "*I am become Death, the destroyer of worlds*" spiels. Now Sandy knew what he meant. The Light Keepers had assured her that her family would be safe and they'd kept their promise.

As Sandy grabbed the dusty wedding photo off the highest shelf to throw in the box, she noticed a tiny camera camouflaged by the black frame. It was the untraceable bug that Mahoe had warned her about, most likely planted there by Agent Miller. Right as she was about to remove the spyware and crush it between her fingers, there was a knock on the door.

Dr Haskell had come by the hospital to wish her luck, dressed for a day of softball with his four girls, his glum eyes more like a father than the usually short-tempered boss. "You don't have to take everything," he moaned. "We do expect you back here one day."

"I'll be back."

Haskell shrugged. "Well, I'm stuck with Agent Miller now that you're leaving. The Feds want me to take your place in the operation." His words were a stark reminder that the hunt for the Light Keepers would only intensify, and now Sandy was one of them.

Acting casual, she said, "In all fairness, you went on vacation and left me with Miller. It's your turn now." Glancing around, she whispered, "And I'd keep my eye on her if I were you."

"Why's that?"

"Agent Miller was illegally recording my sessions for FBI intel." Sandy pointed out the hidden camera. "Not cool, right?"

With a fierce grimace, Dr Haskell folded his arms. "I don't care what it takes to get these assholes," he fumed. "Every single one of those Light Keepers deserves to be behind bars for what they did." He gazed intently at her. "Don't you agree?"

"Of course," Sandy said. "But I do miss the days when I could chat with my patients without the agenda of harnessing intel from them."

"You let me worry about that from now on. Hopefully, by the time you come back, we'll have arrested every single one of those hackers."

"I sure hope so," she lied.

Over the last week, Sandy had asked herself a million times, *Am I in a cult?* She had read every case study from David Koresh to the T-Theory, whose mass suicide had made Heaven's Gate look like amateur hour. The real Light Keepers weren't a cult and the only terrorist front was the Incubi, but there wasn't any proof of that. Not yet. If only she could tell her boss everything, he'd understand – wouldn't he?

"Kalen Green used to be James's counselor," said Haskell. "How's he coping with this mess?"

"He's fine. Luckily she never tried to recruit him. Kalen wasn't always a terrible woman, you know? She did help him get sober once."

"That won't make up for what she did," Haskell said.

"You're right." Sandy plotted a scheme of her own. Her role as a double agent didn't have to be over because she was taking a leave. "You know, I'm still going to be around if you need any assistance with the Feds."

Haskell seemed overwhelmed by his new role, scratching his head at the thought. "One day we'll be able to tell our families that we were the FBI informants who helped take down the biggest terrorist organization in the world, but for now it's true, you're the only one I can talk to about this."

"Anytime you need me," she said. "Don't tell Agent Miller, though. I don't think she liked me that much."

Haskell laughed. "She said you were a pain in the ass, and I told her that's why I hired you in the first place." He summoned Sandy to follow him to the other side of the twelfth floor. "We have a little surprise for you in the conference room."

"Is it a cake?"

"Possibly." That's how they celebrated everything on her floor. "Unless you have to leave."

"I have a little time." She checked her UniTab. "James is meeting me outside in twenty minutes so we can finally tell his mother."

"You haven't told her yet?"

"We were going to do it last weekend, but, ya know, some shit went down."

"Goddamn Light Keepers ..." Haskell muttered as they passed a PSA for the group in the hallway.

Sandy gazed at the image of the infamous avatar, remembering the day she was first introduced to the Light Keeper's spokesperson. It turned out they were the philosophies of one of the two women who created the Sun Follower – Farah Sylvain Ginsberg – but whoever designed the wanted poster had made her black-and-white, taking away all of the beautiful colors. It made her seem sinister instead. After the attack, the ads had quadrupled, and the reward had climbed to ten million dollars for anyone with legit information. No questions asked.

When they got to the break room, Haskell said, "Full disclosure, and so I don't induce labor or anything: some people are waiting to surprise you behind those doors."

He opened the door to the room full of her co-workers and one unexpected guest. Sandy didn't have to act surprised. Her favorite FBI agent, Jen Miller, stood in the back, casually eating a piece of the ceremonial office cake, wearing a spring dress and a devious smirk. It had been over a week since the agent had sent her home an hour before the attack went down. She still hadn't gotten the secret bathroom phone conversation out of her head.

A good amount of people had shown up to wish Sandy good luck on her next chapter of life, a big part of why she loved coming to the Sloan Ketterman every day. Some of her old patients, the ones who were still alive, had even shown up. Before long, she had made her way to the agent.

"Look who it is, Sandy." Dr Haskell's enthusiasm sounded genuine. "She wanted to be here to wish you good luck in the future."

"And I appreciate it." Sandy double-checked her UniTab, noticing James getting close. "It's a shame I have to get out of here any minute now."

Agent Miller requested that Haskell give her and Sandy some space to talk. "You're really starting to show, huh? I was enormous at six months, but of course, I had two on the way."

"Did you come to the hospital just for this?"

Agent Miller narrowed her eyes. "Look, I know you were in the bathroom that day. I waited to see who would come out for twenty minutes."

"Does the FBI know you're working with someone else?"

"Oh give it a rest, Grady," Miller muttered. "You have too much empathy for these Light Keepers. I could hear it in your voice last Friday. You might think what the KOA did was wrong, but no one's going to stop us until we figure out who's running this operation." Agent Miller got close to Sandy. "Xavier Cortez and Monica Klein chose not to cooperate with us so they were dealt with." She winked. "Don't let the same thing happen to you."

After her threatening message, Jen Miller left the impromptu party and Sandy with a bad taste in her mouth. Luckily for her, there was chocolate cake. She had one piece for herself and another for the baby as she said her goodbyes and left Sloan Ketterman for a good while, ready for the next chapter of her life.

As she waited downstairs for James to pick her up, she felt a sense of relief, something she hadn't felt before last Saturday. As far as she was concerned, the Light Keepers would come out on the right side of history.

CHAPTER 47

The summer solstice was still three days away, but it was already close to a hundred degrees. James Grady drove into Delaware County and was only ten minutes out from his mother's home. When he picked up Sandy that morning, she seemed anxious about what Agent Miller had told her. Although Mahoe had promised them they didn't have to worry about the KOA, it was a daunting thought to be a blip on the private militia's radar. The AV hybrid they picked up at the checkpoint didn't have any air conditioner, and the thick air might as well have been a metaphor for the tense ride.

Sandy asked, "Are you nervous?"

Of course, James was. He was now part of a globally targeted terrorist organization with an unborn child who might have to grow up in a foster home if anyone found out. That wasn't what his wife was referring to, though.

"Maybe you should tell her," he insisted. "Bereavement is your expertise after all."

"Which is why I know it's best if it comes from you. I'll be right in the next room if you need me."

James rubbed his beard, and looked Pops's framed burial flag sitting in the back seat. "She must've figured it out after the Army showed up." He stared into Sandy's eyes, his hands on her round belly. "I still don't know why you stuck around that night in the hospital, or why you're still here with me today. I'm a lucky man who doesn't deserve you." When he glanced over at her, his wife gave him a guilty look. "What is it?"

"If it makes you feel any better, I was the one who came up with that terrifying murder hornet scenario in the Cave."

"Of course, it was you who told Nera. You're the only one who knows that."

"It also might've been me who suggested gassing you at the restaurant last week."

"Now that's just fucked up," he said as they both laughed themselves into tears of joy and exhaustion. The last month had been a long strange trip for the both of them. "I guess I needed a kick in the ass just as much then as I do now."

"I think after everything you've been through, you can handle this." Sandy pointed to their baby. "And are you ready for Heath?"

James had finally decided against the name Jimmy, opting to name their little boy after his sister. He smiled. "As ready as I'll ever be."

As they pulled up to the house, they could see Patricia waiting outside. She'd already been filled in on their father's death. James stepped out of the car and asked, "Where's Ma?"

"She's been acting a little strange," his sister warned. "She's been obsessively working in the garden every day for hours ever since Monday. Just like she did during the first pandemic."

"Goddammit!" He asked, "And you don't know why?"

Patricia shook her head no.

"I'm not going to tell her." James mindlessly kicked a stone through their small front yard. "Not today anyway."

His mother slid through the screen door. "What aren't you going to tell me?" She pulled off her yellow gardening gloves and threw them on the porch, greeting Sandy with a hug. When she approached him, her fists were on her hips. "So, what is it, James Michael Grady?"

"It's nothing, Ma. We'll talk about it later."

"No, let's do it now." His mother swiped the key pod from his hand. "I wanted to take you for a little ride anyway." She turned to Patricia and Sandy. "In fact, I think you all should come."

James gave his wife and sister a curious glance. "You haven't driven in years, Ma. How about we take a walk to the church instead?"

She crossed her arms, raising her brows at him. "Would you just listen to your mother for once in your life?"

James got in the passenger side without a word as Sandy and Patricia reluctantly hopped in the back seat. He wasn't even sure if his mother understood how to use the key pod, but it didn't take her long to ignite the hybrid. He gripped the handlebar on the side, glancing at a perplexed Sandy through the side view mirror.

His mother drove a couple of miles north toward the nearby Marple Township. There wasn't much traffic, so James reminisced about the county he'd only lived in for a brief period of his life. They passed the Cardinal O'Hara High School where his first serious girlfriend had dumped him, unable to deal with the turmoil of his sister's suicide. Ironically, the school was right across the street from the cemetery where Heather was buried.

When his mother made a left turn, James figured out that's where she was taking them, driving through the enormous plot of land that must've been at least ten acres. It reminded him of the funeral and the gloomy clouds that had hung over them that day. James hadn't visited in years, never believing that his little sister's soul waited for him there. She spoke to him all the time no matter where he was. His mother finally stopped when they reached a spot near Heather's grave.

"What's this all about, Ma?" James asked. "I'm happy you're getting yourself out there in the world, but this isn't like you."

Ignoring him, his mother got out of the car and walked toward the tombstone. *Heather Marie Grady* was engraved above her short fifteen years between birth and death, alongside a bible quote. "*He heals the brokenhearted and bandages their wounds.*" Patricia and Sandy followed close behind them.

His mother said, "So, you finally figured out what happened to Heather."

James stepped back. "How did you know that?"

"Baby, I've been hiding it for so long that it hurts," she sobbed. "Your father always sugar-coated what he was doing when he was gone. One day before he left, your father finally confessed about what Brian did to you and Heather in those machines."

Patricia seemed confused. "Mom, what are you talking about?" His mother didn't answer. "What is she talking about, James?" He explained to her the Virginia Beach-JTID incident in a condensed version, and through tears Patricia said, "Why would Uncle Brian do that to you both?"

James hugged her. "Don't you worry about him, Patty. He's dead now."

His mother shook her head. "No, James. He's the one who attacked that video game system last week."

"What are you talking about, Ma?"

His mother didn't answer James, banging on the side of her UniTab like an old jukebox. "Gosh dang it! I still don't understand how to use these gadgets." She walked them all back to the vehicle and prompted a photo on the dashboard's large screen. It was the leader of the Knights of Azrael, who only went by Wells. He wore his signature round sunglasses, a synth mask, and a black trench coat. His only recognizable human feature was his curly black hair. She said, "As I told you, Brian is the one who's behind all this."

"I don't understand," James said. "Everyone knows the KOA is after the Light Keepers – them and every government agency on the planet. So, what does Uncle Brian – I mean, Brian – have to do with them?"

"James, honey – the KOA is Brian Connor's creation! He's Wells, the one who's trying to bring down the Light Keepers, and yes, I know you're both one of them. Brian wants that technology for himself and he always has. That's why he faked his death and changed his identity. What he is using now is just some generic version of the Sun Follower he stole from your father years ago."

James tilted his head and shook it. "If you knew I was trying to find the answers, why didn't you tell me before? "

"Besides what happened to you and your sister, I didn't know most of this until this week. They said you had found him."

"Who are *they*?"

"The people who are with your father, I guess."

"Pops is dead, Ma." He pointed to the back seat. "That's his death certificate right there. I saw the videos of him being killed."

His mother grabbed his hand. She led him back over to Heather's grave and pointed to a group of sunflowers planted in the ten feet between Heather's and the next grave over. "Your father told me that if he ever had to go into hiding, he'd put those here to let me know he was still alive. I wanted to see if it was true or if it was a dream." She got to her knees and smelled them. "Now I know."

Patricia asked her, "Is that why you always ask me to check?"

His mother nodded.

"I still don't understand, Ma," said James. "How do you know all this?"

She showed him a handwritten letter. It said, "*No cyber tracks. No paper trails. Burn after reading.*"

In Philadelphia, Mahoe had told them it was the way the Light Keepers would continue to communicate to stay off the radar. The same way they always had. The letter had come in a package addressed to his mother, buried alongside everyday cleaning supplies as part of one of her weekly deliveries.

"I didn't know what it was at first," his mother said.

James read through it and it only reinforced most of what his mother had already told him, written in a cursive form they had long stopped teaching in schools. It spoke of Pops in the third person. "*Your husband became able to communicate when your son, James, activated the program. We have contacted the others to let them know, and will be in touch again when we can.*" It was signed "*F.S.*" James assumed had to be the Farah Sylvain Ginsberg they had mentioned. The creator of it all.

His mother handed him a sealed blank envelope. "And this one's for you."

James stared down at it for a few seconds, before ripping it open and pulling out a piece of paper. It read:

"*Hey Bud,*

I finally got all your emails. That's a lot of deep stuff to unload and hopefully one day I'll get to explain everything to you. But just so you know, you have made me more than proud to call you my son. You have already made this world better than when you came in."

James fell to his knees, knowing right away that Pops was the only one who called him *Bud*. He was the one who gave him that advice too. The handwriting was scrawled across the page, an injury perhaps.

"*I'm just getting used to my avatar, but I'm glad you recognized the signal we sent you and that we were able to get you to the Peak on time. It was the only way to show you that we were the good guys.*"

Finally knowing he hadn't lost his mind, James laughed and cried simultaneously as he continued reading.

"*I'm sorry this will probably feel frustrating, but I have to keep this brief. Tell Diaz I'm sorry for putting her in danger with that investigation we put her on. But people are searching for us, so our communication ability is limited. Trust me, I promise this will all make sense one day. Phase Two is on that flash drive in your computer. Now that you have activated it, you need to keep it safe as Simon told you. We have the only other copy, and it won't be fully operable until the two are together. Once we can figure our way out of here we will get it to the group. That will change everything.*"

Lost for words, James remembered the main folder of the flash drive. Phase Two was in his possession all along, camouflaged with a different spelling – "*FA.Z2*." His mother stood over the sunflowers with Patricia, explaining the situation to his sister. If that was even possible.

Sandy came over and held his hand, which was shaking tremendously. "Is it him?" He nodded. "So, I guess you were right all along."

"I gave up hope so many times."

"And yet here we are." Sandy took the piece of paper from him. "There's something else written on the back."

James turned it around and whatever he was holding back before was unleashed as he began sobbing in joy. It caught the attention of Patricia and his mother, who both came over to make sure he was okay. Patricia read what it said from behind and started crying again. Sandy joined them.

His mother asked, "What does it say, baby?"

James pulled out a lighter from his pocket and signaled to his mother to hand over the other envelope. He read over the message from his father one last time before setting fire to both of the letters. The ashes gently floated into the sky like the flying wish-paper they used to play with as kids, back before their family had been destroyed by one man – one who wasn't Jim Grady.

"Pops says that he misses us so much and he's sorry he'll never be the man we once knew before. And he says ..." James paused to gain his composure. "And he says don't forget ... *Today is the first day of the rest of our lives.*"

The End.

THE
SUN
FOLLOWER

A Novel By Danny Dragone

... For Now.

THE
SUN
FOLLOWER

Made in the USA
Monee, IL
28 July 2024